More praise for
MY FATHER IN THE NIGHT

"[A] momentous period of Irish history . . . Evokes the innocence and exuberance of youth, vicariously taking the reader through adventures and crises that will provoke tears of joy . . . Worth reading."

San Jose Mercury News

"Terence Clarke here writes a dense generational novel with the delicacy and elegance of a poet. He bravely intends to revive a tradition which has largely been left to clumsy hands."

HERBERT GOULD
Author of *Fathers* and *A Girl of Forty*

"With measured grace and a poet's vision, Terence Clarke shows us, as no writer has [shown], how hard it is for one man to speak his heart to another, especially if they are father and son."

SUSAN TROTT
Author of *The Housewife and the Assassin*

"Atmospheric, searching . . . A closely observed, arresting portrait of a boy, his family, and a city in transition."

The Kirkus Reviews

Also by Terence Clarke:

THE DAY NOTHING HAPPENED

MY FATHER IN THE NIGHT

TERENCE CLARKE

BALLANTINE BOOKS • NEW YORK

Copyright © 1991 by Terence Clarke

All rights reserved under International and Pan-American Copyright Conventions. Published in the United States of America by Ballantine Books, a division of Random House, Inc., New York, and simultaneously in Canada by Random House of Canada Limited, Toronto.

Credits for reprinted materials appear on page 241.

This is a work of fiction. Names, characters, places, and incidents either are the product of the author's imagination or are used fictitiously. Any resemblance to actual events, locales, or persons, living or dead, is entirely coincidental.

Library of Congress Catalog Card Number: 90-49561

ISBN 0-345-37567-X

This edition published by arrangement with Mercury House

Manufactured in the United States of America

First Ballantine Books Edition: July 1992

For Brennan Daly Clarke

My father in the night commanding No. . . .
—Louis Simpson

Did others lie down and almost expire under such longing? No. Others swam; others went far out to sea, others dived, others put oxygen flagons on their backs and went down into the depths of the ocean and saw the life there.
—Edna O'Brien

≪ 1 ≫

DOLL'S SOUL

"All right, Pearse. It's time."

Monsignor Hannon bowed toward the crucifix on the wall. Patrick Pearse, his server, bowed with him. Pearse, as he had been called by everyone, even his parents, since he had started serving the daily six o'clock with the stern monsignor, was nervous the moment before the Mass. He turned toward the doorway that led from the sacristy to the altar. The sacristy was a splotched, cream-colored room. The one window, which was high up and translucent, cast little light on anything at this hour of the morning. For Pearse, it did not matter. The real light was in the church itself.

He glanced at the pews as he and the monsignor walked out onto the altar. Because it was Tuesday morning, there were just seven people attending Mass. Sister Marie George and Sister Mary Margaretine, from Saints Peter and Paul School, sat in the first pew. The cleaning lady was there also, in the second row. Pearse didn't know her name, but Monsignor had told him that she was Italian and that she took care of the priests' quarters. Monsignor had showed him on the globe where Italy was.

"You'll go there one day, Pearse," he said.

"Yes, Monsignor," Pearse replied.

"Rome is there. A long way from San Francisco."

"Yes, Monsignor."

"His Holiness is there."

"Yes, Monsignor."

At the rear of the church, Mr. and Mrs. Andreotti stood up and crossed themselves. They came every day to the six o'clock, along with their son Richie, who was in the fourth grade at Saints Peter and Paul. Mrs. Andreotti's mother, Mrs. Pacetti, who was also from Italy, was with them this morning. She wore a black lace doily on her head. Monsignor had told him she was once a famous singer. Mrs. Pacetti mumbled through the Mass, even when she was getting communion. She shut up long enough to take the Host, then returned to prayer. Her constant connection with heaven amazed Pearse, whose mind wandered badly when he prayed.

Pearse recited at lightning speed, syllables coming out of his mouth in a typewriterlike racket, so that when the congregation joined the priest in the Our Father at the end of the Mass, Pearse finished at least ten seconds before the rest of the crowd. But he could not really keep his mind on his prayers. He thought he should be transformed by them, and he was not. He searched for some kind of door to the presence of grace. But his knees hurt, or he did not pay attention to the words, or he worried about his breakfast. He was always Pearse, never Francis of Assisi, never Joan of Arc.

As the Mass began, Pearse looked around the altar at the statues of Joseph and Mary on either side. They were charitable-looking sculptures of painted plaster, as gracious as could be. Joseph reminded Pearse of Abraham Lincoln. The Virgin Mary was sheltered looking, and Pearse thought she was very beautiful. Her skin was white, with a light blue cast to her lowered eyelids. It was the same blue as the long cape that covered her head. She appeared almost to be sleeping, but Pearse knew she was just guarding her blessed secret.

What Pearse loved most about the altar was the white and the gold. The altar was like a wedding cake, with filigreed plaster and gold inlay rising up delicately, in the way of frosting. There were turns, gewgaws, and twists, and a grand cupola far above. An enormous painting of Christ Himself spread its arms over the congregation from the ceiling of the cupola. To either side there was another domed ceiling, where gold crusted the little angels and the bushes in the distance, the clouds, the birds, and the heads of the heavenly saints, all floating about. The church offered a subdued glow that assured Pearse's happiness. God was with them, even though Pearse was worried by Monsignor's occasional dreary statement that the reason he preferred the six o'clock was that it was quiet then. No people.

"Gets it out of the way, too," he said.

As the sun appeared in the windows, the altar was showered with gentle light, in colors, which grew stronger moment by moment. The clouds in the domes appeared to slowly disperse. The painted ceramic of the statues became more distinct and, for Pearse, the altar lifted entirely into the air. As Monsignor prepared the communion, praying with his hands up before him in indecipherable, gorgeous Latin, Pearse's mind opened up and he felt overtaken by grace and beauty, at the edge of heaven.

"Pearse," Monsignor said afterward in the sacristy, "I want you to serve the High Mass at 10:30, the Sunday after next."

Pearse's black cassock hung from his hand. "First Communion Sunday, Monsignor?" He felt his face get hot.

"It'll be good for you. You're a fine server and I think you'll do a good job. I wonder if you'd ask your mother to phone me tonight so I can explain what'll happen. It will be an important event, Pearse."

Monsignor put on his biretta. His own black cassock, with the small jot of white showing from his clerical collar, was so somber by comparison to his strikingly white face that Pearse was frightened by him.

"There'll be some others, of course. Couple of seminarians helping out. And Archbishop Duffy."

"The archbishop?"

"Yes. He'll be our special guest."

Monsignor moved toward the door. He paused a moment as he watched Pearse hang his cassock on the servers' rack.

"How old are you now, Pearse?"

"Eleven, Monsignor."

"You're a good boy."

Pearse ran the three blocks to his home on Mason Street. It was a very cold, sunny October morning, and he was sweating by the time he reached the front steps to his parents' flat. He unbuttoned his jacket and reached inside to his shirt pocket for his key. It would not fit into the lock. Pearse looked at it with disbelief and tried it again. One of his tennis shoes was untied and the cuffs of his pants sagged to the porch. His cheeks were red from the cold, and one end of a dark blue scarf hung down the front of his jacket. Pearse's hair was curly and light brown. He had washed it before going to the church, and now it sprung from his head like twigs. His skin was very clear, and the cold air caused his eyelids to have the blue tint, almost nonexistent, that his mother thought made him look so handsome.

He unlocked the door and ran up the stairs.

"Mom, Mom, I'm going to serve the High Mass," he shouted.

He smelled bacon and eggs. His father, Joe Pearse, sat at the kitchen table reading the *San Francisco Chronicle*, while his older brother Tim balanced a piece of bacon on half an english muffin. Tim's left hand rested on a mug of chocolate on the table. Before him, a copy of *Sports Illustrated* was spread out on the breakfast table. Joe looked over the top of his paper. Pearse's mother, Mimi, was dressed in a white chenille robe and her hair was up in a clip. It was black and very curly.

"For First Communion. And the archbishop's going to be there," Pearse said.

"Oh, Pearse," his mother said.

His father laid the newspaper on the table. He was already dressed to go to work. His jade french cufflinks, a gift from his mother years earlier, gave a bit of color to his white shirt.

"You'll need a haircut," Joe said.

"Can I get some new pants?" Pearse asked. He flung his jacket onto a kitchen chair and sat down at his place. His father poured him a glass of orange juice.

"Sure," Joe said. "You say the archbishop is going to be there?"

"Yeah, and some seminarians. Monsignor, too. Everybody!"

"We'll be there as well, Pearse," his father said, and he clapped the boy on the shoulder. "Wouldn't miss it."

Sister Marie George announced it to the class later that morning.

"Of course, the entire school will be assembled for the Mass, Pearse. Imagine! Such an important day! You'll be bringing God's grace to the first-graders. And we'll be so proud of you, representing Room 12 on the altar."

She turned to the rest of the class.

"Let's offer a few Hail Marys in thanks for Pearse's achievement."

Pearse's position in the class, which had been at best little noticed, now became firmly etched in everyone's mind. The weekly collection of colored pencil drawings on the bulletin board had always featured work by Jeannie Lavin and Ben Del Negro. Jeannie's horses, sedate, dignified, and always stationary next to a fence or hanging out of a barn door, had been the school art contest winners two years in a row. Ben, a skinny, excitable kid who poked fun at everybody, drew custom cars. His hoods and fenders featured leaping panthers. He pin-striped everything, so that the cars became precise pyres of flame.

Now Pearse's drawings from the art lesson the week before were put up, labored copies of an illustration of a sailing ship

Sister Marie George had gotten out of a book. Pearse's rendition bore a resemblance to the model, in that there was a demonstrable hull and some masts. He had forgotten the sails themselves. Three sticklike sailors smiled from the foredeck. He had drawn a yellow sun up in one corner, with a stripe of blue across the top of the paper representing the sky.

The Wednesday before the High Mass, Pearse's mother took him to Roos Brothers for a new pair of shoes. He rode up the escalator alone, preceding Mimi by ten feet. He felt an aura of real importance surrounding him. Pearse was a kind boy, though not noted by the nuns at school as material for Saint Ignatius High, where, as Tim put it, The Brains went. Maybe Sacred Heart, though his mother thought there were too many toughs in that school.

The fact was, Pearse was an average student, well liked by his teachers. But there was the sense that he could do better in school if he would only apply himself. He seemed scattered. He was sometimes late for school, though not because he was intentionally delinquent. He was simply distracted by the store windows on the way. Ratto's Footwear on Columbus, for example, displayed shoes that appeared to be made from the same material as his mother's wicker chairs. Panelli's Delicatessen on Stockton Street, with big salamis hanging from the ceiling, also attracted him. The salamis always reminded him of the *Hindenburg* falling to earth in flames, films of which he had seen on television.

"Do you want black shoes or brown shoes?" his mother asked.

"Black," Pearse said. "It's a High Mass, Mom."

He tried on several pairs, finally choosing some penny loafers like the ones the high-school kids wore. He wore the shoes to dinner that night, a copper penny in each one.

"Pearse?" It was his grandfather MJ on the telephone. "I'll be coming to the Mass this Sunday."

"Good."

"But, you know, Doll won't be able to see it."

Pearse's grandmother, suffering from cancer, had been confined to her bed for two months now.

"I know."

"But I want you to understand that this will be one of the greatest moments of my life. I'll be telling her all about it."

MJ's elderly voice crackled with pleasure. "I served the Christmas High Mass when I was your age, you know," he said.

"You did?"

"Yes. And I made a fool of myself."

"You did?"

"I dropped the wine cruet," MJ said.

"What happened?"

"Oh, nothing. I was very embarrassed, of course. There was wine and glass all over the altar. I never got to serve another High Mass."

"You didn't?"

"Nope. And that's why I'll be there for your Mass. Because I know you'll do a better job than I could ever do."

Pearse blushed at the compliment.

Mimi told him she was going to have a surprise for him after the Mass.

"What is it?" Pearse asked. They stood in the doorway to the living room as Chet Huntley spoke on television with John Kennedy, the senator from Massachusetts. Pearse liked Kennedy because his grandfather liked him.

"Irish boy," MJ had said. "Catholic, of course, and that'll be a problem for him if he ever goes for higher office."

MJ had shrugged, leaving Pearse with no explanation of the senator's difficulty. If he's a Catholic, Pearse thought, everybody should like him.

"But he'll do all right," MJ had concluded.

"It's something that will keep you warm," Mimi said.

"But what is it?" Pearse asked.

"You'll see, you'll see."

Mimi caressed Pearse's cheek. Senator Kennedy joked about how difficult it was to find a nice place to live in Washington.

On First Communion Sunday, Pearse got up at five a.m. He couldn't sleep any more, even though his father had told him the night before that he would wake him up at eight o'clock, in plenty of time for the Mass. But Pearse's usual daily Mass required an early rising, so he woke up on his own. He went to the bathroom, angry that he would have to sit around until everyone else got up. But his mother had arisen as soon as he had, and she encountered him in the dark hallway. He was shivering in his underpants.

"Pearse?"

She took him in her arms, and he nestled his face into her soft, prickly chenille robe.

"Today's the day," she said.

Pearse pressed his arms against his chest so that they too were warmed by his mother's robe.

"And you're going to do just great."

At Saints Peter and Paul, Pearse slipped a bright red, freshly laundered cassock over his head. Intimidated by the seminarians and by all the priests in the sacristy, he stood in the far corner beneath the window. The two seminarians were college-age men. They had a kind of rapport with Monsignor that Pearse himself had never had. They were young, but they were adults. They shared Monsignor's casual attitude toward all the sacred things. They arranged the chalice and the vestments in the same spirit in which Pearse's mother washed the dishes or folded the laundry. They paid no attention to Pearse himself, even when Monsignor introduced him.

"Now, you show these seminarians how it's done, Pearse."

The boy's eyes widened and he swallowed as he averted his eyes toward the floor. He realized, suddenly, that the Mass was about to begin.

"Yes, Monsignor."

Everyone bowed to the crucifix on the wall and turned toward the doorway. Pearse clutched his hands tightly and walked through the door with his eyes closed.

The seminarians led the way, followed by Pearse in his red cassock and white altar blouse; the pastor and principal of the school, Father Dimiola; an assistant, Father Delmonico; and Monsignor. The first seminarian carried a brass staff, about six feet high, on the top of which was a gold crucifix. For Pearse, the cross invested the entire group with the light of divinity which, for a brief second, really did transport him. He felt swept away and floating.

But when he glanced into the pews, his throat suddenly caught. The church was filled with people, including all the children from his school. Their white shirts and blouses formed a flickering cloud through the first twenty pews. The first-graders, who would receive their First Communion, were even more formally dressed, nervous and jumpy in the front rows. The boys wore coats and ties, and the girls' white dresses were covered with frills. Standees crowded the side aisles and the rear of the church. Pearse heard giggles from the students.

Then he sensed the presence on the altar of a sober and remarkable eminence, seated on one of the thronelike seats at the side. The man's cassock gathered about him like drapery. His burgundy-colored biretta rested on his knees like a velvet jew-

elry box. His white hair was combed and neat, and he had a
look on his face of beneficent cruelty as he stared at Pearse.

Archbishop John Michael Duffy stood up, and his action
seemed to engage everyone in the church. Silence gathered about
him. He clasped his hands together before his chest, and, as
Monsignor arranged the altar and prepared to begin the Mass,
the archbishop sighed loudly, with impatience.

Happily, everything went quite well. Pearse's responses came
out in the perfect, rote-learned Latin that he had recited day
after day for the previous year. During the preparatory stage
before communion—the most exciting moment for Pearse, as
the bread and wine were transfigured to the body and blood of
Christ—he glanced a few times at the archbishop. There was the
quality of a painting about the prelate. The robes he wore were
just like those Pearse had seen in the comics in the Maryknoll
magazine, about martyred bishops in China. They were red and
thick, like the curtains at the movie. When Archbishop Duffy
moved, which was infrequently, he did so with aplomb and
fatigue.

Monsignor stood before the altar, his back to the congregation. He was about to consecrate the Host, and Pearse readied
himself. He took up the bells in his right hand. Monsignor genuflected, raised the Host above the altar, then genuflected again.
Pearse rang the bells with each movement, with as much finesse
as he could. Most altar boys made this an opportunity to startle
everyone. Pearse felt it was too delicate a moment for that. After
all, Christ was about to descend. This should be a time when
the parishioners could be peaceful and happy. So he made sure
the sound of his bells rose up sweetly through the church.

Pearse's confidence had returned. He actually felt a part of
the team on the altar, as though he were partially a seminarian
himself. As he took the paten in his hand to assist at communion, Pearse glanced into the audience. The first-graders were
approaching the altar rail, in restless innocence, followed in turn
by the other students. He saw his parents, his brother, and his
grandfather standing in the side aisle. His mother and father
smiled at him, careful to preserve his dignity as a server. Pearse
smiled back. By now, little that was bad could happen. Pearse
raised his eyebrows twice, and his mother looked away, amused.

Pearse preceded Monsignor to the kneeler, where the archbishop waited. He stood to Monsignor's right and extended the
gold paten beneath the archbishop's chin. The prelate leaned his
head back and opened his mouth. A patch of white hair came

out of each of his nostrils. His teeth were yellowed and there was darkness in the intervening spaces.

For a moment, Monsignor fidgeted with the chalice. Pearse glanced up at him, as did the archbishop. Monsignor seemed unable to put his fingers on one of the Hosts, and when he finally did so, it slipped from his grasp. The wafer bounced off the edge of the chalice, and Pearse lunged with the paten to catch it. The Host twirled along the edge of the paten like a skittering dime and fell again. Pearse grabbed for it with his free hand. Then he remembered his first instructions as an altar boy, many months before, when Father Dimiola, rectitude steadying his voice, had told Pearse that it was a mortal sin to ever touch the Host with your fingers if you were not a priest. Pearse gasped and pulled back, his arms flailing in the air. The paten flew from his hand. It climbed past Monsignor's ear, and he turned to watch it sail to the cruet stand across the altar. It caromed from the stand to the marble floor and clattered about aimlessly before coming to rest beneath the altar rail.

There were muffled outbursts of laughter from the adults throughout the church. The children broke up in an explosion of glee, their high-pitched cackles echoing through the building. Pearse took a step toward the rail, where the parishioners waited in confusion. He glanced back at the two men behind him. Archbishop Duffy had laid his forehead on his folded hands. He appeared to be laughing as well.

Pearse looked up into Monsignor's eyes, hoping for commiseration. He could not move. He felt anguish gathering, and he struggled against a flurry of tears. He dropped his eyes toward the floor. The Host at Monsignor's feet was darkened by a smudge along the edge.

"Pearse," Monsignor said after a moment.

The boy looked up. His face felt blotched.

"Pick up the paten, Pearse."

Pearse's knees quavered, and he felt he was about to fall over.

"We've got to get on with this," Monsignor said. "Go get it."

As Monsignor picked up the Host, Pearse moved toward the laughter of the parishioners, keeping his head down, struggling not to weep. He avoided looking at his parents as he genuflected to take up the paten.

In the sacristy afterwards, Pearse removed his cassock in isolation. Monsignor ignored him, as he had done for the rest of the Mass. He chatted with Archbishop Duffy while the two men took off their own vestments. The archbishop put on a black suitcoat, brushed a few flecks of dandruff from the shoulders, and shook Monsignor's hand. He wished the seminarians well in their studies. Pearse stood beneath the window, in the dark corner. Finally the archbishop left with the other priests, and Monsignor, noticing Pearse, crossed the room to him.

"Listen, don't worry about it, son," he said.

To Pearse's mortification, he found that he hated the monsignor's sympathy.

"Happens to the best of us." Monsignor laid his hand on Pearse's shoulder, let it rest a moment, then patted him once on the cheek. "But I'm afraid, for the moment anyway, that it's back to the dungeon of the six o'clock for you." He removed his hand, though the cold feel of his touch lingered on Pearse's skin. "I'll expect to see you in the morning."

Pearse spent the rest of Communion Sunday in his room. Mimi consoled him, and she gave him the new sweater she had bought for him as a celebratory gift. She left the room without his trying it on, and he let it remain on the end of his bed.

MJ entered the room carrying a breakfast tray—bacon and eggs, Wonder Bread toast with jam, fried potatoes, and hot chocolate—all of them Pearse's favorites.

"Here you are, young man." He placed the tray on the bed. "Just for you."

Pearse leaned against the wall. "Thanks. Not hungry," he said.

"Oh, come on, Pearse. You'll be all right."

Pearse looked the bacon and eggs over, then turned away. They looked lumpy on the plate, like glazed rubber.

"I know you don't feel so well," MJ said. He stepped back toward the door. "That's why your mother asked me to bring your breakfast in to you."

Pearse glanced once more at the bacon. It reminded him of the Last Supper. Despite his misery, he thought it was nice of MJ to bring it in.

"Doll wants to hear about it, too, Pearse," MJ said. "It's still a big day, you know."

Pearse's mouth turned down, and he closed his eyes.

"Thanks," he said.

The next morning, Pearse arrived in the sacristy fifteen minutes earlier than usual. He stood in the semidarkness before the crucifix on the wall and prayed. But the prayers came out of his mouth and disappeared. He put on his black cassock, which was wrinkled. Monsinor arrived, and the six o'clock began.

Saint Joseph looked down on Pearse with only slight approval. The saint's skin was gray. Pearse looked out into the church. Mr. and Mrs. Andreotti were there, standing up in the back row as usual, with Richie, who smirked when he saw Pearse. Mrs. Pacetti was not in the church, and Pearse guessed she was ill, or tired. Sister Mary Margaretine had come to the Mass. Pearse was dismayed to see that Sister Marie George had not.

Monsignor mounted the three steps to the altar very slowly, as though each one required a long, distressed exhalation. Pearse glanced into the domed ceiling to the right of the altar. The painted clouds were so dark that there seemed to be little differentiation between them. The angels and the saints were stiffly rendered. Christ appeared to stare at a spot well above Pearse's head. Pearse looked high up at the windows that surrounded the cupola. Dim morning light began to show in them, and Pearse noticed for the first time that there were panes in the glass, barred panes, and that they were clotted with dust.

When he arrived at school later that morning, a general glee followed Pearse about the playground, into the boys' bathroom, into the classroom . . . wherever he went. The other children reminded him of his failure almost every moment. The worst came when a Chinese kid, Forrest Yick, called him Y. A., after the famous quarterback.

Pearse kept to himself and moped. Sister Marie George sensed his disappointment and said nothing about the Mass. During morning recess, Pearse remained in the classroom. When the bell rang, he merely sat and watched the rush. He let everyone go—Forrest Yick, bony Gary Durham, Ben Del Negro, everybody. Even Barry Minnachetti, a favorite of Sister Marie George's, a slim, weak-willed student who was a dork about playing any games at all—even he got a start on Pearse, although Barry was beaten out the door by all the girls.

Pearse remained with his elbows sprawled to either edge of the desktop, looking at the class bulletin board. A photo from *Life* magazine showed Vice President Nixon giving the victory sign with both hands. His head looked like a smiling plate. Other world figures—Christ, Lawrence Welk, and Joseph Stalin, a dead Russian king or something who Sister Marie George had said was one of the worst men in history—were pinned to the bulletin board as well. Across the top was a headline cut from pieces of colored paper that read "Famous People." A paper alphabet was suspended from a wire above the blackboard, across the front of the room. There were charts measuring the pupils' progress in spelling, arithmetic, and comportment. Another wall was decorated with poster-paint paintings done by the children. There were ships and unruly clouds, cows with crude udders in fields, and birds in the distance.

The desks were very old, made of stained wood and metal that was painted black. A storage shelf beneath each desktop held the pupils' books and papers. Sister Marie George insisted that each desk be well organized. But Pearse found neatness dull, so his desk was like his bedroom at home. He made no effort to clean it out, except when he was forced to do so by Sister Marie George. At the rear of the classroom was a small plaster grotto in which knelt a statue of Saint Sebastian, run through with arrows. He had pink cheeks, and his eyes, uplifted toward the ceiling, were glazed with tranquillity.

Pearse leaned his chin on an open hand. Sister Marie George remained at her desk. She wore a long black habit with a black cowl. The wimple was close-fitting to her face and made of stiffly starched white cloth. Sister Marie George's rimless glasses made her appear more serious than she really was, and the effect was heightened by the forbidding darkness of her habit. But her round cheeks stood out from her face in humorous puffs. Pearse especially liked her laughter, which was frequent. He thought she looked like Benjamin Franklin.

"Pearse, you should go outside and play," she said after a few moments.

Pearse remained silent.

"It won't do you any good to stay in here." Sister Marie George fingered the black tassel that normally hung down the side of her habit. The tassel had been mussed, and she held it upside down to straighten it. The strands hanging over her hand reminded Pearse of a hula skirt. She stood up and approached him. The sound of her heavy shoes was like that of a workman's shoes, but her fingers were delicately white. They were similar to the fingers on the Virgin Mary in church, with shapely nails and no cracks or abrasions to speak of. Unlike Pearse's fingers, which were rough with tiny stubbles where he had chewed on them, Sister Marie George's appeared to have been fashioned by someone as though they were intended for display in a shop window. When she placed her hand on the back of Pearse's head and caressed him, her fingers mixed with his hair.

"We all have experiences like you had yesterday," she said. The boy shook his head and grumbled.

"No, it's true," Sister Marie George continued. "I know that doesn't help much, but it is true."

"Why does everyone have to make fun of me, then?"

The nun sat down at the desk next to Pearse's. She hung one hand over the edge of the desktop. The brightness of her fingers, coming from her voluminous black sleeve, was accentuated by the dark wood and metal.

"I don't know," she sighed. "Children always do that, Pearse. Eventually they'll stop."

"No they won't, Sister," Pearse said. He felt like such a fool that even Sister Marie George's commiseration seemed abrasive to him.

"Why don't you read something," she suggested. "It'll make you feel better."

"Read!" Pearse shrugged. What he really wanted was to evaporate silently into the morning air. He looked into the corner of the room, where there was a low round table and four wooden chairs. A set of bookshelves contained animal stories, Mother Goose books, and kids' adventure novels, plus a selection of *Classics Illustrated* comics.

Most of the comic books were dog-eared. The children took them up because they contained more pictures than the other books, but the *Classics Illustrated*s were seldom really interesting to them. The stories themselves were too slow, usually about some family in Russia or a love story filled with rainy thunderstorms and handkerchiefs. The only one that had universal appeal for the children was *Moby Dick*, and that one only in the last part, when the small boats go out after the White Whale. There, things really picked up. The children did not think Captain Ahab should be as angry with the whale as he was, since it was, after all, the whale's ocean.

Pearse kept it a secret that he genuinely liked the *Classics Illustrated*s. The others grumbled that the stories were boring. But, though Pearse could race through a *Scrooge McDuck*, he seldom read it more than once. The drawings were light and frantic, but there was no detail. Those in *Moby Dick* were so much more complex and intricate that Pearse spent hours looking at them, wondering what it would actually feel like to be pulled through the frothing waters by a whale at the end of a

rope, or to be dazzled, hair on end, by the Saint Elmo's fire in
the rigging. The loss of the ship in the whirlpool was Pearse's
favorite part. There was something in the disappearance in a
vortex that appealed to him. The wooden decks and thick ropes,
the smudged tackle and sails all in a circle as the sea water took
them down . . . Wow! Pearse thought.

Sister Marie George folded her hands together. "But if you
don't want to read," she said, "you can sit here and wait. Whatever you like." She stood and placed her hand once more on
Pearse's head. "You were the Lord's own altar boy yesterday,
Pearse. Even though, God help us, Monsignor didn't seem to
see it that way."

She moved toward the door, then stopped and turned around.
"You did a good job. You did, really." She went out.

The warmth of the nun's words momentarily lightened Pearse's
unhappiness. But the memory of the paten parting the air chilled
him and tightened his stomach. He looked out the window, distracted by the noise of the children playing outside. Sunlight fell
across the wall on the far side of the playground. The colors of
the buildings across Washington Square were sharpened by the
clear morning light, so that each façade had its own distinct
design, like a postage stamp.

Pearse stood and walked to the bookshelves. He thumbed
through the *Classics Illustrated*s, coming to one whose cover
showed three girls gathered on a couch. Their long hair was
carefully curled in ringlets, and they were playing with a cat.

Pearse took the comic to his desk. Looking through it, he saw
scenes of cooking and sewing, with a lot of walks in the country.
The comic was called *Little Women*, which, to Pearse, did not
sound promising. He leaned on one hand and turned a few more
pages. He decided to put it back.

Forrest Yick came into the room with the basketball in his
hands. His hair was straight and black, and hung down over his
forehead like a fine, trimmed brush. In every other respect,
though, Forrest looked as though he had been caught in a whirl-
wind. His white shirt had come out from beneath his belt on
one side. The cuffs of his dark purple corduroys piled up on his
scuffed shoes. Outside, the bell rang. Dribbling the ball, Forrest
walked toward the cloakroom. After a moment he looked
around, apparently recalling Sister Marie George's rule against
bouncing balls in the classroom, and spotted Pearse.

"Hey, Y. A. What're you doing in here?" he asked.

"Nothing," Pearse replied. He closed the comic book and

turned it face down. He hoped to sweep the book from the table and replace it with something else while Forrest was in the cloakroom. Forrest bounced the ball once, and there was a moment of silence.

"That's one of those dumb comics, right?" Forrest asked. "The *Classics* ones?" His voice had a flat, monotonous intonation, in which each syllable carried the same weight as the one before it and the one behind. There were only five Chinese kids in the school. Most of them seemed to speak that way, and they were imitated behind their backs, with much laughter.

Pearse did not respond.

"Girls' comics, right?" Forrest grinned.

"No," Pearse said. His cheeks began to warm.

"Yeah, it is." Forrest turned toward the table, and Pearse took the comic onto his lap. "Lemme see it."

"Leave me alone."

"Lemme see it!"

Forrest grabbed the comic book from Pearse's lap. Pearse held on to it, and the book ripped into two jagged sections. Forrest stepped away from the table and looked at the cover in his hand.

"Ugh!" he said. "Dolls!" He looked over his shoulder, saw the room was still empty, and pretended to wipe his ass with the comic.

Pearse and Forrest had never gotten along. The trouble was that, though they were enemies, they were neighbors. Forrest's parents, Mr. and Mrs. Yick, owned the Gold Coin Grocery on the corner across Mason Street from the Pearses' flat. They lived in a small apartment above the store. Mr. Yick was a generous man. Sometimes he gave Pearse a candy bar after school and allowed the boy to sit on a stool next to the cash register in his store. Once Mrs. Yick had gotten after her husband for squandering so much candy on Pearse, and she actually went to the back room of the store in a huff. She continued to yell at him from the back room in Cantonese, a language that sounded to Pearse like a record playing backwards.

Forrest would come in at six o'clock in the evening to help his father close up for the day. Pearse envied how he got to roll back the overhead awning and push the sidewalk vegetable bins into the store. But Forrest was a braggart, a picky sort who made fun of people at school, with the same rough chuckle, every day. He was smaller than Pearse, and he had a kind of gritty indifference to friendship that was unlike Pearse altogether.

"It's about girls, right?" Forrest grinned as he looked at the comic once more.

"Give it back."

"You like dolls, too, I bet."

Abruptly Pearse stood up and took the comic book away. Forrest threw the ball at Pearse, and it hit him in the face. Pearse pressed his hands against his forehead. His skin stung, as though in flames. Forrest's laughter, like the cackle of a panicked chicken, accentuated Pearse's pain. The figure of Archbishop Duffy appeared in his thoughts, guffawing. The classroom door opened. In a rage, Pearse picked up the ball and hurled it back at Forrest. It missed and bounced off one of the girls entering the room.

Pearse shoved Forrest against the blackboard, and both boys fell to the floor.

"Hey, cut it out," Forrest shouted. But his voice gurgled and became a kind of rattle. The boys flailed about. Pearse landed the first blow, and the girls screamed. His fingers got caught beneath Forrest's left shoulder, which was jammed against the wall, and he could do nothing to extract them. Humiliation, like a bright, glistening sore, flared through Pearse's gut.

The door opened once more, and Sister Marie George came in. Immediately she tried to pull the boys apart, but Forrest held on to Pearse's shirt. Pearse hit Forrest in the side. His blows seemed to have little effect, and Forrest began kicking him. But then Forrest's legs got caught between the legs of a chair.

"All right, you boys!"

Pearse felt himself jerked into the air.

"You stop this!"

Father Dimiola held Pearse by one arm and took hold of Forrest's shirt. To Pearse's great surprise, he saw that Forrest was crying, and Pearse began fighting with Father Dimiola himself, to get out of his grasp so that he could pursue the other boy.

"No, Pearse," the priest shouted. He was a thick-muscled man with dark skin and black eyes. Everything in his face was round and filled with flesh. Father Dimiola's fingers dug into Pearse's skin, so that the boy's muscles ached in his grasp. Pearse's legs flopped about. Sister Marie George pushed Forrest toward a chair, and Father Dimiola grabbed Pearse with both hands, gathering him into an embrace. His arms felt like thick straps around Pearse's shoulders.

"Stop it, boy," the priest said. His cassock surrounded Pearse like a black blanket. "I said stop it!"

"But he was making fun of me!" Pearse shouted. His breath came in short gulps. Forrest, now sitting in a chair, snivelled, while Pearse remained in a fury. The fight was like proof to him of his own disgrace and foolishness.

"What did he say to you?" the priest asked.

"He called me Y. A., Father."

Father Dimiola's brow furrowed as he tried to place the name. "Why would he do that?"

Pearse took in a breath, held it a moment to steady himself, and let it out. His teeth ground together as he recalled the clatter of the paten across the altar floor.

"You mean . . ." Father Dimiola broke into laughter. "You mean, Y. A. Tittle?" For a moment, he laughed outright. He moved a hand to his mouth, and barks of glee came out from behind it, each one rattling about Pearse's ears. Both boys remained contrite. Pearse, however, felt a sudden disgust for Father Dimiola as the priest tried unsuccessfully to throttle his levity.

"It was because of yesterday!" Pearse shouted. "Because of what happened at the High Mass!" He stuck his hands in his pants pockets and let his misery overtake him. Sister Marie George sighed, and Father Dimiola finally allowed the smile that had remained on his lips to slip away.

"You shouldn't have done that, Forrest," the priest said.

"Yeah, but, Father . . ."

"And in any case, I don't care who was making fun of whom. Both you boys are coming to my office."

"You're not gonna tell my father!" Forrest said.

"We'll see, Forrest. You follow me."

"Please, Father, don't tell!"

"And you too, Pearse. We'll see about telling both your parents."

The priest followed the boys into the hall. Forrest, his face wet with tears, got the attention of many of the children returning from recess. Pearse pushed his hands into the pockets of his corduroys and walked along silently. He had never been told to go to the principal's office before. That was bad punishment, for the worst offenses. And now he was being escorted there by the principal himself. He did not look at any of the children in the hallway, and he tried to keep his distance from Father Dimiola.

They walked into the principal's office and passed Mrs. Morgan, the secretary, who sat typing at her desk. She looked up, and her mouth fell open with surprise.

"In here," Father Dimiola said, gesturing toward his private office. The boys went in and stopped before the priest's desk.

Father Dimiola paused at Mrs. Morgan's desk. "They were fighting," he said.

"Pearse was fighting?" Mrs. Morgan asked.

Pearse noticed with a kind of saddened pleasure that Forrest's shirt was torn at the collar. A wandering line of snot decorated his lip.

"Yes," the priest replied. "So I'll be in here a few minutes with them. Don't let anyone interrupt, will you?"

"Yes, Father."

Father Dimiola sat down at his desk. The hollow creaking of his chair, like that of an iron gate, filled the room. He wore glasses with thick black frames that obscured his eyes.

"OK. Who started it?" he asked.

"He did!" Forrest said.

"Is that so, Pearse?"

Pearse shook his head.

"Did Forrest here start it?"

"Yes, Father."

"I did not!" Forrest shouted. "I was just coming in to put the ball away."

"Forrest. My name is Father."

Forrest winced and shrugged his shoulders. Pearse chuckled, and the priest turned on him immediately.

"You too, Pearse. There's no laughing in here."

Pearse tightened his mouth. "Yes, Father."

"Now, we will not have fighting on the school grounds, you understand?"

"Yes, Father," both boys replied.

"Especially from one of my altar boys, Pearse. I won't have it."

The children frequently talked among themselves about the boiler room below the school, where Father Dimiola was rumored to have a number of leather straps with which he spanked the boys who were bad. No one had actually seen the boiler room, but Pearse now saw himself surrounded by rusty pipes, cobwebs, and slime, his bottom gleaming bright red.

"You know, Pearse, you got to be an altar boy because you understand the rules here, and you follow them."

"Yes, Father."

"And that means you have a particular obligation."

Pearse could not understand why he was being yelled at, when Forrest had caused the fight.

"Serving Mass is something reserved only for the best," Father Dimiola continued.

"Yes, Father."

"And I know that you are one of the best."

"Thanks, Father."

"Though that could change. Because, Pearse, at Saints Peter and Paul, altar boys do not fight on the school grounds. I can easily keep you from serving Mass, you know. How would you like that?"

Father Dimiola leaned forward and placed his elbows on the papers on his desk. The darkness of the priest's eyes terrified the boy. He seemed to be deeply angry with Pearse. Worse, Pearse sensed that Father Dimiola had always been so.

Pearse felt his own eyes tighten. "But Father, that wouldn't be fair," he said.

"Why not?"

Pearse stuck his hands in his pockets. His mouth turned down at both ends as he sensed that he was at bay.

"It just wouldn't," he said finally.

"We'll see about that."

"Yes, Father," Pearse said.

The priest nodded, then leaned back in his chair. "I think you're a good boy."

This shift in tone felt more positive to Pearse. He hoped Father Dimiola had only been trying to scare him with the talk of kicking him off the altar boys. Indeed, Pearse sensed that the priest was about to change the subject altogether, and, attempting a kind of agreeableness, he nodded.

"But I think you will have to take a little vacation," Father Dimiola concluded.

"You—you mean," Pearse stammered, "I'm getting kicked out of school?"

Both boys stood still, in silence. Pearse felt a movement from Forrest, and glanced at him for a moment. Indeed, Forrest was watching him, and Pearse could do nothing to deflect the other boy's intimidated amusement.

"No, not that." Father Dimiola sat back in his chair. "I'll just tell Monsignor not to expect you at Mass tomorrow, Pearse."

"But Father . . ."

"In a couple weeks, we'll see about letting you serve again. After Thanksgiving, maybe."

"Father!"

"Pearse, don't argue. This is something you brought on yourself. You shouldn't be fighting."

"But it isn't fair!"

"Pearse!" Father Dimiola's fingers were splayed on the desk. Pearse shut up, trying to staunch his surprised anguish before he got into more trouble. His protests whirled about in his throat.

"Now I want you two boys to go home right after school." Pearse looked up above Father Dimiola's head. A small brass crucifix hanging on the wall darkened the office.

"But I want you to go together," the priest continued. "I know your father's store is near Pearse's place, right, Forrest?"

"Yes, Father," Forrest replied.

"Good. You two walk there together. And I mean that." Father Dimiola pointed a finger at them. *"With each other."* The words came out separately, as though each were an order. "You understand?"

Both boys assented.

"And I want *you* to tell your father what happened here today, Forrest."

"But Father. He'll get mad at me. Real mad."

"Too bad."

"Please, Father."

Forrest's hands were clenched at his sides. He seemed to wither. Despite his own unhappiness, Pearse noticed Forrest's fear and was surprised by it.

"Please!"

Father Dimiola joined his hands on the desk. "And I don't want you to say that Pearse here picked a fight with you. Or that you were just going along minding your own business, see. I want you to tell him that *you* were fighting."

The priest turned to Pearse.

"And the same goes for you," he said.

Pearse fixed his eyes on Father Dimiola's index finger, pointed at him like a stubby twig.

That afternoon the sunlight shone on the two boys' backs as they pouted, together, up Columbus Avenue. Fumes swirled from the passing cars. It was warm, and Pearse removed his jacket and wrapped it about his waist. He saw himself reflected in the window of Guardino's Delicatessen, a ghost within the colorful profusion of olive oil tins, packaged almond cookies,

Italian wines, cheeses, and salamis. His hair was mussed, and he attempted to straighten it, to little avail. He was mortified, having to tell his parents what had happened. His stomach felt empty yet heavy, separated from the rest of his body. Forrest walked ahead of him. Pearse wished he could sneak away, but Father Dimiola's voice kept him shackled to the other boy.

It disturbed him to feel that maybe he had been wrong about Forrest, but he did. Forrest's tears had been entirely unexpected, and Pearse had come to suspect, despite his own troubles, that maybe Forrest had not really meant what he had said. In the warm light of the street and its diversions, Pearse thought that Forrest was just being stupid when he called him Y. A. Or that maybe he was just trying to be funny. He stuck his hands in his pockets, stepped into the gutter between two cars, and kicked an empty sardine tin.

The arrival of this sympathy was a complexity that Pearse had not expected, and one that he wished would go away. It was far more satisfying simply to hate Forrest. The tin skittered beneath a parked car, and Pearse stepped up on the sidewalk once more. He took a rubber band from his pocket, stretched it from the end of a finger, and let it go. It caromed off the sidewalk. Watching the rubber band skitter along the cement, Pearse collided with Forrest.

"Excuse me," he said, surprised by the words as they blurted from his mouth. He reminded himself that he was supposed to be sullen. But he noticed that Forrest had hunched his shoulders, fearfully, to protect himself. Forrest had been looking at a pair of tennis shoes in the window, Keds with black hightops and white rubber soles.

Pearse moved on, but Forrest remained where he was. Pearse looked up the street. After a moment, he stepped back toward Forrest.

"Hey, we're supposed to go home," he said.

Forrest tightened his lips and would not look up.

"Together, remember?" Pearse continued.

"I didn't mean anything," Forrest said. There was a long silence. "I was just making a joke."

Pearse became afraid that Forrest would refuse to go any farther.

"You didn't have to hit me," Forrest continued.

"Come on, Forrest!" Pearse looked back down Columbus toward Washington Square. He feared he would see Father Dimiola standing outside the menswear store half a block away, spying on the boys from behind the rack of coats on the side-walk.

"OK," Forrest said, turning again up the street. "But I didn't mean it."

Slowly Forrest followed Pearse up the street to the corner of Columbus and Mason. They paused at the corner, across from the Gold Coin Grocery. Forrest rubbed his cheek with the palm of his hand, as though worried that a teary smudge there would give his guilt away. Pearse kept his hands in his pants pockets. He imagined the oppressive disapproval of his father, who would be waiting for him in the living room. Then Pearse realized that, in fact, his father would not even be home from work yet. That made things worse. At least Forrest would be able to get his punishment over with. Pearse had to wait a couple more hours, each minute passing drearily like a bedraggled float in a parade.

Mr. Yick came out of the store across the street and began going through the oranges in one of the bins. He was dressed in a brown flannel shirt, gray pants, a dark blue apron, and a blue wool watchcap. Forrest did not call out to him. In fact, he seemed to shiver as he watched his father inspect the oranges. Forrest glanced at Pearse and then shrugged, pursing his lips.

"Here goes," he said. He stepped from the curb.

"OK," Pearse replied.

"So, how was school, Pearse?" Joe removed his coat and hung it in the hall closet. Pearse, lost in a maelstrom of nerves, struggled to retrieve what, all afternoon, he had planned to say. But it was gone. Joe turned from the closet and walked into the living room. Unfolding his paper, he sat down in an easy chair near the bay window that looked out on Mason Street.

The windows were covered with starched lace curtains, like snowflakes frozen before the glass. A carved rosewood table in the bay itself resembled a dark crown. A chesterfield—a very puffy couch that sighed as Pearse sat down on it—paralleled the long wall of the living room, beneath a painting of a redwood grove.

"Learn anything today?"

Pearse's eyes moved toward a photo of Franklin Roosevelt that rested in a frame on an end table. Roosevelt was one of Joe's heroes, a president who had supported the working man, just as Joe did when he went to work at his law office every day. Joe often said that it was clear as day that Franklin Roosevelt had been an Irishman. In the photo, Roosevelt wore a hat with the brim flipped up. He grinned widely, and a graceful cigarette holder came out from between his crooked teeth.

The newspaper was open on Joe's lap. Pearse struggled to still his knees. He heard his mother's footsteps in the hall. Mimi came into the room and handed Joe a glass of bourbon. Then she sat down on the chesterfield beside Pearse, wiping her hands with a dishtowel.

Pearse swallowed. His saliva went down his throat in pieces. He placed his hands on his knees.

"I . . ."

"Joe, I talked to your father this afternoon," Mimi said.

Pearse looked away grumpily.

"He said Pearse could come over tomorrow night for dinner if he wants," Mimi continued.

"Where are you going?" Pearse asked.

"To a recital," Joe said. "Tito Gobbi's in town."

Pearse recalled the geography lesson Sister Marie George had given the class the week before. He could not remember the name of the country. She had showed the students where it was on the globe, and there were pictures in the geography book of horses and carts and piles of twigs. There had been a guy named Tito in that country, too.

"He's an opera singer," Joe said. He stood and went to a bookshelf above the record player. He brought out a narrow box of records, on the cover of which was a gray-haired man who was mean-looking and fat, with a pointy beard, a crown, a cape, and sideburns that resmbled shoe polish. "This is him."

Pearse perused the photo. Not the same guy, he thought.

During the fall, the opera was a biweekly event for Pearse's parents, even though they worried that it was too expensive. His father particularly was a devotee, and Pearse had an interest in opera simply because his father liked it so much. Pearse enjoyed the stories, but he had no idea what a performance could be like, except for the screeching on his father's records, which was similar to the screeching on the Texaco opera broadcasts he listened to every Saturday morning. Joe cleaned his golf clubs while he listened to the opera. Sometimes he polished the silver or washed his car in the alley behind their apartment. He conducted with the hose, so that water cascaded through the sunlight up and down, the singers' voices carried along on the beaded spray.

"Would you like to go to MJ's?" Joe asked.

Pearse nodded and sat back. "I guess so." His voice declined
to a whisper at the end.

"He didn't get much of a chance to talk with you, you know,
after the Mass," Mimi said. "And I know he wants to."

Pearse's lips curled against one another.

"He felt badly for you," she continued. "Felt the Mass was
a bad deal. And he just wants to spend some time with you. Let
you sit a while with Doll, maybe read to her."

Mimi stood and took up the towel again. Her dark brown hair
had a reddish sheen that could barely be seen, yet gave it genuine
softness. Her eyes were green and so enormously striking that
they seemed to pause even at those things to which, in fact, she
barely gave a look. For Pearse, Mimi exuded a more specific
kind of love than did Joe, a far better defined love, a gorgeous
love. Often, the way she spoke—in an ironic fashion that made
quiet fun of things—caused Pearse to laugh out loud. He was
thrilled by the whispered profanity she sometimes inserted into
a conversation, because it gave him the freedom to think such
words himself and to ponder the fun of using them. Mimi laid
a hand on Pearse's knee.

"He'd really enjoy it, Pearse," she said.

"Mom, I . . ."

"Good," Joe said. "I'll let him know."

Mimi left to return to the kitchen, and Joe opened the newspaper once more. He snapped it once, to make sure the pages
were clear of wrinkles. It was a ponderous, immediate action
that was identical to MJ's opening of the newspaper. The ex-
panse of newsprint hid the upper half of Joe's body. It was a
paper he received every few weeks in the mail, the *United Irishmen*. Joe sometimes read from the paper to Pearse, articles about
the history of Ireland. They were stories fascinating to the boy,
who was miffed by the mean old English and how they treated
the brave, happy Irish.

The trouble was that the English were the same people who
made the movies his father so loved, like *The Lavender Hill
Mob* and *The Man in the White Suit*. Often, Pearse did not
understand what they said at all in those movies, yet laughed
anyway, amused simply by the way their voices sounded. Pearse
wondered how it was that such humorous people could be so
cruel. They threw the Irish in jail. They took away their potatoes.

Joe crossed his legs, so that one hung loosely before the other,
at an angle. The shoe moved toward Pearse, then away—a leather

pendulum at the end of a sock-covered stick. Pearse had always enjoyed how his father carried himself. Other fathers left for work looking as enthusiastic and gruffly humorous as Joe, but Pearse was convinced that his was the only one who returned from work looking just as fine. The men walking home from the business district in the afternoon seemed frayed. Their shirts hung out in back. They plodded up Columbus Avenue, and their hair flew about. But when Joe Pearse, his briefcase swinging from his right hand, rounded the corner and walked the few yards up Mason Street to the front door of their apartment, he appeared as fresh and talkative as ever. Pearse figured it was just because Joe was a lawyer, though he had noticed that some of the others who worked at Murhpy, Tomlinson were really pretty slovenly. They wore suits, but the suits did not always fit. And even if they did fit, they were quite wrinkled.

Pearse had mentioned that to Joe once.

"It's because we represent unions, Pearse. You don't make any money . . . you don't get elegant, see . . . working for the longshoremen or the retail clerks.''

Joe was a thickset man, with very black, curly hair. His eyes were dark, precise, and large beneath shaggy brows. This evening he wore dark gray wool pants, wrinkled, with a gray pinstripe that was barely discernible, yet which gave the pants a certain lightness. There was a great deal of cloth in them, as there was in the white shirt and ill-tied, striped silk tie that Joe also wore. He was formal but sloppy. It was the sense of amused, careless authority with which Joe dressed that made Pearse so proud of him.

Just now, though, Pearse could not break through the barrier of the newspaper. It was like a flag Joe was holding up to dry. Pearse made out headlines here and there, the biggest one reading "Brits and the Big Lie.'' Pearse muttered to himself, fending off the imagined voices of Monsignor, Father Dimiola, and the Brits—whoever they were—as they bandied about negative-sounding scraps of language and swatches of disapproval—every one of them a lie. Pearse was stung by how much the lies had to do with him. He sat far back on the chesterfield. The front of his T-shirt came out from under his belt, and he stuffed it back in. He looked down at his knees. He waited. Joe laid the paper down to turn the page, and Pearse sat up to speak.

"Dad, I got in a fight.''

Joe seemed not to hear him. He was burly and brusque—big like GI Joe. At this moment, though, he seemed to wander between the paper, which rose up again before his face, and Pearse.

His voice gathered in the air. "What was that?"

"Forrest Yick and me. We got in a fight."

"With who?"

Pearse grimaced. "No, Dad. With each other."

"Oh." Joe's fingers grasped the paper. "Why?"

He didn't like my comic book! Pearse thought. Flustered, he glanced at the floor. Father Dimiola's orders remained in his memory, a dark instruction. Gathering himself to reply, Pearse attempted fairness. But he could not be fair. Forrest made fun of *me*, he thought. He made *me* feel stupid.

"I don't know why," he said.

The newspaper wavered as his father turned a page. Joe uncrossed his legs. His wingtips, both now resting on the floor, were fat and slightly scuffed. Pearse wished it were not so hard to get Joe to listen. Why can't he just put the paper down? he thought.

"Father Dimiola told me to tell you," Pearse said.

Mimi entered the room, wiping her hands again with the towel. She pushed her hair back with one hand. There was a speck of tomato sauce on the towel. "Told you to tell us what, Pearse?" she asked.

Pearse looked once more at the floor. "I got in a fight."

"You did? Why?"

"I don't know!" Pearse shouted. He heard the newspaper falling to Joe's knees. "I mean," he continued, looking at his mother, "Forrest told me the comic book I was reading was sissy, and I didn't like that, and he threw the ball at me, and I didn't like that. . . ."

Pearse could not stand the look his father gave him. It was open and filled with weighty interest in Pearse's explanation. Pearse wished he could figure out what Joe wanted. For instance, the look on his face now was the one Joe always gave when he was about to become angry with Pearse. It was like that a lot with him, so that Pearse and his brother Tim had to navigate Joe's mood before saying anything to him at all.

"What comic?" Joe asked.

"The one I was looking at."

"Which one was that?"

"It was a *Classics Illustrated*." Pearse turned toward his mother. "It was called *Little Girls*."

"*Little Girls,*" Mimi said.

"Yeah. And he laughed at it." Pearse glanced at his father once more, then looked at the floor. "And I thought he should leave me alone. But he didn't."

"So what'd you do?" Joe asked.

Pearse recalled the basketball, its seams twirling before him, then disappearing as the ball collided with his forehead.

"I hit him," Pearse groaned.

"Good!"

"Joe, that is not good," Mimi interjected.

Pearse looked up abruptly at his father, who indeed seemed to approve of what had happened.

"We don't want to have Pearse thrown out of school," Mimi continued.

"But that didn't happen, did it?" Joe asked.

"No," Pearse replied. He bit his lower lip.

"What did happen?"

Pearse closed his eyes. He was buoyed by Joe's support, but he did not understand it. He did not trust it.

"Father threw me off the altar boys," Pearse said. He attempted, vainly, to calm his nerves.

"He's not going to let you serve Mass?" Joe asked.

Mimi wiped her hands with her towel. There was a very long pause, and finally Pearse shook his head.

"Pearse," Joe said. "What did you do?"

"It's just that Father told me I had to tell you about it."

"But what did you do?"

"I mean, to tell you about it as if it was my fault!" Pearse waited a moment as his parents glanced at each other in silence.

"As if what were your fault?"

"That we got in a fight!" Pearse shouted.

"Was it your fault?" his father asked.

"No!"

"Whose fault was it?"

"Forrest's!"

"And you didn't stand up for yourself?"

"I don't know," Pearse said. "I . . ."

Joe's surprising initial patience now seemed about to break down. A burr had entered his voice, a downturn in the tone of it.

"You didn't stand up for yourself?" Joe said once more.

"Father wouldn't let me say what really happened," Pearse replied.

"You told him it was Forrest's fault."

"Yeah, but he wouldn't listen."

"I don't believe that."

"What don't you believe, Joe?" Mimi asked. "That Father wouldn't listen?"

Joe's forehead reddened. "No. That Pearse could just sit there and get thrown off the altar boys without defending himself." He sat back in his chair. "This kid Forrest takes a swipe at him, and Pearse doesn't do anything about it."

"I did, too!" Pearse shouted. "I beat him up!"

"Joe, maybe he couldn't defend himself," Mimi said.

Pearse had gotten caught before in moments like this. His father became abrupt, and then harried his adversary—Pearse, Tim, it did not matter who it was.

"I did try to tell Father," Pearse said.

"You just told us you didn't," Joe replied.

"Pearse got it wrong, Joe," Mimi interjected. "That's all."

Joe held up his hand in an attitude of helplessness. It was a gesture he often made in a conversation, as though a moment had arrived in which the truth, framed like a picture on a wall, must be plain to everyone. "OK," he said. "So, Pearse. Let's try getting it straight."

"He does get it straight," Mimi said. "He's just having trouble explaining himself. Give him a moment."

"Yeah," Pearse said miserably.

He looked up at his mother. Her arms were folded. Joe's mouth dropped at the edges in befuddlement.

"Forrest threw the foursquare ball at me!" Pearse continued. Joe waited, but Pearse could not say any more.

"So Father Dimiola threw you off the altar boys," Joe said.

"Yeah."

"And he made you come home to tell us exactly what happened."

Pearse nodded, holding his breath.

"Were you to blame, Pearse?"

Pearse's shoulders fell. He could not go on. "Yes, I guess so."

A few years earlier, while playing with Tim and some friends in a vacant lot, Pearse had picked up a small piece of cyclone fencing from a refuse heap. He had tried to throw it like a boomerang. One rough-cut edge of it caught in his hand and gashed his index finger from one knuckle to the next. Pearse grasped the hand, blood coursing out over his fingers. He ran home, trailing blood along the sidewalk. The cut had required stitches, and its closure, in neat, puffy sections, had relieved Pearse. It had sickened him to actually peer inside his body, to see the pulse and ooze of his bright blood welling up before him.

Now, silent in front of his father, he imagined a similar gash, larger and shining, filled with his own humiliation. Except this time it contained different colors—gray and shit brown as well as red. The gash was ragged. Its flow was lumpy, profuse, and confusing.

"Are you the only one who's getting thrown off the altar boys?" Joe asked.

"Forrest doesn't serve."

Joe's head moved back and forth.

"I mean, they asked him to once," Pearse continued. "He went to training. But he couldn't pronounce the Latin."

Pearse remembered the other boys imitating Forrest during the training period. He got the words backwards, splitting them up and recombining them in comic ways.

"You must have done something really out of order to get kicked out, Pearse."

"I didn't!"

Mimi dabbed her fingers with the towel. Her eyes hardened, as they frequently did when she was upset. Pearse was surprised to see the look she gave Joe, which included a certain terse bitterness. She did not like what Joe had said, and Pearse waited, hoping she would help him. But Mimi went out of the living room, leaving Pearse alone to face his father.

"I wish my grandpa were here," Pearse muttered.

"Why?" Joe dropped the newspaper to the floor. Pearse's comment had come out of him more or less unexpectedly, and he wished right away that he could gather it back.

"I don't know," he said. He reached into his pocket and brought out a rubber band.

"You think you'd get better treatment from him?" Joe asked.

In fact, that was exactly what Pearse thought. But looking up at his father's face, Pearse recognized that that would be a bad thing to admit to. Joe and MJ squabbled a lot. Pearse's grandfather was always patient with Joe. He waited and waited during Joe's occasional periods of complaint, when Joe seemed unable to be friendly with his father. The complaints particularly seemed to accompany the whisky Joe drank before dinner and the wine he had with dinner. His conversation tripped from moment to moment, and his mood turned quickly from an admiring conversation about Tim's football prowess, for example, to loud grumbles about MJ's being so hard to read.

"Dad, I just think you put things away and guard them," Joe had once said, "so they won't come back and threaten you. You sit and wait."

"What do you want from me, Joe?"

"Rage, maybe. I don't know. Excitement."

MJ had touched his lips with a napkin, examining it afterwards. "Rage leads to wars," he had replied.

Listening to this, Pearse was confused by the two figures sitting at opposite ends of the table. His father was noisy, with his tie undone and the sleeves of his white shirt rolled halfway up his forearms. Joe's hair seemed to burst in curls from his head, and his voice had an immediate volume when he gave an opinion. MJ always wore his coat to the table, a white handkerchief tucked sportily in his breast pocket. The way he let his hand rest on the table, so still that it looked like a model, actually seemed to annoy Joe even further. MJ was always reserved in this way, which made it much easier for Pearse to speak with him than with Joe.

"I love your grandfather, Pearse," Joe said now. "But I grew up with *him* as the father, you know. I know what he can be like."

Pearse winced with the unusual acidity of this remark. He himself felt that MJ would be terrific as a father, taking his kids to Stow Lake in the park, out for ice cream, to the bocce ball courts on Saturdays . . . all the stuff he did with Pearse already.

"And it really angers me," Joe concluded, "that you can think MJ would be a better father than I am."

The bowl of applesauce slipped across the wooden tray and bumped the empty teacup and saucer. MJ shifted the tray onto one hand, rearranging everything the way it had been before. He worried especially about the teapot, which he had once dropped, several years earlier. It had broken into two clean-edged pieces, and his wife Doll had carefully glued it back together. It had been her mother's originally, brought from Ireland. He examined for a moment the curved seam that ran below the spout, through the field of glazed red nasturtiums on the side, and back toward the handle.

He continued up the stairs and turned down the hall toward the bedroom. He had spooned the applesauce from a jar, sprinkling cinnamon on it just as Doll always had, and prepared the

Earl Grey tea in the pot. He had also placed a slice of buttered toast on a small plate, with a cloth napkin in a silver napkin holder. From time to time in the past, during MJ's struggles with the flu or his occasional bursitis, Doll had brought a similar tray to him. She believed that the best expression of love was the completion of small tasks, many of them, for those people for whom you cared. Now that she was so ill herself, MJ tried to complete such tasks for Doll. But his careful imitations paled when he considered how really useless they were. Lately, he went ahead and ate the toast himself. She would not even know he had prepared it.

Doll lay on one side of their double bed, which was made of dark hardwood from Ireland, a wedding gift to them from his older brother Jack. It was typical of Jack to be so extravagant. He had done well selling sheets and blankets wholesale in the Midwest for a New York firm. He was ostentatious, like an American. He could afford the bed, though it had embarrassed MJ at the time because it was so obviously a piece of rich man's furniture, and MJ and Doll were making, between them, six dollars a week the year they were married. Doll had loved the bed from the first. Now her small gray head lay against a pillow that had lace-embroidered borders. She weighed seventy pounds.

He stepped silently into the room and placed the tray on the lace doily that ran the length of the night table. He took up the bottles of pills and shook out the three tablets she would take later that evening. Leaning over her and kissing her, MJ sat down in the rocking chair at the foot of the bed.

Earlier in Doll's illness, MJ had sat in this chair to read to her—usually the gospel for that particular day and articles from the Maryknoll Society magazine. Doll preferred the stories of self-sacrifice on the part of missionary nuns in places like Nanking and the Malay Peninsula. She imagined the isolation of the nuns, out there in the jungle, nursing, as she said, those poor, lost, dark, pagan babies.

MJ looked over his hands, which were lined and darkly freckled. He exhaled as he thought how unexpected it was, Doll's dying before him. She'd never really been ill until now. She was only fifty-seven years old, fourteen years younger than MJ himself. But her cancer had made her gray-skinned, a waste. She had slipped slowly into pain and then oblivion, and MJ didn't know what to do with such solitude. Indeed, he felt that in this dark room he served no function at all, that the darkness made him simply into an old figurine in a chair. As she had lost her strength, Doll had forgotten who MJ was, and he had often stood at the end of her bed wishing he could speak with her.

Finally he had given up, irritated by her breathing and frustrated because it grew more and more difficult-sounding and thin. It seemed to MJ that with each exhalation her illness enveloped her a bit more, like a blanket. Most of the time now her breathing unnerved him, so that he could not remain in the room more than a few minutes. He felt heartless when he left her there alone. But waiting for her to take another breath was just as heartless, because then he felt like Death itself, impatient at the end of the bed.

MJ took up the newspaper from the floor. He read the front page, passed through the first section, then the sports, then the comics. It was a routine he had followed for years. He came to a small article on page six about an IRA man in Maze Prison in Northern Ireland, a political figure. MJ read it over quickly and moved on. A mick in prison, he grumbled. What else is new? He adjusted his suit jacket. It was of brown wool, worn with a white shirt and a dark blue wool tie. It was an old suit, a comfortable suit, and still in quite good condition. MJ was careful about his dress, wishing to avoid the disintegration of himself, what he called the old man's penalty.

He stood up to look out the window. He and Doll lived in a large brick house on Lake Street in San Francisco, near Park Presidio. The bedroom had a view of Mountain Lake Park. The late afternoon sun shed yellow light across the eucalyptus trees on the far side of the pond. The water was dark, almost black. There were tennis courts and a playground as well, a far cry from what he'd played on as a child—rain-soaked cobbled streets in the town of Charleville, in Cork, sixty years ago.

Good Christ, he thought, I'm glad I came here. He had been glad since the moment he'd arrived in Chicago, in 1914, to meet his brother Jack. Jack was dead now, since just after the Korean War. He had gotten MJ a job clerking at Marshall Field and Company, and MJ had done the rest on his own. Fine businessman, he thought now. Everyone said so. He had stayed with Marshall Field for twenty-five years, then gone on the road for O'Brian Brothers, a manufacturer of women's underthings.

He chuckled as he turned back to the newspaper. A man like MJ Pearse peddling women's drawers, he thought. It never made any sense. MJ was conservative, a Democrat, a good Catholic, who smoked cigars and all his life never had a drink. He wouldn't tolerate prurient remarks about what he sold. It's merchandise, that's all, he said, like pots and pans, and he sold it everywhere up and down the West Coast—to the Magnins, to the Daly Brothers in Eureka, to O'Connor-Moffatt.

Downstairs, the front door closed and MJ heard Pearse's footsteps coming up the stairs.

"Hi," the boy said as he entered the room.

"You're early," MJ replied. "Your parents gone to the opera house already?"

"No, they're going out to dinner first. So I just took the bus." Pearse approached the bed. "How's Grandma?" he asked.

"The same," MJ said. "She's sleeping."

"But she's OK."

"Sure. She's fine, Pearse."

The boy removed his jacket and folded it over the end of the bed. He wore a white T-shirt, jeans, and tennis shoes.

"Are you hungry?" MJ asked.

"Yeah."

"Why don't you have some of Doll's applesauce there. She's not going to eat it."

Pearse's love of applesauce was extreme, like the fervor with which he assisted at Mass. He took up the bowl and spoon from the tray. He laid the bowl on his lap and stirred the applesauce, making sure the cinnamon was spread throughout. In three swift spoonfuls, he ate it all. Holding the spoon in his right hand, he placed his left on his grandmother's hand and caressed it. He watched her face a moment.

"Grandpa, why did Grandma have to have Extreme Unction?" he asked. The sacrament, a preparation by the priest of the soul before death, had been given several days before. Doll had been too ill to take Communion, but she was anointed nonetheless. MJ, dressed very carefully, had stood at the end of the bed next to Joe and Mimi, his hand clasped in Mimi's. He had been lost in rage. He thought the sacrament legitimized her passing and assured her death. He imagined that Doll could feel Monsignor's presence and somehow hear the mutter of his prayers. It just tells her that it's all right to give up, MJ had thought. Then he chided himself for being so selfish, because at that moment, he realized, he was not really thinking of Doll at all, of her passage or her soul's welfare. He was worried more about himself and how he would get along without her. His anger churned against this blockish, irritating realization. So damned self-serving, he thought of himself.

It had not helped that Joe had sensed MJ's impatience and had criticized him for it.

"Extreme Unction is a sacrament, Dad. If she *didn't* have it, it'd make her unhappy."

MJ had scowled as Joe said this, though he knew his son was right. Extreme Unction cleansed the soul. What did it matter that the poor woman's selfish husband felt somehow insulted by it?

"She's pretty sick, Pearse."

"But she's not really going to die, is she?"

MJ was pleased by Pearse's delicacy on the subject of Doll's illness. After she had been confined to her bed, Pearse had come to visit several times a week. He read to her from his comic books. Her favorites were those that featured Batman, because Pearse thought he was so exciting and suave. Batman's cars and airplanes, all specially designed and modern with weapons and swept-back wings, made him more than just a hero for Pearse, and he read those stories to Doll with real excitement. Funny kid, MJ thought—he enjoyed the *Classics Illustrated* books as well, especially adventure stories in which the characters fended one another off with elegant swordplay. He had read *A Tale of Two Cities* to his grandmother many times.

" 'It is a far, far better thing that I do,' " Pearse had intoned, " 'than I have ever done . . .' "

"You remind me so much of Ronald Colman, Pearse," Doll had said.

Now MJ sat down on the bed next to Pearse and placed his hand on the boy's back.

"Everybody dies, Pearse," he said.

"But she's not going to die now, is she?"

"No, I don't think so. Doll's got a lot more left in her."

"Then why'd Monsignor give her Extreme Unction?"

"I guess . . . I guess I don't know."

"See," Pearse continued, "they told me at school you only get Extreme Unction when they're sure you're going to die."

"They did?"

"Yeah. Because, if you get the sacrament, you go straight to heaven. That's right, isn't it?"

"Yes."

"But then, if you get better, you could go out and do all kinds of bad things—steal tires, say bad words—and still go to heaven, even if, like, you got run over by a truck."

MJ exhaled and looked off toward the window.

"So," Pearse continued, "they don't give you Extreme Unction if you're not going to die."

"That's right."

Pearse studied the bedsheet a moment.

"But you can receive Extreme Unction many times," MJ said. "It doesn't seem to last, I guess. My brother Jack had it three times before he died."

"He did?"

"Yes. He said he liked it better than going to a ballgame."

"Nah, he didn't say that."

MJ grinned painfully. "Jack said it, yes. But I don't think he meant it."

Pearse licked the last of the applesauce from the spoon.

"So when they told me in school that when you get Extreme Unction you go straight to heaven, that wasn't true?"

"What do you mean?"

"Maybe you stay here on earth," Pearse said.

"It's possible. But at least you won't go to hell."

"Grandma wouldn't go to hell anyway, would she?"

"Of course not."

Pearse placed the bowl back on the tray. "Then why did she need Extreme Unction?"

Confused, MJ shook his head. "I don't know, Pearse." He watched as Pearse put his hand once more on Doll's. "I don't know. Listen, there are some Oreo cookies in the kitchen. You want to have one?"

The room grew silent, unusually so. MJ glanced beyond Pearse at Doll. Something had happened in the moment they were talking. Doll appeared distant, even motionless.

"Where are they?" Pearse asked.

"On the shelf by the refrigerator."

Pearse left the room, and as he descended the stairs MJ turned quickly to Doll. To his horror, she appeared to have died.

MJ took up Doll's hand. He shook it, and suddenly she began breathing once more. Relieved, he adjusted her hair with his fingers. How would you explain to Pearse that she'd died? he wondered. How will you explain it to yourself? MJ thought with sadness of the humor there was in a loved one's demise, the clichés brought up by the priest at the funeral about how it was that so and so had led a full life, that so and so had died fulfilled, completed, and without remorse. Doll would laugh at that. She always knew, he thought, that everyone would do things differently if they could only *stay* alive.

MJ glanced at the photos on her night table. The one of Pius XII showed a plain man in plain glasses. The pontiff's face was black and white, and his vestments were tinted in watercolors. A portion of his face and his left arm were stuck to the glass. There was also a photo of Pearse getting a drink of water in Golden Gate Park, at the age of two. Kind of a golden time, MJ thought. He chuckled to himself as he recalled the paten twirling through the air on First Communion Sunday a few days before. Pearse's mortification, so obvious in his rapidly paling face, had brought many bursts of laughter from the pews, perforated by the sound of the paten landing on the floor. No, when he was two, MJ thought, poor Pearse wouldn't have had the faintest idea how to betray himself like that. In the photograph, Joe held on to the collar of Pearse's coat, restraining him. The stream of water splashed abruptly against the boy's lips.

MJ wondered how Pearse would remember the Communion Mass. Now, the boy was humiliated. But would he think back with rueful humor one day on the archbishop's amusement, or on the cold bacon and eggs in his bedroom? MJ's own memories, which had been constant since Doll's illness had begun, seemed hardly selective at all. He remembered everything, especially things that brought him happiness, like their wedding day and the day Joe was born. But there were moments of chagrin, even of difficulty, like his last days in Ireland, hiding in Dublin, when he had had to cadge meals from his cousin Donal Pearse and his wife, and sleep on their couch. The darkness of that living room was the freshest memory, a piano in a corner, an oak dish cabinet filled with gloomy crystal, and a painted wall, stenciled below the plate rail with a pattern of leaves. The dark had turned the leaves to black thorns.

Next to the picture of Pearse, there was another of MJ and Doll in Chicago when they had first married, in 1918. A happier day, he thought, to be sure. MJ wore a black suit, a black vest, and a white, high-collared shirt with a black tie and a derby hat.

"A funeral director," he grumbled as he looked at it. "Ward heeler."

Doll's white dress and the spray of flowers in her hair . . . the photo never did justice to how pretty she was that day, he thought. Seventeen years old. MJ, at thirty-one, was considered just the right age to marry. But it was odd, he thought now, how little prepared I was for Doll. Like the way she insisted on having flowers all the time. In Ireland he had never thought of flowers at all, and he had been surprised to find how, in Chicago, in midwinter, they were the most important things in Doll's life.

One day, a few months after their wedding, Doll had brought a cup of coffee from the stove for MJ, taking a small pitcher of cream from the icebox and pouring some of it into his cup. The cream settled through the coffee, then moved up from the bottom of the cup in a graceful, muddy swirl. MJ watched it, declining to stir the coffee with his spoon until the cream had slowed of its own accord. Doll replaced the coffee pot on the stove and sat down to finish the wheat toast and jam that remained on her plate. A crockery vase, filled with flowers she had dried the previous summer, stood at one edge of the round kitchen table. A window looked out on a cramped dirt yard, now colorless with snow except along the fence, where a red wheelbarrow lay sheltered from the wind. Doll took up the slice of toast. Her hands, which were small, with slim fingers, cradled it. She seemed to want to protect it, even as her lips closed about one corner of the slice, which was covered with blueberry jam.

"The jam reminds me of summer," she said, looking out the window. She fingered one of the dry thistles, which rattled when it rubbed against the other flowers. "It's so cold here, Michael," she said.

Like bits of broken glass, small petals from a daisy fell to the table.

MJ took her hand in his and kissed it. He was dressed for work in his wool suit, his shirt starched and ironed, his dark blue tie the only bit of color allowed by his department manager at Marshall Field, a kindly, dull-voiced man named Smythe. MJ's face was clean and shaved. His hair, which he combed straight back, was quite dark, almost black, and it shone with oil.

"Was it like this in Ireland?" Doll asked.

MJ caressed her fingers. "We didn't have it as cold as this," he said. "Rain, yes. But this kind of snow . . . I don't know what we'd do with such snow."

"Then why would an Irishman like yourself come to a place like this?"

The smile MJ gave as an answer sustained the moment long enough to avoid an actual reply. MJ had not intended to leave Charleville, where he had lived with his parents in the house where he had been born. He had had a good job as a clerk in a draper's shop owned by a Protestant named Holmes. MJ's plan was to open a shop of his own one day. But now, as he let his reply wander into silence, he remembered how those plans had so abruptly changed.

Doll cinched her cotton robe and wrapped her hands about her own cup of coffee. Her hair was taken up in a black ribbon. She had light green eyes that were very direct and far from simple. They gave Doll such an air of elegance that she seemed far more settled than a seventeen-year-old girl. The fact was, he was surprised that Doll had married him. For one thing, she was an American whose parents had come over from Ireland, quite young, in 1896. She made fun of his accent, although he had worked on it steadily to rid it of the Irish argot, to take on the flat, picturesque Chicago drone. He had even changed his name, from Michael to the more brusque, American-sounding MJ.

When she lay in bed with him, MJ felt he had found some kind of exotic. From his point of view, it seemed that she was the foreigner rather than he. Her upbringing had been so different from his own that sometimes he felt there was almost nothing in common between them. Her parents had Irish girls as servants, some of whom had been in the States longer than MJ himself. Her father, a politician named Kennealy, hardly seemed Irish at all, especially in the way he talked, with his sloppy enunciation. Kennealy felt disposed toward MJ, though, because Kennealy had Fenian sympathies and sent money to the IRB. He liked a man, he said, who knew where his heart should lie. But MJ had not had the nerve to tell Kennealy that he thought they all were idiots, all the Irish, especially the Irish Republican Brotherhood.

Doll's speech as a girl was not restrained or careful in any way. She had thrown off the tight reserve that made the Irish-born girls seem iron-willed, even old. Her casual dress was criticized by other women in the parish, who said her mother had lost control of her. Doll was not sensible-sounding, not bogged down by the nuns, not afraid to move. At first, MJ was a little afraid of her. She had seemed so free with her conversation. She had been scattered, but in the way a garish flower was scattered, petals everywhere, declarative and open.

"Pearse'll be right back," MJ said to her, interrupting his revery. Her skin was gray now and gave off little light. Her hair was neatly combed, but it had lost so much color in recent months that MJ felt she actually looked older than he. He glanced over his shoulder. He was worried that the boy would come back too soon, before Doll recovered herself. She took in a long breath, as though suddenly surprised. For a moment she did not move. She seemed to be contemplating something in a shrouded distance. MJ took her hand, then placed his fingers against the spotted skin of her wrist. Her pulse had weakened. But it had weakened before, often, and come back within minutes. She exhaled, and for a long moment appeared once more to have died.

MJ leaned closer, imploring another breath from her. He put his ear next to her mouth, then felt again for her pulse. Her heart continued, but it seeemed far away.

"Doll," he whispered.

Her pulse receded and stopped.

"Doll!" MJ touched her cheek and ran his fingers over her mouth. There was no movement, and his chest suddenly tightened with fear. But after a moment, the heartbeat started once more and stabilized in a weak, inconstant flutter.

"I've got the cookies, Grandpa," Pearse said as he reentered the room.

"Don't come in!" MJ said.

"But Grandpa," Pearse said.

Frightened, MJ glanced over his shoulder. Pearse held the package of Oreos in his right hand. He had opened it on the stairs and now held one of the cookies. A crescent-shaped bite had been taken from it, and the boy's lips were dotted at each side of his mouth with brown crumbs.

"Pearse, you shouldn't be in here," MJ said.

"But why?" Pearse asked.

"Just wait in the hall. I'll tell you later."

"No, I don't want . . ."

"Pearse, get out!" MJ himself was so afraid that his harsh order strengthened him. He turned once more to Doll. Her upper lip trembled a moment, then became still.

"Grandpa." Pearse stepped back toward the doorway.

MJ heard the rustle of the cellophane wrapper. He pressed his fingers tightly against Doll's wrist. She was not breathing at all.

"Doll," MJ whispered, this time with insistence. His own heart knocked within him. "Please, Doll. Please."

"Grandpa, what's wrong?"

MJ dug his fingers into Doll's wrist, worrying that he would bruise her skin. "Love," he whispered. The sheet was mussed over Doll's chest, unlike how she would have arranged it. He slumped over her. "Please," MJ said.

Her heart gave way, and she died.

"Please, Grandpa!" Pearse shouted.

In the still hand MJ took up, Doll's bones moved, but only because MJ moved them. Her mouth had fallen open. Her eyelids, though shut, seemed too thin and white to actually keep her from seeing. MJ turned his head away. His eyes were shut tight. For the moment he had forgotten Pearse's presence in the room. But now, weeping, the boy appeared at his shoulder, and MJ realized that Pearse had defied his order.

Pearse sat in his grandparents' kitchen, a glass of milk before him on the table. The residue on the side of the glass looked to him like chalk and phlegm. A number of police and firemen stood in the hall. At another time they would have thrilled him, but now they looked monstrously heavy to Pearse—brutes cluttering the house. A policeman sat at the desk in the hallway, where Doll had sat when she spoke on the phone. The heels of his shoes were hooked to the crossbraces of the oak chair, beneath the seat. It was a chair on which Doll had allowed few people to sit, because of its fragility. Pearse, for one, was never permitted to use it.

As MJ walked into the kitchen, Pearse picked up a spoon. He tapped it against the side of the glass. MJ's eyes were watery and sad, as they had appeared when he and Pearse had come back down the stairs and gone to the phone. Pearse, still embittered by his grandfather's shouting at him, had sensed that the old man did not know what to do as he searched for the telephone book.

First, MJ had phoned the opera house. The performance had not started yet, and he did not know at what restaurant Joe and Mimi were having dinner. Then, swearing, he searched for a second number in the phone book and called the fire department.

"Yes," he muttered. He wiped his forehead with one hand. Pearse, sitting at the table in the kitchen, felt isolated by his voice, as though he were dreaming his grandfather's request. "My wife. Yes, she's gone, I think. Yes. But now, please. As soon as possible."

Afterwards, MJ waited with Pearse in the kitchen. They heard sirens far away. Usually, Pearse expected sirens to be frightening but distant, and then to fade. These became louder, though, and louder. The darkness in the hallway turned bright red as light came through the cut-glass window of the front door.

The firemen came into the house with flourishing authority. There were two of them, dressed in black rubber slickers. Pearse was disappointed that they had not worn their helmets.

"What happened?" one of the men asked.

"It's my wife," MJ said. "Upstairs."

"OK. Come on, Eddie," he said. Turning toward the stairs, he almost ran into Pearse. "Excuse me, kid," the man said. "Out of the way."

Pearse was thrilled. But as they clattered up the stairs their red oxygen bottle gouged some paint from the wall, and the boy winced. He waited below, his arm wrapped about the bottom of the oak bannister.

The firemen talked a moment in the bedroom.

"Nah, Eddie," Pearse heard, finally. "She's dead."

The last two words seemed to blacken the stairwell. After a moment, one of the men reappeared. He looked exhausted in his black coat.

Now, in the kitchen, MJ laid a hand on the back of the boy's head. "It's pretty awful, isn't it, Pearse?" he said.

Pearse pulled away. He laid his chin on his open palm, so that his cheeks and lips puffed out.

"Come on, Pearse," MJ said. His voice was gravelly, and it dropped down with impatience.

"You yelled at me," Pearse said.

The policeman at the telephone was laughing, and he sat forward to lean on the writing desk. His fingers, wrapped about the black receiver of the phone, appeared crooked, broken.

"I guess I was scared, Pearse. I'm sorry."

"Why does he have to sit in Grandma's chair like that?" Pearse asked.

MJ looked into the hallway. "You've got me. These fellows aren't . . . they don't care as much about the family as we do."

"But . . ."

"Just doing their job."

The sweat on MJ's forehead shone above his temples, and the strands of gray-white hair seemed laden with liquid.

"I didn't expect so many people, though," he said. "I wish Joe would get here."

The policeman hung up the phone and came into the kitchen. He was sweating as well.

"The coroner will be here in a minute, Mr. Pearse."

"More people?"

"We have to, sir. He's got to be here."

"But . . . What is your name?"

"Jim Michaels."

"Yes, Officer Michaels, this is all too much!"

Michaels's uniform was dark blue and appeared to be full of stuffing. He had a black, neatly trimmed moustache, like Clark Gable's, and a red-mottled face, the kind MJ said went along with "being lost in the drink." Pearse had heard his grandfather's phrase often, in saddened conversations about various relations and old friends. He imagined himself, in a diving suit with a round brass helmet, making his uncertain way through the ice cubes in his father's whisky. The crisp star Michaels wore on his chest was the neatest thing about him. His graying hair stood up wildly from his head, but only here and there, so that he appeared partially electrified. The knot of his blue tie was soiled.

"We'll be out of here in a couple minutes, sir. We've just got to write a few reports and dispose of the remains."

He glanced at Pearse, who averted his eyes to the revolver on Michaels's hip. He wanted to look more carefully at it. Even, maybe, to touch it. Michaels turned and left the room.

"Remains," Pearse thought. He whispered the word to himself. It had a palpable feel in his mouth, like dirt. It was a piece of gum on the street. Stuff. Gunk. His mouth soured with the remembered taste of other remains, like warm sherbet on a plate, separated and grainy. Pearse's heart beat slowly. He thought of his grandmother in her bed, falling apart before him like the leftovers of an old stew. After several minutes, the doorbell rang.

Pearse stood up. His heart raced as he looked for his father to come through the door. Instead, a very tall man with a piece-meal shadow of beard on his face entered the house and followed Michaels back into the kitchen. The man wore a suit that was not wrinkled at all. He looked like he never sat down. Pearse noticed how the knot of this man's tie was not at all dirty. And there wasn't a crease in it, unlike the knots in his father's ties, which looked like crinkled paper.

"Mr. Pearse, this is John Everett, from the coroner's office."

Everett offered his hand to MJ, and Pearse took his chair again at the table.

"Hello, Mr. Pearse," Everett said. "Sorry we have to barge in on you tonight, and for what's happened."

"Thank you," MJ replied.

"I've just got a few questions." Everett looked down at Pearse. "Hello, son. You're . . ."

"My grandson," MJ replied.

"Yes. Well, I feel badly for your grandmother."

Everett's face looked chipped and pocked. He seemed like a kind enough man, but the turn of his eyes toward the folder he carried, so immediately after his expression of condolence, offended Pearse. Tightening his lips, Pearse looked away.

"Maybe we should speak in private," Everett said.

MJ made a fatigued gesture toward the living room. As Everett passed into the hallway, MJ leaned on the kitchen table and placed a hand on Pearse's arm.

"I'll be back in a minute."

"When are my mom and dad going to get here?"

"Soon. A couple minutes, I hope. I'll be in the living room."

MJ left the kitchen and followed Everett up the hallway. Pearse sat waiting a moment. He felt isolated in the brightness of the kitchen. He could see everything in the room. A string of garlic, like small brains, lay coiled in a metal basket by the stove. Pearse's stomach tightened, and he looked down at the floor. One of his tennis shoes was untied. The cloth of his pants legs rubbed against his thighs like insects.

He stood and left the kitchen. No one noticed him as he paused at the doorway to the living room. MJ sat on the couch. His eyes were haggard, and in the dim light they looked dried out and papery.

"We'll need you to sign this, Mr. Pearse," Everett said, "and then we can take her away."

MJ took a pen in his hand and, slowly shaking his head, signed the sheet of paper in Everett's folder.

"Where will she be?" he asked.

"The morgue."

"Oh, Jesus."

Pearse walked to the stairs, saw that he was unnoticed, and ascended to the second floor. He entered Doll's room. Her face had been covered with a blanket. Pearse's mouth became dry, and he could not move. Frightened, he turned to leave. But as he stepped back toward the doorway, he thought how much he wanted to touch his grandmother. He could not allow her to be taken away without doing something for her. He turned back, then paused a moment as he tried to quell the sense of helplessness that made him so afraid. He expected to see movement beneath the blanket, perhaps a hand pushing it aside, or an exhalation as Doll turned her head to look out the window.

But his grandmother made no such adjustment. The blanket was still, and he could just make out the profile of Doll's chin and nose. He swallowed. He had to get the blanket away from her face. Opening and closing his hands, he took in a breath and stepped toward the bed.

Pearse took the blanket between his thumb and index finger, but he was unable to pull it away. In the comics, death had always been exciting—a Nazi, in flames, exploding from a foxhole, or a declaration of some kind from a wounded pirate—the location of the treasure, maybe—before he slumped into the arms of Captain Blood. Death was filled with fire and sacrifice. But his grandmother's passing had not seemed like death at all. It was like sleep. Nothing had happened. He fingered the blanket. Death couldn't be just a nap, he thought, just nothing.

Pearse turned the blanket aside.

He took in a breath. Doll's eyes were open very slightly, so that he saw the reflection of light in the narrow slits between her eyelids. Her lips, which in life had moved and smiled and passed words, now appeared straplike and thin, colored gray like the ocean in winter. Trembling, Pearse touched Doll's cheek.

He implored her silently to take his hand. But as the backs of his fingers moved across her skin, she still did not move. Pearse caressed Doll's hair, then her eyes. Finally he sat down next to her and joined his hands in his lap. His face felt gorged with liquid.

She was dead. She would not say anything to him.

He noticed Doll's napkin holder on the tray and picked it up. It was pure silver and monogrammed with a large *P*, which was nestled in a bed of engraved leaves. There were lacelike cracks in the silver.

Pearse decided to take it. He would put it in his room, on his desk. It was something just for him, a private recollection. Standing up, he walked toward the doorway, where he was met by the smiling Everett.

"Hello, son," Everett said. "I'm sorry, but you're not supposed to be here."

"Why?"

"It's just that we have some things we need to do with her."

Everett gestured toward Doll, then entered the room. He was followed by Officer Michaels, who hurriedly crossed to the bed and replaced the blanket over Doll's face. Sensing the weight of the cloth on his grandmother's eyes, Pearse stepped toward the bed once more.

"Did you do anything in here?" Everett asked.

Pearse stopped.

"Touch anything?"

"No," Pearse replied. He slipped the napkin holder into his pocket. "Just looking around."

Pearse searched for MJ, who evidently had remained downstairs. He moved toward the doorway.

"What about that thing in your pocket?" Michaels asked.

Pearse blushed, feeling suddenly like a thief. "I'm gonna take it with me."

"You've got to put it back, son," Everett said.

"Why?"

"I have to do a report, and we can't have anything removed from the room."

"Especially anything of value," Michaels added.

"But I want it. It's my grandmother's."

"I'm sorry," Michaels interjected. "Not now. You'll have to put it back." He approached Pearse. "Give it to me."

Pearse brought the napkin holder from his pocket and slapped it into Michaels's outstretched hand. Michaels laid it on the dresser, then turned to the boy once more. Putting a hand on his shoulder, the policeman attempted to escort Pearse from the room. In its holster, the handgun was at the level of Pearse's chest. The black metal butt had a piece of polished wood on each side. It was monumental and violent. Pearse imagined the gun going off, taking part of his head away.

"Leave me alone," Pearse said. He pushed Michaels's hand away.

"Come on, son. You've got to go now."

"I *won't*."

Everett moved toward the doorway, to call MJ. Michaels knelt before Pearse on one knee and took him by the arms. Pearse pulled away before the policeman could speak, and Michaels took hold of him more closely.

"Listen, son, I know how you feel. But we have to do some things for her, and then we'll take her away so you won't have to worry about her."

Pearse pulled his arms from Michaels's grasp. "Don't you even know her name?" he asked.

"Of course I do. It's Mrs. Pearse. Margaret Pearse."

"It's Doll!" Pearse shouted. "Doll!" Pearse pushed past Michaels and approached the bed once more.

There was noise downstairs, many voices. Pearse heard footsteps on the stairs.

Michaels turned the boy around by his shoulders. The policeman's face was mottled and dark. "Come on, son," he said. "Stop it."

Pearse swung at Michaels's chest. "Leave me alone!" he shouted. He felt crazy, as though Michaels were an animal attacking him. He hit him again, coming close to Michaels's face.

"Pearse!"

The boy's head snapped about as he heard his father rushing up the stairs. Joe, followed by MJ and Mimi, came into the room and took Pearse by the hand.

"Let go of him," he said to Michaels, who stood and stepped back. "Pearse," Joe repeated. He knelt and took the boy in his arms.

Pearse buried his eyes in the cloth of his father's overcoat. His heart beat clumsily, and he began, once more, to weep.

"Jesus, Dad, how could you let Pearse come up here like this?" Joe said.

MJ, stung by the rebuke, turned away.

"I'm this boy's father," Joe said to Michaels. His voice surrounded Pearse. "This is my mother who's dead here, and we've called her doctor. You know you don't have to be here."

"We were called, Mr. . . . Mr. . . . ."

"Joe Pearse."

Joe let go of the boy and took out his wallet. He extracted a business card and handed it to Michaels.

"My father called you because he did not know what to do. Look, you can see there that I'm an attorney. You don't need to be here. He was scared, that's all. Can't you see that?"

"Mr. Pearse . . ."

"Get out!"

Michaels ran a hand through his hair. "Mr. Pearse, we don't know any of the details here. We were called, and we came. Your mother's died, and we don't know why."

"She's been sick for months."

"Under her doctor's care?"

"Of course!"

Michaels hung his head a moment. "You know, damn it," he sighed, "your father could have called your mother's doctor, and the doctor could have done all this. But he didn't tell us anything.''

"He panicked. He just didn't know," Joe said. "Christ, they've been married for forty years. How can you expect him not to panic?''

Pearse held on to the lapels of Joe's coat. Michaels's face oozed, without definition, through his tears. The policeman moved to the doorway. Pearse, still incensed with anger at him, looked out from his father's coat. The blanket over Doll's face smothered her, and Pearse tried in vain to blot out the sound of Michaels's voice as the policeman apologized.

"Yes, it's a sad evening," Monsignor said. He sat in an overstuffed chair across the living room from MJ. He had removed his coat, so that his white shirtsleeves appeared chalky against the burgundy velvet of the chair. A glass of Early Times rested on the end table next to him. Mimi had given him a cork-bottomed coaster as well, on which to place his drink.

After the police left, Joe had phoned Monsignor and asked him to come over. The priest and his father had been friends for many years. In the thirties, when Monsignor was an assistant at Saints Peter and Paul, he had also been advisor to the Knights of Columbus chapter there, and it was then that they had met.

The two men had taken up golf together. An immediate fan, MJ had hired a professional to teach him. Monsignor played as often as MJ, but he was less of an athlete, and his swing remained tentative and anguished. "Moral failure is the emblem of a game of golf," Monsignor had once said. He always felt that Satan himself was holding his bag. Thus, when Monsignor teed off, his club staggered through its circuit, leaving him leaning dangerously backwards at the end. The ball jetted away at an angle, a rapid dot ricocheting off the base of a nearby tree. His progress was a mixture of divots and lengthy searches. Age had reduced MJ's long game, but Monsignor's had never really existed, except insofar as, after several strokes, he finally got to the green and the rest of the waiting foursome.

He fingered the sand wedge Joe had brought him from the garage, one of a new set of clubs MJ had bought the month before. Monsignor's white hair shone in the gloomy light. His hair made him appear a larger man than indeed he was. On the golf course, he resembled the president of a company or an important politician. He was tall. He ambled along in an Irish sweater and made condescending, pleasant jokes between his numerous attempts to hit the ball.

He put the club aside. "You know, I'll miss her, MJ."

"Thank you. We all will."

Monsignor's arrival had only served to flood MJ with recollections. Monsignor had officiated at Joe and Mimi's wedding, and, in turn, he had baptized Tim and Pearse—both boys, as it happened, on sunny days. MJ recalled with fondness the tableaux in the baptistery, the family warmed by the light from the stained-glass windows. The day of Pearse's baptism, in 1947, Doll had worn a small-brimmed black hat, swept around one side by five feathers, dyed red. Pearse, in his father Joe's own baptismal dress of white linen, had still had the red hair with which he was born. The black-and-white photo of Pearse in his grandmother's arms had not done justice to their colors together, nor to Doll's flushed happiness.

"I imagine Pearse was quite upset, wasn't he?" Monsignor said. "To actually see his grandmother pass away."

"Of course. Yes."

As the police were leaving, Pearse had sat with Mimi on the stairway. His face was covered with tears, yet there remained fresh defiance of all these intruders. It was a defiance that appealed to MJ, even though he too was in Pearse's doghouse. He was sorry he had shouted at the boy, especially because Pearse had later so clearly shared MJ's unhappiness that so many people were milling around, just talking to each other. They were laughing, for God's sake, MJ thought, and my wife had just died. Pearse's insistence on taking the napkin holder had pleased his grandfather greatly.

He's like that in church too, MJ thought. Pearse's religion was sincere and devout in a way that only a child's, or an ascetic's, could be. MJ knew that when Pearse fumbled about on the altar, scratching himself and mumbling like all the altar boys did, he yet felt the transport of his soul to a kind of ecstasy. His father Joe was the same, when it came to the church. And MJ thought that was terrific, even though Pearse was not old enough to notice that the answer provided on the altar was insubstantial in almost every other moment in life. In the end, religion is just show business, MJ mumbled to himself. It gets tarnished by other things as time passes, such as self-betrayal. Foolishness. Death.

"I remember how happy Doll was when Tim was baptized," Monsignor continued. "*And* Pearse. Remember?"

"Yes." -

"When I poured the holy water on Pearse's forehead, do you remember how he cried?" Monsignor broke out laughing, and MJ put a finger before his own mouth, requesting quiet. He pointed toward the ceiling and the second floor, where Pearse now was asleep in the guest room. Pearse and Joe were staying the night.

"You know what's happened to him, don't you?" MJ asked.

Monsignor shook his head, studying the sand wedge once more.

"Your fellow Dimiola won't let him serve Mass any more."

"Why? When did that happen?"

"I don't know. A few days ago. For some kind of fight he got into in school."

"Pearse?"

"Yes. And I'm sure he'll want to serve Doll's Requiem Mass."

Monsignor settled back in the chair and took up his glass of whisky. "I don't know what it is about Jack Dimiola, MJ."

"How do you mean?"

"He throws his weight around as though he were the pope himself." Monsignor leaned back and downed the rest of the whisky. He placed the glass on the table. "Mussolini, that's who he is. But we'll take care of it, you and I. You know, Dimiola was my assistant when I was pastor there. He'll listen to me."

Only half the glass rested on the coaster. The other half touched the tabletop itself.

"Would you and Pearse care to meet me at the rectory the day after tomorrow, after the plans get started for the funeral? I'm sure we can take care of this in a few minutes."

MJ, worried that he would be taken away from the preparations for Doll's Mass, shook his head.

"It'll be a difficult day, MJ," Monsignor insisted, "and this'll be a break, see? Take your mind off things. Come on."

"OK," MJ replied. "I'll be there. I'll pick up Pearse after school, and we'll come right over."

"Fine." Monsignor stood and stretched. MJ stood up as well, relieved that the moment had finally arrived for the priest to go.

"Thank you for having me," Monsignor said. "You know, a priest is supposed to know what to say at times like this." He ran his hand across the back of his neck a moment, looking at the floor. "But it's just a sad, sad day."

MJ, feeling the genuineness of Monsignor's own loss, and wishing to reply, was too fatigued to do so. He waited as Monsignor put on his coat, then shook his hand, a disconsolate gesture that served to hurry the priest out the door.

MJ went to the kitchen, where Joe and Mimi were cleaning up. He took the glass of milk and the Oreo cookie Mimi offered him. He received a hug from her, then turned toward the doorway.

"You going to be OK, Dad?" Joe asked.

"Sure. Don't worry about me. Good night."

As he approached the top of the stairs, though, MJ slowed, frightened by the darkness. He paused and ate the cookie. He loosened his tie. He could smell his own sweat, which nauseated him because it reminded him of how Doll had smelled as she had become more and more ill. He sipped from the milk and stepped toward the doorway of the bedroom, faltering a moment when he saw the lamplight reflecting off the fresh sheets Mimi had placed on the bed. He entered the room.

He sat down in the rocking chair. Mimi had pulled back the blanket, so that the sheet was exposed in a large triangle. The lamplight was dim and threw few shadows. The sheet had no depth. It was gray-white, and MJ imagined himself lying down on it and sinking into it, drowned. He sat back in the chair and crossed his legs. Drowned in loneliness, he thought. He finished the milk and placed the glass on the floor.

He stood up. Calming himself, he approached the bed, removing his shirt. The button on one cuff would not come undone. Finally he loosened it and took the shirt off, swearing at it beneath his breath. He was startled by a movement to his left. But then he saw it had been made by his own reflection in the mirror, that of an old man in a T-shirt, the skin on his arms sagging and lined.

He held the dress shirt loosely. He felt exposed. His arms were very white.

MJ recalled a man he had known in Charleville in 1914, a retired policeman from Cork named Monohan. He was a prisoner, held by the Irish Republican Brotherhood. MJ's involvement with the IRB had been disapproved of by the parish priest in Charleville. After MJ had attended his first meeting, Father Devlin had heard about it and admonished him. "You're a fine young man, Michael, and your parents have been good Catholics all their lives. You can't just throw your future away with this Republican foolishness.'' But MJ had not worried about the priest. And when he had been asked to guard Monohan, he had been proud to do it, though he did not tell his parents.

MJ arrived every evening about seven at the farmhouse of a man named John Creeley. He stayed until eleven, keeping an eye on the old man, at which time Creeley himself took over, padlocking the door to the cellar in which they kept the prisoner.

The first evening that MJ had been taken to the cellar, when he got to the bottom of the stairs he saw the old man standing at a table in the middle of the room. Monohan wore a shirt and wool pants. Because the cellar was so cold, he was wrapped up in a blanket as well. Monohan had round eyeglasses and was semi-bald. A strand of white hair hovered in the air to the side of his head. He was about seventy years old.

You dumb fool, MJ thought, as he looked back at the mirror once more. You look like Monohan only because you're so old. He turned away from the mirror. He was nonetheless frightened by this recollection. He had thought of Monohan often over the years. When he had first met him, MJ had been unable to imagine what such an old man could have done to so offend the IRB.

MJ sat down on the bed to remove his shoes and socks. He let them lie where they dropped, then stood to take off his pants. He looked again in the mirror. His T-shirt bulged above his belt, and his chest seemed small by comparison to his gut. There was a stoop in his shoulders. MJ tried standing up straight, then let the stance go. Doesn't matter, he thought. He shook his head. Doesn't matter any more at all.

He wanted quiet and memory, but not the memory of what had happened earlier this evening in this room. That was too unforgiving, and filled MJ with regret. It caused him to wonder what more he could have done to save Doll, what more to prolong her life. Instead, MJ wanted to remember Doll from years ago. Her hand in his as they lay in bed. The turn of her shoulder beneath his caress, the cloth of her nightgown.

He lay down on the cold sheet. Closing his eyes, he thought how it would be appropriate for him to be afraid, lying in the bed in which his wife had just died. But they had made love here. They had slept with each other through illnesses and arguments. They had gotten old here.

MJ pulled the blanket up around him and turned off the lamp. A streetlight formed a dim swatch of blue through the curtain, shredded by the folds of the cloth. Otherwise the room was

black. MJ waited for sleep. But the memory of Doll's fading
heartbeat intruded on him, repeatedly, in pieces. After several
minutes he allowed the warmth of the blanket to cheer him,
though he lay in the darkness weeping.

"Now, Forrest and Pearse," Sister Marie George said, "I
want you two to sit here together . . ."

Pearse and his mother had decided he would go to school, de-
spite the funeral preparations. "It'll keep your mind off things,
Sweetheart," Mimi had said, as she prepared his bag lunch.
"And Doll will be with you at school, don't worry."

Though there had been a sort of rapprochement between the
two boys during their walk home the day of the fight, Pearse
was still stung by the trouble Forrest had caused him. Pearse
had kept his distance, even though Forrest had actually sat down
next to him the day after their fight, at lunch time, on a bench
in the playground. Pearse wondered whether Forrest was going
to start the whole thing all over again. But Forrest simply ate
his sandwich, placed the wrapper in his paper bag, stood up,
and moved toward the garbage can at the end of the bench.

"See you," he said.

The sun shone directly on Pearse's face. Children ran about
on the playground in a confusion of colors and noise. Pearse
looked to either side. There was no one else on the bench. He
folded his arms and leaned back, exhaling.

He decided that Forrest must have been talking to him.

"And read this book together," Sister Marie George continued. She laid the book on the table in the reading corner where
the two boys sat. Pearse had avoided reading altogether since
the fight, feeling that, for the moment, he wanted to keep from
getting into trouble of any kind. Thumbing through books con-
stituted a great risk.

"What's it about, Sister?" Forrest asked.

"It's a good story," the nun said. "There are two boys, and
they get stuck in a haunted house one night . . ."

Pearse's interest was stirred. In his room at night, he often
thought about haunted houses, with himself stuck in a dark,
cobwebbed kitchen, surrounded by knives. Or in the belfry.
He wondered what it would be like if his parents' flat had
a belfry. He imagined the frightened bats, swirling from the
dark chamber to the street below to terrorize the passing cable
cars.

"They get stuck there all night," Sister Marie George contin-

ued. She handed the book to Pearse, who opened it on the table
and leaned over it, resting his elbows on each side.

"No, Pearse, I want you both to read it, at the same time,"
Sister Marie George said. "Out loud, and *to* each other, please."

Pearse felt Forrest's eyes on him, and he sat up straight, pushing the book a few inches to his left. Forrest thumbed through
it until he came to an illustration that showed two frightened-
looking boys lighting the path before them with a flashlight. On
the hill, barely visible in the storm that swirled about it, stood
an enormous clapboard house that was dilapidated and ruined,
yet still lit up in the upper rooms. The drawing was imbued with
darkness, and Pearse felt his shoulders tingle.

While they read, Pearse and Forrest remained quite formal
with each other. Their elbows rested on the table a few inches
apart. They handed the book back and forth in an almost military way, and few extraneous words passed between them.

Eventually the boys in the story found themselves hiding in
the attic, frightened by the darkness down the stairs. They had
sensed the presence of a ghost in the house, that of an old miser
who, years earlier, had been suspected of foul play. Terrified by
the scrabbling of small animals among the shrouded furniture,
they crawled between two old leather chairs. The panes in the
window clattered with rain, and the boys held tight to their flashlight. They trained it across the floor, beneath the furniture.
There were mice and spiders hurrying about.

"Man, I'd never go into that house," Forrest said. "Too
scary."

"I don't know. I'd kind of like to," Pearse replied. He
read on.

Lightning turned the sheets on the furniture to bright flickers
of ice.

"Pretty good, huh?" Forrest said. He pointed at the illustration, a pair of mysterious eyes staring at the boys from beneath
a sheet-covered davenport.

"Yeah. You think these guys'll get out?" Pearse asked.

"They better."

The ghost spoke from beneath the floorboards, or at least it
seemed to. The fury of the storm made it difficult to be certain.
He moaned and thrashed through the house, and suddenly Pearse
himself began to shiver.

The thought of death, like a swirl darkening before him, made
it impossible for him to read any more. Forrest continued, his
eyes rapidly following the words as he read out loud. Pearse

closed his own eyes. The swirl rose up before him, and he saw his entire family carried away in dark mayhem. First his grandmother, a rag doll turning to a flicker that disappeared altogether. His mother flew apart in the darkness, as well as his brother Tim. Then Pearse noticed, shuddering, there was MJ, Pearse himself, and his father. The storm was inexorable and complete. No one survived.

He struggled to keep the sound of a moan beneath his breath. Forrest stopped reading and looked up at him. Pearse feared that Forrest would laugh at him, and he looked away, grimacing. But Forrest said nothing. He waited, his arms lying on the desk to either side of the book.

Pearse mourned in silence.

"You OK?" Forrest asked.

Pearse wiped his eyes with his sleeve.

"You upset because your grandmother died?"

Pearse's lips tightened and he looked down at the desk. Sister Marie George was working with some other pupils, and had not noticed Pearse's breakdown. He joined his hands.

"Sister told us about it," Forrest said. "Told us to leave you alone, you know."

Pearse moved his fingers about, discomforted by the need to say something.

"I'm sorry she died." Forrest laid his hands on the book. His eyes turned toward the window. He seemed embarrassed, as though he could think of nothing else to offer. Pearse, miserable with the recollection of his loss, remained still. To his relief, he realized that Forrest was not going to laugh at him. Instead, Forrest silently thumbed through a few pages of the book, respecting Pearse's privacy.

After school, Pearse walked home with Forrest. They entered the Gold Coin Market, where the ceiling and walls were painted dark green and the paint was chipped here and there, leaving white markings that looked like soapy bullet holes. The lower shelves were filled with sacks of rice and bottles. Up above, and on all the shelves throughout the store, there were toilet items, loose packages of napkins, seltzer water, and a storm of canned foods everywhere. A faded cardboard model of the Dutch Cleanser girl stood next to the fruit bins, her white apron splotched with dried banana.

"Hi, Dad," Forrest said.

Mr. Yick stood up over the carton from which he had been taking tins of tomato sauce. "Hi. Hey, Pearse. You OK?"

"I'm fine, Mr. Yick." Pearse followed Forrest toward the candy bar rack.

"How school?" Mr. Yick asked.

"It was all right," Forrest said. "We had to do a lot of reading." He took two Hersheys from the rack and handed one to Pearse.

Mr. Yick wore his wool watchcap, and Pearse noticed that it was frayed over one ear, as were the cuffs of his shirt. Mr. Yick was just like MJ, in that he saved things for a long time. The cap and the shirt were very clean. They were simply very old as well.

"What you read?" he asked.

"Geography."

"Any good?"

Forrest raised his eyebrows as he glanced at Pearse. He frequently did this, making fun of the way his father spoke. But it was not a cruel mannerism. Forrest and his father usually spoke in Cantonese dialect, and his father seemed to be quite generous with him. But in English, Mr. Yick could not always be understood. He bustled through each sentence like a speeding car.

"Yeah," Forrest replied. "It's when you study about different places."

"You study about China?" his father asked.

"Sure," Pearse said. "We have a bulletin board about China right now."

"You study about Communists?"

"What?"

"Mao Tse-tung."

"Is that a town?" Pearse asked.

Mr. Yick began laughing. "Yeah," he said. "Big town."

Pearse imagined a bustling street filled with lights and bright signs, people shopping everywhere, the same as the pictures on the bulletin board.

Forrest and his father spoke a few minutes in Cantonese.

"Do I have to do that?" Forrest asked, and his father nodded.

"He wants me to tear up some boxes in back," Forrest said to Pearse. "You know, make them flat?" He turned up his lip. "Yuck. Lotta dust."

"I could help you, maybe." Pearse had seen the back room through the door next to the refrigerator case. It was very dark, like a cavern. He suspected the room held family treasures. As they approached the entry to the room, to see how many boxes there were, he glimpsed a dried-out philodendron plant, its leaves like shriveled brown lampshades. A long red ribbon, on which Chinese characters were written in gold, hung from the plant.

"My dad forgot to throw it away," Forrest explained. "Like a lotta things back there. It's real dirty."

He shook his head.

"OK. You come with me upstairs. I have to change my clothes."

Pearse had never been invited into the Yicks' apartment, and he became quite excited as he followed Forrest up the stairs. There was a yellow linoleum floor in the kitchen, scuffed and soiled with age. The kitchen table—square, with rounded corners, a Formica top, and chromed metal legs—held the linoleum down in one corner.

Forrest opened the refrigerator. "You want a glass of milk?" he asked.

"Sure."

Pearse's attention was taken by a row of framed photographs above the table. All the photos were old, and showed Chinese people in black silk suits. Some of the men wore round little caps, like the one Monsignor wore on feast days. Others had porkpie hats. There was a shrine on the table, a small tray filled with sand. Half a dozen joss sticks stuck up from the sand at angles. Four tangerines were bunched to the side of the tray.

"Who are those people?" Pearse asked, pointing at the photos.

Mr. Yick entered the kitchen. He opened a drawer and pulled out a screwdriver. He stepped toward the refrigerator, then paused, caught up with Pearse's question about the photos.

"Family," he said.

"But what's this?" Pearse asked, pointing at the shrine.

"Helps me remember them."

"Oh. They're still in China?"

"No," Mr. Yick said. He stood before the shrine a moment, and the good humor of his reply fell away. He pushed his hands into his pockets. "They dead."

"All of them?"

"All. This my mother."

Mr. Yick pointed at one of the photos, which showed several children lined up formally for the camera, to either side of a seated husband and wife. A little girl stood at the woman's knee.

She too was dressed in black. A black braid fell down over her shoulder, all the way to her waist. Pearse was interested in the shoes she wore. They were round-toed and shiny, made, perhaps, from satin.

"All dead." Mr. Yick pointed at the incense. He joined his hands below his chin and bowed. "So, I talk to Buddha. And he protects them, see?"

Pearse took the glass of milk Forrest gave him. "You talk to who?" he asked.

"Buddha." Mr. Yick grinned and pointed toward the ceiling. "You know, God."

Pearse looked up. The ceiling had mold on it, especially in the corners.

"But aren't you a Catholic?" Pearse asked Forrest.

"Yeah. My mom's Catholic, sort of. My dad's Buddhist. They came from different places in China."

So the Buddhists must be Protestants, Pearse thought.

"That's why we send Forrest to Catholic school," Mr. Yick said, " 'cause Mrs. Yick go to Catholic school in China. Good place, We send him to Chinese school in Chinatown, not a good place."

"Why not?" Pearse asked.

"We want Forrest to be rich, that's why," Mr. Yick grinned. "You wanna be rich around here, you got to be able to talk to the white people."

"But you talk to white people," Pearse replied. "You talk to me!"

"Different. Different." Mr. Yick pummeled Pearse's shoulder, his teeth bright and congratulatory, then turned back toward the photos.

"Did they die because they got old?" Pearse asked.

"No. Communists killed them," Mr. Yick said, pointing at the photos. The smile drained from his face. "And Kuomintang. Big war, see? So I come here to San Francisco. Long time ago."

Pearse sipped from his glass of milk. Forrest stood next to him, listening to his father.

"Were you little when they died?" Pearse asked.

"Me? Yeah. Just a kid. What you call it?" Again, he asked Forrest a question in Cantonese.

"Teenager," Forrest replied.

"Yeah. Teenager."

Pearse looked up once again at the photos, which were of

such stern formality that the subjects appeared to be passing
judgment on Pearse, Forrest, and Mr. Yick. In the more casual slouch with which the little girl leaned against the
chair, Pearse felt that he discerned some of Mr. Yick's friendliness.

He imagined Mr. Yick as a baby with a wool cap on his head,
sitting in a burning road. The Communists or whatever they
were rode by on tanks, creaking behemoths of mud-caked iron
that paid no attention to the child on the shoulder of the road.
The war would be like the ones in GI Joe, Pearse supposed,
where there were periodic red and yellow blasts flinging dirt all
over, with thunderous noise. The child, raising its voice to a
wail, sought help, but none came. Instead, Pearse imagined,
there was nothing but guns and approaching flames.

Until, Pearse thought, I'd get there, all dressed up like the
missionaries in the Maryknoll magazine. He saw himself in
vestments and sneakers. He took the child in his arms and cut
a swath through the now-respectful tanks. The flames receded.
Beyond the clouds and the mountains, light shone bright and
pink in the huge sunset.

"Doesn't matter how long, though," Mr. Yick said.

Pearse looked up at Mr. Yick, who had removed his wool
cap.

"Still miss them."

Pearse studied his face, his wrinkled brown skin. The sadness
in Mr. Yick's slouching shoulders embarrassed the boy. He
worried that he was butting in on something. He looked at the
joss sticks, then into his glass of milk. He did not know what to
do. For a moment the corners of Mr. Yick's mouth twitched
with unhappiness, and Pearse remembered his own grandmother's hand, turning the page of the Maryknoll magazine for
him. He imagined Mr. Yick's lost family appearing in the comic
strip on the back cover. They were all hungry, and they were all
in tears.

Pearse walked back to the school, where he was to meet MJ,
and sat on a bench at one end of the playground. Most of the
children had gone home, and he watched as a few of the older
boys shot baskets. The trees in Washington Square moved slowly
with the wind, which was quite cold in the shadows cast by the
school building. Fallen leaves rolled across the playground,
blown there from the square. Through the gate in the cyclone
fence, MJ entered the playground from the street. He wore a

black suit and a black hat, and as he progressed across the cement softball diamond his shoulders sagged at an angle.

"Hello, Pearse. We've got the Rosary tonight, you know," MJ said. That morning Mimi had ironed the slacks and sports coat Pearse would wear to the Rosary. He had a red clip-on bow tie as well.

Pearse slid from the bench. He took his grandfather's hand.

"At seven o'clock," MJ said.

In Washington Square, a few elderly Chinese women did exercises, raising their arms above their heads and waving them around. The movements appeared fruitless to Pearse, as though the women were greeting a ship. The recent appearance of Chinese in the park had caused some consternation among the Pearses' Italian neighbors on Mason Street, who thought they should stay put in Chinatown, like they were supposed to. Pearse did not share that feeling, because Mr. Yick exercised in the square, very early every morning.

"Monsignor wants to meet us in the church," MJ said. They walked up the street to the entrance to Saints Peter and Paul. The wooden benches in Washington Square were crowded with people. Far outnumbering the Chinese women, Italian men, in sweaters, berets, and brimmed wool hats worn at a tilt, talked loudly with one another in the sun. They sat sideways on the benches, their legs crossed, facing each other the better to gesticulate. Sunlight brightened the grass, and a large swirl of birds circled the bell towers of the church in the blue air.

Pearse and MJ crossed themselves and walked up the main aisle of the church. A long shaft of light cut across the pews before the altar. It was multicolored yellow and green, filtered through a stained glass window far above. Monsignor walked onto the altar, his hands pressed together, looking out into the pews. It was quite cold in the church.

"Ah, Pearse!" he said. Monsignor grasped MJ's hand, then reached down to pat the boy's head. His fingers felt like gnarled wood.

"Let's go over here and sit down," the priest said. He pointed toward the pews.

MJ carried his hat in one hand, and when they sat down he laid it on the bench next to him, upside down. Pearse sat quietly and looked down at the front of his shirt. He did not wish to go over—yet once more—his fight with Forrest Yick. But his mother had assured him that the meeting with Monsignor and Father Dimiola would be good for him. Nobody was going to yell at him, she said, a further assurance that had calmed him, at least up to this moment.

Monsignor's head was illumined by light from the stained glass window, and his hair was brightly stained. When he looked down at Pearse, the hair that fluffed out from his head took on the look of a neon sign.

"Father Dimiola will be here in a moment," Monsignor said. "And we can talk about this, this . . ." The benevolence of his glance at Pearse, so oddly colored, unsettled the boy. ". . . Well, this misfortune, I guess we could call it, from the other day."

"I won't get in trouble, will I?" Pearse asked.

MJ laid a hand on Pearse's knee. "We just want things to be right for you, Pearse. It was a shame about the fight, that's all. Isn't that right, Monsignor?"

"Yes, that's right, and we . . ."

"We want to make things better for you, isn't that so, Monsignor?"

Monsignor nodded again. His hair appeared charged. Single flecks of dust wandered through the shafts of bright air above his head, turning from dark to glare, disappearing, falling.

Father Dimiola walked out onto the altar, genuflected, and turned into the church. He paused a moment at the altar railing and polished a portion of it with the sleeve of his cassock. Straightening up, he continued toward the pews.

"Good afternoon, Monsignor," he said. He removed his glasses and busily shook Monsignor's hand. His face was colorless, his hair messy.

Father Dimiola turned to MJ.

"Mr. Pearse," he said.

"Good afternoon, Father," MJ replied. "Good of you to meet with us."

"We're all very sorry about Mrs. Pearse, of course." Father Dimiola lowered his head and exhaled. "I hope you'll accept our condolences."

"Thank you."

"And you too, Pearse."

Pearse swallowed.

"Please," Father Dimiola said. He gestured toward the pew. "Sit down."

MJ and Pearse took their seats again, while Monsignor remained standing in the sunlight. Father Dimiola stood as well, his back to the altar. There was a moment of silence, in which no one seemed to know what to say. Pearse noticed that one of his shoes was untied, and he let it remain so.

"We're here, I think, to see about Pearse's status on the altar boys," Monsignor said. "Isn't that right, Pearse?"

The boy looked at his fingers.

"Yes," MJ interjected. "Father, you know this little fight Pearse had doesn't amount to much. Boys do that sort of thing."

"That's certainly true, isn't it, son?" Monsignor said. He glanced at Pearse, his eyes beaming in his garish face. "Why, I remember when I was a boy in Oakland, I got caught throwing firecrackers at the fish in Lake Merritt."

He laughed out loud. Pearse had seldom seen such joviality from Monsignor. He looked toward MJ, whose eyes widened with clear impatience. Monsignor leaned over, his laughter now making its way toward the ceiling.

Pearse folded his hands.

"And my father got so mad," Monsignor continued, "that you know what he did, Pearse?"

Pearse shook his head.

"Took the strap to me, that's what."

"The strap?"

"Yes. Men used to shave with a straight razor, you know. They sharpened it on a long leather strap, like a thick belt. You remember, don't you, MJ?"

"For God's sake!" MJ replied.

"When you got hit with it, Pearse, it stung." Monsignor's teeth resembled seashells, bright between his lips.

Father Dimiola folded his arms. Though he too listened to Monsignor's story, he rocked impatiently from side to side.

"What you say is true, Monsignor," he said finally. "Boys can be restless, Lord knows. I just felt, the other day, that Pearse should have shown a little more judgment."

Pearse knew what was coming. It was going to be another lecture, like the kind his father sometimes gave him, about acting his age, or about acting in a way his father could be proud of, or like he was capable of acting.

"I mean, we can't have our boys giving such a bad example to the other children," Father Dimiola said.

"As bad an example as what, Father?" MJ asked.

"As Pearse's!"

Pearse sought the warmth of his grandfather's jacket.

"As boys who fight," Father Dimiola continued. "It just won't do."

Monsignor raised his hand, startling Pearse with the quick movement. "But I think we can make an exception for Pearse, Father," he said. His tone of voice was cheery, the way Pearse had heard it when he discussed a golf shot. "He's never been in trouble before."

Pearse objected to how they were talking about him. He was like a dead person, listening in.

"That's true," Father Dimiola replied. "Very true. But we can't just . . ."

"Damn it, Father!" MJ's voice was suddenly severe. "You put this boy back on the altar boys."

Father Dimiola stiffened. He rubbed his left cheek. "I beg your pardon?"

"Put him back on the altar boys."

"I don't see how I can, Mr. Pearse. At least for the moment. I mean, what would the other boys think?"

"Who cares?" MJ took his hat between the fingers of one hand. "This boy is my grandson, and there is no good reason for him to be discriminated against like this."

Pearse grimaced as MJ's voice took on a tone of real anger. He tried to remain inconspicuous, because he feared MJ was getting him into further trouble.

"I'm not discriminating against him," Father Dimiola said. "He made a mistake, and I'm giving him the opportunity to atone for it."

"Father," Monsignor interjected, "perhaps I can persuade you . . ."

"Monsignor, I don't think you can. With all respect to you, I have to say that I am in charge of the altar boys, not you."

"Oh, I know that, Jack."

"And I am principal of the school."

"Yes, I . . ."

"We have rules, one of which is that there is no fighting. Would you have me bend the rules, Monsignor?"

"No, no. Of course not."

"Would His Holiness bend the rules?"

"His Holiness!" MJ said. "You mean the pope?"

"That's right." Father Dimiola removed his glasses. "By its rules, as they've been meted out by the Holy See, Mother Church has lasted two thousand years, Mr. Pearse. I see no reason to change that."

MJ stood and edged out of the pew into the aisle. He held his hat at his side. "This kid is eleven years old," he said. He stepped toward the altar. Turning about, he glared at Father Dimiola. "Father, would you step over here with me, please, so we can talk in private?"

For a moment, Father Dimiola appeared confused. Then he assented and the two men stepped up onto the altar.

Pearse watched carefully. His grandfather stood on the altar with his back to the church. His black suit looked like the one Monsignor was wearing, and Pearse mused about what it would be like if MJ were to become His Holiness, head of the holy sea. But Pearse's enjoyment of the idea—MJ, in vestments of tumultuous seaweed, rising from the ocean with a tuna on his head—was obscured by his upset. He was mortified by the conversation the men had had. So seldom the object of conflict in the past, he could not understand it now. He imagined himself arguing with Father Dimiola, and shivered at the prospect. For him, the priests were like God Himself. Hell awaited children who crossed Father Dimiola.

Suddenly there was an argument on the altar. Father Dimiola nodded, disagreed, shook his head, MJ tapped the priest's chest with the back of one hand. His voice rose to an insistent, angry grumble.

"You're going to put him back on the altar boys," MJ said, "because my wife just died, and I'm not going to allow you to let that event go by, and the Mass you're going to say, without my grandson helping out. I'll call the damned pope if I have to, Father."

"Of course, of course," Father Dimiola said.

MJ shifted his hat about between his hands. When the two men turned back toward the pews, his face was pale, his forehead mottled.

"Pearse," Father Dimiola said, right away, "I want you to come back onto the altar boys."

Father Dimiola's eyes were encased in the frames of his glasses. Pearse could not escape them.

"No!" Pearse shouted. Resentment rose from his stomach and clogged his throat. "I won't!" He stood, hurried into the aisle, and ran toward the church door.

He pushed through the door, causing it to rebound from the wall. When he burst into the sunlight, he saw the Chinese women, still waving at the clouds. Birds flew about. Pearse sat down on the steps and locked his head between his hands, trying to block the sound of Father Dimiola's voice from his ears.

"Pearse!"

He shook his head. From the corner of his eye he saw a pair of black shoes, black pants cuffs. He turned away, and two hands grabbed him by the shoulders. Pearse tried to pull away from the hands, but could not. He relented as they forced him about.

It was MJ.

"Pearse, you've got to," he said.

"No!"

"Pearse, please. You've got to do it, for me."

"I can't. They'll make fun of me."

"No they won't, Pearse. The kids won't make fun of you again."

Pearse pulled away. He could not focus on MJ's face.

"Not the kids, Grandpa." He pointed toward the church. "Father! My dad! Monsignor!" He felt MJ's hand as it caressed his cheek. "*They'll* make fun of me!"

MJ leaned close. "Pearse. It's for Doll's Mass."

Caught up in his anguish, Pearse was too flustered to listen.

"It's for her," MJ said.

Pearse looked over his shoulder. Father Dimiola came out of the church and paused on the top step. He was followed presently by Monsignor. They stood together, looking down at him, their hands folded before them.

"Don't you think she'd want you to serve, just for her?" MJ asked. His voice was so low and old that its sound reminded Pearse of broken rocks. Holding on to MJ's waist, Pearse could not speak, until he thought of Doll, smothered and lost in her bed, abandoned.

"OK," he said miserably.

MJ's hands tightened about his shoulders.

"OK."

The following day, Pearse arrived in the sacristy a few minutes before Monsignor. He dressed quickly in a black cassock and a fresh, starched altar blouse. Ben Del Negro, who was also to serve the Mass, came in and dressed as well.

"Sorry about your grandma," he said.

"Thanks."

Monsignor came into the sacristy and put on his vestments. At the required hour he took the chalice into his hands, and the three faced the crucifix on the wall.

"All right, boys. It's time," Monsignor said, and they turned toward the door.

The two boys preceded Monsignor onto the altar. They turned and faced the tabernacle, and Monsignor ascended the steps to the altar itself. As he prepared the chalice and the Host, Pearse stared at his back. Monsignor wore black vestments, and their funereal gloom, which was unrelieved in any way by the sunlight coming down from above, actually calmed Pearse. The gold brocade bordering the embroidered cross appeared to hover above the black satin, like reflected candlelight.

Pearse, his hands clasped before him, glanced at Ben, then over his shoulder at his parents, his brother, and his grandfather, who stood in the first pew of the crowded church. Mimi's face was barely visible, like a dim shadow behind her black chiffon veil. His father stood in bulky fortitude, one hand grasping the back of the pew before him, the other around Tim's shoulder. Tim, comic in an uncustomary tie, looked to the side, imprisoned by his father's muscular fingers. MJ was solitary and saddened in the gleam of the morning light.

Doll's coffin lay open to the mourners, so that Pearse could not see her. He looked instead at all the flowers in the church, which his mother, with help from other women of the Altar Society, had prepared. He lowered his head and folded his hands before him. A long silence ensued. There were occasional coughs, a dropped rosary, a sneeze.

I'll serve this Mass, Pearse thought. He shook his head. But I'm sorry, Grandma, I won't serve any more.

Laughter rippled through the house as Joe attempted to speak. The wake had gotten quite noisy through the afternoon. His large hands smothered the buttons of his suitcoat as he smoothed his tie. There were more than a hundred people in the living room, but nobody seemed to be listening to him. He spoke again. Then, grinning, he got down from the chair.

"Maybe I can help you, Joe," Monsignor said. He placed a hand on Joe's shoulder and stepped up onto the chair himself.

"Quiet, everybody." The guests closest to the two men turned to listen. "We're going to have a talk here, now. So keep your voices down."

Nervous about his upcoming speech, Joe glanced at his father. MJ sat in the far corner of the living room, circled by friends and younger relatives. A white handkerchief billowed from the breast pocket of his coat. Joe had practiced through the morning, attempting to memorize the speech he was about to give. But the distraction of the funeral preparations had made that impossible. He had wandered quite a bit, with occasional abrupt pauses when he had forgotten entirely where he was. Now he carried a three-by-five card covered with notes.

Monsignor relinquished the chair to Joe, who stood up on it once more and looked out across the faces. One of his coat lapels was turned in on itself, and he took a moment to adjust it. When he looked up once again, he saw that he had almost everyone's attention.

"Thank you," Joe began. "I just wished to mention that my mother was a friend to us all, and I think we can say that each of us was touched by her in a loving way, an affectionate way."

He retrieved his whisky from Monsignor, then looked about the living room. He felt Pearse's hand slip into his own. He grinned at the boy, who looked up at him with a kind of prideful melancholy.

"I don't want to say too much here," Joe continued, "except to thank all of you for coming. The regard, the food and wine you've brought . . . all of it is very kind. And my father asked me to say something, to thank you. I'm sure you know what it means to him that you're here."

Joe turned toward MJ, whose face did not convey the same goodwill that existed elsewhere in the room. He was pleased with the number of people that had come to the wake, of course, but his eyes were gray with devastation. His head appeared smaller than usual to Joe. His hands were more bony.

"As for me personally," Joe continued after a moment, "I want to tell you something about my mother that shows how important she was to me. She wasn't much of a reader . . . and when I was growing up, that's all I ever did."

Fresh laughter broke out, an acknowledgment of Joe's open personality, one that seemed hardly contemplative at all.

"No, that's true," Joe laughed. "My dad will tell you it's true. It just passed my mother by, why all that was so important to me. She didn't understand the pleasure I was getting out of it, but she was happy to see me get such pleasure. And to do well in school. She thought I was going to be a priest, I guess, poor woman." Joe grinned and sipped from his whisky. "She sat every evening in that chair, where my father is now, a manhattan in her hand. All of you remember her, I'm sure. A small woman, extremely kind, talking to everyone.''

Joe looked again at MJ, and for a moment he could not speak. He swallowed, looked at his notes again, and finally continued.

"She bought books for me," he said. "Good books, too, at the rummage sales at the churches. She recognized names, like Shakespeare, Dickens, Thomas Aquinas, for God's sake. It was wonderful. I read the great works of Western Man because my mother shopped the church bazaars.''

Joe toasted the onlookers.

"She did the same for everyone here, in different ways, in thoughtful ways," he continued. "So I hope you'll remember my mother, and how she loved all of you.''

Abruptly, Joe had nothing else to say. He remained on the chair, and the audience waited a moment longer. Finally, thanking them with a flustered, garbled appreciation, he stepped down. Applause broke out through the room.

Joe had planned this wake in minute detail, making sure there was plenty of everything to eat and drink. He had even left a large table empty in the dining room, certain that many of the guests would bring dishes of their own, to donate to the party. MJ had told him that that was not necessary, that the family should provide everything. Joe contended that mourners wanted to bring food.

"It gives them a chance to participate, Dad," he had said. Joe now noted that he had guessed correctly. The table was full.

The previous evening, Joe had told Pearse and Tim about other parties like this one, after the deaths of other relatives.

"But why do they have . . . what's it called? A wake?" Pearse had asked.

"It's always been. I don't know. Holdover from Ireland, I guess.''

"But we're not Irish, are we?"

"No. Not exactly. I mean, we're Americans.''

"Even though you read that newspaper?" Pearse asked. He pointed at the wood scuttle next to the fireplace, where there was a pile of yellowed newsprint.

"The *United Irishmen*.''

"Yeah. That's for Irish people, isn't it? I mean, can Americans look at it? Will they get in trouble?"

Marvin Rye, a close friend who was a sergeant on the police

force, now tapped Joe's shoulder. Rye worked at Central Station on Vallejo Street, a few blocks from Joe and Mimi's flat. Joe had gone to school with Marvin at Saint Ignatius High School, and they had been unlikely friends. Marvin felt he was misplaced in the city. He preferred hunting deer and going fishing to doing anything in San Francisco, except perhaps attending Forty-Niner games. As a student, Joe, always in the library, had kept Marvin provided with books about rainbow trout, Kodiak bear, insect repellants. When Joe had entered the University of San Francisco, Marvin had gone to the police academy, and they had remained friends. Now, at thirty-nine, Sergeant Rye had a red, lumpy nose that appeared glued to his face.

"Hello, Marvin," Joe said. "How are you?"

"We're all right. Sorry about your mother, of course. I came over to see her a month ago, you know."

"Yes, my father told me."

"She was pretty far gone. We couldn't really talk."

"Yes, I know. How about things in your parish?"

"We got a new guy."

"Who is he?" Joe asked.

"Father Luther. Imagine that, for Christ's sake! Telling my kids about the Blessed Virgin and grace and all that. Luther!"

Joe chuckled, excusing himself and moving toward the dining room. Larry Goggins, a colleague of Joe's from Murphy, Tomlinson, approached. Both men belonged to the San Francisco Irish Republican Club chapter, which raised money to send to Ireland. Joe had invited only one of the club people, because MJ disapproved of his membership in the organization. Joe had not wished to jeopardize his father's mourning by asking people to the wake who might upset him. Larry and Joe had been acquainted since law school, and Larry would pass simply as a friend. Indeed, though, he was the principal fund-raiser for the chapter.

"I don't know what you see in them," MJ had told Joe a few weeks earlier. They had been sitting in Doll's bedroom on a Sunday afternoon. Doll was asleep, and Joe had told MJ about a chapter meeting the night before, at which a Sinn Fein man from Tyrone had spoken. MJ had not wanted to listen much. "Bunch of bush leaguers," he had said.

"But someone's got to help the IRA, Dad."

MJ exhibited a mysterious flintiness when it came to the Irish Republican Army, and he refused to explain how he had come to such rigid disapproval of them. The British clung to the six northern counties, as they had clung so long to the south. Joe felt that only through the efforts the IRB had made in MJ's time, and, later, those of the Army itself, had the South ever gotten its freedom. Negotiation—like that which had partitioned Ireland in 1922 into the Republic and the North—got you screwed. If they hadn't negotiated, Joe thought, the Irish Republic would have gotten it all, and the English would have been pushed into the sea.

"You don't know what you're talking about," MJ said.

But to Joe's wish that he explain why that was so, MJ simply complained once more.

"The IRA's a gang of frauds, that's why," he said. "And people like your Irish Republican Club . . ." He laid a hand out before him, a gesture of resignation. "That money's going for guns, Joe."

Knowledge of MJ's own involvement in Irish politics had come to Joe many years before, almost by mistake. When he was a teenager, he had learned that one of the leaders of the revolution was Padraic Pearse, who had been killed after the taking of the Dublin Post Office in 1916. Joe had come home from the library with the book he had been reading, happy to have discovered that he shared the great revolutionary's name, hoping that perhaps they were related. He asked his father about Pearse, and MJ had laughed at the romance Joe spun out, about the starry poet dying for his country. Joe had looked down from the book at MJ, who was seated in his rocking chair, a Garcia y Vega cigar sending up a wavering line of blue smoke.

"Maybe he was a cousin of ours somewhere, way back when," MJ had said. "But you know how he died, don't you?"

"Sure, he was . . ."

"Executed. The British executed him."

Joe remained standing before his father, his eyes moving between the print and MJ's face.

"They're vicious, the English," MJ continued. He took up the newspaper, laying his cigar in the ashtray on the table next to his chair. "But then, Padraic Pearse probably had a screw loose. I did actually meet him once."

"You knew Padraic Pearse?"

"It was at a meeting, in Charleville."

"You, Dad?"

"Yes. But it didn't amount to much. I shook his hand, that's all. He gave a speech. It was long before he was well known."

"What was he like?"

"A school teacher. Looked like one, too."

"What was he like when he spoke?"

"Well, there were only a dozen men there to hear him, and there had been a good deal of drinking before he got under way. He had some sort of difficulty in one eye, too, I remember. It drooped, you see. Made him look addled."

MJ drew on his cigar.

"Quite serious, as well," he went on. "I didn't have a sense of Padraic Pearse as a humorous man. To tell you the truth, I don't believe he made a single joke the whole evening."

"But what did he say?" Joe asked.

MJ laid the paper on his lap once more. His white shirt was so starched that its wrinkles appeared jagged.

"Nothing," he replied. He stared for a moment at Joe, whose own excitement now embarrassed him. MJ's graying hair was the same color as the smoke from his cigar. "He spoke about the coming Rising. About a lot of blood, I remember. He said Irish blood would be spilled throughout the countryside, that sort of thing."

"Because of what the British were doing to them," Joe said.

"No! Because of what the Irish would do to themselves!"

Joe shook his head, not understanding.

"Sacrifice, you see. Throwing their bodies upon the barricades, that kind of thing," MJ concluded.

"You mean, kill themselves?"

"Yes. And I saw some of that, too."

Joe, so used to his father's careful consideration of what he wished to say, was surprised by the sudden resignation with which he now spoke.

"Sounds wonderful to a young man. Glory. Wolfe Tone. Parnell. It did to me, in 1913."

MJ leaned forward and pointed at the book in Joe's hand.

"But believe me, Joe, what you're reading there is idiocy. Idiocy."

"Terrible news, Joe, about your mother," Goggins said, breaking into Joe's recollection. His voice was so soft that Joe had to lean close to hear it. Goggins's dark suit was boxy and ill fitting. He wore a red tie. "I'm sorry this has to be my first time in your parents' home."

Joe had greeted so many people during the afternoon, and

heard so much sympathy, that he had grown suddenly sick of it.
He kept his head down, looking at his shoes, as Goggins spoke
with him. Mourning requires reserve, Joe thought to himself.
And here I am, in the middle of a party. The noise surrounded
him, like fragments of glass.

"There'll be another time, Larry," he said. "You'd enjoy speaking with my dad, I think. Old school Irishman
and all."

"But he doesn't care to talk about it much, I gather?"

"That's right," Joe replied. "Ireland. . . . There's something about Ireland he doesn't want to recognize any more. 'Not
my people,' he said to me once."

Several men had begun to sing. They stood in a half-circle,
mumbling tunefully into their glasses of whisky. They sang
the first lines of "Have You Ever Been Across the Sea to
Ireland?"

Goggins reached into his breast pocket and brought out an
envelope. "Incidentally, there are a couple things I wanted to
speak with you about. This, for one." He took a letter from the
envelope, unfolded it, and handed it to Joe. "Emmett Day is
going to be here."

"Emmett Day? When?" Day, an historic figure, an old IRB
man still active in Sinn Fein and the Irish Republican Army, was
an ancient hero to Joe and the others in the club. They had read
so much about him that the opportunity to meet him seemed an
historic occasion in itself.

"Three weeks," Goggins replied. "He's coming to raise
money."

Other guests listened a moment to the singers, then turned
back to their conversations. The men continued nonetheless,
their voices tinny with imprecision. Their singing added greatly
to the noise, and Joe found himself moved by their disorganized
sentimentality. The few lyrics he could make out made it difficult for him to listen to what Goggins was saying. The song had
been one of his mother's favorites.

"We're going to put him up in a motel in Daly City," Goggins
said.

Doll herself usually sang just one song, " 'Twas a man that
was the cause of it all," her high voice watery, on the occasion
of her wedding anniversary every year, after dinner.

"He told us not to spend too much money on him," Goggins
continued. "But I think we ought to feed him, don't you?"

Looking across the room, Joe noted the heaviness that had

come into MJ's eyes as he too listened to the singing. He looked at his cigar distantly, as though his thoughts were quite removed from the room.

Goggins refolded the letter and shoved it back into his coat pocket. "He's going to be having a lot of meals around town, Joe. Like the bishop himself every Sunday. And we're hoping we can count on you to put him up to dinner once or twice."

"Emmett Day?" Joe said. "I'll be glad to."

"Also there's a guy I'd like you to talk with when you have a moment. Another Irishman, a man named Carrington. He's got some immigration problems, and since you know more about that than I do, I think . . ."

"Sure, I'll talk with him. Just have him call me."

The doorbell rang, and Joe excused himself. Pearse followed him into the entry hall. Sister Marie George stood on the porch, accompanied by another nun—Sister Mary Margaretine, who taught second grade at Saints Peter and Paul. Pearse hurried to the door as soon as he saw the two nuns. They leaned over Pearse and took his hands.

"Oh, Pearse," Sister Marie George said. "God bless you."

As he looked on, Joe's breathing slowed and his mouth began to tremble. The nuns reminded him of his own schooling, and the care his mother had taken to help him with his homework. He recalled, as well, MJ's inspections of his test scores. MJ's approval had been forthcoming with the very highest scores, but only with the very highest.

"I hope we're not intruding, Mr. Pearse," Sister Marie George said.

Joe knelt next to Pearse and passed his arm around the boy. Pearse pulled away.

"Intruding?" Joe murmured. "Of course not, Sister. Come in, please. Pearse'll show you into the living room."

Sister Marie George passed Joe by, thanking him. Her arrival had opened a fissure in the calm he had built up around his own sadness. She took Pearse's hand and let him lead her up the hallway.

Joe leaned against Doll's writing desk. Several guests walked out onto the porch, leaving him alone a moment in the entryway. He walked toward the stairway. A lamp on the small table at the top of the stairs illuminated the flowered wallpaper. He took a few steps up the stairs. Pausing a moment, he adjusted one of his shirt cuffs. The voices in the house mixed in a confusing roar. Joe brushed his hair back and turned up the stairs to the second floor.

He stared through the doorway at the empty bed in his parents' room. The sheets, turned down over the blankets, appeared glassy and insubstantial. To Joe, their whiteness was filled with death. Breathing quickly, he entered the room.

He sat down in his father's rocking chair and stared at the bed. There was no movement in it, no shadow, and its emptiness nauseated him. He leaned over and put his face in his hands. The furniture—an armoire in the corner, the round table with the lamp in the window—had a gloom and sullenness that made Joe feel dead himself.

He thought of a conversation between himself and MJ on the day of Pearse's baptism. MJ had loved the boy from the moment of his birth, and apparently Doll had had to advise him to tell Joe that that was so.

"Your mother knows, Joe, how happy I am with Patrick," MJ had said after Pearse's christening. "And she asked me to mention it to you."

The conversation took place in the kitchen of Joe and Mimi's apartment. "I hope you can forgive how cranky I am sometimes," MJ continued. "But I love that boy. And I hope you understand how it is, despite the trouble I have explaining it, that I love you."

The remark had astonished Joe. At first he felt it was self-serving, simply a pleasantry. But the pain that MJ exhibited making the remark had been obvious to Joe. Running through that difficult conversation, Joe realized, was MJ's desire to be affectionate to his son. But the desire reared up against the barrier of MJ's reticence. To most people MJ was a charmingly gracious man, full of good feeling. But to Joe he was like an animated figurine, defying the outside world to probe what lay beneath that animation. Joe himself knew little about him. He felt he had been shut out from MJ all his life.

The conversation had led to little. MJ's reserve remained irritating, especially as he looked away from Joe, hoping not to have to say more. To his son, MJ's request had sounded rehearsed and insincere. Used to spilling his own feelings all over, sloppily, Joe found his father's attempt at candor to be, actually, truthless. And it infuriated Joe that MJ had been goaded to it by Doll.

Joe stood up from MJ's rocking chair, causing it to move back and forth abruptly, empty. But Mother was looking out for me, he thought. At least there was that. And now she's gone. She's air. Clouds.

As surely as he had been drawn to his parents' room, Joe's memory of the conversation with MJ drove him from it. His mourning for his mother gave way to the need to escape. He buttoned his jacket, looked about the dark room, and shuddered. He turned toward the noise and the light.

To Joe's surprise and considerable pleasure, Pearse awaited him on the landing.

An hour later, Pearse pulled himself up the bannister and paused to look down on the guests in the jammed entryway. Monsignor's white head pecked at the air. Sergeant Rye's jaw seemed to hang open, like a bomb bay, with each word. Pearse stopped on the last stair and sat down as he saw Sister Marie George emerging from the living room. She passed through the crowd toward the front door, receiving greetings from everyone. Her black cowl fell down about her shoulders with somber grace, and the other people seemed to fall back, like waves, before her.

Pearse's heart felt like a stone sinking into a swirl of water. But then Mimi approached Sister Marie George, and the two women joined hands, causing the boy's face to warm with happiness.

He stood once more and turned up the hallway toward Doll's room. As he went in, the noise from below was muted. Pearse crossed quickly to his grandparents' bed. The single table lamp was made of panes of blue glass. The light thrown down on the table provided the only warmth in the room. Otherwise, the light was so diffused by the glass shade that it seemed barely to reach the walls. He paused at the edge of the bed and looked at his grandfather's rocking chair, empty as it would be when MJ too died. He ran his hand along the carving on the chairback. MJ's Knights of Columbus blanket lay folded on the seat. It had a green border that surrounded the K of C crest. It was the sort of blanket used for picnics in Golden Gate Park and football games at Kezar Stadium. Pearse had asked his grandfather for it many times, wanting to put it on his own bed. He took up the blanket and spread it out over the sheets before him. Then he lay down and pulled the blanket over him.

Voices filtered through the doorway, and there was a sudden burst of laughter. Pearse allowed the noise to wash over him.

Its rises and falls lulled him, and he luxuriated in the warmth of the blanket. He felt emptied by the evening's gaiety, and he lay embraced by Doll's memory. He could not look ahead. He did not wish to. He merely closed his eyes and waited for the darkness to comfort him—the way, he hoped, it had comforted his grandmother.

≪ 2 ≫

BEATNIKS WERE A MYSTERY

Beatniks were a mystery to Pearse. A year ago, he had barely noticed them. Then suddenly they seemed to be all over the place in North Beach. Pearse's parents had forbidden him to talk with them. But they were so fresh and challenging in their noisy appearance and black clothes that they were exciting to Pearse. Where'd they come from? he wondered.

The day after Doll's funeral, Pearse and his mother were walking up Columbus Avenue from Broadway, where they had been to the bank, when they stopped at Biordi's Italian Ceramics store to look at a platter in the window. Mimi took Pearse's hand.

"That's it," she said. "Isn't it beautiful, Pearse?"

The platter was made of white bone china, with a border of blue and orange nasturtiums about the rim. Mimi stood for several minutes looking at it. She would have liked to buy it right then, but had told Pearse that she could wait another few weeks. She was really hoping to get it as a birthday gift from Joe.

Pearse made a point of agreeing with his mother about how beautiful it was, even though he did not much care for the platter. The white glaze reminded him of meringue, the texture of which made him queasy whenever he touched it. "I guess I like the flowers best," he lied.

Mimi placed the fingers of one hand against her face as she studied the platter. The wind whipped her hair around her cheeks.

"I bet Dad'll get it for you, Mom." Pearse was more interested in other things in the window, like a large terra cotta chicken that looked out at an angle, into the distance. The chicken was evidently sitting on an egg. Its lower half was surrounded by minutely sculpted hay and feathers.

A young man in a black T-shirt, black overcoat, and black pants hurried down Columbus toward them. He had no socks, though his leather dress shoes looked new. Pearse noticed that the ends of the man's coat sleeves ended fully two inches above his wrists. He was about twenty-five, and he had unkempt brown hair and a thick-muscled face, the meatiest part of which was his nose. His dark hair shot out from his head, held down, unsuccessfully, by a navy blue beret. His forearm pressed several books against his chest. Another book stuck out of the pocket of his coat. The ink on the covers was badly scratched. Indeed, the book in his pocket had no cover at all.

Smiling, Pearse looked up at Mimi. But her eyes were so fixed upon the platter that there seemed to be no enjoyment at all of its colors or its sugary, fluted edges. After a moment, Pearse realized that she was afraid of the beatnik.

Pearse was fascinated by him. For one thing, the heaviness of the man's step did not jibe with his voice. He was mumbling, but the voice had a kind of clarion precision. There was authority to it. It was deep. As he passed behind Mimi and Pearse, he continued raving, intimately, to himself. Pearse looked over his shoulder to watch the beatnik, and he saw there was yet another book in his hands.

The man was raving because he was reading.

Mimi held on to Pearse's hand, and it hurt so much that he finally had to pull his hand from her grasp. The beatnik stopped at the corner of Vallejo Street. He slapped the book shut, scratched his head, and looked about, as though surprised by something, then turned the corner past Saint Francis of Assisi church, toward Upper Grant Avenue. Mimi took Pearse's hand again, and as they continued toward Washington Square Pearse looked back to the corner, hoping the beatnik would reappear.

"Those people!" Mimi said. "From now on, Pearse, I don't want you to go anywhere beyond Washington Square without permission." They arrived at the corner of Columbus and Union, where they could look directly across the square at Saints Peter and Paul church and Pearse's school. "Up there, I mean." Mimi pointed up Union Street toward Coit Tower.

"Why not, Mom?" To Pearse, there was little of interest in the neighborhood beyond Washington Square, which was a confusion of houses and narrow streets going up Telegraph Hill . . . except Coit Tower itself, standing over it all, looking like a nozzle. Pearse had occasionally walked along Upper Grant Avenue—several blocks of Italian grocery stores, delicatessens, and bakeries, with apartments up above. He seldom paid attention to any of the shops, especially the bakeries. He did not like the way the loaves of bread were lined up like tanned gravestones in the windows.

He awaited more explanation from his mother. Mimi adjusted the collar of her coat against the wind.

"Because that's where those beatniks are," she said. "I just don't think it's safe up there."

"But why?"

"Because they're such . . ." She bit her lower lip. "Well, such bums!"

Bums seemed so far removed from Pearse and his family, like castoffs from some other country, that Pearse could not imagine having a conversation with one of them. The few times he had seen bums, on Market Street when he went shopping with his mother at Roos Brothers, or from the car window on Sixth Street, Pearse worried about the abandonment they personified. The coarse beards, the wreckage they wore for clothes, and the way they slept on the sidewalk, as though they had been murdered and left to be swept up—the spectacle frightened Pearse. He wondered if bums had been born that way. His parents surely did not think so. Often they told him that those people had suffered grave misfortune of one sort or another, and that others, with families and food on the table, should feel sorry for them and pray for them. Pearse wondered what awful things the beatniks had done, to deserve to be bums as well.

The next day, Pearse went swimming after school at the indoor Crystal Plunge on Lombard Street, a few blocks from his parents' flat. There was little wind, and it was a warm afternoon. He sat down on a bench outside the pool building with some other children and with one of the lifeguards, Debbie Mariano.

"Have you ever seen a beatnik?" he asked her, after a moment.

"Sure," Debbie replied.

"What are they?"

"My dad says they're a bunch of creeps," Debbie replied. "But, you know? There was an article about them in *Life* Magazine."

"There was?"

"Sure. It said they were famous. Poets and artists and stuff like that."

Her leather purse was beat up and shapeless in the way of an old carpetbag. She had put it on the ground between her feet, and now leaned back against the cement wall of the pool building. She was a sophomore at Galileo High School, and her books lay neatly piled on a three-ring binder next to her purse. From inside the Plunge, the swimmers sounded encased and far away. There was a metallic echo to their splashing and shouts.

"But my dad says their poetry is dirty," Debbie continued, "and that if I ever get caught reading it, he'll ground me. So I guess it must be pretty bad."

"My mom told me to stay away from them, too," Pearse said. He was so shy in Debbie's presence that his hands seemed unable to remain still. He put one of them beneath his leg, the other firmly in his coat pocket.

He could not understand Debbie's recent friendliness. Her first day as a lifeguard, she had yelled at Pearse all afternoon for making so much noise. The shouts of the children reverberated back and forth inside the pool building, chaos made watery by the splashing. Pearse had felt he was doing nothing wrong. But Debbie had finally caught him running to the diving board, and had forced him to change into his clothes and go home.

During the weeks that followed, though, she started being actually kind to him. She sought him out one day and gave him a lesson in the backstroke. Another time, she let Pearse wear her whistle and be the assistant lifeguard for a while. He could not figure her out.

Now, sitting in the sun outside the pool building, he noticed how casually she acted around him. She was so much older, yet she treated him like they were friends.

"We could go to one of those cafés," Debbie said. Pearse discerned a smile on her lips. "You know, the coffee houses, where the beatniks sit and talk."

Pearse blushed. "No. I don't like to sit and talk," he said.

"It'd be fun!" Debbie continued. "We could dress up."

"Like them?"

"That's right. Come on, we'll get Tim to come with us."

"No," Pearse said. "My parents wouldn't like it."

"But it'll be OK, Pearse."

Pearse looked at the ground.

"Come on, ask Tim, will you?" Debbie said. Her hair hung down as she surveyed the ground as well. Pearse wanted to reach up to touch her hair. His knees tingled.

"OK, I'll ask my Mom," he said. "But she won't say yes."

As he had predicted, his parents had forbidden the visit to Upper Grant Avenue. Indeed, his mother had sighed and muttered ''Pearse'' below her breath, shaking her head. Joe had simply laughed.

But Pearse did not want to tell Debbie that he could not go. That evening, as he tried to get to sleep, he thought how embarrassing it would be, having to admit to her that his parents wouldn't allow it. Debbie would think he was just a baby. And then she would probably ignore him altogether. Light from the windows across the street shone through his lace curtains. Pearse's record player was turned low. He listened to the Coasters, as he did every night, singing ''Charlie Brown, he's a clown.''

Debbie had approached him again later that afternoon. He had been swimming alone, treading water, doing nothing. His hands fluttering about like fronds beneath the surface, he watched her prepare to jump into the pool. Her hair was very dark brown and straight. As she stood at the edge of the pool, she ran the hair between her hands. Her skin was shiny-dark, like the girls in suntan oil ads. Pearse noticed that she had forgotten to remove her whistle, and that she was about to dive into the water. He took a stroke toward her, his hand in the air, but she suddenly remembered the whistle herself and reached up to remove it. When she laid it on the crumpled white towel behind her, Pearse watched the movement of the muscles across her back. She turned back to the pool and dived in.

She came up after a moment, quite close to him in the deep section, near the diving board.

''Hi, Pearse,'' she said. Now, suddenly, her hair was pressed down flat about her head and down her shoulders. It glistened. ''You going to swim?'' she asked, a suggestion of humor in her voice. ''Or you just going to tread?''

Pearse shrugged his shoulders. His head sank into the brimming water. ''I don't know,'' he gargled. He coughed and spat.

Debbie dipped her head in the pool again and swam toward the ladder. Pearse watched, waving his hands once more below the surface of the water in order to hold himself upright. She pulled herself up to the pool deck and ran her hands over her hair, this time to wring water from it. The black cloth of her suit gleamed, and Pearse, as he watched her, allowed his arms to drop. Water welled up in his mouth once more. He slipped beneath the surface.

* * *

The clank of the first morning cable car straining up the hill had once had a kind of celebratory importance for Pearse. It had told him it was time to get up, to go to church for the six o'clock.

Now, though, he turned over and tried to go back to sleep. He had told his parents he did not want to serve any more, and this was the first Sunday of his general strike. He heard the next cable car pass, all ringing bell and rattling metal. And the next. Several following, as well.

"Pearse?" Mimi looked into Pearse's room at about seven. "You didn't go to the early Mass?"

Pearse placed his hand over his eyes. The Sunday morning sunshine turned the white curtains before his windows into a bright cloud. He studied the red and yellow sleeve of his flannel pajamas.

"You can go with your father and me and Tim at noon," Mimi said.

Pearse rolled over and tossed the blanket from his bed. He wiped his eyes. One leg of his pajamas had crept up his leg. He scratched his head.

"I'll go to the eight o'clock," he mumbled.

Mimi entered the room and put her arm around Pearse. She wore a thick silk robe, colored pink, which pillowed his right cheek.

"Do you feel all right?" Mimi asked.

"Yeah." Pearse had not told his mother the complete truth, that he had no plans to ever go to the six o'clock again.

"You do want to go to Mass today, don't you?" Mimi asked.

"Sure," Pearse shrugged. "It's Sunday. I have to." Pearse grimaced as he thought of Monsignor—no, it would be Father Dimiola saying the eight o'clock—of Father Dimiola walking down the altar railing, approaching Pearse as he knelt, embarrassed, waiting for his Communion.

"That's good." Mimi stood and turned toward the mirror. "I wish you wouldn't stop serving Mass, Pearse. They want to take you back, you know. It made me happy to think of you helping out like that."

As he leaned over to pick the bedspread up from the floor, he saw his bow tie, left on his dresser after Doll's wake the week before. He picked it up. If he said nothing, he hoped, his mother would leave him alone.

Mimi knelt down before him again. She took a nickel from the pocket of her robe and gave it to Pearse.

"Say a prayer for your grandmother, will you? And light a candle for her. I know she'll be watching for it."

Pearse nodded as Mimi kissed him.

Half an hour later, Pearse knelt in the rear of the church, on the aisle across from a bank of flickering white votive candles. He was early for Mass, and the church was nearly empty. A somber echo receded through the silence. There seemed to be no actual cause for the gonglike hum, but it lasted several seconds. Pearse folded his hands and remained still.

Mr. Russo, the sexton, dusted the pews. He had left the melted wax of the votive candles in the tray below them, so that the residue resembled piled-up whipped cream. Above the votive candles, in terraced racks, remembrance candles flickered in smoke-tinged, red glass jars. Pearse enjoyed the playfulness that the candlelight brought into the church, despite the fact that the candles were intended to recall the memory of the dead. Each flame moved in its own way, touched by a breeze so delicate that it could entwine a single wick before moving on into the emptiness.

He stood and approached the candles. Above them a statue of the Virgin Mary stood poised, looking into the distance over Pearse's head. A ceramic scroll on the pedestal, made to look like paper curling at each end, read "Mother of God, Pray for Us."

He lit one of the candles and sensed the immediate arrival of his grandmother's spirit, which felt like an opening, a refreshing, of his mind. It was not just a physical warmth, rather a release from the clutches of his sadness. After a moment, Pearse stood up and crossed himself. He glanced toward the coinbox, which was tarnished black. Fingering the coin in his pocket, he imagined the slice of onion focaccia that it could buy at Liguria Bakery after Mass. Over the years his grandmother had bought him several pieces of the bread, many of them quite secret, all delicious. He looked up at the Virgin, who continued surveying the vista of half-filled pews. The candlelight wavered, reminding Pearse of Doll's presence. Reassured, he turned from the candles. The coin was still in his pocket, and he sat down once more in the pew to await the beginning of Mass.

At first Pearse tried following the Mass with his own missal. But the words jumped before him in the low light. So he tried praying for the repose of Doll's soul, but little came of that either. The altar missal lay open, and Father Dimiola's back was to the congregation. Pearse could see the side of the priest's face—fleshy and lit brightly by the glow from the stained-glass windows. Father Dimiola's hands were held up before him, the palms facing each other. His head bobbed back and forth. Pearse did not understand Latin, but he had enjoyed the sound of it when he had served for Monsignor. It was God's language, and speaking it on the altar, even by rote, had made Pearse feel separated from the others in the church, closer to the clouds and the blue air.

This day, though, God's language was just a mumble.

He watched Ben Del Negro kneeling on the altar with Gary Durham. Ben's black hair was squared off in a flattop, so that it looked like a sponge. And he was so skinny! Pearse wondered if he himself had looked as fidgety on the altar as Ben looked as he moved from side to side, leaned far forward to pray, and mumbled the responses. And Gary's soiled Keds looked ridiculous with his black cassock. The tread at the heels was almost worn away. Pearse became chagrined as he realized that he too had worn Keds when he had served Mass. Indeed, Pearse had them on now.

Yeah, but Ben and Gary can't serve Mass as good as I can, Pearse grumbled. Resentment of all these people telling him what he should do—and not do—welled up in him. But even though he struggled to put it aside, the resentment made him feel better. Nonetheless, Pearse's forehead grew cold with sweat. He found he could no longer stand the murmuring from the altar. I should be up there, he thought. It's not fair, me being out here with everybody else. I didn't do anything wrong.

"Excuse me, please," he said. He leaned toward the man next to him.

Startled, the man looked down at him.

"Can I get out, please?" Pearse asked.

The man sat back. Pearse scurried in front of him toward the aisle, interrupting the prayers of several others.

"Excuse me," he said. He leaned over the pew back, walking on the hardwood kneeler. "Excuse me." When he got to the aisle, he genuflected. He was worried that someone he knew would see him leaving the church. The sunlight formed a precise line beneath the door, and he headed straight for it. He heard Father Dimiola's voice, still mumbling, still far away. Pearse suspected that everyone in the church had seen his lurch toward the aisle, and that they were all watching him.

He hurried toward the entry, looking once over his shoulder. The Mass went on. He reached out to push the door open, then, swearing, stepped back to the holy water font and plunged his index finger into the water. Crossing himself, he ran out into the sunlight.

He felt right away the warmth on his face. The grass in Washington Square formed a broad bowl of luxurious green. Pearse rubbed his fingers together. The holy water had barely evaporated from them.

He stretched and looked to his left. Three people stood on the path a few benches away. They were being harangued by a young man in a black coat, who stood on one of the benches reciting very loudly from a book. Others—passersby carrying shopping bags or pushing baby carriages—hurried along as they passed before him, trying to escape his stormy mutterings.

"Hey, get outta here, you idiot," someone yelled.

Pearse leaned forward to look once more, then walked along the blacktop path toward the gesticulating man. It was the beatnik, the man he had seen outside Biordi's a few days before. As Pearse watched, the beatnik's suspended arm rose up. He made a circle with his hand toward his face and wiped his mouth. There was an exhalation, filled with phlegm. The hand dropped to his chest, then slid out over the book. He reached a particularly feverish part of whatever he was reading and began to shout. Pearse looked around, embarrassed. He saw a green scarf on the path below the bench. One end of it lay in a puddle left by the sprinklers earlier that morning.

Pearse had never had a chance to look at a beatnik so carefully. After a moment he concluded that, really, the man did not look so bad. His shirt was buttoned incorrectly, so that a flap of cloth stuck out from the middle of his white stomach. His beret lay flat on the bench, having fallen from his head, which was covered with thick, curly hair. But he appeared to be dressed at least semi-neatly, something Pearse knew his mother was always trying to get *him* to do.

"Pearse! Pearse!"

He turned about, his heart clutching tight.

"What are you doing out here?" Joe's face was framed by the driver's-side window of his Ford Fairlane. His arm hung out over the pavement, the palm facing up in a gesture of surprise.

"Gee, Dad, what're you doing here?"

Pearse glanced at the beatnik.

"I thought you'd like a ride home," Joe replied. "But Pearse, you're supposed to be in church."

"I know, I . . ."

"Mass isn't over yet."

"I know." Pearse stepped toward the car.

"You just snuck out?" Joe asked.

Pearse pushed his hands deeper into his pockets. He had no excuse, and, about this, he could not lie. Not about Mass. Not about church. If he had left Mass truly sick, he would have been on his way home. Definitely not studying a beatnik, as he was, in the bright morning. He nodded his head.

"Come here, Pearse," Joe said.

Pearse looked over his shoulder once more, as the beatnik raised the book above his head. His voice rose again to a shout, but Pearse could not understand what he was saying. The man's audience had already broken up, so that, really, no one was listening. Finishing his reading, he stepped down to the pathway, put the book in his coat pocket, and reached for his scarf.

Pearse hurried to the car and got in beside his father. Joe turned the Fairlane onto Columbus. Pearse discerned that his father was very angry with him. But he continued looking into the park. The beatnik stretched a long moment in the sun. He buttoned his coat. Then, with a sporty gesture, he tossed the scarf around his neck. The end of it splashed against his face.

"Did you even go to Mass?" Joe asked.

"I just left a little early."

"But why?"

Joe's hands held tightly to the top of the steering wheel. He kept his eyes straight ahead. Pearse could not just say that he had left Mass because he was bored, or that he was still angry about being thrown off the altar boys. He feared that the resentment he felt was just another kind of temptation, an invitation to do bad. Sister Marie George had told his class many times that the Devil crept about looking for unsuspecting children to corrupt. Sometimes her telling of the story made the children laugh, because she so expertly imitated the Devil, hiding behind a tree.

"I don't know why," Pearse replied. At least, this was the truth.

"You have to know," Joe said.

"But . . ."

"Pearse, you're not in any trouble, are you?"

"Trouble?"

"Yes. Like . . . well, you do believe in God, don't you?"

"Dad!"

"You do, don't you?"

Pearse grumbled to himself. "Oh, leave me alone," he said. "Pearse!"

Pearse brought a closed fist down on his leg. The nervous suspicion of himself—that he was just being a bad boy—now seemed a certainty. Even his father thought so.

"I don't want to go to Mass," he said.

"I beg your pardon?" Joe's voice did little to comfort Pearse, though it sounded suddenly quite commiserating. One hand rested on his leg, the other remained fixed on the steering wheel. "Do you think we're all against you or something?" he asked.

Pearse, still in confusion, shook his head. "I don't know."

"No, come on. Tell me what you think. I won't get angry."

The car slowed as Joe awaited an answer. He wore the dark gray suit pants he had put on for the twelve o'clock, a white shirt, and a dark blue tie. The shirtsleeves were rolled up. His eyes were severe. Pearse, faced with the need to articulate what he felt, could not do so. A trickle of anguish seeped through him. The figures of the priests rose up in his mind, filled with certainty in their black wool suits. Like his father. He felt his stomach tighten, as though all of them—the priests, Archbishop Duffy, Joe Pearse—were grabbing at it and wringing it dry.

"I guess I don't think Monsignor cares about me," he said. "Or Father Dimiola."

"But Pearse . . ."

"I don't think they care about me at all."

Pearse had always revered the priests, thinking that they could do nothing wrong. Indeed, he felt, in a kind of swoon, that he loved them. They were kind and firm and funny. Like God Himself, they walked around giving advice, their brocaded vestments heavy in the comfortable gloom of their calling.

So Pearse's admission confused him, because he felt so relieved having made it.

The way Pearse sat against the car door—his hands in his coat pockets, and his chin resting against his bow tie as though it were glued there—convinced Joe that there was more to this for Pearse than just being bored with Mass. A schism of some kind had taken place, and Pearse was floating free, angrily.

Joe continued out Columbus toward the bay, headed for the municipal pier. This was a troubling moment for Pearse . . . even a crisis of faith, maybe, when really the boy should be enjoying his time at Saints Peter and Paul, like the other kids. Pearse had been insulted by the priests, but he had taken that slight to mean that he was not worthy of God's grace. So he sat in the car now like a rumpled outcast.

The importance to Joe of raising his children in the church was more than just religious. His work, in school and as an attorney, had come from his wish—almost a wish in self-defense—to lead a proper life that would please the expectations God had for every Catholic. It was a matter of being charitable and honest, not much else . . . plain virtues that, among Joe's business and law colleagues, were seldom in evidence. But that was not a problem. That was just business.

To his distress, though, he found that he often lacked those virtues himself. He was too impatient, too argumentative, and angry in a disorganized way that frequently confused his family. But, at least, striving for those virtues had helped salve some of the wounds he had inflicted on himself with his unruly personality.

In many respects, all Joe wanted was to do what was expected of him . . . a resigned-sounding phrase. But even "what was expected of him" had been made up of things that, especially as a young man, he had not understood very well. He had felt the presence of some silent figure behind him at a distance, waiting. Christ Himself, he had thought once, with some humor, keeping an eye on you.

As a freshman at the University of San Francisco, Joe had read about the immigrants at Ellis Island, about President Roosevelt and what the New Deal was doing, and about the union movement, and had decided that the figure he sensed was really the difficult past that others before him had suffered—people like his father learning the business at Marshall Field, the garment workers in New York, the Chinese laborers stooping over in the Nevada desert to scrabble rocks from the dirt for the Union Pacific. They were like all the people who had been turned away, disgruntled and sour, by the sign that read "Irish Need Not Apply." It was no wonder to Joe that there were so many Catholics in the union movement. Those guys, he thought, had the strength of their beliefs, and they were not going to let a bunch of dull-spirited Protestant thieves use them up.

So his faith had a hardened purpose, a political one. Besides, Joe loved the church and all its ceremonies. He knew that clerics often just muddled around, semigarrulous men timidly dispensing Communion and caring for the dead. That even when they *were* invincible, they seemed to act from a kind of deliberate uncertainty about it, as though they were harassed by their calling. But Joe was a friend to the priests anyway, and had done all sorts of *pro bono* work for the archdiocese.

Through the years, the figure standing behind him had changed. It had become far more clear. It did not speak. It was calm. But it did not expect to be pleased, and Joe feared that, no matter what he did, he would not be able to change that almost arctic indifference. For the figure now was MJ. Joe had discovered that his pursuit of the faith had also been made with the purpose of achieving some sort of grace in his father's eyes. So Joe's faith had become important because it had become desperate.

"You know what happens to people who lose their faith, don't you, Pearse?"

Pearse looked out the window in silence.

"They begin to wander, you know, and they get caught, aimless. They lose their . . . their footing."

Joe parked the car at the foot of the pier, which extended into the bay in a half-circle. Several swimmers made their way back and forth in the cove that was formed by the pier.

"And it's tough to get it back, once you've lost it."

Pearse watched the swimmers. Joe knew the boy was listening to him, because his head remained so still and intent upon the view before him. Pearse was engaged in the conversation, though he had no reply.

"It's important to me that you go to Mass, Pearse," Joe said. He leaned on the steering wheel. "I'm just afraid that you don't know what you're getting into, see? I know Monsignor makes you angry, and Father Dimiola and so on. But you've got to put all that aside."

For a moment, Pearse turned toward Joe. But his jaw was motionless, the way it was whenever his father criticized him. It meant he was not going to reply.

"Pearse, listen to me!" Joe said.

Pearse flinched.

"Don't just ignore me, Pearse. Don't just turn your back on me."

"But Dad!"

"I'm trying to help you!"

"Dad, I didn't do anything . . ."

"Pearse, you ran out of Mass. What do you think church is, a movie or something? You think you can just walk in and out as you please?"

"No, Dad, but . . ." Suddenly, Pearse began crying. Joe, in

a moment of shocked calm, saw that Pearse did not know how to defend himself. But he felt his anger thriving on the fact that Pearse was fluttering before him, wildly seeking some place to rest, where he would not be yelled at.

"Pearse," Joe muttered. Quickly he started up the car and hurried it from the parking space. Pearse wept in the seat next to him. His open hands lay in his lap, and tears fell across them. Joe stopped the car at a signal light and looked down at the boy, realizing that he had abused him. He had berated Pearse, when what Pearse needed was to be asked, calmly, why he had left Mass. More important, he needed to have someone listen to his answer. Sensing all this, Joe still could not ask the question. He feared that the response would make him angry all over again.

"Pearse, look, let's just go home," he said. "We'll talk about it after your mother and I get back from the twelve o'clock. Don't worry about it just now."

Joe's counsel achieved nothing. The signal light changed, and Pearse brushed aside his tears, spattering his shirt with them.

"OK, Pearse," Joe said, a few hours later, "I'll wash, you rinse."

He walked toward the faucet while Pearse took the hose into his hand and held it at the ready. Pearse pointed the nozzle at the Fairlane. He began playing with the nozzle, as though he were Matt Dillon taking aim. He shot at an imagined bank robber, letting him have it as he crossed the alley, then raised the pistol to his lips to blow away the smoke. Barely watching, Joe reached down and turned the faucet handle.

Water ricocheted from Pearse's forehead.

"Pearse! Spray the car! Spray the car!" Joe ducked behind the Fairlane as spray arched across the alleyway. Recovering himself, Pearse aimed the water directly at the car door, then toward the trunk and the rear wheel. Water dripped from his face.

"Yeah, like that," Joe said. He came out from behind the car, sneaking away from it. He carried a bucket of soapy water. "Come around here, too," he said.

Pearse walked behind the car. He sprayed the top, the back, then all of it. Finally, laying the hose in the gutter, he went to the back steps of the apartment building, brushing the water from his hair with his hands.

The Sunday opera broadcast was playing, and Joe hummed along with the music while he worked. He had not mentioned

Pearse's leaving Mass again. But Joe had spent a good deal of the intervening hours questioning what he himself had done. Throughout the twelve o'clock, he had grumbled at himself for his treatment of Pearse. The fact was, Pearse had reminded Joe of himself as a child, deteriorating before his own father when MJ had picked at him. MJ's criticisms had been less bombastic than Joe's, but the effect had been the same. It was for that reason that Joe had asked Pearse to help him wash the car. Wielding the hose was a favorite entertainment of Pearse's.

"They're doing *La Bohème* today," Joe had said, as they descended to the alley behind their apartment. "You'll like it."

He had set up the radio on the back porch, and the sound of the orchestra filled the alleyway. Pearse sat in the hot sunlight. One wet tennis shoe tapped a stair. Soapy water covered the hood of the car, and Joe pushed the wet rag in a circle.

The orchestra began a soft, complicated passage, which was followed quickly by a baritone voice. Joe walked to the radio to turn it up.

"Listen, Pearse, this is terrific," he said. "This fellow's a Bohemian, his name's Colline, and he's singing about having to sell his coat to get money for medicine."

"But why would anybody want to sing about that?" Pearse asked. He pushed a hand through his hair once more. His shirt was wet as well, and he pulled it from his skin.

"They're *all* Bohemians, and one of them has a girlfriend who's dying of tuberculosis. So they're trying to help her, because really, I guess, they're all in love with her. And that's what most music is about, anyway, isn't it? Love, I mean. That's why it's so wonderful."

"I don't know. I think love's kind of boring."

They listened a moment longer.

" 'Course, there is that Little Richard song," Pearse said.

"Who?"

"A guy on the radio." Pearse's head nodded with the words as he sang them. " 'You ran off and married. But I . . . I love you still.' "

His blue jeans and navy blue checked shirt seemed somber against the lemon sheen of the stairway behind him. Amused by the boy's comparison, Joe studied the way Pearse's free hand twitched with the rhythm of the lyrics he sang.

Joe enjoyed Pearse when he listened to his rock and roll, even though he could not understand the stuff himself. Rock and roll was a lot of yelling, as far as Joe could tell. Pearse had a collection of 45's, to which he and Tim often listened. The music sounded different to Joe, record to record, but the boy's attempts to explain the differences made little sense to him. "See, that's Buddy Holly, Dad," he said, of a round-voiced singer whose voice had no tremolo. Pearse would lie on his bed, the side of his shoe tapping the wall. "Cool, huh?" The next record would drop, and Pearse would caution his father that this one was pretty weird.

"Splish, splash, I was takin' a bath . . ." The singer's voice seemed to rip through the lyrics.

Pearse was seldom able to listen while sitting down, and he danced around to the music, especially in those parts where something big seemed to be happening, when the guitars thundered and the singers screamed. Joe, glancing into the bedroom as he passed, would see Pearse playing pretend guitar and singing to himself in front of the mirror, his eyes shut tight with excitement. " 'Great balls o' fire!' " Pearse's enjoyment of the music was complete. He strode about and waved his arms. He shook his head. And he sang, his high voice monotonous, razorlike, and reedy.

"What are Bohemians?" Pearse asked.

"Old-time poets and artists. Sit around in cafés all day, that kind of thing."

Pearse pointed in the direction of Upper Grant Avenue. "You mean, like the . . ."

"Pearse, do you mind if I rinse?" Joe interrupted.

Pearse assented and leaned back against the steps. Joe took up the hose and began spraying the car.

"See, right here," Joe said, distracted again by the music, "the guy is saying, 'what good's an old coat if it can't keep someone from dying?' It's companionship he's singing about. Friendship."

Joe held the hose at his side, water careening off the surface of the alley. He felt drowsy, but it was due to the music, which put him in a kind of sunny, saddened ecstasy. He closed his eyes. Slowly, he began conducting with the hose.

"Hey, damn it, what the hell you doing?"

Joe snapped from his languor. A man walking up Columbus Avenue had stepped from the curb to cross the alley. He threw up his arm. Water peppered his jacket, and a few books skittered from his hands across the blacktop.

Joe turned the hose back toward the car. "Excuse me," he said. "I wasn't paying attention."

"Yeah, you sure as hell weren't!"

It was one of those beatniks. A young guy. The same guy, in fact, that Pearse had been watching this morning in the square. He wore a beret, and now it dripped with water. He examined his wet pants. One of his books had landed in the gutter and was washed over by soapy runoff.

"Pardon me," Joe said, "I'm sorry."

Joe glanced over his shoulder at Pearse, who had sat up to watch. Pearse lowered his hand—which, Joe noticed, he had inadvertently raised above his head, as if to wave. The beatnik picked up the book and wiped it on his coat. Joe walked toward the steps, where Pearse sat, and grabbed a rag.

"You know this guy, Pearse?"

"No. No, I . . ."

"Here, use this," Joe said. He turned again toward the beatnik, holding the rag before him.

"I'd rather use my damned coat."

Joe took in an impatient breath, and the beatnik moved away, still muttering complaint.

The singer's voice arrived at a low, rumbling note. The beatnik looked back. His eyes paused a moment on Pearse's.

"Damned pages are stuck, damn it," the beatnik said, and he disappeared around the corner.

"This is bacon?" Prodding the round slice with his fork, Monohan had raised his eyebrows as a child would, bewildered by some mysterious gift.

"Sorry?" MJ asked.

"They usually send some bread, you see," Monohan said. He took up a thick slice from his plate, split it in two, and took a bite out of the smaller piece. "Like this. Some soup." He sipped from his cup of tea while the bread was still in his mouth, then pointed once more at the piece of bacon on the plate, the fat of which was crimped about the edges. "But a rasher like this . . . it's the bloody Last Supper, that's what it is."

MJ watched him cut up the bacon. Monohan held the blanket close around his shoulders. His collarless shirt was wrinkled.

"Why are you wasting your time doing this, lad?" Monohan asked. His face was very white in the lamplight, and a pouchlike jowl hung below each cheek. The light glinted across the edges of his steel-rimmed spectacles as he lowered his head over his meal.

"Trying to take Ireland back from the English," MJ replied.

Monohan looked up at him abruptly. "You're quite the patriot," he said.

The old man enjoyed his meal. MJ, ill at ease in his shop-assistant's wool pants and coat, felt sorry for him, so obviously cold as he was. But MJ was afraid to do anything more for him than to visit while he ate his supper.

"Why don't you go to America?" Monohan asked. The last piece of bacon lay on his plate, and he cut it into small pieces. "Before you get too caught up in all this. I mean, don't you feel like an idiot, guarding me while I eat this fine Irish supper?"

Monohan's jowls wavered about his chin. The grin that appeared on his face, so bright by contrast to the darkness of the cellar, caused MJ suddenly to like him.

"Are you Catholic?" MJ asked.

"As Jesus Himself is in heaven," Monohan muttered, gesturing toward the ceiling.

"Then why are you here?"

"Because your friends think my son's betrayed you to the English." Monohan raised a napkin to his lips, then replaced it on his lap. "When all he's done is to defend the name of the king. As any other proper citizen would do."

Monohan reached across the table for his billfold. He pulled a brown-tinged, wrinkled photograph from it and handed it to MJ.

"That's him."

The photo showed a young man with a moustache, dressed, it appeared, for church, in a wool suit.

"The image of his mother," Monohan said, looking over the top of the photo. He shivered and pulled the blanket close to his shoulders. "Can't they bring a stove down here?"

"I don't know," MJ replied.

"We're all going to perish in hell anyway, aren't we?"

Monohan leaned over as another shiver went through his back. MJ laid the photo on the table and poured him a second cup of tea.

"So why can't we have a few of the flames here and now?" The sound of Monohan's wheezy laughter floated into the air, isolated glee in the darkness.

He seemed so kind-hearted, MJ thought, laying his newspaper down on his lap. He checked his watch. Pearse was due to come over in an hour. And wasn't it a curious thing, how humorous Monohan was? Imprisonment like that, away from his family and hidden . . . he didn't even know where he was. Yet

Monohan's incarceration was like time spent studying a tribe of Red Indians. He seemed interested in everything the IRB had to say, instead of resentful that they were holding him. He hated being held, of course, and he resented being so cold. But he made fun of it, like his remark about hell. He *was* in hell—a dark place, no pleasures to speak of—and of course he worried terribly about what would happen to him.

MJ was startled from this recollection by the ringing of the phone. He put his cigar in the ashtray and stood to go into the hallway. Outside, the wind-blown fog swirled in from the Golden Gate. MJ sat down at the writing table.

"Dad? This is Joe."

"How are you?" There was silence for a moment. The fog passed by the front of the house in gusts. Across the street, the parked cars were enveloped in the settling mist. As the cars faded, they became dull outlines, gray-drawn on gray paper.

"We've got a problem with Pearse," Joe said.

"He can't come over?"

"No, he can't."

"Isn't he feeling well?"

"He snuck out of Mass this morning."

"Why?"

"He says he doesn't know."

MJ leaned forward, dropping his elbows to the table. He ran his fingers through his hair.

"He's got to know why he left, though, don't you think?" MJ said.

"I guess so. That's what we all thought. But he actually told me that he doesn't want to go to Mass at all."

MJ sat back in his chair.

"Will you talk with him?" Joe asked.

"Sure, I will. Has anyone else spoken with him?"

"Mimi and I both have. She doesn't seem as worried about it as I am."

"Why?"

"She thinks Pearse is still mad about getting thrown off the altar boys."

"Makes sense." MJ remembered Doll's intervention in the confrontations he had had with Joe. She had always defended her son to MJ. He remembered how Doll had shouted, sedated as she was just after Joe's birth, "Michael, we have a boy!" Her voice was high and excited. MJ's later reserve about Joe had made no sense to her. She accused MJ of being jealous of Joe

and the attention he got from her. MJ's silence at those moments
had convinced Doll she was right, and she had told him so.

"I'll be glad to talk with Pearse," MJ said.

"Good," Joe replied. "He's in his bedroom now. I'm really
worried about him. I mean, maybe he should go see Monsignor
or something."

"No, you're making too much of this, Joe. Pearse just snuck
out of Mass. Haven't you ever done that?"

"Well, not since I passed the bar," Joe laughed.

"Give him the benefit of the doubt. It's been difficult for him,
your mother's passing and so on."

"I know. But I think that would make him want to spend
more time at church, not less."

MJ sighed. It was a surprise to him, sometimes, the naivety
of his son Joe. Big guy. But moony. Head in the clouds.

"You know, he's got a day off from school coming up this
week," MJ said. "Some kind of retreat for the nuns. Why don't
we meet you for lunch? Make something fun out of the day, just
for him. And then we can talk it over, over a ham sandwich."

Joe let out a sigh, and in the sound of it MJ recognized a kind
of gratitude for the suggestion. He's so self-centered, MJ grumbled to himself. Can't he see that all Pearse needs is sympathy?
His sympathy?

"I think that's a good idea, Dad."

"OK. Invite him. And ask him to invite me."

"All right. Yes, thanks. I'll do that now."

Joe put aside the folder, swearing at himself that there was so
little he could do for Tom Carrington. His efforts amounted to
a delaying action, an effort to hold off the government for a
moment, maybe. But indeed Carrington would be extradited.

He had fled from Ireland two years ago, pursued by the British
on a murder charge. A native of Belfast, he had originally come
to the United States when he was seventeen and had lived in
New York for six years. But he had not enjoyed it, finding the
US a facile place to live, so isolated from the difficult troubles
of Ireland. He had gone back finally, though he always took care
to renew his permanent visa to the US. He worked as a cabinet
maker in Derry and joined Sinn Fein. He denied to Joe that he
had ever belonged to the IRA. And he denied having anything
to do with the bomb attack in which three British soldiers were
killed.

"Of course it did take place, Joe," Carrington said during

their first meeting a week earlier. "Can't be denied. There was a big hole in the ground after all. I saw it!"

"Were you there before the police arrived?"

"Oh no. The next day. There was a crowd from the neighboring village. I went out there with them. It was just over the border from the Republic." Carrington drew an imaginary, wavy line on the desktop with his fingertip. "The British keep an eye on the border there because the IRA can slip across into Ireland on that road when things get hot."

"The Republic hides them?" Joe asked.

"No, but they don't look for them either." Carrington smiled, sitting back and shrugging his shoulders. "England's troubles are Ireland's opportunity. Though they don't talk about that much in Dublin."

"And you're sure you weren't involved."

Carrington shook his head. "May the Devil himself take me if I'm lying to you, Joe," he said. "It may have been someone I knew, but I swear to you that I wasn't there myself."

Joe had no way to determine whether the Irishman was telling the truth. And in some respects the truth did not matter, because even if Carrington admitted to the murder, he would no doubt say that it was a political matter, wasn't it? A military operation, and do we owe the English anything anyway, after what they've done to us? You can't say it's murder when they're holding so many of our men and letting them die in those miserable prisons. There's the truth, Joe. There it is.

Yes, but it would be so much simpler, Joe thought wearily, if you could just say that the truth was the truth, that a murder was a murder. Although he was a lawyer, to whom such plain thoughts were anathema in the defense of an accused, there was a relieving beauty to them.

"You don't think we have much of a chance," Carrington said now. His thick red hair hung down over his forehead. It was remarkably messy. Carrington was so thin that he appeared to have been on a kind of hunger strike. Joe had taken him to lunch a few times during the week they had worked on the case, and Carrington had had an enormous appetite. But the food seemed to go nowhere, to have no effect on Carrington's bony, languishing sadness. The Irishman's body appeared to reject his efforts to nourish it.

"It hasn't helped that you've had no legal representation until now," Joe said. "But at least you've held them off."

"I know that, and I'm grateful for what you've done in just

these few days. It isn't easy putting in all this time on a lost cause.''

"It's not a lost cause, Tom."

"What's not?"

"Ireland."

Carrington smiled again. It made him look older. "You're right there, Joe. But I think it's fair to say that *I'm* a lost cause."

"Oh but we've still got . . ."

"They'll put me in the dock and accuse me of every possible offense.''

"Tom."

"Then they'll convict me, and I'll spend the rest of my life shivering in a cell."

"Maybe not."

Despondency took Carrington over for a moment, a frown punctuated nonetheless by a sudden, large grin. "But not before I protest my innocence," he sat up, straightening his coat, "make an eloquent case against the oppression of the Irish people, and let my voice ring with justice and right."

An index finger rose into the air in an exclamatory, victorious gesture. Despite the playact, Carrington's voice plodded at the end with defeat.

"They'll listen for a minute." His voice fell off to a mutter. "And then they'll pack me off."

Joe straightened the folders on his desk. "We'll see what we can do Thursday," he said. "You might be surprised."

"Lord help us, I hope so."

Joe stood and shook Carrington's hand. "My son's coming to see me then, to have lunch with me. After your hearing."

"You have two sons, don't you?" Carrington asked.

"Yes, and this is the younger one. We call him Pearse. He enjoys meeting me for lunch every now and then."

"Sure. Father and son, that sort of thing."

"That's it."

Carrington folded his arms and looked down at the floor. "You're lucky, Joe, being able to see him whenever you wish. One day I'll see my own children again."

After Carrington left, Joe returned to his desk. His effort to organize what he would talk about at the hearing the following week was interrupted by the confusion he felt about Carrington's character. In fact Carrington had five children, to whom he wrote regularly. He was always lamenting his absence from his family, and he felt aimless in the United States. "There's been this tremendous big immigration to the US,'' he once said to Joe. ''Don't you think they'd like to have one or two of us back?'' Carrington put in his time every day working for Dan Sullivan, a contractor friend of Joe's who bought old houses in the Sunset District, refurbished them, and resold them. Carrington was a good worker, Sullivan had told Joe, but a sad one. He came to work every day on time. But he was spiritless. He did what he was told.

Seeing how he loved his wife and children, Joe had difficulty imagining Carrington planting a bomb by a country road. Would Carrington congratulate himself as he ran from the wreckage of a troop lorry? Would he look back and wonder what was going through the mind of the soldier writhing in the ditch by the road, his leg severed by the force of the blast, its stump in blackened, maybe even burning, tatters?

Trying to reconcile these two images was almost impossible for Joe. Someone who, sighing sadly, could show off a photo of his youngest daughter—a little redhead named Padraigeen, in a red sweater—would not be that kind of person.

Of course there's nothing to keep a family man from doing someone in, Joe thought. Familial peace doesn't mean you're any less oppressed by the English, after all. Joe smiled to himself. Indeed, maybe in Ireland, a murderer would be just that kind of person.

''Where are you taking me, Pearse?'' MJ asked.

''It's a surprise.''

''To the zoo? To Playland?''

''Uh-uh.''

Pearse flagged the bus—the 15 Third Street—and led MJ up the stairs. Pulling change from his pocket, he paid both fares and moved toward the rear seat, his favorite. Pearse had told his grandfather that he had gotten a special, secret invitation and, he said, he was real excited about it. But he had refused to tell MJ what the invitation was, and now he led MJ down the aisle as though the old man were blindfolded, holding his hand while they proceeded to the back of the bus.

They rode downtown, and Pearse lamented the new raised freeway that had just been built along the Embarcadero, right in front of the Ferry Building. ''It's so ugly,'' he complained, wrinkling his nose at the structure as the bus crossed Market Street. ''Do they have to put it there?''

''I guess so,'' MJ replied. He looked out the bus window at

the squat cement pillars. "The government does what it wants, you know."

Pearse shrugged. He folded his arms before him and leaned his head against the window.

They transferred to a trolley car going out Market Street. It was a sunny day, and the fall light settling across Pearse's shoulders warmed him, causing him to drowse. He had told MJ they were to get off the car at Civic Center, and MJ woke Pearse when they arrived at the stop.

Pearse lurched sleepily from the seat. His excitement took him over once again. He pointed at City Hall as they descended from the trolley car. "Come on, Grandpa. That's where we're going. My dad's going to take us to lunch."

"Has he got a trial going on?"

"I guess. He said we should go to Room 209."

MJ took the boy's hand when they arrived at City Hall and led him up the steps into the building. A policeman stood just inside the door. He directed MJ and Pearse toward the grand marble stairway, the mottled white steps of which as always reminded MJ of *Gone with the Wind*. Except that there was a crowd of irresolute, seedy people walking up and down the stairs. Some of them—lawyers, obviously—carried briefcases and were shabbily dressed in gray suits and wrinkled ties. Others seemed merely to wander, witnesses maybe, political hangers-on, or relations of accused prisoners, MJ guessed. They shuffled about, looking for courtrooms, the city planning office, the voter registrar. Most of them were lost. There were as well numerous policemen.

"There it is!" Pearse walked ahead, pointing a finger at the brass numbers above two swinging wood doors, each with a small window. Joe stood in the hallway in the company of a red-headed, worried-looking man whose hands resembled bags hanging at his sides.

"Pearse!" Joe excused himself from his companion, who turned into the courtroom. Pearse ran the last several feet toward his father, and Joe grabbed the boy by the shoulders. Joe glanced at MJ and straightened up. His demeanor took on an immediate reserve as he extended his hand. "Hi, Dad," he said. "Pearse decided we needed another witness, eh?"

MJ laughed. "It *was* a great mystery, where he was taking me."

"I'm glad you came."

"But you don't usually work here at City Hall, do you, Joe?" MJ asked. "What have you got going on today?"

"It's a hearing. An immigration thing. We're borrowing one of their courtrooms."

"Immigration?"

"An Irishman. The guy's being harassed by the English because they think he was involved a couple years ago in a crime. But he wasn't there. He's an innocent man, and I'm just trying to help him out."

"You're doing this through your firm?"

"No. It's private. I'm helping him for free."

MJ's overcoat hung open like a bolt of cloth unraveled across his shoulders. He fidgeted with the buttons. Joe, turning his attention once more to Pearse, did not notice his father's nervousness.

"The immigration panel's about to give him their decision, and he's worried about it." Joe leaned close to his father and whispered, "So am I, if you want the truth." He looked again at Pearse and placed a hand on the boy's shoulder. "But it'll just be a few minutes, Pearse. Why don't you and MJ come in to watch, and we'll go out afterwards."

"Is he an Irish citizen?" MJ asked.

"Northern Irish," Joe replied. "But he's got a permanent visa here, so he gets due process. We can't throw him out just because the British want him."

MJ shrugged. "I suppose not."

"Wouldn't be fair, right, Pearse?"

"S'pose not."

Joe gestured toward the door. Pearse led the way into the courtroom. MJ held back a moment, watching Joe's broad back. Joe wouldn't represent a man for free if there weren't a compelling reason to do so, MJ thought. And an Irishman hounded by the English? He's IRA. Got to be. MJ approached the courtroom door, looking in through one of the windows. The Irishman sat at a table inside the court, his shoulders slouched, his fingers wrapped together in a kind of tight knot. His red hair provided what color there was in the room. He was startled from his isolation by Joe introducing him to Pearse. He shook the boy's hand and a brief smile appeared on his face.

His heart racing with the wish to leave, MJ pushed through the door.

* * *

MJ carried his hat in his hand and looked about the courtroom as though he were going to be incarcerated in it. His eyes seemed to jitter as he cast brief glances at Tom Carrington, at the semi-somnolent bailiff who sat at a desk to the side, at the hearing table that was covered with neat piles of typed paper, and finally at Joe.

Joe pointed to the chair next to Pearse, who was seated alone in the gallery.

"There won't be anyone else here today, Dad," he said. "This isn't a trial, so there isn't an audience or a jury."

Carrington turned in his seat and surveyed MJ. His skin had the yellow tinge native to many red-headed Irish. His eyes were reddened as well, the result of too much drinking, that's for sure, Joe thought. Carrington had the famished, truculent look of many Irish poor, of the working class. He stood and approached the railing between the court and the gallery.

"This is your father, Joe?"

"Yes. MJ Pearse, this is . . ."

"Carrington's the name, Mr. Pearse. Pleasure to meet you."

MJ took Carrington's hand. But he reacted with so little enthusiasm that Joe became immediately irritated by his indifference. MJ did not reply to Carrington at all. Rather he sat down next to Pearse and laid his hat on his lap, looking once more around the room. He seemed to be disregarding Carrington out of hand.

The Irishman glanced at Joe and turned back to the table.

"There's something wrong, Dad?" Joe asked.

"No. Not at all."

"Well, why . . ."

Three people walked into the courtroom from the judge's chamber. Interrupted, Joe turned toward Carrington. The others sat down at the table. A fourth man came into the room from the hallway and sat down as well. He was thin, dark, and very well dressed. Already seated, Carrington looked desultorily over the few papers before him.

The room contained no decoration other than a printed announcement regarding what to do in case of fire. Joe felt that the very air in the courtroom was plain and dark, as though there were no possibility of refreshment from it. The yellow-brown of the paint on the walls, stained by many years without touch-up, gave the room a kind of tired weight, as though it had survived long illness.

"Mr. Carrington, the panel has had the opportunity now to go over all of the matters that pertain to your case. We've considered Mr. Winslow's contentions . . ." The speaker, a crisp, black-haired woman whose eyeglasses reflected the folders and papers arranged before her on the table, gestured toward the government attorney, the man who had come in late. "And Mr. Pearse's, as well. And I'm afraid that the evidence supports Mr. Winslow's point of view, and that we have no recourse but to have you return to Northern Ireland to stand trial for the crime of which you are accused."

"But Mrs. Pinella . . ." Carrington said.

Mrs. Pinella paused and looked up from the papers in her hand. She lowered her head slightly, to get a clearer view of the Irishman over the tops of her bifocals.

"It's a serious crime, Mr. Carrington," she replied. Her voice maintained its tone of bureaucratic cheerlessness. Joe tapped a pencil against the tabletop. "And we believe you should have the opportunity to present your point of view to a duly appointed court of law in your own country."

"Jesus," Carrington whispered.

"Of course," Mrs. Pinella continued. She dropped the papers to the table. "You have the right to appeal the decision, if you wish."

"Fuck your decision, miss!"

The pencil skittered from Joe's hand. Carrington quickly stood up. His hands formed bony fists, which he placed squarely on the table. Mrs. Pinella sat back, her mouth open as she looked up at him.

"You don't know what you're asking me to do!" Carrington shouted.

"Tom," Joe said. He stood and took Carrington by the shoulders. The Irishman pushed him away, then leaned far over the table.

"You're asking me to go back to my own country, as you call it, so that I can spend the rest of my life in prison. But it is not my own country! And anyway the whole place is a prison!"

"Tom!" Again Joe placed his hands on Carrington's shoulders. He glanced over his shoulder. The bailiff, shaken from his repose, stood up and moved toward Carrington.

"Sit down," Joe said.

"I won't!"

"Sit down!"

"You look over your papers there, don't you," Carrington

continued, his index finger quivering before Mrs. Pinella's folder. "You talk about me among yourselves in the calm of your . . . your chamber back there. Like goldfish in a tank."

"Mr. Carrington!" Mrs. Pinella said.

"And you send me to Northern Ireland, the country of my origin you call it . . . Jesus, to face a jury of my peers, and every one of them is a goddamned Englishman. That's what you're sending me to. Sure incarceration and nothing else!"

The bailiff approached Carrington. Joe realized he had to shut Carrington up. "Tom, you've got to control yourself."

Carrington moved to speak once more, but Joe interrupted.

"This is a legal proceeding, damn it, and you can't act this way here." Joe looked around the table. "Mrs. Pinella . . . gentlemen. Please forgive this outburst."

Carrington grimaced. "Joe, how can you let them . . . ?"

"Sit down!" Joe placed his hand on the Irishman's shoulder and forced him to his chair. Carrington resisted a moment, then gave in to Joe. His face appeared shrunken. He was suddenly aged.

There was a noise behind him, and Joe glanced over his shoulder into the gallery. Pearse remained seated. But MJ was standing, his hands grasping the back of the seat in front of him. His hat had fallen from his lap onto the seat itself.

"He'd deserve it, the bastard," MJ said. "Send him back!"

Pearse looked up at MJ, startled by his sudden movement. MJ's eyes ticked violently toward Joe's.

"Sit down!" Joe said.

"Sir," the bailiff interrupted wearily, facing MJ himself. "You'll be asked to leave if you don't . . ."

"Please, Dad. Sit down," Joe said.

MJ's eyes widened and, as though suddenly coming out of a dream, he looked around himself. He seemed to weaken. He glanced at his hands, biting his lower lip. He picked up his hat and sat down. Mortified, he mumbled an apology.

From the perspective of the thirty-foot platform, the children playing in the pool below resembled gray-white gardenias twirling about the surface of the water. Their silver arms, and the splashes their arms made, fluttered like splayed petals. Though Pearse had jumped frequently from the platform, he contemplated, with ticklish pleasure, the fall he was about to make. The shouts from below were distant echoes. Water flowed through everything, even the children's laughter, so that a splash continued for what seemed several seconds, until it became obscured by other liquid noises.

Pearse bent his legs and jumped. Cold air rushed past him, cluttering his ears. The walls of the Crystal Plunge went straight up—suddenly—as though they had been blown into the air. He took a breath, awaiting the impact, and landed in the water feet first. The roar of bubbles all around buoyed him up, and he struggled to reach the surface.

He swam to one of the ladders and pulled himself from the water. Looking over his shoulder for Debbie Mariano, he saw that she was at the far end of the pool, watching some other children. He turned and ran along the pool deck to the metal stairway that led to the platform and ascended once more.

This time he lowered his arms to his sides as he fell, to make as little resistance as possible when he entered the water, which he hit like a bomb. The bubbles surged about his head. He swam about, recovering from the giddiness of the flight.

"Hey, Pearse, that was great." Tim stood at the edge of the pool. A towel hung from his neck. "Are you going off the board?"

Pearse climbed from the pool once again. He waited in line at the diving board, stood up on it, and dived headfirst into the pool. Pearse's passage through the air was marred by imperfections. His feet were apart, he drifted to one side, and his legs went over his head as he entered the water.

It was fun anyway.

Debbie stood on the pool deck with a towel, and when Pearse emerged from the water she wrapped it around his head, drying his hair.

"You love to jump, don't you, Pearse?"

"Yeah. I like the bubbles," he gasped. After a moment Debbie let him go, then looked over his shoulder to where Tim stood, talking to some friends.

"I like the fall," Pearse said. He turned to follow her glance.

"You know, Halloween is next week," Debbie said.

"Yeah, I'm going out trick-or-treating with some kids from school."

"What kind of costume are you going to wear?"

Pearse began shivering. He wanted to get back into the pool.

"I don't know. A bum, maybe," he said.

"I've got some things you could wear."

"You do?" Pearse folded his arms before him, trying to fend off the cold.

"I could come over Wednesday afternoon, after school. I've got a costume Tim might like, too."

"Maybe. He used to dress up for Halloween. But I don't think he likes it, now."

Debbie crumpled the towel between her hands and tossed it onto the bench behind her. "The three of us could go around in costume Halloween afternoon. You know, just to see what people would think?"

"You mean, not that night?"

"Oh, sure," Debbie laughed. "That, too!" She fingered her hair. Her fingernails—fire-engine red, glossy ovals—shone with polish.

Pearse nodded, and Debbie walked toward the far end of the pool. Wow! Pearse thought. This'll be fun.

Debbie arrived at Pearse's the afternoon of Halloween, carrying two paper bags filled with clothing. Pearse had been waiting for this all week. The previous afternoon he had paid little attention to the movie Sister Marie George had shown at school, a documentary about the water purification plant in Oakland. It was the third time he had seen it. When the lights went on after the film, Pearse was startled from a daydream in which he and Debbie were wandering through a haunted house.

"Oh, Debbie, you look wonderful," Mimi laughed, as Debbie greeted her at the top of the stairs. Mimi stepped back to let the girl pass toward the living room.

Debbie's costume so surprised Pearse that his pleasure at seeing her was almost overwhelmed by his shock at what she wore. A pair of ceramic earrings looked like black eclipsed moons. Pearse guessed that the black seashell necklace was painted, since he had never seen such shells himself at the beach. They were chipped here and there, so that a few of them resembled ancient teeth, unearthed from a site. She wore a black, sleeveless sweater, and Pearse glanced with embarrassment at the white bra strap that came from beneath the sweater. Her black skirt came down to the middle of her calves, and she wore a pair of patent leather flats.

Her hair hung down straight, treated with wax or oil or something, Pearse decided. It was not at all like her usually soft and frivolously curling hair. Her colored lips reminded him of the red bell peppers in the bins at Mr. Yick's market. They appeared quite swollen. Also her eyebrows were much darker than normal. Black, actually.

She was a sultry, gorgeous beatnik.

"I brought these things, too," Debbie said. She dropped the bags onto the couch in the living room. "Is Tim here?"

"He will be," Mimi replied. "He's over at the playground."

"Playing touch, I bet," Debbie said. She rummaged through one of the bags. "You know, every time I pass by there, he can't talk to me because he's got some kind of game going on. All through the summer, it was baseball. Now it's football."

Pearse grew irritated. His mother seemed happy to commiserate with Debbie, as though the two of them had some kind of shared interest in Tim's activities, from which Pearse was excluded.

"Anyway, Pearse, I hope you don't think these things are dumb," Debbie said. She took a beret from the bag and put it on Pearse's head, at an angle above his left temple. He went to look at himself in his bedroom, and he liked the authority with which he gazed back at himself from the mirror. Debbie and Mimi came into the bedroom with a coat, and he put that on as well. It was dark gray herringbone, ragged at the sleeves.

"I got it at Saint Vincent de Paul," Debbie said. She rolled the collar up so that it surrounded Pearse's neck. The coat came down to just above his knees.

"And what do you think of these?" Debbie said. She took a pair of sunglasses from the bag and gave them to Pearse. "I got them at Saint Vincent's too."

Pearse put them on, and they fit perfectly. But the rims were made of black plastic and looked, he thought, like butterfly wings. There were holes in them, as in Joe's wingtip shoes, and they flared out from the sides of his head.

"I don't know," Pearse mumbled. "Aren't they a girl's?"

Mimi knelt down before him. She held him by the shoulders and stared at the glasses.

"Of course not," she said. "Besides, if you're going to be a beatnik, you've got to dress out of the ordinary."

"That's right," Debbie agreed. She reached into the bag again. "But this'll fix it for you." She pulled a moustache and a small bottle from the bag. "See, you can put a moustache on with this stuff. Spirit gum."

She took the cap from the bottle and applied some of the liquid to Pearse's upper lip.

"I borrowed it from my drama class. It's pretty awful," she said.

Pearse recoiled from the odor, as Debbie pressed the moustache to his lip and tapped it down at the edges with her index finger.

"There."

Pearse turned toward the mirror. The moustache formed a black hedge on his lip. It was rectangular and specific, not following the line of his mouth at all. Pearse liked it a great deal.

The front door opened. The sound of Tim's footsteps came up from below, and Debbie turned toward the hallway.

There was a flurry of greetings. Pearse remained in his room, looking at himself in the mirror. Something was missing from the costume, but he could not discern what it was. The detail was insignificant, but without it the costume was not complete. He put his hands on his waist, then turned to the side and glowered, thinking it a gesture or an attitude that was needed. But that was not it. He turned his chin up, the way Sister Marie George did when she was mad. At those moments, she took on a look of imperious, insulted deflation, as though the children, with their tossed erasers and giggling, had betrayed her. But that was not it either. Pearse shrugged and stared at himself.

Tim followed Mimi into the room. Pearse turned and faced his brother, who immediately grimaced.

"How do you like it?" Pearse asked.

Tim's football remained in his hands. He grinned. "You look like a dork," he said.

This word, used frequently by the children at school, conveyed a kind of disdain not achievable with other insults. Pearse himself used it every day, though not in the presence of his parents. He knew it had something to do with the penis, but there seemed to be a lot more to the word than just that. A dork was a reprehensible person, the sort of kid who had buck teeth or whose glasses were held together with adhesive tape.

Tim noticed the bag on the floor next to Pearse's desk. "What's all this?" he asked, pulling a black felt porkpie hat from the bag. Debbie had included a bright red turtleneck T-shirt, as well as a string of wooden beads. They were old and imperfectly round, with scuffs and scratches all over them. He put the beads over his head and turned toward the mirror.

He preened a bit, his hands on his waist. Pearse, sitting down on his chair, felt ignored. He adjusted his beret, then suddenly realized what it was that was missing from his costume, the nuance that would give it real authenticity. It was the books, the soiled books.

"Yeah, I think they're terrific," Tim said.

Pearse moved from the chair and went to his shelf. The books he had were quite beat up, suitable enough on that score. As well, a lot of them were gifts from his grandparents, and pretty old. But he rejected them all. It would not do to walk around North Beach with a copy of *Little Toot* sticking out of his coat pocket. He slipped from the room and went down the hall into the kitchen. An issue of his father's *United Irishmen* lay on the kitchen table. Pearse fingered the paper a moment, recalling the trolley ride home from City Hall a few days previously. MJ had apologized to Pearse for being so out of line in the courtroom.

"I shouldn't have said that, Pearse. I don't know what got into me." MJ had looked out the window at the crowds on Market Street. "It's just that your father defends those IRA people so much, and he doesn't understand them."

Pearse kept his hands in the pockets of his jacket. He sympathized with Joe, in that he didn't understand what had happened either.

He slipped the newspaper into his coat pocket, but the look still was not right. Bright and neat, the paper was too much like one of his grandfather's handkerchiefs.

Pearse spotted a Hills Brothers coffee can on the sink, the one into which Mimi poured her excess bacon grease. He took some of the grease onto his fingers. Removing the *United Irishmen* from his pocket, he crumpled it several times and smeared it with the grease. Placing the paper back in the coat pocket, he returned to his bedroom.

Debbie and Mimi were fixing Tim's costume, laughing with him as he talked about how funny *he* looked, as well. Pearse surveyed himself in the mirror. The sunglasses hid his eyes and made him appear mysterious. His moustache lay tacked to his lip. The newspaper drooped from his coat pocket like something he had found in the gutter.

It's perfect, Pearse thought.

They walked through Washington Square toward Upper Grant Avenue. But as they crossed the square, Pearse reminded Tim that he was not supposed to go any farther.

"Come on, Pearse," Tim said. He too wore sunglasses. "We won't tell. We won't get caught."

Reluctantly Pearse followed along, putting down the anxiety he felt. They turned onto Upper Grant Avenue itself. They passed a hardware store, an Italian vegetable market, and several bars. The wooden buildings confronted one another across the narrow street, and the sidewalks were stained with tossed-away gum and papers. Debbie's hands flashed about as she walked, and Pearse was distracted by their movement. She broke into laughter, touching Tim's shoulder as they shared a joke. A feeling of sadness welled up in Pearse. He had thought this was going to be his afternoon with Debbie, and that Tim was just coming along for fun. But Debbie's indifference made him worry that she too considered him a dork.

Pearse looked in the window of an Italian bakery. The display case was filled with rows of focaccia and french bread. But the cracked crusts of the loaves seemed rain-worn and elderly, leaning against one another like bloated pieces of wood. He decided to buy a slice of the focaccia, and he looked in his pocket for some change. There was a tapping sound on the window. The baker inside wore a white apron and a white shirt. His sagging eyes were pouched. He waved his hand at Pearse, yelling at him and motioning him away from the window.

Offended, Pearse turned down the street.

A group of beatniks walked toward him. Dressed in blacks and browns, they were quite somber looking, and they talked at great speed. They gestured, looked at the sidewalk, and walked along as though angered by the smears and spittle. Intimidated, Pearse turned back and faced the bakery window. The wings of his sunglasses made a dim pattern on the glass. Inside, dead flies lay scattered on the windowsill. The baker began yelling at him again, telling him to get going. To Pearse's dismay, the beatniks broke into laughter behind him.

It was a bright clatter of noise. He stuck his hands in his pockets and kept his eyes on the bugs. The beatniks were laughing at him. He knew they were.

The baker held one hand up before his face, the fingers facing his lips, together at the tips. Though Pearse knew he was the object of the man's insults, he did not want to face the beatniks, who scared him even more. He could not move.

"That's a wonderful costume," a woman's voice said.

Pearse looked around. The woman, a beatnik, stood right before him. A scarf fell down across the shoulder of her turtleneck sweater. Her hair was mussed, and she held a cigarette in one hand. She picked a piece of tobacco from her lower lip with her long fingernails. Her eyes squinted with cigarette smoke.

"Thanks," Pearse said.

"Do you live around here?"

"No, I live over on Mason Street," Pearse replied. He remained distracted by the baker, who, though he had ceased shouting, now stood behind the display of breads, glaring at Pearse and the woman.

"The beret's my favorite part," she said.

Pearse blushed.

"You're going trick-or-treating tonight?"

"Yes, I guess so."

"Happy Halloween, then. See you." The woman hurried after her friends.

Pearse stood still a moment, confused by the conversation. He had never realized that beatniks could be so friendly. He reached up to adjust his moustache, and noticed there were beatniks everywhere. Dressed in slovenly clothes, somber and private, they all seemed to be walking along with their collars up around their necks. Sunglasses. Beards. Music came out the door of one of the bars, but it was formless. A saxophone and trumpet exchanged moments of stuttering noise. Pearse looked across Upper Grant Avenue. He did look like the people walking up and down. The fact was, he decided, he looked just like them.

The Caffè Trieste was a small coffeehouse with windows on the front and one side, looking out on the corner of Vallejo Street and Upper Grant Avenue. Pearse caught up with Debbie and Tim as they walked, somewhat cautiously, through the door of the café. On the lefthand side, a bench paralleled one long window. Several people sat on the bench, conversing as they sipped from small cups of coffee. Pearse noticed a number of women, but none of them looked like his mother. Dressed as morosely as the men were, the women were yet more attractive, supplying a vivacity that the men lacked altogether. Cigarette smoke filled the room.

Beyond the telephone booth, another bench turned the corner to the right and followed the back wall. There were several rectangular tables in the middle of the room, with chairs everywhere. Because of the windows, the light in the café was very bright, although the yellow-brown walls projected a gloominess that matched the mumbled conversation through the room. The patrons paid little attention to Tim and Debbie, but laughter broke out when they saw Pearse. The counterman leaned far over the counter and addressed him as he walked through the door.

"Hey, buddy," he said. "Happy Halloween!"

Pearse stared into the glass case at the end of the counter, where a pile of gnocchi sat, like thumbs, in one corner of a serving dish.

"Trick or treat, man," one of the customers said. He sat at a table in the middle of the café. Pearse's eyes widened as he recognized him. It was his beatnik, now dry, no longer sullied by the operatic spray of his father's hose. His beret lay on the table, next to three empty coffee cups. Several books were spread out on the table as well. There was a pocket dictionary and an ashtray filled with cigarette butts. Gray smoke surrounded his head. His smile came out of the smoke, a soiled, misty wedge.

"Pearse, you want a Coke or something?" Tim asked.

Pearse turned around. "I don't know," he said.

"You don't drink coffee, do you?" Debbie asked Tim.

"Me? No, not me," he replied. He adjusted his porkpie hat, looking around to see whether he was being watched.

Pearse raised his hand. "I do!" he said.

"Come on, Pearse," Tim grumbled.

"I want coffee," Pearse insisted.

"OK, so what'll it be?" the counterman asked.

"I guess we'll have . . ." Debbie shrugged. "Oh, I don't know." She looked around the café. Pearse waited for her to order. Her eyes moved back and forth across the tables. She held her fingers to her lips, pressing them against her teeth.

Pearse pointed at one of the cups on the beatnik's table. "What's that?" he asked.

The beatnik placed his hand on the saucer and pushed it forward. "It's called espresso, man," he said.

"Espresso?"

"Yeah. It's from Italy."

Espresso. Pearse liked the word. It reminded him of the name of a car. "That's where the Holy Father lives," he said. Maybe that's what the Holy Father drives, he thought.

"Could I have one of those?" he asked Debbie.

"OK." There was relief in Debbie's voice, a return to the pretended self-assurance with which she had led the way into the café. "Two espressos, please," she said. "And . . ." She looked toward Tim.

"A glass of milk," Tim muttered.

The counterman prepared the coffees, and Debbie ordered three pastries as well.

"Pearse, go get that table, will you?" she said. She gestured toward the beatnik. Almost all the customers had noticed Pearse by now, and the level of conversation had dropped off in the café, as they watched Pearse pull back a chair from the table next to the beatnik's.

"Can we sit here?" he asked. Pearse worried that the waver in his voice was quite noticeable.

"Sure," the beatnik said. He stood and helped Pearse with the empty coffee cups and sodden napkins that had been left behind. Pearse noticed with interest the book in the beatnik's pocket. They carried the dishes to a small cart laden with dirty cups and saucers.

"I dig your costume," the beatnik said. "Especially the beret."

"Oh. Thanks," Pearse said. He did not know what to do, remembering how, on the sidewalk outside Biordi's a week and a half before, his mother's hand had tightened on his own.

"My name's Ed Finney." The beatnik extended his hand. Pearse noticed that his fingernails were abraded.

"Patrick's my name," Pearse mumbled.

"Patrick what?"

"Pearse. But that's what everybody calls me, anyway. Pearse, I mean."

"All right, Pearse." Ed grabbed Pearse's hand, and a smile came back onto his lips. His teeth were clean and bright. "How do you do?"

"Fine."

At the counter, Debbie leaned against Tim, who stepped away with embarrassment. Debbie slipped her hand through his arm.

"I'm here with my brother, see. Over there. And the lifeguard, from the pool."

Debbie laid her head on Tim's shoulder.

"We're dressed up for Halloween," Pearse said.

"That's what I figured," Ed replied. He leaned back in his chair and picked up the two ends of his scarf, the same scarf that had lain in the puddle in Washington Street. He tossed one of the ends around his neck. "Me too," he said.

"You mean, you're not a beatnik?"

"Oh, sure I am, I guess."

Ed took up his cigarette from the ashtray. He held it tight between the tips of his index finger and his thumb as he drew on it. His hand cupped the cigarette itself.

"But I like to dress up as much as the next guy," he said. As he spoke, small putters of smoke came from his mouth. He finished the sentence and exhaled the rest. The cloud contained an acrid, biting odor, from which Pearse recoiled. Ed moved the ashtray to the far side of his table.

"Sorry," he said. "It's a Gauloise."

"What's that?"

"A brand of cigarettes. Tough to get around here, I can tell you that." Ed reached into the breast pocket of his coat and pulled out a wrinkled purple pack of cigarettes. He handed it to Pearse. "Expensive, too. But, when you've gotten used to them, you've really got to have them."

Pearse wondered how such an awful-smelling cigarette could come in such a pretty wrapping.

"How come they're hard to get?" he asked.

"They come from France." Ed took up the cigarette once more. He put it in his mouth, then replaced the pack in his coat pocket. The cigarette drooped from his lips. "I heard that Baudelaire smoked them. Ever been to France?"

"No. But it's next to Italy, isn't it?"

"Sure is."

"Someday I'm going to go to Italy."

"Not a bad place. Why do you want to go there?"

"To visit the Holy Father."

"Who?"

"The pope."

"The pope!" Ed blinked again, as more smoke got into his eyes. He removed the cigarette from his mouth and spat out a piece of tobacco.

"Yes," Pearse replied uncertainly. Ed's eyes had grown round with censure. A frown gathered on his face.

"Here's your pastry, Pearse," Debbie said. She looked at Ed. "Hi," she whispered.

Ed shook his head, pushing the books around the table in front of him. "Pope's a damned fascist," he said. He grumbled as he finished the sentence.

There was a silence, and Tim sat down to his pastry and glass of milk. Debbie placed an espresso before Pearse, who leaned forward to smell it. He did not know what a fascist was, though he had heard that word before on one occasion. His father had used it during a conversation with MJ a few weeks before, talking about the English.

"Fascists!" MJ had laughed. "The English? Joe, Joe. Until you've met an IRA man with a bomb in his hand, you haven't even come close to meeting a fascist."

The two men had argued at length, and Pearse had gone to

sleep on the chesterfield, their lengthy and irascible assertions clashing in his ears,

"What are you reading?" Ed asked. Conversation had picked up once more in the café. Still, wherever Pearse looked, people grinned at him. He pulled the paper from his pocket and tossed it onto the table.

"It's my dad's," he said.

"Pearse, where'd you get that?" Tim asked.

"From the kitchen," Pearse said. "It was on the table."

"But that's the latest issue."

Debbie took a bite from her cinnamon roll, laid it back on her plate, and touched Tim's hand.

"This is my brother," Pearse said to Ed.

"What d'you say?" Ed replied. Ignoring him, Tim cut into his pastry with a fork. It was stale, and Tim had to push the fork back and forth with his fingers.

Pearse took his cup between his hands. It was chocolate brown on the outside and white inside. Taking a breath, he slurped some of the coffee into his mouth. The expresso tasted like hand soap.

"What is this *United Irishmen*?" Ed asked. He thumbed through the paper.

Pearse stuck his tongue out to wet his lips, hoping to weaken the taste in his mouth with saliva. He shivered violently. The coffee had a bright aftertaste that reminded him of Vaseline.

"You read this?" Ed asked.

"What?" Pearse whispered.

"You OK, Pearse?" Tim asked.

"This newspaper. It's from Ireland," Ed said.

Pearse took a bite from the pastry, watching as Debbie lifted her cup to her lips. But when she sipped the coffee, there was no reaction. Then, to Pearse's surprise, she took some more.

A fading bit of steam circled Pearse's coffee. Noting that Debbie was actually enjoying her expresso, he picked up his cup again and took in a bit more of his own. It tasted just as bad. But this time, he found much satisfaction in forcing the bitter coffee past his lips. Pearse laid the cup in its saucer, then removed his sunglasses and placed them on the table.

"This is OK," he said.

"I like it too," Debbie replied. She turned to Tim. "You really ought to try it."

"Yeah, Tim," Pearse agreed. He saw his brother's uncertainty. "You should."

He turned toward Ed. "You know, I saw you in Washington Square a couple days ago."

"What was I doing?"

"Standing on a bench, reading out loud."

"Oh, yeah," Ed replied. He put the cigarette out in the ashtray. "I do that now and then. Not a lot of people read poetry in this damned country, so I go out there and read it to them."

"Do they pay you?"

"I don't get any money for that," he said. "But who cares? See, I don't believe in money."

"What, are you a . . . a bum or something?"

"Me? No! What do you think?"

Pearse shrank back against the seat. "I don't know."

"I mean, I fought in Korea!"

Sipping his coffee, Pearse glanced up quickly at Ed.

"It's just that the bastards don't pay me for what I do," Ed said.

"What's that?"

"Verse."

Pearse pondered the answer in silence.

"Poetry, I mean," Ed said.

"Oh, the stuff Sister makes us read at school sometimes."

"What's that?"

" 'Now I lay me down to sleep.' Like that?"

Ed's laughter burst out into unaffected noise, very pleasurable to hear. "Yeah, that's it," he said. He turned again to his coffee, chuckling.

Across the table, Tim appeared even more uncomfortable. Debbie still attempted engaging him in conversation, to no avail. Suddenly Pearse realized that Debbie liked Tim. She wants to be his girlfriend, Pearse thought.

Disappointed, he sipped his coffee while Ed returned to the *United Irishmen*. Pearse was glad the beatnik liked the paper, even though Pearse himself felt that the *United Irishmen* contained just a lot of boring pictures of men in black suits, and big headlines with words he could not understand. Now and then, a picture of a destroyed building brought something of interest to the paper. Otherwise, he could not understand why his father liked it so much.

Now Debbie and Tim were holding hands. Pearse leaned on a fist and stared into his coffee. Debbie's hand caressed Tim's where it lay on the table. Pearse, isolated in his jealousy, surveyed the costume-jewelry ring on her finger. It had a number of pearllike stones surrounding a red glass ruby. To Pearse's dismay, Tim looked at Debbie and smiled.

"Hey, this is interesting," Ed said. "Look at this." He spread the newspaper over the table and pointed at a photo of a man sitting on a cot, wrapped in a blanket. "It says his name is Paddy McGillicuddy."

The name reminded Pearse of popcorn cooking on the stove.

"Yeah, it's wonderful, isn't it?" Ed continued. "But he's in trouble, it looks like. He's a prisoner of the English, in Northern Ireland, and he's on a hunger strike."

Ed looked toward Pearse.

"You know what that is?"

Pearse shook his head.

"It's when someone stops eating, hoping he can get the government to change its policies."

"But why do they make him wear the blanket?" Pearse asked, pointing at the photo.

"They don't," Ed replied, "not according to this article. He's doing it on his own, and it says there are a lot of Catholic prisoners doing the same. They refuse to wear prison clothes, because that makes it seem like they've committed crimes. And they don't think they're criminals, because all they've done is to disobey the government. So they don't want to wear the prison uniform, and they wrap themselves in a blanket instead."

Ed looked at the photo again.

"I guess it's as if they're saying, 'You can do all you want to me, but I'm still Paddy McGillicuddy.' You know, 'You can keep your clothes, because this flannel gives me more warmth than you bastards ever could.' "

Ed nodded, approving the idea.

"But they don't eat," he continued, pursing his lips. "And that's tough."

He turned the page to look at a few more headlines.

"You got this from your father?" he asked.

"Yeah. You want to keep it?"

"Can I?"

"Sure."

Ed looked into the newspaper once more, then tapped Pearse's knee. "Thanks, Pearse. But you should keep it. If it's your dad's, I wouldn't want to get you in trouble."

"He doesn't care."

"I'll bet he does." Ed turned back to the first page and pointed to a spot above the masthead. "Like your brother says, it has this week's date on it."

"I guess so," Pearse said.

"But I'll tell you what. Why don't you bring it back next week, after he reads it? I'll borrow it from you then."

Ed leaned across the table, smiling in a conspiratorial way.

"No one'll know I've got it," he said. "And you can sneak it back after I'm done."

Across the table, Tim was beginning to give in to Debbie's affections. He laid his hand on hers, on the leather bench. His fingers appeared wooden and straight.

Pearse finished his coffee and rose from the table. "OK," he said, "I guess I'll see you then."

Ed nodded and gave him the newspaper. "Right. I'll be here, eh?"

Pearse folded the paper and replaced it in his coat pocket. Tim's hand was entwined in Debbie's.

"OK," Pearse replied to Ed. He waited a moment longer, hoping for Tim's and Debbie's attention. They had not noticed his move to leave.

"See you at home, Tim," Pearse said.

His brother did not respond. When Debbie finally looked up at Pearse, as though from an afterthought, Pearse's heart felt like a smudge. It actually hurt with disappointment that she had paid so little attention to him.

"See you tomorrow, maybe, Pearse?" she asked. She looked at Tim. "I mean, if I can come over?"

"I guess." Pearse turned toward the door.

"Hey," Ed called out. He took up Pearse's sunglasses and held them up over the table. "Don't forget these."

"Oh." Pearse stepped back to the table and took the glasses. He was sorry to leave the noise and smoke of the café.

Ed waved once. "I'll see you next time," he said.

"Yeah," Pearse smiled. He put on the sunglasses, adjusted his beret, and walked out of the café.

Though marred by clouds coming in from the ocean, the afternoon sunlight fell directly against the façade of the Caffè Trieste. Pearse looked across the street. The doors of Saint Francis of Assisi church were open, and shadows fell across them. Pearse adjusted his sunglasses and crossed over.

Passing before the church, he heard laughter inside, and he stopped to listen. A high-pitched shout echoed through the door, an unusual sound to come from a church. Pearse walked up the steps and looked in. The church was so dark that it had the appearance of a threatening cave.

As he entered, he noticed the painting to the right of the altar, which showed Saint Francis of Assisi talking with several other friars. Saint Francis had a teacherly look, and Pearse assumed he was telling them something about kindness or charity, stuff like that. There were birds on the ground, birds in the air, and little angels, like fat babies with wings, all over. High above the scene, an adult angel hung in the air. Light came from behind the angel and lit the clouds that surrounded him. It tinted his pink legs with gold.

On the crucifix, Christ's arms extended uncomfortably from His shoulders. The blood flowing down His forearms toward the elbows seemed like decoration, like ribbons on a birthday present.

Pearse walked up the side aisle. He genuflected and sat down in one of the pews, in the gloom next to a pillar. The silence in the church was interrupted by footsteps at the side of the altar. Then he heard a dropped coin and the descending whine it made as it rolled across the marble floor. Sunlight shone through one window, up high on a wall. Otherwise, everything was shadowy in reflected light. The confessionals, like rectangular chambers carved into the side of a cliff, were quite black. Pearse heard giggles from the altar, then a clap of sound, as if a book had dropped to the floor.

A skeleton came out from behind the altar. He stopped at the pulpit and looked into the church, but he did not see Pearse in the shadows. Pearse laid a hand on the back of the pew before him. He blinked and took in a breath.

A moth circled up a shaft of light over the altar. Pearse looked about for a priest. The skeleton turned, walked up the steps onto the altar, and stopped, looking up at the vestibule. He waved toward the side of the church, and two more apparitions came out.

Kids, Pearse concluded. Fifth, sixth grade, maybe. One was a pirate, the other a sorcerer with a white beard and a conelike hat. They ran up the steps and began helping the skeleton up onto the altar. The skeleton pulled aside the vestibule curtain and examined the small brass door. It was locked, and he jumped back down from the altar. He walked with the other boys to the cruet stand, where he took up one of the small bottles and poured the wine from it onto the marble floor.

Pearse's stomach grew tight. When the boy dropped the water cruet, it shattered on the steps, and Pearse jumped out of the shadow and ran to the altar.

"Stop it," he shouted. He grabbed the skeleton and pushed him back against the stand. It skidded away from the two boys, toppling over on its side. Pearse grabbed the skeleton's hair, and the skeleton pulled back.

Pearse stumbled to the floor. The boys grabbed him, and he threw his arms up around his head to protect himself. Someone kicked him, and he began shouting, no words, simply an anguished wail. A man's voice broke through the confusion, and suddenly the other boys were running away. Pearse held on to the skeleton, whose muscles were taut beneath the costume. Pearse grabbed his leg.

"What are you boys doing?"

A priest took the other boy by the arm. His mask fell off, but Pearse did not recognize him. His face was quite red from the effort of trying to get away. His sand-colored hair flew about, and there were scratches on his neck where Pearse had attacked him.

"It wasn't me," the boy yelled. "It was him. He was trying to take the glass things, the pouring things . . ."

He doesn't even know their names, Pearse thought.

"I did not!" Pearse shouted. He stood up and attacked the boy once more.

"You boys stop this. Stop this now," the priest said. He grabbed the skeleton.

Pearse sucked in a breath and ran as fast as he could for the door of the church.

"Come back here," the priest yelled. He chased Pearse up the aisle. Pearse dashed his hand into the water, crossed himself, and ran out. The priest caught him just as he got to the top step of the porch.

"Let me go!" Pearse shouted.

The priest took him into his arms, but Pearse was able to free himself, and he turned once again toward the street. Across the way, Ed Finney closed the door of the Caffè Trieste and walked down the sidewalk toward Columbus. He carried all his books in one arm.

The priest grabbed Pearse again at the bottom of the steps. "Where do you live?" he said.

Pearse avoided the priest's hand as it reached for his moustache.

"Tell me your name!"

Pearse shook his head and fended the man off. His sunglasses flew away and skittered across the sidewalk.

"I said, tell me your name."

Suddenly Pearse glimpsed two hands crumpling the priest's cassock at the shoulders.

"Schmuck!" a voice said. "Let go of him!"

Pearse saw a scarf, a book sliding across the cement.

The priest backed away, throwing one arm up over his head. Ed pushed the priest farther back. His coat flailed about him, and the scarf came unraveled from his neck. He took the priest by the front of the cassock.

"Let go of him!" Ed shouted.

Pearse came free as the two men struggled. The priest tried to escape, but Ed followed him up the stairs. Pearse searched for his sunglasses, finding them propped up against the bottom step. One of the stems had been broken off. Ed pushed the priest into an alcove at the far end of the porch. Pearse looked up once more and gasped. Ed was hitting the priest with one of his books, and the priest slumped down against the wall. He held his hands up for protection. Ed rolled the book into a kind of tiny billy club and let the priest have it on top of his head.

"Come on, kid," Ed said. He took Pearse's hand and led him quickly up the sidewalk. Pearse looked over his shoulder. Like a pile of black-robed sticks, the priest sat breathlessly in the alcove.

Pearse was shocked. He had never thought that a priest could actually be knocked down. Yet, having knocked one down, Ed still lived. No lightning struck him, as it had Saint Paul. Indeed, Ed was now laughing. No thunderous clouds. No heavenly disapproval. Pearse stumbled behind, running as fast as he could across Columbus Avenue. They hurried around the backside of a bus that was just leaving the stop in front of Molinari's Delicatessen. Ed pounded his fist against its side, and the bus stopped to take them in. Pearse followed Ed down the aisle. Looking out the window, he saw the priest rising from the alcove in defeated disarray. The bus accelerated from the stop, and the priest scratched his head, searching the street for his attacker.

Gee, Pearse thought. Maybe God didn't even see it.

"Ah, you never get a chance like that," Ed laughed as he recounted his rescue of Pearse, once more, to Pearse, twenty minutes later. "I mean, to actually put a stop to that kind of . . . oppression, see?" For him, the entire bus ride, and the transfer to the N Judah trolley on which they now rode toward the ocean, had been a celebration. Pearse himself felt guilty, not able to sort out his own responsibility in an attack that, despite its having rescued him, had also shocked him.

He flinched when Ed made a fist and raised it into the air before his face.

"To put it to them like that." Ed grinned. The smile was fresh, uninhibited. "Reminds me of Spain."

"Spain?"

Ed looked out the window of the trolley. "They had a civil war there, about twenty years ago, when I was a little kid. I've been reading about it."

Pearse pulled his coat around him. Heavy clouds darkened the sky, and it had gotten quite cold in the trolley car. He rode in silence as Ed continued talking.

"You know what a civil war is, don't you?" Ed asked.

Pearse shook his head.

"It's when one group of people in a country fights against another. Not two different countries, like us and them. A civil war is when everyone's from the same country."

"Like us and us," Pearse replied.

"Yes, that's right."

"But isn't that against the rules?" Pearse asked.

"Sure it is." Ed dangled one end of his scarf from his hands. He studied the loose, worn strings. "But it happens anyway. And they had a war like that in Spain. Probably about the time your parents got married. And, see, my father went there to fight."

"He was a soldier?"

"Yeah," Ed sighed. He sat up straighter and took in a breath. His exhale sounded measured and prideful. "Lincoln Brigade."

"But they weren't fighting the Japs."

"No! They were fighting the Fascists!"

Ed leaned his head against the glass and watched the trees pass by the trolley window.

"What's that word?" Pearse asked. "A fast, a fast . . ."

"Fascist?"

"Yeah. What's that?"

The smile went from Ed's face, though Pearse sensed a kind of residual excitement as he searched out his words.

"A fascist . . ." Ed paused again and laid his hands in his lap. "Well, my father used to say that a fascist embodies the worst kind of repressive, dictatorial bullshit you ever heard of."

Ed's voice grew louder and higher as he raised a hand and shook an index finger. The finger rattled before Pearse's face. "I kind of liked it, when he said things like that. The enemy of freedom, he called them."

The trolley creaked as it came to a stop to take on a passenger.

Pearse thought of the seminarians he had met at the First Communion Mass. Ed seemed to be about the same age, like twenty-five or something, and he knew about weird stuff, like they did. Spain. Fascists. Stuff that Pearse had never heard of, really. But there was a significant difference between Ed and the seminarians. They were quiet, prayerful, and kind of boring, Pearse thought, while Ed was everywhere disorganized. He talked rapidly about all kinds of different things, all at once. But because he was so scattered, he wasn't a know-it-all. And for that, Pearse liked him.

"My dad was a stevedore in New York," Ed continued, "and he hated the Fascists. So there was a war in Spain, when a bunch of those bastards tried to take over an elected, Republican government, you understand?"

Pearse did not, though he asserted that he did.

"And my dad went with a number of other guys from the docks, to fight in Spain against the Fascists."

"What happened?"

"Most of them died."

Pearse's face reddened. "Your father died?"

"No, he didn't. But his friends did, in the first couple weeks." Ed tightened his mouth and sighed. "In fact, that was the problem with my dad and me."

"Was he mad at you because you didn't want to do what he said?"

Ed played for a moment with the ends of his scarf. "In a way."

A man in a dark green suit boarded the trolley and sat down across the aisle. His eyes appeared to work independently of each other, so that he looked somewhat screwy. His hands were long and white. The trolley lurched once more into movement.

Ed turned toward the window. His voice gave way to a murmur, a ramble, that Pearse had difficulty hearing.

"My father didn't like it that I went to Korea, after high school. I got drafted. You know, when they make you go into the army. When I told him what had happened, he asked me what I was going to do in Korea. And I told him I guessed I'd be fighting against the Reds."

Pearse recalled the Marines and GI Joe and all the comics characters, prevailing against the mean-hearted North Koreans.

"The commies," Ed continued. "And you know what he did, Pearse?"

Pearse shook his head. Ed, slumped against the window, seemed suddenly distressed. He cleared his throat, as though the phlegm had appeared unexpectedly. The woman in the seat in front of them reached for the cord for the next stop. She was the same size everywhere, and reminded Pearse of a muffin.

"He threw me out. Told me he'd fought on the side of the commies, and no son of his was going to go out and kill the bastards, if he had anything to say about it."

Ed grimaced and pushed his hands into his coat pockets. "But what could I do?" he asked. "The army told me to go."

"Did your dad stay mad at you?"

"He didn't speak to me any more. He still lives in the Bronx, and he still thinks the commies are the answer to all our prayers. And I went off to war. Fought at Inchon. Seventh Infantry Division."

"You did?" Pearse's admiration for Ed became, at that moment, instantaneously complete. He had a comic about the invasion of Inchon, and he realized he was in the company of a true hero. He imagined the pitched battles, hand to hand, with Ed and his buddies, their backs to the water, menaced by waves of Reds defending the beach. There was artillery and the "pop!" and "thwock!" of bayonet fights in the foxholes.

"Wow, that's great," Pearse said.

Ed looked down at him. The change in his expression, from a frown to a kindly smile, filled his face.

"Thanks, Pearse," he replied.

The trolley stopped to take on another passenger. The car itself was dark and shopworn.

"Do you enjoy the beach?" Ed asked.

"Sure," Pearse replied. He removed his beret, scratching his itchy head. "I go sometimes with my grandfather. It's just that it gets a little cold out here."

Ed looked out the window once more. The clouds were becoming very dark gray, settling over the verdant sprawl of Golden Gate Park. The trees appeared to have no vibrancy at all. If they moved back and forth in the wind from the ocean, it was with heavy, colorless grace.

"It does get cold," Ed said. "But the ocean, on a day like this . . . I mean, look out there."

He pointed through the front window of the trolley. Far ahead, at the end of Judah Street, the surface of the ocean was spattered with whitecaps. Large gray waves gathered up slowly in several lines that moved, breaking, toward the beach.

"Those waves, you have to sit and look at them to really get the idea of them. I mean, no two of them are alike, right?"

Pearse sat up straight and looked out the window. "I guess so."

"Believe me, Pearse, it's true. I'll show you when we get there."

The trolley arrived at the turnaround, across the Great Highway from the beach. Pearse and Ed descended from it, scurried across the highway and walked out onto the sand.

The ocean was gray and gray-black. The elegant collapse of the waves belied their initial appearance, that of ridges of dark iron. Those farthest out curled over in a somnolent way. Pearse could hear the deep roar of them over the more immediate sounds of the shorebreak, which was itself the color of mud. Pearse pulled his coat tightly about him. Ed walked ahead, gathering his own coat against the wind. When he turned to address Pearse, his face had changed color as well. His skin was pink with cold.

"See that out there, Pearse? Great things have been written about that."

Pearse looked out to sea. Gulls struggled through the wind like black flowers.

"And I'm going to write great things about that," Ed grumbled. "Turbulence. Seaweed."

"Seaweed?"

"You bet." Ed pulled a piece of paper from his coat pocket. "Like here's something I wrote." He handed it to the boy, who glanced at the typescript, which was blurred and covered over with pencilled corrections.

"What's it called?" Pearse asked, perusing the title. *"The Sword . . . The . . ."*

"The Sword Down the Throat of the Poet!"

"Yuck."

Ed's lips turned down. "Maybe the title's not so good. But the poetry's pretty nifty, I can tell you that."

"I don't think I'd like it."

"Do you read poetry in school?"

Pearse's long coat flapped about his legs. "Not so much. But there's a lot of it on my 45's. Like, 'Whoopin' cough'll foolya, chickenpox'll coolya, but poison ivy, Lord'll make you itch.' "

"Yeah, that's The Coasters," Ed muttered.

"And there's another one my brother Tim likes. It goes . . ." Pearse assumed the look of a disaffected teenager, like the one he had seen in *Rebel Without a Cause*. He pulled a tuft of hair down over his forehead. His eyes surveyed the ground, his shoulders at an angle. " 'Oops lollipop! Put my feet on the floor' " he began. His voice attempted the tune, but could not bring it off. He tapped the sand with his toe. " 'I wrapped a towel around me and I opened the door. But then, uh, splish splash! I jumped back in the bath.' "

"Hey, I know that," Ed grinned.

Pearse hunched over, and a smile came onto his face. " 'How was I to know there was a party goin' on?' "

"Sure. Bobby Darin!"

"Right!"

Ed tapped Pearse on the shoulder, and both broke into laughter.

"You ever swam in water like this, Pearse?" Ed asked.

Pearse shook his head. "No. It's too cold."

Ed looked out to sea. The wind rattled the hair that stuck out from beneath his beret. His scarf blew out behind him like a frayed flag.

"I come here to swim now and then," he said.

A gust staggered Pearse.

"In fact, I think I'll take a dip right now," Ed continued. He removed his hands from his pockets and quickly unbuttoned the coat.

Pearse noticed that the daylight had lessened. "Now?" he asked. He looked about. The beach was deserted.

Ed removed his shirt, took off his shoes, and tried to remove a sock. He jumped about on one foot, clumsy in the wind. Finally succeeding with both socks, he took off his pants and began walking toward the water.

"I'll just be a couple minutes, Pearse," he said.

He loped to the ocean's edge. His bulky waist lumbered against the elastic band of his boxer shorts. His legs were so pale that they shone like metallic straws.

He ran into the water and was knocked down by a wave.

Pearse stepped toward the waterline. Ed's body emerged, spray coming from his mouth and hair. He held his arms out and shook them.

"Cold! It's cold!" he shouted, before another wave washed

over him. It was a thick surge of water. The foam was the color of asphalt.

Pearse could not see him anywhere in the ruin of the shore-break. Helpless, he groaned as he imagined Ed rolling about beneath the surface, trying to save himself. Pearse had been tumbled by waves before, though smaller ones on much less stormy days. He knew how the sand was cluttering Ed's hair and how the rough force of the sea tumbled him about like a rag. Seaweed brushed your face, he remembered, like agonized hands. He envisioned Ed's white body washing up on the beach. More waves burst onto the sand. The water between them rocked and surged. Seized with fear, Pearse saw there was little he could do. He began screaming Ed's name.

He saw an arm reaching up between the waves. Then a dark head, bobbling like a errant buoy. Ed swam toward the shore, was overtaken by a wave, and continued swimming. He suddenly appeared in the shorebreak, thrown up on the sand. He rolled over twice, his arms flailing. Pearse moved to help him, and Ed got up to his hands and knees. He was knocked down by the remnants of a final wave. Rolling about, he stood and staggered to the shore.

Ed shivered as water ran down his body in dark rivulets. One leg of his boxer shorts was tucked up below the waistband. The other adhered to his leg, and his hair lay pasted to his head. He took his coat and began drying himself. His lips were blue.

"Help me, Pearse," he said, holding out a hand and pointing to his shirt. Pearse got it for him, then waited with Ed's pants. After a moment, Ed had dressed almost completely, and he shoved his feet into his shoes. He pulled the beret down over his hair and put on his coat. His hands were to cold to button it, and Pearse did it for him.

They walked from the beach. The daylight was almost gone.

"Why did you do that?" Pearse asked. He was furious.

Ed hunched his shoulders. "Fun," he said.

Pearse closed his eyes.

"I just wanted to do it!" Ed continued. He seemed to sense Pearse's disgruntlement. He started to run as a trolley entered the turnaround across the highway. Pearse caught up with him.

"Sometimes you throw yourself away," Ed said, his voice wavering as they ran. "I guess just to see what'll happen."

They reached the curb across from the turnaround.

"Besides," Ed said, folding his quivering arms before him, "I love the ocean. I love what's in it."

There was a line of traffic, and as they waited for it to pass, Pearse and Ed turned to look once more at the beach. The white-caps were invisible in the darkness. All they could see were black waves falling to a black sea.

By the time the bus left Pearse off at the corner of Mason Street, the moon had come up. The street rattled with noise. There were platoons of children everywhere, goblins, clowns, and vampires up and down the steps of the houses on Mason Street. Large yellow smiles with broken teeth looked down from the windows. The pumpkin Pearse had helped carve was not out on the porch, as his father had told him it would be, and he worried that it had been forgotten.

Pearse put his beret back on. He took the broken sunglasses from his pocket, balanced them on his nose and one ear, and approached the stairway. Unlocking the front door to the apartment, he ascended the stairs.

"Trick or treat!" he shouted.

There was a hurried gathering about the top of the stairs. Joe, Mimi, MJ, Tim, and Sergeant Rye, in uniform, appeared, looking over the railing. Joe descended two steps and stopped. His eyes were narrow. Mimi's face was blotched. Tim had been crying as well, but Pearse immediately sensed that Tim's unhappiness was due to his being in trouble.

"Pearse! Where have you been?" his father demanded. Pearse paused on the stairs. Although there were no clouds painted on the ceiling behind his family, and no broad shadows of early morning gloom, they all looked down at Pearse as the saints did from the cupola at church. His heart thumped against the front of his chest.

"I went to the beach," Pearse responded.

"The beach!" Joe replied. "What the hell were you doing at the beach?"

Profanity was normal to Joe, and it was usually one of the things Pearse enjoyed in his father. When Joe swore, it made his family laugh.

This time, though, Joe's profanity intimidated the boy.

"I . . . I was just there," Pearse said. "I wasn't doing anything."

"Pearse! Don't you know we didn't know where you were?" Mimi shouted. Her handkerchief hung before the railing. "We thought you'd been kidnapped!" she said.

"Kidnapped!"

"Yes!" Joe replied. He walked down the stairs and took

Pearse by the shoulder. "Who was that guy dragging you up the street?"

Pearse glanced at Tim, who was dressed in a pair of Levi's and a T-shirt, his feet bare. He stood with his hands in his pockets. Swollen as they were, his cheeks tightened as he ground his teeth. He did not look at Pearse.

"What guy?" Pearse asked.

"The beatnik!" Joe shouted. "Tim told us . . ." He looked back up the stairs at Pearse's brother. "Tim, tell Pearse what you told us!"

Tim allowed his breath to fill his cheeks. He remained silent. Joe pulled Pearse up the stairway and pushed him toward his brother.

"Go on, tell him," Joe said.

Tim stared at the floor. "I don't know," he said miserably.

"Tell him!" Joe insisted.

Tim flinched with the anger of Joe's order.

"Debbie and I were walking around Columbus, Pearse," he sputtered, "and we saw you and that other guy, running across the street. It scared me. I thought he was some kind of . . . I don't know, some kind of creep or something."

"Who was he, Pearse?" Joe interjected.

"His name's Ed," Pearse said.

"Ed. Ed who?"

Wincing, Pearse stripped the moustache from his upper lip. "Ed something, I don't know," he muttered.

"Who is he, Pearse?"

"He's a guy I met."

"That's what we figured. But who is he?"

"We met him at the Caffè Trieste," Pearse replied. Tim looked away, groaning.

"What's that?" Joe asked.

"A coffee house. Up on Grant Avenue."

"You took Pearse to a beatnik coffee house?" Mimi asked. Her voice took on a tone of teary disappointment. "Tim, you didn't tell us that." Her eyes were dark and greatly saddened.

Pearse noticed MJ, standing back and waiting, almost hidden behind Sergeant Rye. He had said nothing, but he appeared to want to interrupt. His dark brown suit and holly-green vest, lively by comparison to his hand-tied, royal blue bow tie, were wrinkled. His eyes were watery. He appeared so opaque and gray as to be almost faded.

"Yes," Pearse replied to his mother, scraping the floor with his toe. He knew, now, that he had caused her pain, and he cursed himself. "It *was* one of those coffee houses."

The phone rang, and Joe went into the living room to answer it. Mimi knelt down before Pearse and embraced him. He was still surprised by the wild indirection of her crying. Her cheek against his forehead was gummy with tears.

Joe returned after a moment. "That was Debbie Mariano's mother, Tim."

Tim removed his hands from his pockets.

"She's been grounded for two weeks."

"She has!"

"Her parents had told her never to talk to any of those bums."

"Beatniks!" Pearse interrupted.

"Call them what you will, Pearse." Joe pointed at the boy, his finger like a blade. "They're bums."

For Pearse, the most complicated kind of guilt came from being caught, absolutely, in the act, like the day he stole a roll of caps from the shelf of the National Dollar store on Stockton Street. The manager of the store apprehended Pearse as he popped the caps on the sidewalk out front, one by one, with the butt of his cap pistol. Pearse had been sent to bed without his dinner. Hungry, disappointed in himself, he had been somehow triumphant just the same. For the moment, Pearse was not just "that *nice* boy." He did not automatically get a smile when someone entered the room and noticed him. In short, he was notorious. After a while, though, in the darkness of his room, his guilt returned, so that his festivity had a dulled edge. He had not been able to celebrate freely.

This time, there was no celebration at all.

"And when your mother told you not to speak with those people, what was it she said exactly, Pearse?" Joe asked.

"She said she never wanted me to go farther up the hill than Washington Square."

"That's right. And you did, didn't you?"

Pearse's shoulders sagged. His father's breathing shivered with anger.

"That's right," Joe said, noting Pearse's silence. "So I think the two of you will be grounded, also. You get to spend the next two weeks here at home. You can go to school. You can help out a little more around here. You know, actually volunteer to help. You can go to Mass."

Joe looked down at Pearse, who removed his beret and let it hang from his hand, like a rag.

"You can *serve* Mass, if you like, Pearse."

Pearse remained impassive. He thought of the dark, embracing waves, and of himself running into them, laughing.

"But that's all," Joe concluded.

≪ 3 ≫

THE BLANKET, PATRIOTISM, AND MURDER

"There. How's that?" Tim asked.

Pearse looked into the mirror. He and Tim both wore sports coats and slacks, ready for the big evening ahead. Joe had loaned Pearse a tie, a green one with diagonal orange stripes, that Tim had just tied for Pearse, once, with no mistakes.

"I like it," Pearse replied. "Do you think Mom will?"

"Sure she will. And Mr. Day'll like it too, I bet."

Tim's tie was gray wool, and the collar of his new shirt was too large for him, so that there was space between the collar and his neck all the way around. He looked in the mirror and tightened the tie, but that caused the collar to crumple. He loosened it once more, then stood before the mirror debating, it seemed, which alternative looked worse. Finally he chose the loose look, and let it remain.

"Shit," he whispered, despondently shaking his head.

"But Mr. Day'll like it," Pearse said.

"When's he getting here?"

"At seven, Dad says," Pearse replied. "And a lot of other people are coming, too. Dad told me Mr. Day is real important."

Tim sat down at Pearse's desk, carefully pushing aside the homework papers that Pearse had scattered across the desktop.

"I hope so," Tim said. "I was going to try to call Debbie tonight, you know, to ask her to go to the movie with me after we get ungrounded."

"You were?"

"Yeah. *Creature from the Black Lagoon.*"

"Cool."

"But Dad told me there'll be a lot of people here, so I won't be able to use the phone, you know, in private, so . . ."

Pearse sighed and fiddled for a moment with a button of his coat. He knew that Tim and Debbie had been trying to call each other. Indeed, that fact had quelled Pearse's hope of being her special friend. He had, in short, given up, though he had not known what it was he was abandoning. To Pearse, it had been the chance just to sit around and look at her.

"Are you and Debbie going to go steady?" he asked.

Tim returned his gaze, then looked away. "No," he said. He smiled to himself.

Pearse knew that Tim was lying. "She probably didn't mind you calling her, though," he replied. "Debbie's pretty nice."

"Yeah, she is," Tim said. There was a sort of longing in his voice, similar to the yearning that Pearse heard in his mother's Perry Como records.

"I guess we better go out to the kitchen," Tim said. "Mom'll want some help."

Both boys looked again into the mirror. Straightening his tie once more, Tim looked at the floor of Pearse's room, reflected in the glass.

"Don't you think you ought to clean up a little, though?" he asked.

Pearse turned and looked over the clothes that littered his floor liked labeled tatters.

"Nah," he said.

They went out.

There were already several men in the kitchen. One of them was ruddy faced, with round cheeks and an orange, bloodshot nose. When he spoke to Sergeant Rye, he sounded like he was swearing, though the words he used, like "bleedin' " and "shite," made no sense to Pearse at all. Joe took the boys by the shoulders and introduced them to the man.

"Tim and Patrick, this is a new member of the Republican chapter, Tom Markham."

Mr. Markham had long lips, and when he sipped from the glass of whisky in his hand they formed broad plates on either side of the rim. "Hello, boys," he said, shaking the hand of each.

"Mr. Markham works for a moving company out in the Mission, Pearse," Joe said. He too shook the man's hand. "Fresh off the boat, eh, Tom?"

"That's it, and glad of it," Mr. Markham said. "Bloody wonderful country, America."

"And you know Larry Goggins, don't you, Pearse?" Joe continued.

Mr. Goggins was dressed the same way he had been at Doll's funeral. His sagging bow tie looked comically formal. He shook Pearse's hand.

"Good to see you, fellows," he said.

Joe turned the boys toward the kitchen counter, where another man was mixing a drink.

"And this is Mr. Doherty, Pearse, who maybe you've met. He helps out with the Knights of Columbus at church."

"Hi," Pearse said. He had seen Mr. Doherty at Saints Peter and Paul. He was an usher for the twelve o'clock.

"How do you do?" Mr. Doherty asked. He removed the cigarette from his lips and toasted the boys. "First best drink of the day," he said, not awaiting their answers.

Mimi came in from the bedroom. There was a general surge of interest in her white silk dress. She had had her hair done, and the normal curl of it was emphasized by its new, darker tint. Pearse noticed how the men's eyes seemed to flicker about his mother when her back was turned. Her dress had a line of black buttons down the back, from top to bottom.

Mimi was pretty without having to do anything about it, and when she did do something about it, as on this evening, Pearse thought she looked like a movie star. She greeted everyone so gracefully that it seemed to Pearse she must never be nervous, as he always was when being introduced to a crowd. His mother's smile actually softened the language of the men in the room. There were few other women among the evening's guests. All of them were wives, and they began helping with the food and drink as soon as they arrived.

The conversation among the men was riddled with self-importance. Pearse had noted this before, when men got together. Their voices seemed to weigh a lot. But few of the men ever asked questions, and it was hard to interrupt them. There was none of the hilarity of conversations among women, which Pearse preferred.

Soon the apartment was filled with men, and Pearse stood at the top of the stairs, leaning against the railing listening to his father talk with Sergeant Rye.

"You know, Emmett Day is one of the important people in the movement now, a kind of *éminence grise*, I guess."

"An old man?" Rye asked.

"Eighty, at least. He makes a tour of the States every six months or so. He's a major influence, and controversial."

"Why?"

"He's never given up, for one. You know, he was with the Irish Volunteers before World War I. He did some time in jail, in 1914, on a murder charge. A policeman was killed. But the government couldn't make it stick, so they sent him to prison for a couple of months on a weapons offense. He was at the Post Office siege in 1916, and spent a few years in prison for that. Then he went underground again when the British were allowed to stay on in the north. There was no question about it, as far as he was concerned. He figured Arthur Griffith had sold everybody out, forcing the treaty on the new Republic, and he fought through the civil war against the Irish Free State. He was even imprisoned for a couple days when Michael Collins was killed."

Sergeant Rye's eyebrows rose and he shook his head.

"Who was that, Dad?" Pearse asked.

"Michael Collins was in charge of the Irish Free State Army, Pearse, after they got rid of the British. About thirty-five years ago. See, to get rid of the British, a man named Arthur Griffith and some others had agreed to let them stay in the north of Ireland, and a lot of the Irish thought they didn't have to do that. They thought they could have driven the British out entirely, without agreeing to anything. So there was another war, after the one against England."

"A civil war?"

Joe smiled, laying a hand on Pearse's arm. "You know what a civil war is?"

"Us against us!" Pearse replied.

The two men looked down at the boy a moment. "Smart kid, there," Sergeant Rye said.

"Like in Spain, right?" Pearse asked.

"Where'd you learn about that?" Joe asked.

Pearse retreated. "I don't know. Heard about it on TV or something. I don't know."

The bell rang, and Pearse hurried down the stairs to open the door. It was just seven o'clock. In the darkness outside a man stood, slightly hunched, on the porch. He was very old, and Pearse noticed right away that he shook with some kind of palsy. He frightened Pearse, looking down on the boy from beneath the brim of a large black hat. Pearse was especially unnerved by the old man's eyes, which, magnified by his thick eyeglasses, appeared large and starved.

"Is this the Pearse residence?" the man asked.

"Yes, sir," Pearse replied, his voice uncertain.

"And what is your name, boy?" This man spoke the same way as Mr. Markham. But there was a feverish, liquid waver in his voice. The breath making its way from his lungs sounded granular.

"Patrick Pearse."

"Patrick Pearse." The old man removed his hat. The few hairs on his head glimmered, like wisps of bone. "Jesus, Mary, and Joseph," he muttered, "Patrick Pearse is his name."

"Do you want to come in?"

"Is your father here?"

"Yes, I am," Joe said, suddenly appearing behind Pearse. "You're Mr. Day?"

"That's it."

"Please come in."

"I've been speaking with your son, here," Day said. His teeth were crooked and very yellow, covered with saliva. His unkempt eyebrows were iron-gray. "Polite lad. He's a poet, I hope."

"Pearse?"

Joe took Day's hand and ushered him into the house. Pearse smiled up at his father, proud to be acknowledged by a man as famous as Mr. Day.

"I believe Pearse is a kind of poet, yes," Joe replied. Together, Pearse and his father led the old man to the top of the stairs, where about fifty people awaited him.

There was a great deal of talk throughout the evening, buoyed up on the smell of whisky. Warmth surged through the cigar smoke and heavy frivolity, as though disagreement among the guests was simply out of the question. Everyone was prideful. Everyone was happy. And Pearse felt that he was the happiest of all.

He wanted to sit down next to Mr. Day on the chesterfield, but the press of the crowd around the old man prevented him from doing it. However, Joe had asked Pearse and Tim to help with the drinks, so the Irishman held a full glass of whisky in his hand the entire evening. He was surrounded by men asking him questions. Joe himself, with Larry Goggins, went about the room with an envelope, into which he put checks given to him by several of the guests.

After nine o'clock the guests began leaving, and Pearse was able to secure a spot on the couch next to Emmett Day. A few men remained, standing about the living room. Joe sat on the couch next to Pearse.

"Without you, you know, and the funds we get from America, the poor lads in Belfast wouldn't stand a chance," Day explained. "It's terrible up there. For the men on the blanket, it's as bad as it ever was."

"Do you know what that means, Pearse?" Joe asked. "Being on the blanket?"

"Yeah, that's . . ."

"Irishmen are still in prison in the north," Joe interrupted. "And they don't feel they should be, of course. The British have no right to put them there."

"The British have no right to be there," Day interjected, sampling his whisky.

"Of course," Joe replied. "And these men are being put in jail because they want to have their own Irish state, their own government. So they refuse to wear the prison's clothes, and they stay in their cells all day, wearing the blankets off their beds."

"And it gets cold there, you know," Day interjected. "Rain hurtling from the sky year 'round."

He held himself in a mock shiver, looking down at the boy at his side.

"Bloody awful place, northern Ireland," he continued. "Arctic wind. I hope you never have to suffer something like that."

"I'd have to be pretty bad, I guess."

Day shook his head. He let his hands drop to his knees and leaned close to Pearse.

"Just brave, son, that's all. Just brave."

He coughed once and took a handkerchief from his coat pocket. He brought the handkerchief to his mouth.

"Luckily," he continued, folding the handkerchief and replacing it in the pocket, "the blanket, as forbidding as it is, makes them free." Day looked around the room. "Doesn't it? Just a bloody piece of cloth. But there's a curious, redeeming grace about the thing, nonetheless. They shake with the cold, those men do. Sometimes they die. But at last, at last, they're free. You wouldn't think such a thing could have such power, would you, fellows?"

Pearse grew excited by the idea that he could be as brave as those guys on the blanket.

"Do you know who you're named after?" Day asked him.

"Somebody famous in Ireland," Pearse replied. "That's right, isn't it, Dad?"

"Padraic Pearse himself!" Day exclaimed. He touched Pearse's knee. "Sure, he was famous. And, I hope, for all the right reasons."

Pearse shook his head, awaiting an explanation.

"Oh, he was a fair poet," Day continued. "But Padraic was a better revolutionary."

"How so?" Joe asked.

"Because he made a mark for himself as such. He made a difference."

Day took up his whisky and sipped from it. Grimacing, he placed the glass on the table.

"It isn't easy, fighting a war. You may not know anyone who ever has."

Pearse sat up. He started to speak. Then, thinking better of it, he let the moment pass. He had thought of Ed and the invasion of Inchon.

"My father knew some of the people involved," Joe interjected.

"From Ireland, is he?"

"Yes. He told me once he had met Padraic Pearse. But I don't think my father had much to do with the Rising. Nothing, actually. Because he came here before 1916."

"Like many another," Day said. "We could have used them."

"But there was every reason to abandon Ireland in those times, I think," Joe replied.

"Of course. I don't blame your father. His name was Pearse?"

"That's right."

Day pondered the name. "There were a lot of them. I don't suppose I knew him."

"He lived in Charleville."

"In County Cork?"

"Yes."

Again, Day considered the information, slowly shaking his head. "No. No. It's too long ago."

Pearse heard a phlegm-laden sigh, as though there were no muscles inside Day, just bones and soggy lungs.

"But what about Padraic Pearse, Mr. Day?" Pearse asked.

Day's eyebrows went up. "A schoolteacher, with a love of words, and didn't he write about what it meant to be an Irishman, poor fellow."

Sergeant Rye stood in the bay window, holding a glass of whisky, while Mr. Doherty, sitting on a chair at the far end of the chesterfield, seemed preoccupied by his shoe. The few other guests remaining in the living room listened attentively as Day sighed.

"He died wanting the best for us, you know. Sacrificed himself so that Ireland would be free. Shed his blood . . ." Day's evident sadness grew as he spoke. His fingers gripped each other like old twigs. "Defending the homeland," he continued.

He turned toward Pearse.

"And when you've done this as long as I have, Patrick, you wonder if you'll ever see the end of it."

A darkness seemed to take hold of the room. No one spoke as Day lifted his glass to his lips, and through the silence, Pearse wondered how he *could* help. He did not think that there would be much interest in the neighborhood in buying subscriptions to the *United Irishmen*. Pearse had trouble enough selling the archdiocesan newspaper.

"Did he win?" Pearse asked.

"Who, lad? Did who win?"

"Padraic Pearse."

"Did he win what?"

"The civil war!"

Day smiled and raised a hand to speak. "Oh, he died long before the civil war," he said. "Padraic was murdered, in cold blood, by the British. Heartless bastards, every one of them."

There was a rumble of agreement through the room. The darkened mood was interrupted by the sound of the doorbell.

"I'll get it," Pearse said, and he stood up from the chesterfield to walk to the top of the stairs. He descended the stairs two at a time, holding on to the railing. When he opened the door, he found MJ standing on the front steps, holding a large paper bag.

"Grandpa!"

MJ removed his hat. "Hello, Pearse. I was having dinner with Monsignor, and I thought . . ." He looked up at Pearse. "Are your parents home?"

"Sure. They're upstairs."

"Good. I brought something for you, something special." MJ entered the apartment and dropped the bag on the first step. "Since I was in the neighborhood, you know. It's this . . ."

He reached into the bag and began pulling at the contents.

The surprise of MJ's arrival was heightened by the mysterious gift. Pearse looked down at the bag, trying to get an idea of what was inside. MJ made a mock show of struggling with the bag, causing Pearse for the moment to forget about the party upstairs in the apartment. There was a sudden clamor in his heart.

"Dad!" Joe stood, with Tim, at the top of the stairs.

"Oh, hello, Joe."

"Come on up."

"No, my car's parked at the corner," MJ said. "Lights are on. I just wanted to give this to Pearse."

"But what is it?" Pearse asked.

Joe came down the stairs and stopped next to the boy. "Won't you come up, just for a few minutes?" he said. "There's someone here I'd like you to meet."

MJ glanced out the front door window. "Maybe just for a while."

Pearse waited impatiently as MJ continued hiding the contents of the bag from him.

"He's a countryman of yours," Joe said.

"What is it, Grandpa?" Pearse asked, as they started back up the stairs.

"Oh, it's just this," MJ replied. He reached into the bag and pulled out a corner of his Knights of Columbus blanket.

"You mean it's mine?"

"That's right," MJ said. "You can put it on your bed, just like we talked about. You know, other kids have got Notre Dame flags, or UCLA or something. Like, Tim's got your dad's, from USF. But you've got the K of C!" He slapped Pearse's back.

"Dad, look at this," Pearse said to Joe. He pulled the blanket from the bag.

They reached the top of the stairs.

"Hello, Timmy," MJ said.

"Hi, Grandpa."

Joe led the way into the living room. Sergeant Rye recognized MJ right away, and came across the room to greet him.

"Hello, Mr. Pearse. Good to see you."

"Marvin Rye," MJ said. A smile came onto his face, and he shook the policeman's hand. "How are you?"

"Just fine."

"Your parents?"

"The same, thanks."

Joe put an arm around MJ's shoulders. Emmett Day stood as the two men approached.

Pearse, taking the blanket out from beneath his arm, held it up for Tim. "See what I got here?" he asked.

"Dad, I'd like you to meet this man," Joe said.

MJ extended his hand, and Day took it in his.

"This is my father, MJ Pearse," Joe said. "Dad, I'd like you to meet Emmett Day, from Dublin, Ireland."

MJ's eyes flickered, and he looked down at Day's chest.

"Pleasure to meet you, Mr. Pearse," Day said.

MJ pulled his hand away.

"I understand you're from Ireland also," Day continued. "But I don't remember any Pearses myself, in Charleville. Were your people from Dublin originally, or somewhere else?"

There was such a long pause that Pearse looked up from the blanket MJ had given him. He was struck by the look of hatred that had come into his grandfather's face. MJ's eyes were fixed on Day's.

"Emmett Day," MJ said.

"That's right, yes."

"And you were with the Irish Republican Brotherhood, the Volunteers, before 1916."

Again, there was silence. Day dropped his hand to his side and sat down.

"I was," he said.

MJ remained standing. The continued silence seemed to discomfort the other men in the room.

"Would you care for a soda, Dad?" Joe interjected. "Cup of Lipton's?"

Slowly, as though he and Day were alone in the room, MJ lifted his hand and pointed at the Irishman.

"Did you know . . ." he said. He turned toward Joe. His hand remained suspended before Day. "Did you know that this man is a murderer?"

Pearse's heart banged against the front of his chest. The blanket remained in his hands.

"I beg your pardon?" Day rasped.

"You murdered a man, in Charleville, in May, 1914. Monohan was his name."

"I did no such thing."

"Dad, what are you trying to do?" Joe interjected once again. "This man is my guest."

"It is the truth, Joe," MJ muttered. His voice broke, and for a moment he could not speak.

"I murdered no one," Day whispered.

"You did it, and I know because I saw it."

Day remained sitting, seeming to lack the strength to defend himself.

"Dad, you can't stay here if you keep on with this," Joe said. His voice frightened Pearse.

"You don't want the truth, Joe?"

"Emmett Day is a fine man. He's fought all his life for the Irish people."

"Sure, he murdered a defenseless man one day in the road." Pearse was struck by the odd accent with which his grandfather uttered this sentence. It was a rolling, lilting sound, with rough-sounding *R*'s.

"What are you talking about?" Joe asked, taking MJ's arm.

"I'm not staying here while Emmett Day is in your house, Joe. This man is a killer."

"I haven't any idea . . ." Day said. "I did no such thing."

"You left him to die," MJ continued.

"I did not, Mr. . . . Mr. . . ."

"Michael Pearse!" MJ shouted. "Pearse is my name. Michael Pearse!" He turned away and headed for the door.

"Dad!" Joe said.

Pearse jumped up from the couch to follow him. The two men walked down the stairs, and MJ pulled the door open with a lurch.

"You give him your whisky as though he's the mayor or something," MJ said.

"He's a patriot, Dad," Joe replied. "He's been in prison for what he's done."

"And he should be there now," MJ replied. He hurried down the front steps toward his car.

"Don't say that, Dad," Joe replied. His voice deepened and grew more angry.

MJ turned on the sidewalk. In the darkness his face was itself dark, like a blank shadow.

"You're a fool, Joe." Each syllable carried equal weight. The sentence came out like a pronouncement.

"About what? Tell me what this is all about."

"You're a fool about the Irish, and about that man up there." MJ pointed at Joe's apartment. "You're sending them money so they can murder people."

"But what about the British?" Joe shouted.

Pearse stood on the top step. His heart throbbed, and he felt tears coming to his eyes. He feared the two men were going to fight, and he did not know what to do.

"The British! It's clear as day, Joe. The British are criminals too!" MJ pointed again at the window that looked out from the living room of the apartment. "But there you have an honest-to-God killer, right there, drinking your whisky. You can read about the British, Joe, in the papers. But there . . . there is an Irishman, sitting on your damned couch. He's like that fool you were defending at the City Hall. Both of them Irishmen, and they'll both murder you just as dead as any Englishman will. When are you going to learn that?"

MJ descended the hill to his car, leaving Joe standing on the sidewalk. As MJ drove away, Joe turned back toward the front steps of the apartment. He touched Pearse's shoulder as they went through the doorway.

"Don't worry, Pearse," he said. "We'll talk to him tomorrow." His voice was clipped with anger.

Pearse ascended the stairs and reentered the living room. He stood before a floor lamp at one end of the chesterfield. The K of C blanket lay, still folded, on the cushion next to Mr. Day. The other men in the room could say little to Day, and they talked quietly with each other, embarrassed.

"I'm sorry," Joe said to the Irishman. "I didn't expect that response from my father."

Day huffed and crossed his legs. "I don't know where he got that guff about my being some sort of criminal."

"I don't either," Joe replied. "I apologize." He gestured around the room. "We all apologize."

"Michael Pearse is his name?" Day asked.

"That's right."

Day considered the name for a moment. Finally he shook his head.

"I never met him." Day lifted the glass of whisky toward Joe. "I never met your father before this evening, Joe. He's got the wrong man."

A weak conviviality appeared on his face as he turned toward Pearse. His glasses reflected light from the lamp above the boy's head.

"That's all there is to it, isn't it?" Day asked. "The wrong man."

When he arrived home, MJ removed his jacket and tossed it over the stair railing in the entry hall. How could it be, he thought, Emmett Day in my own son's house, regaled and adored? And Pearse, did you see Pearse so stricken on the front steps like that, with no idea what had happened? No idea what foolishness his father had brought into the place?

The entry parlor was hung with pictures Doll had collected, and he looked them over, trying to calm himself. Most were photographs of the family, and there was a religious picture as well, of Doll's favorite saint. Teresa of Avila had founded the Carmelite Order, to which Doll's Aunt Mary had belonged. In the reproduction of the painting on the wall, Teresa swooned toward the figure of the Sacred Heart, which hung from heaven like a bleeding moon. MJ put a pot of water on the stove. He thumbed through a magazine for a moment, then put it aside as he waited for the water to boil.

Not every memory was a menace for MJ, and he savored his recollections of his grandchildren. The day Pearse was born, for example, when Doll had cried simply because the baby had such beautiful red hair. What mattered the most to Doll was her family, and she provided for them all the time, especially her grandchildren. On Holy Days of Obligation she sent cards to Tim and Pearse, with portraits of individual saints printed on them. Pearse collected them as he did bubble gum baseball cards. In fact, he kept them in the same card file, so that a Maria Goretti was followed by a Mickey Mantle, a Don Bosco by a Don Drysdale.

The difficulty had come with Doll's insistence, toward the end, that MJ look at his memories with more precision, and that he include her in the process.

For years, Doll had acquiesced to MJ's explanation that he had come to the United States just as her own parents had, to escape the Irish drudgery and cold in order to find some way to live better. "It was economics," he would say. "My brother Jack was here, see, and he had an opportunity. He arranged it for me." He took care making such an explanation, because an effective lie required poise. Doll knew that MJ had been involved with the IRB, but the IRB had sounded to her the same as the Gaelic Athletic Association, an organization to which her father had belonged for a few years before *he* had left Ireland. Early in their courtship, MJ discovered that Doll knew very little about the IRB's politics. As far as she was concerned, the organization was like many another, made up of football and Guinness, harmless gatherings of Catholic men. The meaning of MJ's involvement in the IRB was submerged in his evasive documentary.

Until Doll began to die.

Every Sunday evening they watched "What's My Line?" Doll always enjoyed the show, with the screwy professions and incomplete answers. They continued watching the show during Doll's illness, MJ sitting next to her bed in his rocking chair. One evening she had combed her hair after a tiny meal MJ had prepared of toast and Campbell's chicken alphabet soup. She still worried over her appearance, and indeed MJ had been helping her apply her makeup when visitors were to come over. He had gotten quite adept at the lipstick, the application of which was too fine a task for Doll's weakened hands. He had found it humorous, an elderly man like him so delicately touching his wife's lips, like an ardent boy at the front yard gate.

The panelists on "What's My Line?" interviewed a man who was a matchmaker, who arranged marriages between American men and Irish women. His name was Fogarty. It took the panelists only a few minutes to find out Fogarty's profession. Everyone was charmed by his humorous accent, but he was nervous on camera, and he told more than he had to. He was bald, and his head shone in the reflected light like a silver puddle.

"A nincompoop, isn't he?" Doll said, as the show came to an end. "You'd think he'd be able to give better answers than those."

MJ, removing the tray from her lap, agreed. He turned off the television. Doll rested her head on her pillow. She had a handkerchief in her hand, and she dabbed her forehead with it, trying to relieve the clammy moisture that seemed always to cover her body now.

"How do you feel?" MJ asked.

"Not very well. It hurts."

"I know. I'm sorry."

Doll intertwined her fingers with MJ's in a small gesture they had exchanged for years, a sensual reminder.

"I'm sorry we never went to Ireland, Michael," she said. She rested her hand on the embroidery of the sheet turned back over her blanket. "Would you have taken me to Charleville?"

"Of course."

"Shown me where you lived?"

"Yes, certainly."

MJ's mother had cared for his room in Charleville until the day he left and, he understood from her letters, for years afterward. The iron bedstead in one corner left enough room for a single oak chair and a tall armoire, also of oak. MJ had always made sure that his clothing was neatly organized. Arthur Holmes, his employer, insisted that those who worked for him dress properly. "Our patrons expect it, don't they? We give them no less than what we would expect ourselves." Holmes had been a fine-looking man. Even the lines in his face were elegant, and everyone who worked for him liked him. Had he not been a Protestant, they said, he would have made a very fine pope. As he inspected the shelves of his shop every morning, his face was so prissy that the clerks joked about how he resembled the apostle Thomas, turning his nose up at the wound in Christ's side.

"Why didn't you ever want to go back?" Doll asked.

MJ gestured with one hand. "My life was here," he said.

"But you cut Ireland off so."

"Yes. Yes, I did."

"Why?"

MJ shook his head.

"Please, Michael, tell me."

MJ knew that the version he had presented of his past had never satisfied Doll, really. He had become an American so quickly, even in his speech, that Doll had worried he had abandoned everything. He had passed it off, all of it, making compliments that he hoped would divert her questions. He had her, he said, which mattered more than anything he had ever had in Ireland. And then they had had their family—the baptisms, Communions, and weddings, all of them as lovely as could be. The lie in such bland assurances went unrevealed.

"Michael," Doll said. She sighed, a suggestion of disappointment. "I'm sorry to leave you."

"No, Doll." MJ leaned forward and took her hand. "Don't say that."

"Michael, I've wanted to know, so badly . . ." She paused and extended her hand across the blanket toward MJ. "I love you, Michael. We've given so much to each other . . . to Joe and the grandchildren."

Avoiding her eyes, MJ leaned forward to kiss her hand.

"Tell me more about Charleville, Michael. Please."

MJ sat back. "Oh, there was the rain," he said. His voice was almost silent itself. "Lovely green, all year . . ."

"But tell me why you left."

MJ touched his fingers together, to keep them steady.

"Tell me."

One afternoon, very early in Monohan's incarceration, MJ had been looking about the cellar, which was lit during the day from two paned windows at either end. He had brought Monohan his supper of two eggs, potatoes, toast, and tea. The windows were at ground level, and MJ could see little through them, other than the scraggly ends of weed-grass that shivered in the gray wind.

Monohan's captors had set up a small bed for him in a corner of the room. There was a soiled rug. Jailed as he was, Monohan read a great deal, and his light came from the wax candles with which he was supplied by John Creeley. "I won't stand for my bloody eyesight being taken from me," Monohan had said, "as my bloody freedom has been." MJ sympathized with him, for the most part because Monohan was so humorous in his complaint.

"I'm sure they'll be looking for me," Monohan said, as he approached the table to have his supper. "You can't keep a man hidden forever in a place like this. And your lot aren't worth much, anyway, are they?" he continued.

The blanket hung from his shoulders like a cape. He seemed to have grown weaker just in the few days he had been here, so that he was becoming gray-white, entirely. He wheezed and expectorated, and punctuated his speech with unhappy, phlegm-ridden sighs.

"They don't even have the confidence to let me have proper heat."

He took the edge of the blanket between the fingers of both hands. Looking up at MJ, Monohan shook his head with chagrin.

"Do they think that keeping me frozen will make me even less able to escape?"

Monohan turned back toward the table, sat down, and took up the fork and knife. He cut into an egg and hurried a piece of it to his mouth, then pointed with the knife at his bed.

"Sit down, lad."

MJ had brought Monohan a fresh supply of candles and a book of stories by Thomas Hardy. The book lay unopened on the table.

"They'll have to let me go," Monohan said. "It's a hanging matter to harm a policeman, you know."

"You're with the police?" MJ asked.

"I was, at one time." He looked up from the plate. "They didn't tell you?"

MJ shook his head.

"They don't tell you much, then, do they?"

It was true, MJ knew nothing about Monohan. The others had told him to bring the food and to keep quiet.

"Don't speak to him about politics, Michael," Creeley had said. He was about fifty, a prosperous farmer. "Don't tell him your name, because he'll run circles around you with all his kindness and good humor. You can't trust him."

Pointing a finger at MJ's chest, Creeley gave him another, very specific order.

"And for the love of Mike, don't tell him where he is. If he were to escape, he could bring the entire constabulary up here on us—and on you, of course—and we'd have a hell of a time of it."

"It's a shame, that," Monohan continued. "It's the most interesting thing about me, the fact that I was with the constabulary. For thirty-five years. And my son is with them now."

MJ pursed his lips. So, he thought, this man is the enemy.

"But that's why I'm here, you see!" Monohan said, his hand held out before him, as though in explanation. "Does the news disappoint you?"

He pushed the plate across the table toward MJ.

"Do you want this back?"

"No. Sorry." MJ waved his hand.

"Shall I starve myself, too?" Monohan retrieved the plate. "You know, it's possible to be with the police and be a human being," he said.

MJ shook his head, and Monohan laughed.

"I'm glad you agree," he said. He wiped the plate with a piece of toast and shoved the last bit of food into his mouth.

"I grew up like you did," MJ had replied to Doll. He worried for a moment that the conversation and the wave of memory it engendered would drive him mad. A private, solitary loss of reason. "I've told you about my parents. You read Mother's letters."

"She longed for you to come back, Michael." Doll exhaled and coughed. Her face, which had become gray and less distinct as she had grown ill, tightened with each paroxysm. After a moment's rest, she spoke once more. Her voice cracked as she talked. "It's just that I could see how little she understood you, and why you left. You weren't like your brother Jack. Why would anyone leave a place he loved so much?"

MJ did not reply. But in the silence, he sensed from Doll that there would be little talk after this. She continued coughing. Death swirled into the room.

"It's just that I . . . I became involved, once, with a group. A group of lads," he muttered. He stopped speaking. He had not used the word "lads" for decades.

"What does that mean?"

"They were . . . we fought against the English."

"The IRA, you mean," Doll said.

MJ grew rigid with embarrassment. "It was like the IRA, yes. In a way."

"What happened?"

MJ crossed his legs and rocked back and forth in his chair a moment.

"I was very young."

"I know, Michael."

"In my twenties. I was a kind of courier."

"But what did you do?"

"Delivered bicycles in the middle of the night, for God's sake. Messages here and there."

Doll coughed a moment. "If that's all there was to it . . ." she sighed.

MJ hoped, through his silence, to evade an answer once again. But, to his surprise, he found himself wishing to tell Doll about old Monohan.

"But that isn't all there was," he said. He took up his cup of tea from the tray. "I met a fellow once, in that time. An elderly man, like me now."

"Was he on your side?"

"Jim Monohan? No. He was the enemy."

Doll continued watching MJ, awaiting an explanation.

"I was given the job of guarding him and bringing him his supper," he said. "He'd been captured by the IRB because he'd been with the constabulary, and they thought that by kidnapping him they could influence the police to stop pursuing them. It was his son they wanted to . . . 'convince,' I guess, is the proper word."

"Who was his son?" she asked.

"A policeman as well. And a Catholic. He was helping the British against the Rising. And he relished sending our men to jail. I think he hated the Irish."

"And so, your group . . . what were they called?"

"The Irish Republican Brotherhood."

"They were holding his father?"

"That's right."

"Michael, you took part in that?"

"Yes," MJ muttered, "I'm sorry to say that I did. And the interesting thing was, his son did nothing about it. We sent him ultimatums, for weeks, apparently, telling him that his father's life was in danger, that he'd be killed . . ."

"You did this?"

"The Dublin people did it, yes. The fellows in charge."

"What happened?"

"Nothing. Monohan's son did nothing. He refused to answer us." As he spoke, the nervousness left MJ's hands. "A lot of us liked the old man. I did, especially. I brought him books from time to time. I sat and talked with him."

"They didn't harm him, though."

MJ sat sipping his tea, trying to bring back exactly what had happened. The truth stood, like a broken image, before him . . . the palpable odor of blood, the slow turn of a bicycle wheel in the rain, the gray sky.

"No, they didn't," MJ said finally. His heart tumbled. He leaned his head against the fingers of one hand, trying to avoid Doll's eyes. He was afraid of the disappointment she must feel in him. In those moments, through the years, when the memory of old Monohan had come back to him, MJ's gullet had closed, and he had not been able to swallow. It was the same now. He glanced at Doll, ashamed.

"The Irish Volunteers had brought old Monohan to a house outside Charleville, on the River Blackwater. To keep him there."

"And that's when you left, isn't it?" Doll asked. "You thought it was wrong, what they were doing." Doll's eyes were extraordinarily clear and directed. MJ realized, with surprise, that she was not angry with him. But he could not allay the anger he felt for himself, while Doll appeared almost pleased with the revelation of her husband's past. She held his hand in both of hers. Her fingers seemed barely capable of grasping anything.

MJ's heart beat more slowly.

"Yes," he replied. "Soon after that."

"Oh, I don't blame you, Michael," Doll said, taking him into her arms. "You felt so guilty. And so saddened for the poor man. Was he a bad man?"

"No, Monohan was quite a good man. For one thing, he was a family man. He loved his son."

The ring of the phone in the entry hall brought MJ from the memory of this conversation. He did not want to answer the phone, suspecting it was Joe calling to ask if he was all right.

The bright trill served to illuminate the shameful lie he had told Doll that night. Just a lie of omission, of silence, enabled by her quick assumption that MJ's only crime was that he had brought an incarcerated man his food. There was nothing to that, she seemed to have said. A youthful mistake, and understandable. But the phone reminded MJ also of how angered he was by what had happened at Joe's earlier in the evening. He had guarded himself so well for so many years that the confrontation with Day had taken him completely by surprise. MJ had often wondered what such a meeting with Day would be like, but none of the possibilities had included such a volcanic betrayal of himself. When the phone stopped ringing, MJ's eyes remained on it, as if he were waiting for it to start up once more.

MJ slept that night, but so badly that true sleep eluded him altogether. Whenever he turned over, he felt new discomfort. His chest ached.

He lay on his back in the morning. The fresh sunlight coming in through the window dazzled him, and he placed his forearm over his eyes. Emmett Day had been so reserved a man when he was young, MJ recalled. And now, if you saw him in the street, you'd think he was just another grandfatherly fool, like myself. And he still doesn't have an ounce of meat on him, does he?

The memory of shouting at Joe on the sidewalk brought a pained groan from MJ. Joe was so surprised, MJ thought. He looked like I'd just disowned him or something, and he still doesn't have an explanation.

Unless Day did recognize me, and told him . . . told my own son . . .

MJ sat up in bed and pushed aside the window curtain. Outside, the blue morning light seemed to detach the Mountain Lake pond from the shore around it. The water appeared quite cold. Patches of wind traced the surface, scouring it delicately.

MJ turned to the phone.

Joe and Mimi's line was busy, and MJ stood looking out the window for a few minutes. He had met Emmett Day in 1914, at the Wolfe Tone, a pub in Charleville. There had been only a few men there that night, farmers who had come into town for the day. They sat at a table discussing a horse one of them had sold that afternoon. Their reddened cheeks appeared swollen, and a kind of bored slovenliness filled their laughter. They were chunky men with rough hands. Their pint glasses of porter were tinged inside with wrinkles of drying foam.

MJ had received a note at Holmes's Arcade, handwritten from the IRB, telling him to come to the pub at six. Emmett Day, of the Irish Volunteers, wanted to meet him, it said. MJ had no idea who Day was, but the Volunteers were brave men. They were the military wing of the IRB, and MJ had heard all about them and the extraordinary things they were doing to bring arms into Ireland. Sitting alone over a cup of tea, he waited, excited. A tall man entered the pub and spotted MJ right away.

"Is your name Michael?" he asked. He removed his bowler and laid it on the table. MJ was surprised to see so formal a hat in Charleville, where the usual headgear was that worn by the farmers at the other end of the pub, wool caps notable for their finger-worn, dirty brims.

"Yes." MJ stood up.

"Emmett Day." Day offered his hand. His face was angular, and he wore a pair of rimless spectacles. He was about thirty-five. His oiled black hair was parted in the middle, and he wore an English cravat and a heavy wool suit. "The men in Cork told me you were here, and that you were helping John Creeley with the prisoner."

"Yes."

"How has it been, then?" Day asked as he sat down at the table. "What sort of man is this Monohan?"

MJ turned his teacup about on the saucer. "He's unhappy. He doesn't like being imprisoned."

"Do you know why we took him?"

"No. I asked John Creeley, and . . ." MJ laughed. "He told me it was none of my business. He said it with a good deal of authority."

"John's being careful, as he's supposed to be. We can't be too free with our information, you know."

"But I'm with the IRB."

"Yes, but if the constabulary were to question you . . . There's much that *I* don't know, as well, you see. It's a precaution."

"May I ask, though, who you are?" MJ sat back in his chair.

"Yes. I have an interest in Monohan, too. He's a man we needed to have, to provide a kind of military diversion, I suppose."

The answer contained so little information about Day that MJ thought to ask him again.

Day leaned over the table, suddenly businesslike. "It's important that what we talk about remain private, Michael. Can I have your word on that?"

"Certainly."

"Good, because, you see, there's going to be a shipment of arms . . ." Day looked down at his hands. "I'm telling you this because I've been told you're a good man."

MJ grinned at the flattery.

"There'll be a shipment of arms coming to Ireland in a few months, and it'll come in at Howth."

"Near Dublin."

"That's right. But there's someone working with the English there—an Irishman, God save us, a captain with the police, whose name is Monohan, as well—who we suspect knows something about the plan."

"Why do you think so?" MJ asked.

"A lot of our men have been taken recently. They put them in jail in Dublin, you know." Day shook his head. "There's nothing new there. But they're men who've been involved in this plan, and the constabulary has gotten information, somehow, about who they are. We think this man Monohan is the source of it. So . . ." Day removed his glasses and took a handkerchief from his coat pocket. He cleaned the glasses and put them back on, adjusting the stems about the backs of his ears. "So, we've taken his father."

"Mr. Monohan."

"As a means to an end, you see."

"But what's the end?"

"To supply the diversion," Day grinned. "If this chap is worried about his father, maybe he'll leave our lads alone."

MJ recalled how excited he had become at that moment, to be involved in such a plan. His hands grasping the teacup had begun to tingle, the palms suddenly wet with nervous sweat. Turning from the window, he picked up the phone once more and dialed Joe's number.

"Hello, Pearse," he said, when the boy picked up the phone. "Is your father there?"

"No, Grandpa. He's taking Mr. Day to the train station in Oakland."

"I see. Listen, Pearse, I'm sorry about last night."

"It's OK," Pearse replied. "I slept under your blanket."

"You did! Did you like it?"

"Yeah. It just fits my bed."

MJ smiled. "Would you care to go on The Tour today?" he asked. "A special issue, just for fun?"

"Sure!" Pearse said, his voice rising with expectation.

"Ask your mother, will you, if that'll be all right?"

Pearse laid the phone down, and there was a moment's silence.

"Have you told Monohan anything about yourself?" Day had asked.

MJ sipped his tea. "No. I was told just to watch him, and to button my lip."

"But I hear you've gotten friendly with him."

"That's true. Mr. Monohan seems a kind man, that's all. Lonely, of course."

"Careful, Michael. He'll take any opportunity . . ."

MJ grew irritated and allowed the teacup to clatter in the saucer.

"I don't suppose I have to tell you that," Day said. "Sorry. Forgive me."

"Of course."

"The IRB needs men like you, Michael. That's really the only reason I'm here. When we find someone who we feel has the right sentiments in his heart, as you have . . ."

MJ held up a hand, embarrassed by Day's compliments.

Pearse took up the phone once more. "Mom says OK," he said. "Where can we go?"

"I'll tell you when I get there."

MJ took the curtain between two fingers. The dyed cotton, threaded here and there with gold, was fading.

"I'll pick you up in an hour," he said.

"Today we'll go out to Polk Street," MJ said as Pearse looked around his room for his jacket. "We'll get a piece of lemon crunch."

"Oh," Pearse replied. He found the jacket next to his desk, under a pile of comic books. Putting it on and zipping it up, he looked at MJ. "You do mean Blum's, don't you, Grandpa?"

"That's right."

"Oh boy!"

The Tour was a regular event, long established between Pearse and MJ. Sometimes it meant going to a football game at Kezar Stadium, the Forty-Niners versus the ever-triumphant Los Angeles Rams. More frequently, it was a bus ride to one of the San Francisco neighborhoods and a walk up and down its main business street. Pearse liked Clement Street, for one, because of Ivan the Terrible's, an old Russian bakery at Twenty-Second Avenue, with yellowed, dirty windows, where MJ bought him polmenyi for lunch. Tasha, the waitress, was about seventy and wore a white nurse's dress, a name tag, a black hairnet over a black wig, and quantities of gold-encrusted costume jewelry. Lipstick covered far more of her face than just her lips, and she actually skimmed the plates of polmenyi across the tabletop rather than laying them gently upon it. Pearse enjoyed the sour cream on the broth, the texture of which enriched the soup and made it sweeter.

Their favorite tour, though, was of North Beach. Pearse and his grandfather walked about the neighborhood so that MJ could stop and look into the shop windows, chat with shopkeepers as he wished, or have an ice cream on a bench in Washington Square. MJ joked a lot about how different the Italians were from the Irish . . . how they talked all the time in that sputtery language and waved their hands and seemed to have so much fun. But he had the same regard for large wheels of cheese and ornate olive oil tins as the Italians had. MJ's voice hurried itself with rattly humor as he talked with the men at Panelli's Delicatessen. At those times, he felt the kind of enjoyment that he expressed to Pearse when he talked of doing business himself as a younger man.

He pronounced the word "binness," an error Pearse copied. When you were on the road, MJ said, you missed your family, and you tired of the endless train trips up and down the coast. But "binness" was at least a humorous endeavor, "a long talk, that's all it is," from Fresno to Portland to Boise to Spokane. "That's why I like The Tour, Pearse," MJ had once told him, over a Coke at Mel's Diner on Geary Boulevard. "You go around and talk." MJ imagined being with his grandson on the train, the Cascade Mountains milky with snow. "You see how people live."

Pearse's enthusiastic response to the news that they were going to Blum's relieved MJ, because he had felt so distracted when he had first arrived. He had been enervated walking up the stairs, his feet padding against the runner. In the mirror on the landing, he had seen how the skin around his mouth was drawn down and mottled. His eyes were washed in liquid.

Descending the stairs, they stepped out onto the front porch, where a gust of cold wind stood them up against the door.

Huddled beneath the awning of the Gold Coin Grocery, MJ and Pearse awaited the cable car coming up from Fisherman's Wharf. The wind numbed their fingers, and both of them thrust their hands in their coat pockets. Riding the cable car, Pearse stood on the running board, in front, his teeth bared, confronting the buffeting wind. He savored his bravery. Now and then he waved importantly to his grandfather, who had elected to remain inside.

They transferred to the California Street car. Pearse took the running board again. At the corner of Polk and California streets, MJ and Pearse descended from the car and headed for Blum's. Pearse had never ordered anything in the coffeeshop but the lemon crunch cake and innumerable glasses of milk. His grandfather had introduced him to the lemon crunch when he was two, and they had made a regular pilgrimage every few months since then. The cake combined a sugary delicacy with a suggestion of tart lemon in the frosting. What made it Pearse's favorite were the crushed walnuts stuck to the frosting outside.

He and MJ ate their pieces quite differently. MJ integrated the frosting with the cake, so that each forkful contained some of each. Pearse opted to eat all of the cake first, leaving the frosting to stand on its own, like the walls of an ancient fortress. Then he sliced the frosting into small strips, which he ate one by one, slowly, allowing the frosting to dissolve in his mouth. The walnuts added a saline crunchiness which he loved above all.

MJ liked to watch him as he ate the frosting. MJ savored the lemon crunch cake as much as Pearse did, and he hoped Pearse knew that he was not being laughed at. Rather, MJ admired Pearse's thoroughgoing enjoyment of the experience, the sweet gush of the melting frosting, the grittiness of the nuts, the glorious mixture.

"Hello, Mr. Pearse." Betty was their waitress, an older woman whose hair was bright red-gray and curly. "Hi, Pearse. A piece of lemon crunch for each of you?"

"Thanks," MJ replied. He removed his hat and hung it from the attachment on the back of the pink counter seat. "A cup of coffee for me, and . . ."

"A glass of milk?" Betty asked, looking at Pearse.

"Yes, please."

As Pearse addressed his lemon crunch, MJ looked into the mirror behind the counter. The other patrons were old women, dressed in furs, with shopping bags. They sat at little round tables, conversing over tiny sandwiches and pink bowls filled with ice cream and syrups. MJ and Pearse were the only patrons sitting at the counter, and the blues and browns of the clothing they wore seemed dull to MJ, overwhelmed by the pink walls and sugary pillars of Blum's decor, the pink and white dresses worn by the waitresses, and the pink cellophane wrappings on the cakes and candies.

"Not bad, eh?" he said, carefully cutting a wedge of cake and letting it fall over onto his fork.

Pearse did not answer. His mouth was full.

"You know what would go good in here Grandpa?" he said after a moment. A piece of cake teetered on the end of his fork.

"What?"

"Your Knights of Columbus uniform."

"You think so?"

"Yeah. The sword and the hat, especially."

One of the photos on Doll's dresser showed MJ in his uniform, on Columbus Day, 1952. He was to march in the parade through North Beach, an annual event for the Knights of Columbus chapter from Saints Peter and Paul. The hat was fashioned after that of a naval officer of the eighteenth century. It was high and narrow, with a feathery white fringe coming out of the top. Each Knight also carried a long sword, hanging from a thick leather belt. MJ felt that he looked like a clown in the uniform. But he also thought there was a kind of antique panache in it that did not exist in anything else he owned. The humor of the hat's feathers intruded upon the K of C's view of itself, that it held the line against those who would bring down Mother Church. Like the commies, for example. The Knights of Columbus were, MJ thought, a comic defense of the faith.

"But why here? Why at Blum's?" MJ asked.

"Because you could be guards. You know, stand at the door and make sure nobody steals anything."

MJ glanced into the mirror. The women sitting at the tables were, for the most part, his contemporaries. Elegant shoppers, gray-haired and monied.

"I suppose you're right," he shrugged. He addressed his cake once more.

"What do the Knights of Columbus do?"

"They help out at church ceremonies . . . parades, that kind of thing. And they raise money to send to charities."

Pearse scraped some crumbs from an inside section of frosting, then continued chipping away at the cake itself.

"Are the Knights of Columbus soldiers?" he asked.

"No," MJ replied. "They just pretend to be. Though some of them actually were, in World War I and II."

"Against the Japs."

"Yes, and the Huns."

"Who was that?"

"The Germans."

"Huns?"

"That's right. That's what they were called in the First World War."

"The Knights of Columbus fought against the Huns?"

"No, Pearse," MJ sighed. "Some of the fellows who are in the K of C now fought against the Huns when they were young, a long time ago."

"When the Huns were young," Pearse said.

"Yes," MJ replied wearily. He turned to his cake. "That's right, yes."

"It'd be fun to be a soldier, though," Pearse said. "Wear your sword and march around."

MJ had heard this from Pearse before. The boy loved things that were done with brio, and that was why he so enjoyed the K of C hat. Artifice fascinated Pearse. He still talked, enthusiastically, about the night he went to see the old movie *King Kong* with his parents. The darkness and the jungle, he had said, had made him feel that he was in Borneo or somewhere, with wild men and fierce snakes. Also, Pearse listened to so much of that—"What is it?" MJ thought. "Rock 'n' rock? Rollin' rock?"—and knew so precisely so many of the lyrics, that MJ had concluded there must be something to it. When Pearse recited lyrics like "He walks in the classroom cool and slow," he imitated the slouched indifference of the juvenile delinquent. "Who calls the English teacher Daddy-O?" His version of the songs made MJ laugh, because the boy so expertly conveyed the snot-nosed arrogance the lyrics contained. The music reminded MJ of loud traffic clamoring up the street. But he saw, through Pearse, the possibility that it had value.

"Being a soldier isn't enjoyable, though, Pearse," MJ said. "You know, people die in a war."

"Were you ever a soldier, Grandpa?"

"Me? No." MJ lifted a piece of cake to his mouth.

"But did you ever see anybody die, like in a battle? I mean, did you ever see blood? Or somebody getting shot, like in John Wayne?"

MJ held the fork before his mouth. The brown walnuts adhering to the side of the frosting began to sicken him. He laid the fork down on his plate and reached for his cup of coffee.

Pearse, still talking, swirled his own fork about his plate. He pushed several pieces of walnut into a tiny pile.

"Guts and things," he said.

MJ sipped a bit of the coffee, and it caught in his throat. He coughed, and the coffee splattered out of his mouth onto his hand.

"Gee, Grandpa," Pearse said.

MJ reached for a napkin.

"Are you OK?" Pearse asked.

"The problems we face are endless," Day had said, that evening at the pub. "So fresh blood is a pleasure to see."

Day searched his overcoat pocket for a match.

"And this Captain Monohan—your prisoner's son—is coming here to Charleville," he said. "He's here now, actually."

MJ poured more tea into his cup. Before Monohan's capture, his duties for the IRB had been minimal, and he had wanted more involvement. He had been attending meetings for about a year, enjoying the exhortations of the visiting speakers to Ireland free and Ireland forever. But really, he had imagined himself doing something more like this, actually helping the Rising, giving his name to it, as it were, crossing the line to expel the damned English.

"We understand he's staying the night at the home of a woman here in Charleville," Day said. "A Mrs. Daly."

"Mrs. Con Daly?" MJ asked.

"That's it."

"What are you going to do?" MJ asked.

Day lit the match and brought it to his cigarette. "We're going to take the son as well."

"Kidnap him?"

"To hold him until after the Howth operation. To keep him from harm's way, I guess you could say."

MJ brought the teacup to his lips.

"Will you help us do that, Michael?" Day asked. "We need another man. And there's liable to be danger."

After a pause, MJ nodded. "Yes, I can show you Mrs. Daly's. It's up the road, not far."

"Tomorrow morning, then? First thing."

"Tomorrow morning," MJ replied.

The next morning they bicycled the half-mile to Mrs. Daly's house. Besides MJ and Day there was a third man, an upholsterer from Dublin named Bob Costello. He was a large man, dressed in a wool suit, tie, and overcoat, who had trouble negotiating the road on his bicycle. He swore at the ruts, causing MJ and Day to laugh at him as they made their way through the dark. In the early morning gloom, the countryside appeared weighted down. The stone walls rose and fell over the distant hills like black necklaces. MJ's bicycle rattled beneath him. There was a kind of soaked mist between the hills, which dissipated where the slopes rose into the daybreak.

"Here we are," MJ said as they cleared a rise and looked down on Mrs. Daly's house. There were a few other buildings across the road from hers, smaller, whitewashed structures that belonged to neighboring farmers. Con Daly had passed away a few years previously. He and Mrs. Daly had been considered well-to-do, but that turned out not to have been so. Not wanting to lose her house, Mrs. Daly now rented rooms to guests on a nightly basis.

The three men descended the hill, walking their bicycles. They stopped several yards before the house and leaned the bicycles against the corner of a wall.

"We'll wait until there's more light," Day said. "He should be coming out presently."

"What do we do then?" MJ asked.

"We'll want to have a talk with him." Day's voice sounded quite casual, as though, really, he were not much interested in the task. He put up his collar and leaned against the wall, reaching into his pocket for some tobacco and papers. "Do you smoke?" he asked MJ.

"No."

"Bob?"

"Yes, thanks," Costello replied. He accepted a paper and tobacco from Day, lit the cigarette he made, and, cupping it between his fingers, looked off into the fields. He was a heavy-faced man with blue eyes. His hands were scratched and thick.

For several minutes, there was no talk. The light turned gray and began to brighten. Two men walked from a yard father down the road. They were driving a horse before an empty cart, and did not notice MJ and the others standing by the wall. There was no wind, and the mist between the hills began to disperse, making them appear even softer than they had appeared before. MJ loved the countryside around Charleville. The air was damp and caressing in the spring, which made the warming mornings particularly fine, even when it was going to rain. He unbuttoned his coat as the dawn cold diminished. Perhaps it would rain later on, but there was a finesse to the morning so far that made it quite pleasant.

At ten minutes past eight, a man walked from the front door of Mrs. Daly's house.

"There he is," Day whispered. He dropped his cigarette to the ground. Costello pursed his lips and nodded, pushing his hands into his pockets.

The man wore a dark coat and pants, a wool tie, a scarf wrapped around his neck, and a gray, brimmed wool cap. He walked through the garden toward the front gate, pushing a bicycle. Even at this distance, MJ recognized him. He was the man in the photograph Monohan had showed him.

"Bob," Day said in a low voice, touching Costello's sleeve. "You'll go down there and speak with him a moment."

MJ leaned close, to listen.

"Begin a conversation, you see," Day went on. "Can you show him the way into Charleville? That sort of thing. Ask his name."

MJ interrupted. "May I do that?" he asked. His heart quivered. He was frightened by his suggestion.

Day studied MJ's face a moment.

"There's no harm in it," he said. His soft voice sounded quite proper, and put MJ at ease. "We've never seen this Captain Monohan, Michael. So you'll speak with him, and when we're certain we've got the right fellow, Bob and I'll take hold of him, and he'll get to join his father, you see. It's a simple matter, really. I want you just to ask him his name, somehow. We want to be sure we have the right bloke, don't we?"

"I'm certain he is," MJ said.

The man approached the gate.

"Go on," Day said, and he laid a hand on MJ's arm, pushing him into the road.

MJ took a few steps, his shoes crunching in the gravel by the side of the road. He paused and glanced over his shoulder at Day, who nodded in the direction of the house. Taking a breath, MJ turned down the road.

"Good morning, Captain," he said.

The man looked up. His hands rested on the bars of the bicycle. He was in his forties, a little overweight, with a large moustache. MJ noticed that the skin around his eyes was lined.

"What is it?" the man said.

"Nothing. I just thought . . . well . . . ."

"What is it?"

A voice came from behind MJ. "Is it you, Captain Monohan?"

The man's head snapped around, in the direction of the voice. His mouth opened. There were two explosions.

Monohan spun about and fell against the stone wall. His bicycle rattled to the ground. MJ's heart felt like it would come out of him. Monohan's coat lay open, and blood flowed from the torn wounds in his chest. His mouth was open. His eyes ticked back and forth, electrified with pain. MJ knelt over him, and the serrated wounds bubbled in the soft light.

"Oh, Jesus," MJ said. He took Monohan's coat by the lapels and pulled him a few inches from the ground. One leg was turned beneath him. An arm lay propped against the wall.

"What . . ." MJ stammered. "What . . ."

The man tried to speak, but his voice was inundated with liquid. After a moment, a spurt of blood pushed from his mouth across MJ's fingers. Horrified, MJ let go of the coat. Monohan's head cracked against the wall.

There was a movement next to MJ. Bob Costello shoved a pistol into his coat pocket. Looking a moment at the body, he tapped MJ's arm.

"Come on. We've got to go."

He ran up the road toward his bicycle, leaving MJ staring at Monohan as he silently died.

The sound of Costello's footsteps ground into MJ's hearing. He could not bear what he saw. He wanted to take the dead man up by the coat, to make him stand, make him walk. But he was too afraid to touch him.

Day grabbed MJ by the arm. "Come on, you bastard," he said. The alarm in his voice broke through MJ's terror. "Run! We've got to get out of here."

MJ turned and ran, gasping as he pushed his bicycle to the crest of the hill. The dead man's blood, slick between MJ's fingers, smeared the handlebars, and MJ struggled to wipe it away. Looking back, he saw that a glimmer of morning sun had touched the house. The body remained in the road, twisted in the light.

Pearse sat waiting, his eyes darting with concern, as MJ glanced at himself in the mirror behind the counter at Blum's.

"Yes, I'm OK, Pearse."

"Did the cake make you sick?" Pearse handed MJ a fresh napkin, with which MJ dabbed his stained cuff.

"No. No," MJ replied. He took out some dollar bills. "It was just something I thought of, that's all. Are you finished?"

Pearse hurriedly took the last piece of frosting into his mouth, nodding.

"Let's go, then."

"You're not mad at me, are you?"

"No, no," MJ grimaced. He left a few bills on the counter, then stood and reached for his hat. "Come on, I just want to get out of here."

Emmett Day reached into his coat pocket for a handkerchief. He leaned forward, coughing once, and his face reddened. Joe kept his eyes on the road ahead, but he worried about Day. The old man seemed genuinely ill, though Joe wondered whether he were not, more specifically, hung over. Thanks to Pearse, Day had had five whiskies the evening before.

"Did the boy do that by himself, Joe?" Day asked. "Or did you put him up to it?"

"I told him to keep your glass full," Joe replied. "But Pearse doesn't do things with such determination unless he really wants to."

"Well, he's a good boy." Day examined the phlegm in the handkerchief before folding it and replacing it in his pocket. "He reminded me of my own sons, you know."

"How many do you have?"

"Two, and four daughters."

"What do they do?"

"One of my sons is a banker. The bright one. Chartered Bank of England, Lord help us! The other works for a printer in Dublin." Day smiled, leaning against the car door. "I never thought, when I was a teacher myself, that I'd have children. You don't think about those things when you're a young man traveling at night, planning the new order of things. The Rising, you know."

"You never saw yourself as a man who changed diapers?"

"No," Day laughed. "The wife took care of that."

"Is she . . . is she still . . ."

"No, my wife died two years ago. And I miss her, Joe. You don't know what it's like to have to go on alone, do you?"

"No, but my father does."

Day adjusted his coat as Joe pulled into the Southern Pacific Fruitvale station and parked in a space looking out onto the tracks. It was a humid morning, yet Day kept his coat on. He wore a brown sweater as well. The collar of his shirt was stained yellow with age. There was space between the collar itself and Day's wattled neck.

"Ah, your father," Day replied. "You know, I remember him now."

Joe glanced quickly at the Irishman. He placed his fingers on the steering wheel.

Day watched two children run past the car, a red-headed boy playing with his little sister. Their parents sat, with another, older couple, on a bench outside the station. Grandparents, Joe guessed. The children ran around to the back of the station building and emerged once more from the other side. The sound of their running was dotted with high-pitched laughter.

"You did know him, then?" Joe asked.

"Yes. There was something that happened down there in Charleville. We had a problem with one of the police, and we had to do something about it. It was a serious matter."

Day watched as the children began a game of tag on the platform.

"Do you know anything about the Howth operation?" he asked.

"The guns? The daylight landing?"

"That's it."

"1914. Of course," Joe replied. "The Volunteers brought in thousands of rifles right under the British noses, in the middle of the day."

"Just past morning tea time, as I recall." Day began laughing, a damp rasp. "It was a grand moment for us."

In the far distance a train appeared, slowing for its entrance to the station.

"Kate!" the boy shouted to the little girl. "Here it comes!" The children went to the edge of the platform to watch, calling to their parents.

"But we had to do some things we didn't wish to do, to ensure its success," Day went on. "There was an officer with the Dublin constabulary, a tenacious bastard if there ever was one. He knew something was up, and we had to get him off the trail, you might say."

Joe turned toward Day and waited. An odd, painful fear entered his heart as Day spoke. But he pushed his hand out before him and blurted the beginning of a question.

"Did you . . ."

The words were scuttled in his throat. He could not continue. Day turned his head from the window. His eyes surveyed

Joe's, who realized the old man felt pain of his own with the telling of the story. But it was not the kind of pain that comes with the recollection of the facts, the mere recitation of what had happened, as difficult as that may be. Rather, Day feared that he was going to do harm to Joe's feelings for his father.

"We killed him, yes," Day muttered, finally, quickly. He looked away once more. "Had to."

"Why?"

"There were lives at stake, Joe. Many men had been put in prison because of this man. He was a collaborator with the British, and he had to be removed."

Joe tightened the fingers of one hand around the steering wheel. "Did my father kill him?"

"And the funny thing is that, last night, I didn't realize it was your father who was with us that day."

"Did *he* do the killing?"

"We'd wondered why he ran away, you see. He . . ."

"Mr. Day!" Joe grabbed the sleeve of Day's coat.

Startled, Day pulled his arm away.

"Was it my father who killed him?" Joe asked.

"No. No. It was not."

Joe let go of the sleeve.

"Your father took us to him. He identified him for us. He was a young man, of course, then. I barely knew him."

"He helped you murder the man, though."

The train, bound for Los Angeles, came into the station. Joe opened the car door, went around to the trunk, and got out Day's bag. Helping Day from the car, he accompanied him to the platform, where they approached the red and orange Pullman car. A porter stood at the bottom of the metal stairway. Joe placed a hand in his pocket for some change.

"Yes, gentlemans," the porter said. He was a very large black man, wearing thick glasses. He carried a handful of change, which he rattled before him as the two men approached. "All 'board the Daylight."

Day went up the stairway and turned about on the landing. The brim of his hat had flipped up, so that he looked like a sporty, dying ancient, dressed in wool. His scarf hung down before the lapels of his coat. His eyes, enlarged by his glasses, resembled transparent gray marbles.

"It wasn't murder, Joe," he said. "It was patriotism."

"But . . ."

"Your father risked his life," Day said. "Put it on the line, you see, for what he believed. And maybe he was frightened. Maybe he ran away. But that day, Michael Pearse was a hero." The old man's voice wavered. "And if you can tell him that without getting him angry," he continued after a moment, clearing his throat, "you'd be doing the Republic of Ireland a great service."

Anguished, Joe pondered the conversation with his father, what it would be like. He would have to tell MJ what he knew about him now, the two or three crystalline facts, and MJ would sit in his rocker, furious and embarrassed. This is why Dad's silence was always so censorious, Joe thought. He wanted to put me off the trail. But I wonder, did he want to talk about this all those times, to tell us?

For a moment, Joe reflected on what MJ had shared with his family about Ireland. There had been a great deal of description. But all of it . . . all had been mere bland recitation of the beauties of the landscape, kind-hearted anticlerical humor, and the occasional song. Advertising copy, in short. This information, about the killing of the policeman, had been impossible to tell. It was a doleful secret, and it must have cost him terribly, Joe thought.

"Cowardice is difficult to explain, you know," Day said.

"Cowardice!"

Day shrugged, wincing at Joe's sharp reply. "Your father disappeared after that," he said. "And now we know where he went."

"But my father was no coward."

"Oh, Joe. You should understand that cowardice is not always a bad thing," Day said, looking over his hands.

The porter ascended to the car. He closed the half-door and excused himself, moving into the car itself. Day leaned forward and reached down for Joe's hand.

"There were moments when I wouldn't have minded a little of it myself," he continued.

Joe shook his hand, but he did so with growing bitterness. Day's self-assurance had begun to nauseate him.

"We all know the English are murdering brutes, now, don't we, Joe? It makes sense a man would lose heart against a people like that."

Joe could not imagine how Day had looked as a young man. His sagging, emaciated face and baggy clothing seemed permanent, so that Day appeared, in Joe's notion of the past, as he was now. Joe imagined Day gunning down the policeman, sodden in the rain and mud. He was a decrepit, murderous elder, almost unable to breathe. The rain fell across Day's glasses, shattering his view. His coat hung from his shoulders, and the policeman's body—smoking cloth and blood—lay exploded before him. The thought of it horrified Joe. His stomach turned, and bile rose to his throat.

"Was it you who pulled the trigger?" Joe asked.

Day remained leaning forward, thinking a moment. "You know, I don't remember," he replied finally.

Joe let go of his hand. A residue of dampness remained on Joe's fingers, and he placed his hand in his coat pocket, wiping the palm against the cloth.

"It was a while ago," Joe muttered.

"Sure, Joe," Day replied, "it was that."

An hour later, Joe stood in his living room window, looking out at MJ's Buick. MJ had wheeled the car from its parking place and now headed down the hill to the corner, while Pearse remained on the front steps to the flat. At the last moment, MJ glanced back and looked up at the living room window.

Hurriedly, Joe waved to him.

MJ parked the car in front of the Gold Coin Grocery, got out, and ascended the hill. When he arrived at the steps to the flat, Joe stood on the front porch, his hand on Pearse's shoulder.

"I . . . Joe, I owe you an apology," MJ said.

Joe surveyed his father with a mixture of unhappiness and regard. "Won't you come up for a cup of tea?" he asked.

"No. I just wanted to say that that fellow you had here last night reminded me so of someone I knew in Charleville. It was an uncanny resemblance."

"You never met Emmett Day before?" Joe asked. His disbelief seemed to scatter MJ's explanation. The lie had no conviction. He looked down, unable to meet Joe's gaze. Knowing the truth, Joe hurried nonetheless to put his father at ease. But the interjection was too nervously abrupt.

"Dad, you know who that man was last night."

Wincing, MJ turned away, and Joe descended the stairs to his side.

"Dad . . ."

"I've got to go."

"Dad. Please. Let me talk with you." Joe raised a hand to the back of his neck. He looked at Pearse, who remained on the steps.

"There was a man named Day, Joe," MJ continued. "Or

something of the kind. But that fellow last night couldn't have been the man I knew. The man I saw was well into his fifties at the time, and I'm certain he's in hell by now, isn't he?''

Joe placed a hand on MJ's arm. "Dad, what did you do? What happened?''

MJ shoved a hand into a coat pocket. "Oh, in those times, there were street demonstrations, parades. There was a killing at one of them. A terrible thing, and I saw it. I was in the crowd, that's all. It was awful. I hadn't thought of it for years. But last night, it's just that that fellow Day reminded me of the man who . . . who'd been apprehended. That's all.''

MJ picked a thread from his coat sleeve.

"I hope you'll forgive me, Joe,'' he said. "It was an awful thing I said last night. An awful thing.''

"Of course, Dad,'' Joe muttered.

"It's difficult, you know, with your mother gone.'' MJ shrugged. "I get confused.''

There was a pause. Joe looked over his father's face.

"Dad, was it Emmett Day that murdered Monohan?''

"No, like I just said . . .''

"That shot him down? Was it somebody else? Was it you?''

MJ's shoulders quivered. His heart seemed about to give way, as though it would cease beating and abandon him, abandon the lie he was trying to tell.

Joe leaned against the front of the building, awaiting his father's answer.

"You've felt like a murderer all your life,'' he said, after a moment.

"Joe.''

"And you've smothered the secret, so that none of us would know. So that you wouldn't have to think about it.''

"Get away from me,'' MJ whispered. His hands twitched before him, trying to find in one another some kind of repose. He closed his eyes.

"Dad. Please. The truth,'' Joe said.

Waving his hand behind him, MJ turned away, retreating toward his car. His black overcoat flailed in the breeze that blew up the street.

"Tell me the truth,'' Joe said, following his father down the hill.

Silently, MJ got into the Buick. He started it and swung it out into the street. The car stopped at the bottom of the hill, then disappeared around the corner onto Columbus. Joe stood on the curb. Presently, he was joined by Pearse, who took his hand.

"Are you OK, Dad?" Pearse asked.

Joe exhaled. "You can't pry anything from the son of a bitch," he said.

Pearse's hand slipped from Joe's. The boy zippered his jacket up to the throat. Distracted, Joe did not take notice of him for a moment. But when he looked down at Pearse, he saw that there was clear annoyance in his face, as though, in Joe's angry expression, Pearse had found disapproval of his question as well. The boy turned up the hill and ran toward the apartment.

"Pearse. Please. Wait a minute," Joe said.

"What do you think this is?" Day shouted at MJ, as they cycled up the road from the Daly house. "Do you want to be a slave in your own country all your life?"

"But he didn't have a chance," MJ said.

"Doesn't matter, you fool. He was the enemy. The enemy of the people."

MJ's mother had prepared tea for him, but MJ was unable to take any. His heart was leaden with anguish for what he had done. Murder was something he had read about as a schoolboy, in Dickens. He remembered dark criminals escaping from prison ships, and bodies floating in the filthy Thames. But the man this morning, innocently walking his bicycle to the road . . . the moment of his death flooded MJ's mind over and over. He wanted to confess, immediately, what he had led the murderers to do, but Mother Church's assurances would be laughable. How could he describe to a priest the way the wisp of smoke had risen from the man's foaming wound?

He went to Holmes's shop as though simply to begin another day's work. He removed the bolts of wool from the shelves. Wrapping white paper around his sleeves to keep them clean, he leaned over to dust the backs of the shelves. The paper came away barely soiled. MJ performed this task twice a week. Even the storeroom in back was spotless, where Holmes's desk and the woodstove were, with all the makings for tea, the cups and saucers.

Rain fell heavily outside, and a horsecart passing by appeared shrouded in water. The sign above the door to the Wolfe Tone across the road swung like a crotchety pendulum. Replacing the bolts on the shelves, MJ made sure they lined up properly. He enjoyed the kind of discipline Holmes imposed on the shop, because it made the place so enjoyable for the clientele. The bolts lined up in so military a way were vivid with lovely colors. The buttons Holmes sold, which were arranged by price in myriad little drawers below the bolts of wool, were the best in Charleville. He also carried shirt collars that were made in New York City by a firm called B. Zuckerman, a rarity anywhere in Ireland, and very fine.

MJ went to the back to make a pot of tea. Noting the rain, he figured that Holmes would be wearing a heavy suit this morning. His appearance changed little, day to day, and what subtleties there were were determined by the weather. It'll be the brown one, MJ thought. Pressed, as usual, with a white collar taut like a fence, and a black cravat.

MJ opened the tin of Earl Grey and placed two spoonfuls in the pot. Putting water on to boil, he rubbed his hands before the stove. They remained cold, and MJ continued rubbing them.

A gust of wind buffeted the window. The shop door burst open, then closed just as rapidly.

"Mr. Holmes!" MJ said. He straightened up and folded his hands before him, inadvertently preparing for the inspection Holmes gave the clerks each morning.

"Michael. I'm glad you're here." Holmes removed his hat and hung it on the rack next to the stove. He sat down in one of the chairs before the stove. His hair was mussed.

"They murdered one of the police this morning." Holmes exhaled, and there was a nervous waver in his voice. "Killed him as he left Mrs. Daly's, poor chap. It happened just an hour ago."

Shaking his head, then lowering it a moment with a kind of sorrowful moan, Holmes clasped his hands together.

"Bloody Catholics, what do they want?"

MJ could not move. A hanging matter, he thought. After a moment, Holmes glanced up at him, embarrassed.

"Forgive me, Michael. I didn't mean that."

"Yes, Mr. Holmes."

"I don't . . . I have no argument with your religion. I'm sorry."

MJ kept still.

"In fact, the Catholics, they're fine people, many of them. And your priests . . . fine men. It's these damned criminal Irish . . ." Holmes sighed, then stood and removed the pot of water from the stove. "I don't know what they are. Perhaps you can tell me," he said finally.

"Sorry, sir?''

"What do these people want?''

"I don't know, sir,'' MJ replied.

"You're better for it,'' Holmes said. "Sit down to your tea, here, Michael. And then I want you to go out to Mrs. Daly . . .''

"Pardon me?''

"That's right. To see if we can help her. Poor woman, she must be terribly distressed with all this.''

"Yes, Mr. Holmes.''

MJ rode his bicycle to Mrs. Daly's. He was miserably wet when he cleared the rise above the house. There were several policemen standing in the garden, sodden-looking in the rain. A new lorry, one of the first MJ had ever seen, was parked in the muddy road. The clouds above had little distinction. They were swollen, and oozing water. MJ pulled the brim of his wool cap down to protect his eyes from the rain and began the descent of the hill to the house.

He stopped at the gate, where a constable stood watching his approach. There was a slight, sweet odor that MJ did not recognize. A bicycle lay in the mud outside the gate, its front wheel turning in the wind. A large puddle, in which part of the bicycle lay, was colored deep brown with blood. A brighter swatch of it tinted the grass by the stone wall.

MJ touched his index finger to the rim of his cap.

"Pardon me, sir,'' he said to the constable. "I've come from Holmes's Arcade, in Charleville. Mr. Holmes sent me.''

"And what do you want?'' the policeman asked. His accent was quite heavy, from the west of Ireland. But his voice was muffled, as though the rain were subduing it.

"Just to ask whether Mrs. Daly is getting on all right,'' MJ replied.

The constable shook his head. "We're not letting anyone in. And sure you're asking about the wrong person.''

MJ looked up, his eyes sheltered by the cap.

"There's nothing you can do for her,'' the constable continued, "and less for Captain Monohan.''

MJ placed his hands in the pockets of his overcoat.

"Do you know anything about this?'' the constable asked.

MJ imagined old Monohan seated at the table, pushing a slice of fried egg about his plate, wondering when the bastards were going to let him go. His hands were quite spotted with age and wrinkled, yet they gripped the table utensils with considerable delicacy, as though he had been trained to be God's own waiter in a fine Dublin establishment instead of a policeman hidden in a decaying room. MJ's heart felt riddled with sorrow for Monohan, even as the constable grilled him about why he had come to visit Mrs. Daly.

"No. No, sir, I do not."

"You're certain of that," the constable said.

MJ's guilt wrapped about him like suffocating wool.

"Yes, quite." His shoulders sloped beneath the rain. He resolved in that moment to go see Monohan. He was compelled to do so. He felt that if he did not, the sin he had committed would push him into madness.

"And your name?" the constable asked.

The cloth of MJ's coat took in the rainfall. Each drop buffeted the heavy wool.

"Michael," he said.

"Michael what?"

"Pearse, sir. Michael Pearse."

The bicycle's dark rear wheel was absorbed by the darker pool in which it lay, like the body of an animal.

MJ cycled to John Creeley's farm. The hedges along the road were gray, like thrown-away slabs of iron. The clouds formed an imprecise canopy, losing its shape where it was raining. MJ, trying to calm himself, wished that they would envelop him. He felt as though every angle of his profile and every fold in his black overcoat must gleam precisely, in complete detail, making it impossible for him to hide anywhere. The murder had exposed him to anyone who might wish to pursue him. He was bright and legible, a criminal.

"What is it, Michael?" Mrs. Creeley asked, as she led him from the front door into the kitchen.

"I've just got to speak with Mr. Monohan for a few minutes."

"Were you sent by anyone?" Creeley himself asked. He was sitting at the table, having a cup of tea.

"Yes," MJ lied. "But it's not important. There'll be no trouble."

Creeley glanced at his wife. He was so rough-hewn a man that MJ found his kindness rather surprising. That he was so obviously a traitor to the British authorities had made MJ think that Creeley should be more harsh than he was.

"I suppose there's no harm in it," Creeley said finally. MJ breathed more easily, relieved that Creeley apparently did not yet know of the attack on Captain Monohan.

He descended the stairs. MJ took brief, sad pleasure in the fact that the old man was reading the Hardy stories he had brought him a few days earlier.

"Hello," Monohan said. "Come to spend the morning with me, have you?"

"No, I haven't." MJ paused at the foot of the stairs. Water dripped from his coat to the floor.

"But something's up, isn't it?" Monohan asked. The candles flickered in the gray light from the windows. "You're nervous."

"Yes, I . . ." MJ removed his coat and sat down in the chair opposite Monohan's table. The task of bringing up what had happened grew so forbidding that speech deserted him. But he was determined to tell Monohan before someone else did. He could not stand his own cowardliness.

"What's happened?"

"It's Captain Monohan."

Monohan closed the book before him. His fingers remained on it. "You mean my son."

"Yes. Something terrible's happened."

Monohan's face showed little expression.

"He's dead," MJ muttered. He lowered his head, growing queasy as the words came out of him. "I'm sorry."

"He was murdered, was he?"

"Yes."

"And who did it?"

MJ could not speak.

"Who?" Monohan's voice made a rattling sound, as though he were trying to stifle the very question he was asking. "Was it you, you bastard?" he asked.

The candle flames riffled in a draft from one of the windows. MJ was alarmed by Monohan's sickly menace.

"No," MJ replied.

Monohan leaned forward. "But you saw it. You saw it, didn't you?"

MJ placed a hand over his eyes. "Yes. I saw it. I didn't mean it. I couldn't stop it. They'd killed him before I knew what was happening."

"Were you armed?"

"No, I wasn't! I was there because . . . I don't know why they wanted me there."

"It doesn't matter," Monohan whispered. He crumpled in his chair. "Jesus, my son."

"Please."

Monohan's head twitched.

"May I apologize, please?" MJ asked.

The old man's eyes widened with loathing. "You fuck your apologies, Mick."

"Please, Mr. Monohan. I didn't intend this."

"You've brought me my poor supper for weeks, kept me down here in this piss hole where I'm close to destroyed, losing my health. You try to lighten your burden of guilt by bringing me little trinkets, like this book, every now and then . . ."

Monohan pushed the book aside with the tips of his fingers.

"Shit. That's what this Englishman's book is. Like you and your IRB men. The purest sort of shit." Monohan grasped his hands and lowered his head once more. "And now you've taken my son from me."

"I couldn't have stopped them."

"You could have. You could have turned them in, for God's sake, long ago."

"But Ireland . . ."

"*Bugger* your Ireland!"

Monohan's sorrow caused him to pale even more. Only now, suddenly, he could no longer speak. MJ remained sitting for several minutes while Monohan grieved. Surely, MJ thought, this is what happens in risings. People are killed. Especially people who oppose the will of the masses. The dark-flowing blood of the Irish would drown the English murderers, wasn't that what Padraic Pearse had said?

But now the exhortations of the pamphlets MJ had read seemed sniveling and lying. *This* was the Rising. Captain Monohan had been obliterated, MJ thought, an enemy of the people, as Emmett Day had called him, and a son searching for his father.

Finally MJ stood to leave. He risked the old man's anger by laying his hand across Monohan's.

"He was against you," Monohan grumbled.

MJ removed his fingers from Monohan's.

"I am against you."

The old man lowered his head a moment, then lifted it and stared into MJ's eyes.

"They'll get rid of me, you know," he said.

"They wouldn't! What have you done?"

"Jesus, you are an idiot. What else could they do with me? They'll kill me like they killed my son. But you—you'll stay on this island forever, in your little shop or your classroom or your pub, whatever it is you do, and you'll never be forgiven.''

MJ himself began grieving, wishing he could salve Monohan's anguish.

''You'll grow to hate yourself,'' Monohan said, ''and you'll never be forgiven.''

« 4 »

THE TRUTH AND THE HOTEL DANTE

Still grounded, Pearse skirted Washington Square for the next few days. Wind-blown November leaves scudded over the grass in the gray light. He looked out now and then from the window of his classroom, hoping to glimpse Ed sitting on one of the benches. Cutting out paper maple leaves one day, Pearse imagined what it would be like were it ever to snow on the square, like it did on the Cascades in Washington, something MJ had told him about. He saw a Chinese woman doing her exercises, and two other women, heavily bundled against the cold, pushing baby carriages on the pathway around the square. But there was no snow. And there was no Ed. Pearse sighed, convinced that the Halloween trip to the beach had meant nothing and that the beatnik had forgotten him. He laid the scissors on the window sill, recalling, regretfully, Doll's enjoyment of the leaves he used to make for her, which she always taped to her refrigerator door.

Pearse slouched about the apartment, resisting his parents' worried efforts to "bring him out of it," as Joe put it. For one thing, the dispute between Joe and MJ was still going on. MJ had not visited or even called. And Joe had told Pearse that *he* could not call MJ, an order that had precipitated a loud argument between his parents.

Mimi had prepared a baked ham that evening, with scalloped potatoes and french-cut green beans. As Joe had served Pearse seconds, he had asked the boy if he understood why he and MJ were arguing.

Pearse did not answer. His resentment felt like cold gravel in his throat. It isn't fair, he thought, that I can't go see Grandpa. I always get to go see him.

"Pearse!" Joe said, dropping the slice of ham on the plate. "What's wrong with you? Why won't you answer?"

"Nothing's wrong!" Pearse said. He held his fork in one hand, on the table. The tines pointed at the ceiling.

"But you won't talk to me!" Joe said.

Mimi interjected. "He's just trying to enjoy his meal, Joe."

Grateful, Pearse nodded.

"But what happened to the Pearse we used to know?" Joe asked. "The happy Pearse. The Pearse who enjoyed things."

"Joe, stop it," Mimi said.

Surprised by the heat of Mimi's response, Joe did not notice as Tim held out his own plate for seconds.

"Just stop it!" Mimi repeated. "You won't let him visit his own grandfather! Even though it's clear as day that you miss MJ as much as the rest of us, Joe. The poor man got a terrible shock the other night with that guy Day, and you're in a position to help him."

"He's got to come to me for that," Joe said. "To ask me."

"Oh, Joe, you're so foolish. It's no wonder Pearse mopes. I think he's got a right to mope."

The argument ensued.

The next afternoon, Pearse sat with MJ in the living room of MJ's house. He had snuck out, telling his father he was going to the Salesian Boys' Club at Saints Peter and Paul to play checkers. MJ reached into his vest pocket for a Garcia y Vega. Removing the paper ring, he gave it to Pearse, who secured it on his little finger.

"Is everything OK with you, Pearse?" MJ asked. There was a fire in the fireplace, and the flames crouched about the small pieces of wood. The manner in which MJ put his question was far less abrasive than Joe's. Nonetheless, Pearse felt the muscles of his face tighten, and he struggled against the tears that came to his eyes.

"What is it?" MJ said. "It'll be our secret."

Pearse felt his anger subside. He took in a few short breaths, and let them out in rapid succession.

"It's because Mom and Dad won't let me see Ed," he replied.

"Who?"

Pearse groaned. "You know, the beatnik guy."

MJ lifted the cigar to his lips, drew on it once, and let the smoke out.

"They're just afraid, Pearse," he said. "Your father doesn't want you running around with bums."

"He's not a bum!"

MJ held out a hand. "OK. OK. But maybe Joe and Mimi

don't know much about those beatniks, and sometimes adults get upset about people they can't figure out." He took up the cigar once more. "You think this fellow Ed is OK?"

"Yes!" Pearse said. "We just went to the beach on Halloween, that's all. It was fun! And he knows how to rhyme stuff."

"He does?"

"Yes. Grandpa, Mom and Dad don't know. Ed's a nice guy. He's not a bad guy."

MJ stuck out his lower lip, seeming to accept Pearse's opinion. "Then look, if that's the way you feel, I think you better go see him," he said.

Pearse turned the paper ring about his finger, contemplating it. "But, Mom and Dad . . . I mean, won't they get mad at me again?"

There was a pause. MJ sat back and took a long draw on his cigar.

"You really like this fellow, don't you, Pearse?" he said.

Pearse inclined his head.

"All right. We've got to keep this a secret. But tomorrow's Saturday," MJ said. "And Joe and I and Monsignor have a golf game, at about ten."

"You do?"

"And the Altar Society has a table at the cathedral rummage sale. Your mother's going to help out. So maybe you could . . ."

MJ looked at the cigar in his hand.

"You could just take a walk over there," he whispered, "to that café." He crossed his legs, leaning back in a luxurious way into the couch.

Pearse looked up at him, thoughts swirling about in his head. But how can I . . . I mean, wouldn't it be . . . ?

MJ watched the smoke rise from his cigar to the ceiling. Then he took out the small pair of scissors he carried with him everywhere, to trim the soggy end of the cigar.

The next morning, Pearse snuck down Upper Grant Avenue toward the Caffè Trieste the same way he had seen soldiers doing it on *Victory at Sea*, door to door.

"Ed Finney? Lives around corner." The man behind the counter pointed out the window, toward Columbus Avenue. He spoke in a heavy accent that Pearse had trouble understanding. "Hotel Dante. You can't miss it."

"What's it called?" Pearse asked.

"Dante." The sound came out as a festive bark. "Sounds nice, yes? Good Italian name." He turned a fluted gray knob on the espresso machine, and a high-pitched whooshing sound emerged. "But that hotel is a . . . how you say, a dump? Yes! Hotel Dante is a dump!"

The gleeful clatter of his words punctuated the steam.

Pearse found the hotel and walked up a flight of linoleum-covered stairs to a counter, behind which sat a middle-aged man in a plaid shirt.

"Is this where Ed lives?"

"Ed who?"

"Finney."

The day clerk's eyebrows, like small hairy bruises, rose up as he stared at Pearse's face. "Yeah," he said finally. He pointed up the stairs. "Second deck. Two-oh-one."

"OK. Thanks."

Pearse climbed the stairs. The rubber safeguards were cracked and falling apart. On one stair the rubber had disappeared altogether, though the metal runner remained, nailed to the wood. The hallway, which was painted dark green, made him feel imprisoned. The linoleum floor crackled beneath Pearse's shoes, and the light bulbs running the length of the hall were circled with wire mesh. As he arrived at the door to 201, his stomach hardened, and he felt a surge of intrusive guilt. His parents would ground him until he died if they were to see him in the Hotel Dante. Swallowing, Pearse raised his fist and knocked on the door.

There were footsteps and a single cough. The door opened, and a piece of torn paper blew into the hallway.

"Hi, Ed."

Ed stood before Pearse in a black T-shirt and black slacks. His wingtips were exceedingly scuffed. He had a cigarette in his hand, and the smell of Gauloise smoke blew into Pearse's face. The boy waved his hand before his nose.

"So, I'm supposed to know you?" Ed asked.

Pearse's mouth quivered with surprise.

"What do you want, man?"

Pearse looked down at the floor. Ed *had* forgotten about him. Immediately embarrassed, he wanted to turn and run away. But as he surveyed his Keds and the Levi's he wore, their cuffs rolled up, and the flannel Eisenhower jacket to which his mother had sewn a set of sergeant's stripes he had bought at a war surplus store, Pearse realized he did not have on his moustache. He was not wearing his sunglasses.

"Yeah, Ed," Pearse smiled. "Don't you recognize me?"

Ed's face tightened.

"I'm Pearse!"

Ed took a drag on the Gauloise and gazed through the smoke at the boy. "It's you?"

"Yeah! See . . . I just look a little different today, that's all."

Quickly, Ed extended his hand. "How are you, Pearse?" He clapped the boy on the arm. "Hey, it's nice to see you."

Pearse smiled, relieved.

"Come on in," Ed continued, stepping away from the door.

But suddenly Pearse found that he had little to say. He entered Ed's room, where a bare light bulb hung from a wire coming down from the ceiling. There was an overstuffed chair and a radio, a bed, a hot plate, and a small, rusted refrigerator in one corner. Bookshelves hid every wall. They seemed to squat, torturously burdened with books and scattered papers that were stuffed into folders jammed between the books, loose, folded, and crumpled everywhere. A wine bottle stood on top of the refrigerator, its label stained with burgundy-colored splotches. There was a single table beneath the window looking out on Columbus Avenue. A white cardboard carton, which contained chop suey, stood open on the table, with a spoon sticking out of it. Ed's typewriter also sat on the table, surrounded by paper. The even lines of the typescript were sullied with messy pencilled corrections. There were arrows and scratch-outs, single words followed by insistent exclamation points, and long, grumbling notations. The typewriter was a black Royal with round keys that came out in an underbite. The two cannisters that held the ribbon looked like raised eyebrows. In fact, the typewriter reminded Pearse of Groucho Marx.

"So, what do you think?" Ed asked, gesturing about the room.

"Great," Pearse replied.

Ed went to the table. He pointed at a canvas army chair. "Sit down, Pearse. Take off your coat."

Pearse walked to the chair, but it too was piled with books. He paused a moment, his coat hanging from one hand.

"Oh! Sorry," Ed said. He pushed Pearse aside and swept the books onto the floor. Arranging them into a kind of pile with his feet, he pointed again to the chair. "Have a seat."

Ed sat down at the table. He leaned forward, placing his elbows on his knees. The smoke from his Gauloise rose up past his face. Pearse noticed that he had a tattoo of a woman in a grass skirt on his right arm.

"So, how've you been?" Ed asked.

There was a moment of silence, until Pearse dropped his hands to his lap and, sighing, began to speak.

"I got home pretty late on Halloween," he said.

"Yeah, I wondered about that. My shoes were filled with water when I got back here. And sand. It was like walking around in a damned puddle all night."

"I'm sorry I haven't come over to see you," Pearse said. He looked up at Ed's face, worried that he would find disapproval. "I just . . . my Dad had told me, see, that I wasn't supposed to talk to you, and I kind of got grounded."

Ed's brow crumpled.

"I mean, I had a lot of fun at the beach."

"Pearse. Wait."

"I didn't know what to do," Pearse continued. He stuck his hands into the pockets of his coat. "And I wanted to come up to the Caffè Trieste again, too, but my parents . . ."

"Hang on a second."

"My parents were real mad at me."

"Pearse, Pearse. Hang on!"

Ed laid his hand on Pearse's knee. His brown hair was very thick and had not been combed. He brought the cigarette to his mouth. Pearse did not speak, though he felt the words ranging about his gullet, corralled there.

"Do your parents know you're here now?"

"No!" Pearse replied.

"Then won't you get in trouble again?"

"I don't know. I just wanted to . . . I guess . . . you know . . . to say I'm sorry."

"You're *not* worried about what your parents think?"

"Yeah, I am." Pearse slumped back into the chair. "I'm scared," he mumbled. He lifted his feet and let them drop, so that the heels of his tennis shoes kicked against the books lying on the floor. "But I came over anyway."

Ed put out the cigarette in an ashtray on the table. Together they watched the butt fall over on its side.

"I like that," Ed said finally. "And I appreciate it, Pearse, but maybe we should keep it a secret, don't you think? I mean, I don't suppose you want your parents to know you're here, right?"

"No."

"OK. I got it. So . . . what's new with you?"

"Nothing."

"Have you been learning anything at school?"

"I'm learning about Italy in my geography book. Rome."

"Where the pope is, I bet."

"There's a big picture of him right at the beginning of the chapter."

"I can imagine."

"Making the sign of the cross."

Ed reached across the table for his packet of Gauloises. "You really like all that, don't you, Pearse?" he said. He lit up, shaking the match until the flame went out. "The church, I mean."

"I don't know."

A thick strand of smoke rose up about Ed's head.

"I feel kind of like I'm in jail sometimes," Pearse continued.

"But you believe in God, don't you?"

"God? Oh, yeah. God's great."

"Why?"

For a moment, Pearse did not have an answer. "He makes me feel good. Like when my grandmother died."

"When was that?"

"Three weeks ago. I mean, everybody tried to be nice, you know. But I was pretty sad when she died."

"And what does God do?"

"Makes it so I don't cry."

"And the priests at your school? They can't do that?"

"Oh, no. Like Monsignor, he just gave me a lot of rules and things."

Ed tapped the cigarette against the edge of the ashtray, nodding. "That's the way they always are," he muttered.

"What do you mean?"

"Oh, these guys set up a bureaucracy, and legislate to keep people in their place." Ed stood up and put his hands in his pockets. " 'Keep them unhappy, right, boys? Keep them poor.' It's always been that way, Pearse. The people get down on their knees and pray to God, get some joy out of that, and the priests tell them they must have committed some kind of sin, because how could they be so happy, otherwise?"

Pearse didn't understand what Ed was saying. Ed raised a finger in the air.

"Right? I mean, they screw the damned faith they're supposed to defend. Right?" Ed pointed the finger at Pearse. "They can't be happy unless you're unhappy."

Pearse lowered his head. "That's not what I meant," he said.

Noticing Pearse's discomfort, Ed relaxed and sat down once more. "Anyway," he said, "that's what I think. You should have heard my father when he talked about it."

Pearse looked about the room at the bookshelves. "Do you read all this stuff?" he asked.

"A couple of them are books I wrote," Ed replied. He stood and crossed the room toward one of the bookcases. Browsing, he pulled half a dozen volumes from various places. A few pieces of paper, dislodged from the shelves, floated to the floor. "Like, look at this. I published this last year."

"Great," Pearse said, looking over the cover of the book Ed handed him. "It's called . . . what's it called?"

"The Duluth Tantra Blues."

"What's that?"

"Hard to explain. But how about this one?" Ed said, giving Pearse a book with no real cover. It was wrinkled and stained with coffee. "See? It's called *Sanctioned Rot.*"

"What's it about?" Pearse asked.

"The United Fruit Company."

"Wow," Pearse replied. Again, he did not understand.

"Yeah, it's one of my better sellers so far. Seventy copies, something like that." He held the book before him, thumbing through it.

Pearse looked at the tattoo on Ed's arm. "Where'd you get that?" he asked.

"In Japan. I was on leave, you know, from Korea."

"What's it like, being in a war?"

"A war?" Ed dropped the book to the table. "Pearse, it's great." Again, he began pacing. This time, though, as he spoke, Pearse felt more included in the monolog, sensing Ed's real, abrupt happiness. His voice took on a raspy warmth as he praised the guys in the Seventh Infantry, the bravery of the sons of bitches, and the glory they had all found in the long, damned, bloody nights up by the 38th Parallel.

"Did you get to shoot guns?" Pearse asked.

"Did we!" Ed clenched his fist with enthusiasm. "Pearse, we fought those North Koreans to a standstill."

"Did you win?"

Ed stood in a kind of hunch before Pearse. After a moment his eyes fluttered, and he dropped the fist to his side.

"Sure, I guess. I mean, the Reds got the north."

"You lost?" Pearse asked.

Ed lifted his cigarette to his mouth, scratching his head.

"You didn't win?" Pearse asked.

"Well, at least I got this out of it," Ed replied, going once more to the bookshelf. He pulled down a pamphlet that was six pages long, stapled. It was written in typescript and entitled *Blues in My Seoul*. The corners curved back, smudged.

Pearse looked at the cover, then up at Ed.

"It's my first book," Ed said.

Pearse shrugged, handing it back to him.

"Look here, Pearse," Ed said. "You may not think so, but poetry is dynamite."

"You like it that much?"

"What do you mean?"

"Well, I think that swimming at the Crystal Plunge with my brother is dynamite. But not poetry."

"Pearse, I mean it can cause revolutions! It can bring down governments!" Ed reached for the sheet of paper in his typewriter. Pulling it out, he held it before him. "Like this one. It's my new one, and it's about the atomic bomb. You know, they just fired one off last week. You want to hear it?"

"OK."

"See, it's things like this, Pearse," Ed continued, tapping a finger against the sheet of paper, "that'll bring an end to wars and starvation and all that." His voice grew congested as he spoke, and he coughed to clear it. Finally he began reciting.

Pearse made out a few phrases, like "the end of the angel-studded world," delivered with ponderous resonance. And something about eternal atomic nights and the death of the hipster. Debbie Mariano had told him what a hipster was. "Something like a beatnik, I guess," she had said. But there were no rhymes at all, and especially with Ed's spirited reading, Pearse was rather frightened by the poem. Ed's free hand formed the shape of the mushroom cloud. It was an expert gesture, perfect in conveying Ed's descriptions of individual deaths, terrifying Pearse as the poet moved on to the millions killed in such a holocaust.

Ed shouted the poem. He stood planted in the center of the room, the paper quivering in his clenched hand. He raised a fist and thrust it forward at the beginning of each of the litany of acrid phrases. Ed's chest and arms appeared colossal to Pearse, who wanted him to stop halfway through. But Pearse remained quiet, trying, finally, just not to listen. After a stentorian crescendo, during which Ed crushed the paper between his fingers and proclaimed against the government in Washington, he grew silent and rested against the edge of the table. There was heavy quiet for several moments.

"That's all I've got so far," Ed said after a while. "But it'll be done in a couple days. It's got to be done, because I'm going to read it next Saturday at the Trieste."

"Out loud?"

"Of course!" Ed replied. "It happens every Saturday. You want to come?"

Pearse lowered his head, chagrined by the impossibility of joining Ed at the café.

"I mean, did you . . . did you like the poem?" Ed asked.

Pearse could not answer. Words scattered in his mind, and he swallowed, trying to find something to say.

"I guess maybe you didn't get it," Ed concluded. He sat down at the table. He kept his head lowered for a moment. "Look, there's one thing that you have to remember in poetry, Pearse," he said. "There's only one thing that matters."

"Whether it rhymes?" Pearse asked.

"No. Whether it's the truth!"

Pearse leaned on the table. "But how do you know?" he asked.

Ed raised a finger before his face.

"I think you can always tell when you're being taken for a ride. Right?" he asked.

"Yeah, I guess."

"Like when someone says things that make you feel good, but only for a while, before they start making you feel bad. Or when you're told to go into battle and you realize, the minute you're climbing up out of the trench, that you've been fucked again, right?"

Pearse grew hot with embarrassment.

"I mean, you know when someone's lying to you." Ed stood and walked to one of the bookshelves. "Like those turkeys in Washington. Eisenhower and Nixon? Now, you know they're lying to us."

"The president wouldn't lie," Pearse said.

"Listen to this," Ed said, paying no attention. He took one of the books from the shelf and opened it. "*This* is the truth, Pearse." He stood before the boy and cleared his throat. "It's by a guy named Corso. It goes, 'Ah tower from thy berryless head I'd a vision in common with myself the proximity of Alcatraz and not the hip volley of white jazz & verse . . .' "

Ed's hand rose up before him, and he took an enthused breath. Pearse didn't get it.

" 'Or verse and jazz embraced but a real heart-rending constant vision of Alcatraz marshalled before my eyes . . .' "

Pearse kept quiet. This stuff was dumb. Ed closed the book with a gesture of respectful quiet. To Pearse, he looked like one of the kids at the communion rail, after having taken the Host.

Slowly, Ed looked down at Pearse and seemed to sense the boy's confusion. "It's a description of Coit Tower," he said.

"Coit Tower!"

"See, Pearse, truth like *this* truth is the only thing that matters. The truth! You know what that is?"

"Sure. The truth is just . . ."

"It's the truth!"

"Yeah, I guess."

"And you know how it is that poetry's the truth?"

Pearse shook his head, and Ed replaced the book on the shelf.

"Look," he said. "In the Middle Ages, a long, long time ago, people used to go on pilgrimages. You know what those are?"

"Like the *Mayflower*."

"Yes . . . yes. And sometimes they went on pilgrimage to a big church or cathedral, like at Canterbury, in England."

"Why?"

"To visit the place. To pray to the memory of Thomas à Becket. That kind of thing. But in those days, the cathedral was surrounded by all kinds of narrow alleys, dark, with candlelight and mud and rain. The alleys were filled with shops. There were bars, cafés. It was fun!"

"I bet."

"It was dangerous, too. Thrilling! And, sometimes," Ed continued, wiping his lips, "a lot of times, the pilgrims went on the pilgrimage for those things, rather than for the cathedral."

Pearse nodded.

"And I see the truth as all of that, put together. The grime, the dirt, and the mess . . ." Ed looked at the floor, lost in his description. "Whores and porter and all the smoke and the shit, all of it. And out of the center rises the cathedral, big and muscular with stone, rising up to the glory of God's might." Ed raised his hands before him. "And that's poetry, Pearse. All of it, gathered together at the tip of the highest point, all the sickness and filth, the dust on the saints' statues, the thievery, the cobwebbed gold on the altars, the buttresses, the grace of God, all of it. It's poetry. It's art. It's the truth.''

During the rising heat of the description, Pearse's head tilted backward as his eyes followed Ed's hands. Pearse felt washed away by the beatnik's certainty. He could not understand the description, but Ed's voice commanded him with its fervor. Pearse did not speak. Finally he stood and moved toward the door.

"I guess I should go," he said, overwhelmed.

Pulled from his distraction, Ed turned about. "But where are you headed, so soon?''

"Home. I think I should go home.''

"Monsignor?''

"Yes?''

"This is Joe Pearse.''

There was a pause. Monsignor had the habit, shared by many clerics, of not remembering names well. Whenever Joe phoned him, a moment followed during which Monsignor had to recall who he was.

"Joe! How are you?''

"Fine, thanks. Listen, I'm not going to be able to make it out to the golf course this morning.''

"Why not?''

"I'm involved in something at the office and I've got to go in for a couple of hours for a meeting.''

Another thing about Monsignor was that he took badly to changes of plan. Now he would have to go out to the Lincoln Park golf course with MJ alone, which meant that they would have to play the round with another twosome. To add just a single fourth player would be more acceptable to the priest because Joe, Monsignor, and MJ would be an intact group, while the fourth would be a grateful, cooperative appendage. Now, though, Monsignor would have to contend with two strangers. And they might be as good as, say, Ben Hogan.

"You can't make our tee-off time?'' Monsignor asked.

"No. Sorry.''

"You can't . . . can't change your appointment?''

"No,'' Joe replied. "See, my client and I have had some, well, reversals in a case he's hired me for, and he's in terrible shape. I've got to help him. I can fill you in on it later.''

"Oh.''

Joe tapped his fingers on the table.

"MJ will pick me up?" Monsignor asked.

"Right. Just as we'd planned."

Joe felt bad about breaking the appointment. The golf game was a monthly event, and he enjoyed playing with his father and Monsignor. Besides, Joe had looked forward to this particular match as a way of starting a reconciliation with MJ. At first Joe had resolved not to approach his father at all, feeling insulted by MJ's refusal to tell the truth about Emmett Day. Though it was not the truth that mattered so much, since Joe thought he knew what that was. But once again, as many times before, MJ had not paid his own son the compliment of trusting him.

Since the argument with Mimi, though, Joe's resolve had wavered, a process helped by the memory of the conversation he had had with Day at the train station. Day's observation—about murder and patriotism—had made Joe feel compromised and sleazy. So now he felt he had to talk with MJ once more.

But Tom Carrington had disappeared, failing to show up at the immigration hearing appeal that had been scheduled the previous week. It had taken Joe several days to track Carrington down, and even now he did not know where he was living. But he had gotten a message that Carrington would come to his office on Saturday morning, and Joe did not want to miss him. Carrington had obviously panicked, convinced the extradition was now certain to take place. Joe wanted to do what he could to calm Carrington down. Hiding from the hearings would only hasten their final outcome.

Joe walked down Columbus toward the financial district. The offices of Murphy, Tomlinson were in a yellow brick building next door to Harrington's Bar on Front Street. As Joe mounted the stairs to the second floor, he considered Emmett Day's advice, that he tell MJ what a hero he had been. The distaste Joe had felt watching the train leave the station had become palpable during the days since. Day's explanation of the murder had been altogether breezy, Joe thought, with its casual forgetfulness of what had really happened. Doing the Republic of Ireland a service? Jesus, Joe thought, what heartlessness!

He took a moment to dust the photos of Mimi, Tim, and Pearse on the table behind his desk, then straightened the papers that had accumulated the afternoon before in preparation for this meeting. The frosted glass door to the office—with the intensity of his name, "Joe Pearse, Esquire," in gilt lettering on the outside—let in some light from the hall, and Joe raised the venetian blinds to reveal the street below. Mimi had helped him decorate, buying some framed original prints of sailing ships and a map of San Francisco that had been made in 1847, showing the anchorage at South Beach. It was as much an illustration as a map, depicting Rincon Hill, its few clapboard buildings, and a wharf, all hand watercolored, a village unaffected by the explosion of the gold rush that would come two years later.

Joe's office decor was similar to that of other attorneys' offices. It contained an air of conservatism and place, so that the illustration of South Beach looked like an illustration of Nantucket or maybe Back Bay. Joe knew that such decor made his clients feel comfortable, as though they were in the office of a kindly ship's chandler. This had always amused Joe, since, as far as he was concerned, the practice of law and, specifically, the winning of cases was a matter of whim and heat. Certainly there was research to be done at every turn—the *California Appellate Review*, after all, and all its crippled language. But juries were swayed by pity and shock, or at least the seeming shock expressed by attorneys presenting their case. And that was what Joe so loved about practicing law—that it put aside, finally, the endless qualifications of the law books. The Law was much more like the city that had grown beyond South Beach, with its conglomeration of dumpy neighborhoods and passions, the acrimony of city politics, and the constant, disorderly dockside strife.

There was a knock at the door. Through the glass, Joe saw a hat worn at an angle, a gray suit and a gray tie. He swung the door open and greeted Tom Carrington, though he barely recognized him. Carrington was so surprisingly well dressed that his appearance took on the nature of a disguise. His previously disheveled appearance was now neatened by a crewcut. Carrington looked like an American businessman. Joe smiled. A haberdasher, maybe. The only things that gave away how he really made his living were his hands, which were cut here and there and scraped. His eyes moved from Joe's face to the office behind him. He walked in and tossed the hat onto the rack behind Joe's door.

"Listen, thanks for searching me out, Joe."

"Sure. But what's . . ."

Carrington moved to the desk. "I can't stay long."

"What's the problem, Tom? Where were you the other day?"

Carrington sat down in the chair across Joe's desk. He looked down to the side. One toe tapped against the rug beneath the chair. "It's just that I can't keep going like this, Joe," he muttered.

"Of course not. It's not easy," Joe nodded. "But Tom, you've got to."

He went to his own chair and sat down. He took up a pencil and moved to speak once more. But Carrington seemed unable to look at him. His shoulders appeared thin and wasted, as though they could barely hold up the jacket he wore.

"They *will* put you away," Joe said finally, "if you refuse to come to the hearings. The law does not look kindly on that. But I've gotten them to agree to another hearing next Tuesday, at three."

"I can't." Carrington gestured with his hands, a kind of fevered shrug. "I can't do it again."

Carrington slouched in the chair, joining his hands. The dejection that appeared in his eyes was so complete that Joe laid the pencil on his desk and waited.

"They're after me all the time, Joe," Carrington said. "Always trying to put me away, and fellows like me. I'm tired of it!"

"I imagine you are," Joe replied. He waited again, looking for the flicker of humor that more usually accompanied Carrington's complaints about his troubles.

"I mean you've done so much to try to help me," Carrington said. He pointed at the table that ran the length of one wall of Joe's office. It was covered, neatly, with briefs, depositions, and correspondence, all relating to Carrington's battle with the immigration service.

"Is that what a revolution is supposed to be?" Carrington sighed. "All that paper? This nice, oak-lined office? Is this it?"

"In this country it is, if you want to win."

Carrington waved a hand, shaking his head. "Well, I think it's better yelling at the bastards from the barricades and bashing a couple heads. That's what wins revolutions, Joe."

Joe recalled the photos he had seen of the British army escorting Padraic Pearse and the others from the Dublin Post Office in 1916, just prior to their executions. They had yelled from the barricades.

"All this paper . . ." Carrington joined his hands once more and shrugged.

"But, you're alive," Joe said.

"What's that got to do with it?"

"A lot of people are killed in Ireland every year."

"Jesus, don't I know that?"

"And now we're able to use a set of laws . . . laws that were intended to order society . . . we're able to use those laws to keep you out of the slammer. Imagine that! There's a revolution right there."

"But I wonder if it's worth the effort."

Carrington stood, went to the rack to retrieve his hat, and placed it on his head. He adjusted the hat, to the same angle it had had when he had entered the office. Buttoning his coat, he turned toward the door.

"Because no government ever gives up, Joe. In Ireland we know that. Sure, I'm alive. But I get tired of having to run to you for help all the time. Very tired."

Carrington opened the door and stepped out into the hallway.

"That's not to say that I don't appreciate what you do for me," he said. "You've kept me going, you know."

Because Carrington was so thin and his face so small, his nose appeared to jut from it, like a monument. The tightness of his skin gave him the look of a lean boy in a movie from the thirties, hawking papers on Times Square.

"Without you," he continued, "I'd pretty much be doing time, and all just because the poor Irish want the rights God gave them."

He looked down the hall toward the elevator.

"Sure it's a pain in the arse, Joe."

Joe stepped into the hallway and took Carrington's hand.

"How come you've never been to Ireland?" Carrington asked.

"I'll go," Joe replied. "One of these days."

Carrington shrugged. "You can't fight the revolution eight thousand miles away, you know. If you're going to put up a fight about something, you've got to be right there, right now." He grinned. "That's what those poor fellows in Belfast do, dressed for the winter in their blankets."

Carrington's shoulders shivered as he hunched over, chuckling, in imitation of a man shaking with cold.

"Look what it gets them," he said. He turned up the hallway and waved to Joe as he proceeded toward the elevator.

"But will you be at the hearing?" Joe said.

Carrington paused. The elevator door opened and, for a moment, Joe feared that this was the last time he would ever see the Irishman.

"Tom, I can't advise you to break the law," Joe said. "The fact is, if you don't show, I can't help you. I won't help you."

For a moment, he thought how such a remark would please MJ. At last, Joe, a refusal to help the Fenian murderers. But now Joe realized why that would be so important to his father. The trouble was, there was a kind of personal settlement that Joe felt he had to make with these men. *My father may think I'm a fool. But, Jesus, I've got an obligation to help them.*

"All right, for God's sake, I'll be there." Carrington entered the elevator and the door closed behind him.

Joe left the folder on his desk, then descended the stairs and went out into Front Street.

The bright air seemed to etch the few clouds from their blue backdrop. There was little activity downtown, and Joe walked quickly toward Kearny Street, enjoying the solitude of the empty buildings, the light, the sense of clarity given to everything by the exceptional morning.

He walked up the hill to Broadway and Columbus, where he could see the two spires of Saints Peter and Paul above the buildings in the distance. Passing Molinari's Delicatessen, he paused a moment to look at the display in the window, a collection of tins of olive oil from Italy. Each had a profuse drawing of a country scene, young boys escorting milkmaids through the olive groves, that kind of thing, enjoying a tête-à-tête beneath a brocaded arbor. Turning away, Joe glanced across Columbus Street at Biordi's Italian Ceramics. He wanted to pick up the platter that Mimi was hoping for, for her birthday. He waited at the corner for the signal light, enjoying the warmth of the sun on his face. This would be the last such warmth for a while, as autumn progressed into winter. The sun weakened even as he waited for the light to change, cooled by a breeze from the bay. He crossed the street and stopped to look in Biordi's window.

There was a movement to his right, a black suit, a splotch of white hair.

"Oh, hello, Joe."

"Monsignor!"

"Yes, I . . ."

"Didn't you go to the golf course?"

Monsignor's head moved back and forth, a slow-moving flag. "I thought we could wait for another day," he said. "Keep things as they should be."

"So you called my father?"

"Yes. And that was OK with him."

For a moment, Joe felt the possibility of an insult.

"He said he'd miss seeing you," Monsignor continued. He

looked into the window of the shop and surveyed the platters, his hands joined behind his back. "Said he hasn't seen you in a while, that maybe we could do it next week."

Next door to Biordi's there was a transient hotel, the front door of which suddenly opened. Buttoning his coat, busy and distracted, a boy stepped out onto the sidewalk.

"Pearse!" Joe said.

Pearse's face reddened and took on the look of trapped guilt that Joe had seen frequently during the last few weeks. His fingers dropped from the coat buttons. It was boyish trapped guilt, of course, and thus contained the wish to run away as fast as possible. Joe thought of the day MJ had discovered a copy of the *Police Gazette* beneath his mattress, when Joe was fourteen. MJ had waved the magazine angrily before his face.

"Why do you have to read such things?" he had said. The woman on the cover, wearing a torn slip, undulated before Joe. MJ's voice was so downtrodden with disappointment that Joe felt he must have, at that moment, opened the door through which he would pass without ceremony into hell.

"I'm sorry, Dad," Joe remembered replying. "I won't do it again!"

"Gee, Dad," Pearse muttered. "Hi."

"What are you doing here?" Joe asked.

"Hi, Monsignor," Pearse said.

"Good morning, young man."

Joe pointed at the door to the hotel. "I mean, in this dump," he said.

Pearse's breath fluttered. "Oh, uh, nothing. Just hanging around."

"Is that the truth?" Joe faced the boy. The door behind Pearse opened, and Pearse looked quickly into the window of Biordi's. A young man stepped out onto the sidewalk behind Pearse, a man whose voice swirled about Joe and the boy—a young voice, strong and clear.

"Who's this, Pearse? Your dad?" it said.

Pearse tightened into a small, hunched pillar.

"Good morning." Ed put the cigarette in his mouth. His eyes squinted from the smoke.

Joe recognized him right away.

"I'm Ed Finney. I'm a friend of Pearse's."

Ed removed the cigarette and dropped it to the pavement, stamping it out with his shoe. Incredulous, Joe surveyed the action. Pearse winced.

"What do you say?" Ed asked.

Getting no response, he glanced briefly at Monsignor. But really he paid little attention to the priest, and his eyes took on a contemptuous-seeming darkness as he turned again toward Joe.

To Pearse's astonishment, his father did not bludgeon him after Pearse pulled him away from the conversation with Ed. Of course, Joe criticized Pearse, and the conversation ended in mutual exasperation on the front steps of their flat.

"Why do you think you're already grounded, Pearse?" Joe asked.

"I guess it's 'cause . . ."

"Can't you use a little sense?"

"But Dad!"

"No 'buts.' "

"But Dad!"

Resentful, embarrassed, feeling betrayed by his own stupidity, Pearse yet decided that he had to see Ed read his rhymes at the Trieste. But he thought he had better get some support from someone who had a little more authority than he, who might be able to stand up for him if he got caught again. So he asked MJ—in secret—to take him there.

"I'm not so sure we should, Pearse," MJ said. "Your dad, you know."

"Yeah. He *always* catches me. I always get caught doing stuff."

MJ put a hand to his lips as he laughed. "It just looks that way. You're a kid, Pearse! So it appears you get nabbed no matter what you do. But really, that has more to do with being a child and less with being guilty of anything."

MJ's advice made no sense to Pearse, but he pressed on. "We could go to the Trieste on The Tour, couldn't we?" he asked. "Just pretend we're going up to the Liguria Bakery or something? See, we'd pass by the place. You know, go in kind of by mistake."

MJ listened, but Pearse felt he would not get agreement. "There's something happening that'll be fun, too," Pearse added.

"What's that?"

"You know my friend Ed?"

Troubled, MJ nodded.

"He says there's going to be . . . it's going to be kind of like a speech, in class. They do it at the Trieste every Saturday afternoon.''

"A class?''

"Yeah. They recite stuff. You know, like I have to do in catechism.''

"What stuff?'' MJ asked.

"It's kind of like a show, I guess.''

"Other beatniks, you mean?''

"I guess so,'' Pearse replied.

MJ shook his head. "Not quite my crowd, Pearse.'' He reached into the breast pocket of his coat and took out a cigar. "I don't know much about all that.''

"Maybe we could just go and stand outside the window, though.''

Pearse attempted nonchalance, though really he ached with the wish that his grandfather would agree. To Pearse's delight, MJ lit the cigar after a moment, and seemed to indicate that he would think about it. It was not an actual reply. Rather, it was a foggy indication of something that was, maybe, possible. Pearse guessed . . . Pearse hoped that MJ had agreed to the idea, and that he was just engaging in the kind of care that would be necessary to pull the thing off.

"Here's your lunch, Pearse,'' Mimi said the following Saturday morning. "I've made a ham and cheese sandwich for each of you.''

"With pickles on mine, Mom?''

"That's right. And a thermos of fruit juice. But I didn't put in any cookies.''

"You didn't?''

"No. Because your grandfather told me he was taking you to Blum's for desert.''

Pearse accepted the paper bag from his mother.

"And I think . . . I mean, I'm not sure, but I think your father's going to pick you up afterwards,'' Mimi said. "He's got something going on with Monsignor this afternoon. In any case, your grandfather says he's going to take you first to Coit Tower, to look at the view.''

Pearse sensed MJ's deception of Mimi.

"Then down the Filbert Steps to the wharf.'' Mimi looked out the kitchen window at the sky.

Clutching his secret within him, Pearse paused a moment to enjoy the view with his mother.

Indeed, there were very high white clouds, bunched up like

serene haystacks over the bay. The fall air brightened everything, making even the frames around the windows of the dingy
buildings appear new and freshly painted.

Pearse breathed easily once he saw that MJ had no intention
at all of going to Coit Tower. MJ continued straight down Columbus, passing by Washington Square entirely. That meant he
had another plan. But as they proceeded, MJ became preoccupied with the small stores and coffee houses on Columbus. He
did not even mention the Trieste, and Pearse impatiently groused
as his grandfather chatted for fifteen minutes with Mr. Azzolini,
who ran a tiny knife-sharpening store next to the Portofino Café.
Finally they continued down Columbus toward the corner of
Vallejo Street.

"What do you say we go into Saint Francis's, here?" MJ
asked. He pointed up at the doorway to the church. "There
might be a bazaar or something."

Pearse, shuddering as he recalled the battle with the priest on
the steps of that church, shook his head. Also he had the idea
that MJ was fooling around with him, making fun of his anxiety.
He followed MJ toward the front door of the Trieste, where a
group of beatniks stood about. MJ, as usual, was dressed in a
suit and tie. Because of the cool morning, he had brought along
a camel's-hair overcoat. His elegance caught the attention of the
beatniks, who wore old black T-shirts and black slacks, unkempt skirts, black sweaters and stockings.

Pearse reached into the pocket of his jacket and pulled out his
beret. He placed it on his head at an angle.

"Grandpa," he called.

MJ turned to look, and frowned in reply. But he reached for
Pearse's shoulder and pushed him toward the door.

There were about a hundred people inside. The café smelled
of cigarette smoke laced with coffee. An inversion layer had
formed about halfway up the wall, so that the cloud of smoke
flattened out just above the level of the phone booth. Beatniks
gestured at one another in the gloom.

Pearse led MJ toward a small table next to the phone booth.
"Let's sit here," he said, placing his lunch bag on the table.
Pearse noticed that MJ had stiffened, and that he kept his eyes
directly ahead, so that Pearse worried that he already wanted to
leave. But as MJ sat down, he removed his hat and placed it on
his lap. He snuck a glance at a woman at the next table. Her
legs were wrapped about one another as she leaned far over the
tabletop, resting her head on one hand. She was listening to a

man read out loud from a book. The cigarette in her hand—
Pearse noted, rather assuredly, that it was not a Gauloise—sent
a gauzy line of smoke past her ear.

"Grandpa, would you like something to drink?"

"Hm? Oh. A cup of Lipton's. Do they have that here?" MJ
asked.

"I think so."

"I'll have that. A little milk, too, please."

Pearse remained standing beside the table as MJ ventured
another look about the room. After a moment, Pearse tapped
MJ's knee.

"May I have some money?" he asked.

"Oh, excuse me. Yes," MJ replied. He unbuttoned his overcoat and reached into his breast pocket for his wallet. He pulled
out two dollars.

Pearse went to the counter and ordered a cup of Lipton's tea
for MJ and an espresso for himself. He looked back toward his
grandfather. MJ looked like a kind of private tableau, an emblem of warm, elderly politesse surrounded by noisy gesticula-
tion.

"Here you are, kid," the counterman said, and Pearse handed
him the money. Getting his change, he picked up the drinks and
turned again toward his grandfather. MJ was still seated, his
overcoat slouched over the back of the chair. Pearse halted
abruptly, the drinks slopping over into their saucers.

Ed stood before MJ, talking rapidly and grabbing the old
man's hand.

MJ appeared stricken. His head was pressed against the wall
behind him. Clearly, he was listening to Ed. Indeed, there was
no way Ed could be avoided, as he pulled a book from his coat
pocket. Holding it out before MJ, he pointed at the cover, his
lips moving rapidly in an insistent description of something. MJ
sat still, his hat in his hand.

"Hi," Pearse said as he placed the tea and the expresso on
the table.

"Pearse!" Ed clapped the boy on the shoulder. He had not
shaved in a few days, and he appeared wildly nuts. His hair flew
about. The pupils of his eyes were isolated in the surrounding
white, and they seemed to jitter.

"I was just telling your grandfather here . . ."

"How'd you know he's my grandpa?" Pearse asked.

"I saw you walk in with him." The book remained, shaking,
in Ed's hand. "And then I asked him, see?"

"Oh."

"And I think it's terrific you came out to see me read," Ed continued. "Actually, I'm a little nervous about it."

"What is this going to be, though, son?" MJ asked. "Pearse told me that a lot of you . . . beatniks? . . ."

Ed shrugged, assenting.

"That you beatniks are going to recite?"

"Yeah, that's it. Poetry!"

"By who? By Shakespeare or someone?"

Ed took the book between the fingers of both hands. He appeared not to have understood MJ's question.

"Shakespeare?" he asked.

"Yes."

"No, man. We're going to read our own stuff."

"Your own?"

"Yeah. We . . ."

"OK, everybody." A tall, sandy-haired man, wearing horn-rimmed sunglasses, spoke into the microphone that stood before the jukebox. His T-shirt was rolled up at the sleeves. "So, Michael McClure's going to read," he said, "and Allen, of course."

There was applause as the announcer indicated two men standing by the jukebox. One was blond and looked like a teenager. The other was willowy-limbed and dark, clean-shaven, with the thickest glasses Pearse had ever seen.

"And we're going to start with another poet everyone here knows, Ed Finney, who's going to read from his new manuscript, *The Ecstatic*, which will be out next spring from Seaweed Press."

Several patrons whistled, to the accompaniment of applause.

"You ready, Ed?"

Ed nodded and walked to another table, where a folder lay open, revealing many pieces of paper on which he had evidently been writing before Pearse and MJ had arrived. There was more applause. The loudest clapping came from Pearse.

Ed took the microphone.

"Yeah, I want to start with . . . with . . ." He could not find the piece for which he was searching.

There was brief talk among the audience.

"It's a little something about the atomic bomb," Ed said finally.

This time, Pearse did not listen to the words. Rather, he concentrated on Ed's delivery. Ed stalked about the open floor. His voice was more vibrant than it had been in his room at the Hotel Dante, and there was a sense that he was carried away by the words. Ed was upset by the atomic bomb, that much was clear. But he apparently thought he could change things just by yelling at the source of his discouragement. His face changed from rage to saddened humor and back, up and down, his eyes flitting about through the entire recitation. His voice surged and grumbled. He menaced the audience.

When he finished the poem, Ed received quite loud applause. He read several more pieces, and Pearse noticed how silent the audience became as he made his way through them. Everybody seemed to respect Ed. Indeed, Pearse wondered if there had ever been a priest like him, though he figured Ed was maybe too young to be a priest. But he recalled Monsignor's sermons, delivered in a strong-willed monotone, in which hell, sin, and heaven were all described with the enthusiasm of a bored tree. What would it be like if Ed gave a sermon? Pearse wondered. He imagined the wreckage on the altar, the flowers tossed about, the clenched fist.

When Ed's reading ended, the announcer told everyone there would be a break of several minutes. Ed made his way toward Pearse and MJ, interrupted by patrons clapping him on the back and shaking his hand. He was sweating. When he reached the table, he laid the manuscript down on the open folder and took a chair next to Pearse. Gratified by the attention Ed paid him, Pearse forgot about his grandfather.

After a moment, though, he glanced toward MJ. The old man sipped his tea with single, noisy slurps. He looked across the table at Ed, who was being congratulated again by one of the audience. Ed turned back to the table, flushed with pleasure.

"So, what'd you think?" he asked, looking toward MJ.

A long silence ensued. Worried, Pearse hoped for some favorable reply from his grandfather.

"Fact is," MJ said, finally, "the fact is, son, I didn't understand a word."

Pearse groaned, stung with embarrassment. He had forgotten, for the moment, that he had not understood any of it either.

"But, I'll tell you," MJ continued. "I'm not so sure I have to understand."

Pearse fingered his expresso cup.

"It's what you feel that matters, I guess, isn't it?" MJ asked. "That's the important thing. So, if it comes out in a muddle . . ."

Smiling, he cocked his head and shrugged, a sort of apology. "That really doesn't matter."

Pearse did not understand.

"I mean, it's obvious that there's heart in what you write. A full heart. That's clear."

"Thanks," Ed muttered.

"Clear as day, if you ask me," MJ continued.

Ed began shaking his head as he took a Gauloise from his coat pocket.

"Doesn't that make sense, Mr. Finney?" MJ asked.

During the long silence, as Ed fiddled with the matches, Pearse's embarrassment grew even more. He saw that his grandfather was still struggling for an explanation. Finally, Ed lit a match and held it, burning, a few inches in front of the cigarette he had taken between his lips.

"It's not an insult?" MJ asked.

Ed fixed MJ with a surly smile. "Hell, no!" He lit the Gauloise. "A lot of people don't get poetry at all. Or at least, my poetry. It's surprising how few poets, even . . ."

He tossed the match in an ashtray, then leaned close, looking around the room and lowering his voice.

"How few of these poets understand what you realized after listening to only a few minutes of, uh . . ." He tapped the manuscript with an index finger. "Of this crap."

He took a drag from his cigarette.

"Even though I think it's pretty terrific crap."

Abruptly, he pushed the pack toward MJ.

"Sorry, I didn't mean to be rude," he said.

"No, not at all," MJ replied. "I don't smoke cigarettes. Not strong enough for me."

"But Grandpa," Pearse interjected. "Have you ever had one of these?"

MJ looked down his shoulder at Pearse. "No, Pearse. Have you?"

Ed broke into barking laughter.

"No!" Pearse adjusted his beret. "Course not."

"Try one," Ed said to MJ. "Pearse has a point."

MJ reached across the table and took one of the Gauloises. Pearse picked up Ed's packet of matches and lit the cigarette for MJ, who removed it from his lips as he inhaled the smoke.

"Not bad," he observed.

"Pearse told me you're Irish," Ed said.

"That's right."

Ed nodded. "My grandmother was from Mayo," he said. "Little place called Corraun, on Clew Bay."

"I don't know it," MJ replied, sipping his tea.

"Me neither," Ed concluded. "Never been to Ireland at all. One hell of a lot of poets there, of course."

MJ agreed.

"And it's you who gets that paper Pearse showed me? The *Irish* something-or-other. What is it, Pearse? *The Wild Irishman*?"

"*United Irishmen,*" Pearse said.

MJ let his fingers lie along the edge of the saucer. "No, that's my son who takes that paper. Pearse's father. I don't . . ."

"How do you like that?" Ed replied. He turned toward Pearse, a congratulatory tap of the finger on the table sealing the moment. "Terrific, isn't it, Pearse, that there are people here in this country willing to rub the English nose in the shit they've left to the Irish?"

The authoritative speed with which Ed delivered his opinion, and the bite that the swear word gave it, thrilled Pearse. He nodded his head, giggling.

MJ sniffed, shaking his head. "I had some personal experience of all that, though."

"In Ireland?"

"Yes."

"You mean with the IRA?"

"It was long ago, Mr. Finney, before the Army."

"You mean, we've got a whole family of revolutionaries here?"

"No, no."

"It's no wonder Pearse likes to come to the Trieste," Ed moved on. "Here his grandfather understands matters of the heart, and he fought with the goddamned Irish Republican Army!"

"Listen, Mr. Finney . . ."

"*And* he's got a son himself who carries on the cause."

Unable to quash Ed's rising fervor, MJ tapped his finger abruptly on the tabletop. "Damn it, you're too young to know about any of that."

"Friggin' Limeys."

"No. No. We have a difference of opinion, here."

"Spill blood anywhere they damned please!" Ed gestured with disgust.

"Mr. Finney. You can't just embrace somebody like the Irish Republican Army!"

Pearse turned his head from side to side, trying to understand how it was that Ed and his grandfather had so quickly started arguing.

"Why the hell not?" Ed said. "Aren't they defending the interests of the people? Aren't they the ones taking the fight to the rummy English oppressor?"

The patrons at the next table interrupted their conversation to watch Ed. MJ's face began to redden. Pearse, powerless to stop the argument, sat back in his chair and glowered. He reached up and removed the beret from his head.

"Mr. Finney, I have seen what they can do," MJ said. "Both sides. But especially I have seen what the Irish can do."

Pearse's mouth twitched as he listened to his grandfather. MJ had taken up his hat, and now crumpled the brim between his fingers.

"Like what?" Ed asked.

MJ lowered his head, refusing to answer.

"I imagine they complain about political oppression," Ed said, answering his own question. "I mean, isn't that what the Irish talk about?" Wrinkles formed about his mouth as he spoke. He raised a finger in the air. "They strike out at the subjugation of innocent peoples, right?"

"Nothing as foolish-sounding as that," MJ replied.

"Then what are you talking about?"

"Killing!" MJ said.

Pearse gripped his beret. He leaned forward, uncertain of what he had just heard. MJ appeared lost in anger, and his eyes savaged the table before him as he searched for more to say. His cheeks were sunken and very florid. His eyes were what surprised Pearse the most. MJ, usually a temperate man, now glared at Ed as though he wanted the young man jailed. A few more patrons turned from their own conversations to listen.

"Don't you know? . . . ." MJ asked, with sharp bitterness. "Have you ever seen what happens in a war? Especially a civil war?"

Suddenly, Pearse wanted to run from the Trieste. He knew that Ed would reply with a loud retelling of the Inchon invasion, and how the Seventh Infantry had saved the day against the marauding Chinese.

But Ed's answer did not come. Instead, he seemed as surprised by MJ's outburst as was Pearse. Smoke rose from the cigarette in his hand.

"No one should ever be murdered . . ." MJ said. His voice quavered. He glared at the floor. "People talk so carelessly about revolutions, Mr. Finney. They talk as though there were nothing to them. Have a revolution! Nothing to it. And we'll come back to this dingy café for a coffee afterwards. Bodies in a ditch? Fresh with blood? Old men left without their children? What does it matter? We have our self-assurances. We have our . . ." MJ pointed toward Pearse's coffee. "What is that stuff called, Pearse?"

"Expresso," Pearse groaned.

"That's right. We have our expresso, and everybody else gets the wreckage. But I've actually seen that, Mr. Finney." MJ touched his eyelids. "With these eyes, at a range of a few feet, and I know that the only revolution worth a damn is this one."

He lowered his hand to his chest.

"This one. The one in here."

He stood, and the patrons at the adjoining tables whispered with one another as MJ took up his coat.

"And I don't see any reason to stay here. Pearse, I'm afraid I have to leave."

For a moment, Pearse could not move.

"Are you coming with me?" MJ asked.

Images swirled through the boy's head, of murder, of fire, of his grandfather at war. He could not imagine what had happened to MJ.

Placing his hat on his head, MJ moved through the crowd.

Pearse put his beret back on. He slipped into his jacket and buttoned it. He took the lunch bag into his hand.

"I gotta go, Ed." He stood and hurried from the table.

"Pearse!"

The boy looked over his shoulder. Ed, his cigarette hanging from his lips, gathered his manuscript together. Stray pieces of paper fell to the floor, and Ed genuflected to pick them up. He clutched the folder to his chest. Corners of paper stuck out at angles, as though excited by the ride they were to take.

"I'm coming with you," Ed said. He took the boy's shoulder and pushed him toward the door.

Pulling the door shut behind him, MJ walked a few steps down the street, then leaned against the front of the café. His overcoat, slung over one arm, slipped toward his hand. His shoulders and chest were covered with sweat. He rubbed his eyes, trying to expel from his mind the conversation that had so electrified him.

MJ could not bear what he had just told Pearse and Ed. He had so successfully put those things aside, for so many years, that their sudden rush from him had emptied his heart. Even Doll, to whom he had told a great deal before she died, had not caused in MJ such a painful need to explain himself. Neither had Joe. Neither, even, had Emmett Day himself. But what he had said to Ed, MJ realized, was what he had always wished to say, if only to obtain, finally, from someone, a moment's forgiveness. But Ed Finney didn't have any idea what I was talking about, MJ thought. The happiness he had found with Doll and his family—it disgusted MJ to know that, in a way, even that represented just an attempt to escape from his own memory. But you never escaped, he thought, as he turned his back to the building and looked up at the sun. The day you killed him, his chest sucking at the fresh rain . . . right there, you wasted your life.

The clatter and pain of his heart caused him, for the moment, to miss Doll terribly. If he could give his family happiness, MJ had believed, he could go on living. He could stand what he had done, as long as his family loved him.

"Grandpa!" Pearse ran up to MJ. He took the old man's hand.

Pearse's jacket was buttoned incorrectly, from haste, MJ guessed. He looked to the boy for sympathy, and could tell from the evident relief on Pearse's face that he must not look as bad as he felt.

"Mr. Pearse," Ed interjected. "I'm sorry. I didn't mean to cause you such pain."

"Christ! It wasn't you," MJ replied. He cursed himself for bringing Pearse to the Trieste at all. He had done it to defy Joe, he now realized. A petty thing. A childish thing. To get back at him for exposing the truth MJ had hidden so well for so long.

Ed scratched the back of his neck and looked out into the street. "I make assumptions all the time," he said. His mouth tightened, and he clutched his folder to his chest. "Assumptions that don't bear up . . . I mean, I put my foot in my mouth a lot."

MJ pulled Pearse close.

"I talk too much," Ed said. He looked with dismay at the

gum-strewn sidewalk. "I don't know a damned thing about the Irish."

Pearse's fingers clutched MJ's shirt. As MJ held the boy close, sunlight glinted from the café window. The buildings across the way were reflected, like shards of wood, in the glass. Pearse still wore the ridiculous beret that he hoped, MJ suspected, made him look like a bohemian. It was a bit of panache that amused MJ, and that he respected, because it was so guileless.

"I'm not angry, Pearse," MJ said. He stood and laid a hand on the side of the boy's head.

"Can we still go to Blum's?" Pearse asked.

MJ unbuttoned the boy's jacket and rebuttoned it correctly. "What, you want a piece of lemon crunch?"

Pearse looked away. He put his hands in the pockets of his jacket. "Yes."

Ed looked down at Pearse as well. The beatnik's ragged hair and the limp cigarette hanging from his lips made him appear eccentric and quite poor. I bet this guy's never had a job! MJ thought. And Pearse—worried that he had erred somehow and that he had to seek forgiveness from MJ—seemed to admire Ed for all that. MJ recalled for a moment his standing before Ed in the café, invoking the human heart. MJ knew it had not been for Ed that he had made his admission. It had been for Pearse—the boy losing his faith, in trouble with his father, the scattered boy.

"All right, let's go," MJ replied.

"And Ed can come, too?"

After his unintelligible poems, delivered in a wordy squall, MJ had assumed that Ed was just a firebrand, a spark. Obviously, though, he cared for Pearse, so that the discussion about the Irish Republican Army no longer mattered much to MJ.

"You want to come?" MJ asked.

Ed took the Gauloise from his lips and dropped it to the ground. Stamping it out, he tossed his scarf about his neck.

"Thanks," he said. "Yeah, I'd love to."

They rode the cable car out California Street. Pearse sat between the two men, on the long bench outside the car. Ed and his grandfather seemed to have hit it off, though Pearse could not have imagined, half an hour earlier, how that would happen. Ed was filled with questions about MJ, and MJ gestured and talked, offering slow observations that were pelted once more by Ed's inquiries. MJ's answers interested Pearse, because they had to do with when he was a very young man. For Pearse, before this day, MJ's past had been laid out in long reminiscences about "binness." The things of which he now spoke to Ed were new. All new.

"But what did you do for them?" Ed asked.

"Not much, at first. I was a shop clerk, that's all. And I had been to a couple of meetings, in Charleville, where I grew up. The Rising seemed to me a romantic thing. Throw off the English yoke. Ireland for the Irish."

"I can imagine," Ed muttered. "Goddamned Brits."

"But I was a fool, Ed."

Pearse watched some clouds pass behind the Pacific Union Club. The enormous, rust-hued mansion was about the same color as the Golden Gate Bridge. Pearse had decided that it must be some kind of apartment building for very old men, a few of whom tottered up the front stairs just now. Pearse's father often made fun of it. "You've got to be rich, approaching death, and Protestant to belong to it," he said. It was the most beautiful building Pearse had ever seen. It reminded him of Oz.

"I gather you witnessed some terrible things," Ed said.

Pearse leaned against his grandfather and listened.

"I saw a policeman murdered," MJ said.

"That's all?" Ed asked.

MJ put an arm around the boy. "But that's a heartless thing," he said. "It didn't matter that he was on the other side. I knew the man's father."

"How did it happen?"

"Some Republican men shot him down in a road. He was unarmed. Getting on his bicycle."

Pearse's heart began to flutter as MJ spoke. He snuggled closer to his grandfather, trying to envision the "pow!" of the pistol, the "krak!" and the spatter of flame.

"Why were you there, Grandpa?" Pearse asked.

MJ removed his hand from Pearse's shoulder. "I fingered him, Pearse. I led them to him."

"The man was Protestant?" Ed asked.

"No. He was a Catholic. You see, the Irish struggle was not as clean as one might wish. There were numbers of Catholics who didn't want a war with the English. Faithful to the Crown, and all that. There were Protestants who lived in peace with the Catholics, who let them live their lives. And even Protestants who led the fight against the British."

Ed shook his head.

"Oh, it's true, Ed. Charles Stewart Parnell himself, for God's sake. Yeats! That's one of the disconcerting things about a civil war."

Pearse took hold of the pole in front of him as the cable car began its descent of Nob Hill.

"You destroy families in civil wars. It's inevitable." MJ gathered the collar of his overcoat around his throat. A gust of wind blew up the hill, chilling everyone.

"But what about the potato famine?" Ed asked. "The English were responsible for that, weren't they? We've all read about it."

"Oh, there are times when the people have to rise up," MJ replied.

The cable car approached the corner of Polk Street, and MJ stood, taking Pearse's hand.

"But not in Ireland, Ed. Against Hitler, sure. Stalin. But the IRA—and those Protestants up in Ulster, too—they're so self-involved, they haven't noticed how bad it can get elsewhere."

The cable car came to a halt. The two men remained a moment on the running board, as MJ finished his thought.

"The truth is that the poor souls who survived Auschwitz must laugh at the Irish. And that's it . . . the trouble with the Irish is that they're blind," he said. "They should take a look around. See some of the far worse places that exist. Or at least take a look at each other. They've got the same weather to endure, you know, the Protestants and the Catholics. The same foul rain."

MJ helped Pearse from the car.

"They've got the same souls."

Watching for traffic, MJ and Ed followed Pearse toward the curb. Pearse led the way to Blum's. He ran the last several feet to the door, opening it and heading for three open stools at the counter.

"Hi, Pearse," Betty said. She was carrying a large chocolate sundae. "Your grandfather with you?"

"Yes, he's coming."

The door opened once more, and MJ walked in. Betty's teeth glimmered. The pink Blum's ribbon formed a windmill behind her head. Greeting MJ, she pointed to the counter stool next to Pearse's.

Just then, Ed entered the café. He shuffled along the counter behind MJ and Pearse. His beret remained on his head.

There was little conversation in the café, as the customers

addressed their bowls of peppermint ice cream and cherry-banana splits. Ed's appearance disrupted this silence. An air of surprised disapproval filled the room. A man at the counter turned from his sundae. The spoon in his hand dripped with chocolate.

"Here! Sir!" Betty placed her pencil in her hair and pointed at Ed.

Ed came to a halt. Like a slowly closing door, his head turned toward the waitress.

"See that sign?" Betty pointed above the mirror.

Pearse turned his head and began reading to himself. *We reserve the right . . .*

"Yeah, so what?" Ed said.

"Sir, we don't serve people like you."

"Betty," MJ interrupted, pointing at Ed. "This boy's with us." He hung his hat from the snap on the back of the stool and sat down. "He's a friend of ours. And I'm buying."

The pencil stuck out from Betty's hair like an arrow. "He's with you, Mr. Pearse?"

"Yes. And we'd all like a piece of lemon crunch, please."

A flood of relief burst through Pearse, and he settled on the counter stool next to his grandfather. Ed sat down also, though Pearse sensed an arousal of hostility in him, first at Betty, then, as Ed looked over his shoulder, at everyone else in Blum's.

Folding his hands, Ed leaned forward and addressed MJ.

"You know, we didn't chase the damned North Koreans back over the Parallel," he said, "just to get turned down in a dump like this."

Betty winced as she took up a knife to cut the cake.

"You fought in Korea?" MJ asked.

"Sure as hell did! And I'll eat a piece of cake with anyone in this room, because I *fought* for the right to be a goddamned anarchist."

A shocked buzz ground through the café.

"Ed," MJ responded. "These people are friends of mine."

"You *like* these people?"

"That waitress is, anyway," MJ replied. "Please. Keep your voice down."

Ed remained silent, his head at an angle as he stared at the counter. His breath came from him dotted with phlegm.

"I mean, I didn't make fun of your beatniks," MJ said. "And I didn't laugh at your . . . what were they, Pearse?"

Pearse looked about at both men. "They're rhymes," he said. "Isn't that right, Ed?"

Ed broke into a large grin, his eyes surveying the counter.

"Right," MJ said, "I didn't laugh at your rhymes."

He accepted his piece of cake from Betty. She laid a second plate of lemon crunch before Pearse, who began his delicate surgery of it. Then she clattered a plate onto the placemat before Ed, who took up a fork and cut right through the wedge of cake.

"So, enjoy yourself," MJ concluded.

Ed lifted one of the halves toward his open mouth. Pearse nudged a small square of lemon crunch onto his fork, which he hurried to his lips as well.

"Hello there, young man." It was a familiar voice, deep and tinny, the voice Pearse had listened to every morning for months. "Save a little of that cake for me."

Monsignor's hand caressed the back of his neck. The morsel of cake dropped to the counter. Pearse chased after it, but knocked it to his lap.

"Oh," Monsignor said. "Sorry." He removed his hat and clapped MJ on the back. "Joe's waiting outside, in the car. He asked me to come in to see how you fellows were doing."

Fear lurched through Pearse's stomach. Glancing through the café's glass door, he saw the headlight and hood ornament of his father's Ford Fairlane. Joe stepped onto the curb, placed a coin in the meter, and headed for the café himself. Pearse grabbed his beret from the counter and stuffed it into his jacket pocket.

Monsignor stepped back from the counter. He looked toward MJ, who had turned on his stool to follow Pearse's gaze out the door. The priest's mouth fell open as, shocked, he realized that Ed was there too, also enjoying a piece of lemon crunch.

"Do you know who this is?" Monsignor asked, pointing a finger at Ed.

"It's Ed Finney," MJ replied, distracted.

Ed pushed the remaining crumbs against the brim of the plate.

"I don't know his name, MJ," Monsignor replied. "But do you know who he is?"

"A friend of Pearse's," MJ said.

Joe walked through the door. The smile that Pearse managed felt like broken ceramic on his face.

"And you're allowing this?" Monsignor asked.

"Yeah, he's allowing it," Ed interjected. His fork rattled against his plate.

"I . . . Yes, I'm afraid I am allowing it," MJ said.

"Mother of God," Monsignor muttered. He turned toward Pearse's father. "Saints preserve us, Joe. Will you look at this?"

Ed dropped the fork to the counter and splayed his hands out before him.

"Goddamn it!"

The anger that had previously kept him bent over his piece of cake now straightened him up. He turned on the stool and pointed at Monsignor, who took a step back.

"Goddamn it!"

"Take it easy there, young man," Monsignor said, pointing a finger at Ed's chest.

" 'I saw you, Walt Whitman,' " Ed muttered. His voice had a kind of low burr in it, like a ghost in a haunted house.

Joe stopped, confused by the tableau.

" 'Childless, lonely old grubber.' "

Monsignor waved his arms before him, as though trying to bat Ed away. Mortified, MJ and Pearse turned toward Ed, whom MJ attempted to shut up.

" 'Poking among the meats in the refrigerator,' " Ed intoned. He pushed MJ aside, then stood up from the stool and moved toward Monsignor. His scarf fell to the floor.

"Ed!" MJ shouted.

Ed tapped Monsignor's chest with his index finger. " 'And eyeing the grocery boys!' "

The priest did not move. The folds and creases of his suit disappeared in the obdurate black of the cloth. But the tiny white square of his clerical collar seemed to brighten and grow larger. His jowls hung loosely from his enormous head. The gray eyes trembled.

There was a gasping, elderly scream from one of the ladies in the restaurant.

Monsignor's hands had gathered into fists, and the skin in his face reddened, flushed with what appeared to be actual fury. Pearse imagined a lightning bolt making its crackling way from the clouds above, to collide with Ed's quivering hand, to knock it aside, to obliterate it. He actually glanced upward, expecting to see the lightning shatter the pink ceiling. Worst of all, he dreaded Monsignor's silence, as the priest stood his ground against Ed.

"Get out!" Monsignor shouted finally.

Pearse's heart battered like a stone.

Joe took Ed by the shoulders, to turn him about.

"You let go of me!" Ed shouted. He knocked Joe's hands away.

Pearse pushed against his father. "Dad! Don't!"

"Get out!" Monsignor said once more.

Ed retreated toward the door.

Joe grasped Pearse's hands and turned him around, holding him across the chest. Ed looked back at the three men until MJ waved a hand at him.

"You better go, Ed."

Ed's eyes fell toward Pearse's.

"Go on!" MJ said.

Ed turned and left the restaurant.

Pearse, released from his father's grasp, knelt to pick up the scarf.

"Leave it, Pearse," Joe said.

"But Dad!"

"No. Just throw it out the door."

"But . . ."

"Pearse, do what I say!"

Moaning with dejection, Pearse opened the door and tossed the scarf onto the dirty cement outside.

"You didn't have to humiliate him, Joe," Mimi said, as the front door closed behind MJ. He had left the flat in a silent huff, insulted by Joe's accusation that he was turning Pearse against his own family.

"He's always had Pearse's best interests at heart," Mimi continued.

"Yes, but this was a betrayal. And I'm the boy's father."

"MJ knows that."

"And what I say should be . . . it should be listened to, at least."

Pearse moved to the couch and sat down. He rested his elbows on his legs and put his hands over his ears.

"That's always been the problem with my father," Joe continued. "I read. I'm a great student, thinking it'll mean something to him, and I guess it did! But he couldn't express it. He couldn't say it. I go to law school, and he barely asks me about it. And just the other day, he insults a guest of mine, somebody I've wanted to meet for years, with a very inflammatory and uncertain accusation, in this house. Doesn't explain it to me, and I have to learn why he did it from the man he's accusing. And then I feel bad because, in the end, I think my father was right. Mimi, it's been that way all my life. I love him! But he won't let me tell him that."

Joe sat down on the chesterfield. He glanced at Pearse, who would not look at him.

"And I think he loves me. But I'm not going to just let it go, this time. Pearse is being led astray by this guy Finney, and I seem to be the only person in the family who understands that. So I'm going to stand on what I believe. I don't like Pearse hanging around with hipsters. That's the term, isn't it, Pearse?"

Pearse did not respond.

"And I'm not going to allow my father to just ignore what I want," Joe continued.

Mimi sat next to Pearse and placed a hand on the boy's knee. "What are you going to do?"

Joe's white shirt was splotched beneath the arms with sweat. "No more tours, I guess, for the time being," he said.

"Dad!" Pearse cried out.

"That's right, Pearse. And I don't know how we're going to police this, but you are not going up to that café, ever again."

"But what did I do?" Pearse asked.

A sudden precision came into Joe's features. His cheeks grew taut.

"Pearse, I want you to be a good Catholic."

"I *am* a good Catholic."

"I hope so. But I think you're too young to understand what it means to be going around with those people up there on Grant Avenue. And I can't imagine how it is that my own father . . . It's affected you, Pearse. It's changed how you act."

Pearse could not understand why the things Joe described were so bad. He felt that the way the priests had ignored him and his embarrassment had been the real betrayal. That was surely worse. The lovely colors and giddiness of the Mass had disappeared. Monsignor's labored sermons now led to sleep. And above all, Pearse's prayers went nowhere.

"So it's a new day here," Joe continued. "No tours."

"Oh . . . ." Pearse's voice sank as he turned toward the doorway.

"And no beatniks."

Pearse ran from the room. He slammed his bedroom door behind him. Through the door, he could hear his father's muffled voice.

"I'm not going to give in this time, Mimi. Pearse has got to learn."

Pearse awaited some kind of defense from his mother, to no avail. Her disappointment, when she learned what had happened, had discouraged him, because it had been so genuine. She had knelt before him, taken his hands, and kissed them. The afternoon's pleasure still sustained Pearse, despite its harsh aftermath. But Mimi's eyes had been luminous with worry.

"Oh, Pearse," she said, "are we losing you?"

His mother's question made Pearse imagine himself tumbling through the welcoming doors of hell. People who were lost were those who abandoned themselves to the devil, like boys who said "shit" and did not go to confession. That kind of thing. Sin sucked them in and laughed at their remorse.

Pearse waited on his bed. Finally his parents walked from the living room to the kitchen. He rummaged through his jacket pockets and found he still had sixty-three cents, the change from the Caffè Trieste. He opened the bedroom door and stuck his head into the hallway. His father had started talking, once more, about MJ. Pearse snuck down the hall to the top of the stairs, descended them in silence, and went out the front door.

He put on his beret and ran down Columbus. The sun had just gone down, and the lights in the shop windows revealed shirts, salamis, and loaves of bread, all passing by in feverish succession. None of them interested Pearse. Halfway through the intersection at Union Street, an Oldsmobile edged into the crosswalk, almost hitting him. He scurried to the curb and ran from the car's angry horn.

As he approached the Hotel Dante, Pearse saw a movement, like a narrow snow flurry, in front of the building. The flakes were very large and rectangular. The squall floated toward the sidewalk from the window of Ed's room. Ed's arms waved out of the window, tossing more of the flakes into the air. They floated serenely toward the cement. Running across the street, Pearse stopped before the hotel. About a hundred poems were scattered across the sidewalk, all of them scratched with erasures and illegible instructions. Pearse looked up at the hotel. Ed had disappeared, and the window was now closed.

Pearse gathered up some of the poems, entered the hotel, and went to Ed's room.

"Who is it?" Ed shouted. "What do you want?"

The door flew open. Pearse's knuckles stung with his hurried knocking.

"What?" Ed peered down at Pearse. He held a cigarette in one hand and a glass of red wine in the other.

Pearse held the poems out before him.

"Oh," Ed said. He raised a hand to his head and stepped back from the door. "Pearse."

"Can I come in?"

"I guess so, sure." Ed stepped away from the door.

Pearse entered the room and immediately saw the papers that lay strewn across the floor. A few shelves of books had been attacked. In an apparent rage Ed had tossed the books to the floor, where they lay crumpled and stiff.

"What happened?" Pearse asked.

Ed retreated to his table. He took up a bottle of wine and poured more of it into his glass.

"I don't know," he replied. The words slid together. "Just didn't like them any more."

"But why?"

"Just didn't."

Pearse had seen people in Ed's condition before. But at the parties he attended with his family, drunk people were usually older people, respectable adults, not guys like Ed. They disappeared sometimes during those get-togethers, to be discovered asleep, fully clothed, on a bed. But Ed's drunkenness was far more erratic. He staggered as he put the bottle back on the table. He burped, then lifted the glass of wine to his lips and tossed it down.

Pearse picked up a few of the books.

"Leave 'em," Ed said. He dropped the glass to the table.

"But it's such a mess."

"Leave 'em." Ed took the books and poems from Pearse's hands and tossed them back to the floor.

Pearse let his arms drop to his sides.

Ed sat down and rested an elbow on the table. "What do you want, anyway?" he asked.

"I don't know," Pearse said. Ed's friendliness had given way to such volcanic anger that Pearse could do little to combat it. "I just . . . I just ran away from home."

Ed seemed not to have heard. He sat at the table, tilting the glass before him. Pearse had hoped for an approving declaration from Ed, something to help him through his misery. But instead, Ed acted as though he wanted to get rid of Pearse.

"What's wrong?" Pearse asked.

Ed began shaking his head. "I'm disappointed, Pearse." He leaned far over the table, reaching for the bottle. He could not quite get it, and his elbow slipped. Just catching himself with his free hand, he straightened up. Trying again, he secured the bottle and poured out more wine.

"What's the matter?" Pearse asked, breaking into the silence.

"It's because nobody ever reads any of the stuff I write," Ed replied. "I mean, I read all those books in high school, the stuff I used to love, Shakespeare and Keats and so on. And I thought, I can be like them! Famous. Sensitive. Instead of playing football and screwing around with cars. And my dad used to tell me what it was like in the thirties, you know, with the Wobblies and the protest songs and all that. And, I thought, hey, I'm gonna write poetry. I'm gonna be like Carl Sandburg."

Pearse grimaced.

"Never mind. It's not important who he is." Ed lowered his head, pushing his hair back with a hand. "But you know what? I'm just beginning to learn that there are a million poets hanging around here, all kinds of guys just like me, and nobody reads anything we write. And I wonder, is this the way it's gonna be? Is this it? I mean, I look around and think that maybe my stuff drains the world of something, instead of adding to it."

"But all those people liked it, Ed. Today, at the Trieste."

Ed shook his head in denial.

"They liked it! I liked it," Pearse added.

"And then your dad and that priest treat me like some kind of criminal. I resented it!"

Pearse's mouth turned down. "But what about my grandfather?"

"He's a great guy!" Ed exclaimed.

"Is there something wrong with him, too?"

"It isn't him, Pearse. It's me. Your grandfather . . . your grandfather pointed out what a liar I am."

Ed's shoulders dropped, making him resemble a jacket hanging from a hook.

"Damned fraud, that's all," he said.

Pearse sighed. "What's that?"

"A fraud? It's somebody who tells you something about himself that isn't true. Deliberately."

"Gee. You're not a beatnik?"

"That's not it." Ed's chest filled with breath. Pearse had thought him incapable of tears, but it looked like Ed was about to begin weeping. "It doesn't take anything to be a beatnik, Pearse. You just have to dress up in black and talk about Guillaume Apollinaire."

Pearse frowned, waiting.

"Jesus. He was a poet, Pearse," Ed said.

"Then what'd you lie about?" Pearse asked.

"That Inchon crap."

"Inchon didn't happen?"

"Of course it happened. It's just that my own involvement with it . . . that's what didn't take place." An exhalation preceded another long sip of wine. "I wasn't there," he said, scratching his head.

"You weren't a soldier?"

"Yeah, I was. But I didn't fight."

"What'd you do?"

"I worked on an army base."

"In Korea?"

"Sure."

"But what'd you do?"

Ed placed the glass on the table and sighed. "I filed reports."

"You didn't fight the Reds to the last man."

"No. The only Red I ever really saw was Joe Stalin. And that was on television, through a department store window."

"I remember him. He's on the bulletin board at school."

Ed waved a hand. "Yeah, well, he was the great hero of my father's life, too." His shoulders drooped once more. "I lied to you, Pearse. I wasn't at the invasion of Inchon. A lot of other guys were. I just wrote down their records, after it happened."

"What records?"

"The ones that reported how they had died there." Ed's forehead began to furrow, and finally he let his hands drop to his knees.

After a silence, Pearse turned from the table. His hands were in his pockets, and he stepped carefully over the books on the floor. Turning back toward Ed, he leaned against one of the bookshelves.

"And your grandfather," Ed continued, "when he told me what happened to him, that he was right there, that he was there in Ireland when it happened, and it all went bad, I realized I was just a phony. I mean, I knew I was, when I started telling people all this stuff. But . . ."

Pearse moved toward the door.

"I was a PFC," Ed concluded. "A clerk-typist." He stood up, shoving his hands into his own pockets. There was a wine stain on his shirt. "I don't guess you understand any of this, do you?" he asked.

Pearse turned the knob and stepped out into the hall. Ed followed him, picking up some pieces of paper from the floor.

"Pearse, it was just a few of the facts that were lies. Not the feeling."

He held the papers up before him, crumpled between his fingers.

"Not the feeling. And at least I lied to everybody."

Pearse walked to the stairs.

"I lied just the same to everybody," Ed said.

Outside, Pearse zipped up his jacket against the cold. The headlights of the cars on Columbus seemed to lurch toward him, to push him around, to intimidate him. He wiped his eyes with his fingers and continued walking. He approached Mason Street and paused at the corner below his apartment. He was sick with the prospect of returning home. He noticed a light on in the living room of Forrest Yick's apartment. Hurrying across the street, he rang the bell.

Forrest's face broke into a smile as he opened the door. "Pearse!"

"Hi, Forrest," Pearse whispered. He looked inside, up the stairs. "Are your parents home?"

"No, they went down to Chinatown tonight. Got a mah-jongg game." Forrest held the remains of an egg roll in one hand. His fingers glistened with grease. He took it into his mouth.

"Can I come in a minute?" Pearse asked.

"Sure."

Pearse followed Forrest up the stairs. The two boys went into the kitchen, and Forrest offered Pearse the plate of egg rolls his mother had left for him. Mr. Yick's family stared down at the boys from the wall.

"I ran away from home," Pearse said, shoving a roll into his mouth. He took another from the plate. At first Forrest did not seem surprised at all, which disappointed Pearse, who had expected a show of commiseration at least, maybe even of amazement, at the drama of the situation. After a moment, though, Forrest grew appropriately worried.

"What are you gonna do?" he asked.

"I was wondering," Pearse muttered, "do you think I could hide, maybe, in your parents' store?"

"Tonight?" Forrest shook his head. "My dad'd get awful mad."

"I'll be gone in the morning. I'll leave before he comes to work."

"I mean, he might think you were robbing stuff."

"Please, Forrest. I just don't want to go home tonight."

"Why? What'd you do?"

"Nothing! But my dad got real mad at me and my grandfather. Everybody's been yelling at me."

Forrest wiped his fingers with a paper napkin and handed one to Pearse. "Yeah, my parents yell at me too." He tossed his napkin in a wastebasket. "Kind of makes you . . . know what I mean? . . . nervous?"

Pearse nodded agreement.

"So I guess . . . I guess, OK," Forrest said. "But you gotta leave early."

He moved toward the kitchen doorway. Pearse held back a moment, until Forrest stopped and looked back over his shoulder.

"Would your mom mind if I had that egg roll?" Pearse asked. He pointed at the plate, where a single egg roll lay in a puddle of oil.

"No, that's OK."

Pearse snatched it up, wrapped it in his napkin, and followed Forrest down the hallway.

Forrest looked up and down Mason Street, then unlocked the front door to the store. He led Pearse down an aisle toward the back room, stumbling over a metal milk crate his father had left by the refrigerator case. "Jesus, Mary, Joseph," he grumbled, pushing it aside. Opening the door, he led Pearse into the back room and turned on the light.

"See, you can sleep here on this table. Got lots of cardboard, so you can make a bed."

Forrest folded his arms before him, his T-shirt doing little to protect him from the cold.

"And we even have a cover, see? To keep you warm." He reached beneath the table and brought out a neatly folded army surplus blanket that, Pearse thought, had the odor of a cellar.

"Yeah, it's been here a long time," Forrest said.

He handed the blanket to Pearse, then went to the doorway.

"It gets kind of dark in here at night," he said. "But we got a flashlight."

He went into the store and returned with a large chrome light. Pearse examined it, comforted by its length and its weighty feel. He opened it and discovered that the flashlight contained six Eveready batteries. He recalled the ads in the funny papers every Sunday, which told of boys saved from drowning and rescued from cliffs because of the long-lasting qualities of their Eveready's. Pearse decided he would be safe with this flashlight. He switched it on, casting a splotch of bright light into a corner of the ceiling. Cobwebs flickered like snow against the brown paint.

"And there's food all over the place," Forrest said. "Bologna. Bananas. Have anything you want."

He pointed through the door.

"Candy bars. Got lots of 'em. Just be sure to keep the door closed, so the light doesn't get into the store. That way," Forrest grinned, "I won't get in trouble with my dad."

He looked out into the store.

"So, I'll see you."

"But, but, Forrest . . ."

Forrest slammed the door behind him. Despite the questions Pearse had, about whether there were bugs and where was the bathroom and so on, he was grateful for his friend's help. Forrest's speech had rattled monotonously, but his concern was obvious. The trouble was that he had disappeared so abruptly that Pearse's sudden isolation filled him with fright. After a moment the door opened once more, making Pearse jump.

"These are pretty good, too." It was Forrest again. He handed Pearse a pint of milk and a stale jelly doughnut, wrapped in waxed paper. "So, good night," he said, closing the door once more.

"Good night," Pearse muttered.

He listened as Forrest locked up the store, then he spread the blanket out on the table, on top of the flattened cardboard boxes. It was already quite cold in the storeroom, and he secured the collar of his coat about his neck. He turned out the light and tried opening the storeroom door. The knob turned, but nothing happened. Pearse rattled it, and still he could not get the door open.

He turned on the light once more. The doorknob was missing a pin, and Pearse realized he had to use the fingers of both hands. When the door finally came open, he turned off the overhead light, then grabbed the flashlight and snuck into the grocery itself.

Pearse went up the aisle in the darkness, toward the fruit bins. The silhouette of the Dutch Cleanser maiden waved toward the window. He reached for an apple, and a small animal scurried across the aisle before him in the moonlight.

Pearse froze.

He thrust the light before him and turned it on. There was no sign of the rat on the stained linoleum. At least, he thought it was a rat. He bent down to try to look beneath the counters. Still he saw nothing. Standing once more, he heard skitters of sound, small fingernails hurrying along one of the aisles. He stepped back toward the storeroom. He splashed the light across the vegetable bins, and there was—Pearse was certain of it—the sound of chewing. Bok choy leaves hung toward the floor. Long, wormlike green beans and, worst of all, knotted fingers of ginger, resembling dead slugs, seemed to move about in the bins. Pearse became quite wretched. He thought of rats leaving their hair in the potatoes. He shuddered, and the sounds continued. Finally, he imagined yellow teeth gnawing at the fruit, then at his shoes, trying to get into them.

He ran back to the storeroom, closed the door tight behind him, and jumped up onto the table. Shivering with fear, he lay down and pulled the blanket over his head.

MJ lay back on the bed, loosening his tie. Vivid images flooded his mind, things he remembered from different times of his life, with no regard for order. They ran together like talk in a crowd, driven, mechanistic. Pain curved down his arm, like metal through the musculature. His breathing aggravated it. His tie lay crumpled across his chest. He looked into the hallway. The task of getting up again, to phone Joe for help, was insurmountable. The sweat that broke out across his forehead felt like cold grease.

Joe had phoned MJ earlier that evening, at nine. "Dad, Pearse is gone," he had said. "Will you come over, please? We need you."

MJ had searched Pearse's neighborhood, driving up and down Columbus Avenue. He had stopped once, at about ten, outside the Trieste. The café was closed, but the counterman, sitting alone over a newspaper in the back, told MJ that Pearse had not been seen at all since the afternoon.

Finally, MJ had stopped to tell Joe and Mimi that he did not feel well and he was going home. The search had come up with nothing. Pearse had disappeared.

"Do you think that I . . . do you think what I did to you and Pearse this afternoon caused this to happen?" Joe asked.

"I don't know," MJ replied. But of course that was it, he thought.

The pain in his chest grew crystalline and more intense.

MJ stared at the telephone. After a moment, he turned and clutched his chest. His shirt felt like burnt paper. He was too frightened to move, and he looked up at the ceiling, searching the darkness.

There was no good reason for his difficulty with Joe. Joe was a family man, a good lawyer, a good Catholic. MJ loved his son. But Joe had never accepted MJ's privacy. And ever since he had learned what had really happened to MJ in Ireland, Joe had seemed bent on a show of kindly understanding, as though MJ were an invalid in need of charity. Joe had always been so happy with the legacy he felt he had received from MJ. He attributed such marvelous mystery to the Irish, when MJ knew that just being Irish carried the same mystery as just being alive. It was not worth inquiring into.

But then MJ sorrowed that he had given Joe so little, really. He wished it had been easier to acknowledge Joe, that he had given him more than just his teenage allowance—what was it back then? a dime a week?—his upbringing, the begrudged acceptance of his fine grades in school. MJ felt that his diffidence had just been cowardice, really. Why not tell the kid what you knew? he wondered. Why deny him your failure?

There had been lights on inside Creeley's house when MJ arrived the evening after Captain Monohan's murder. The curtains had been closed to the road. MJ passed through the gate, and immediately the front door opened. Bob Costello beckoned to him, and MJ hurried inside. There were eight men in the parlor, all dressed against the rain. MJ recognized only Emmett Day, Costello, and Monohan. Monohan was completely dressed. He sat on a divan, held there by one of the men. The look of relief on his face when he saw MJ was momentary. He lowered his head. He grew distant with grief and fear.

"What's this, then?" MJ asked.

"Michael," Day said, not introducing him to the others. "There's been a change of plans. We're taking Monohan out of here. We think it's too dangerous, and we're moving him back to Cork."

"Tonight? Now?"

"Yes, we'll leave in a few minutes."

"But why do you need me?"

Day, his thin lips moving about as he ground his teeth, finally gave a tense smile. "You're one of us now, Michael."

Monohan swore beneath his breath.

"So it isn't that we need you," Day continued. "We're saving you."

Several of the men found this amusing, noting MJ's fearful look about the room.

"Now, take this." Day reached into his coat pocket. He pulled out a revolver and thrust it into MJ's hands.

"But I don't know how to use these things."

Again there was disdainful laughter, and Costello placed a hand on MJ's shoulder.

"You aim it at the poor bastard, Michael," he said. "And then you pull the trigger."

MJ stepped away from him.

"Come on," Day said.

The men put on their caps and gathered themselves against the weather outside. MJ shoved the revolver into his pocket, as Day shook Mr. Creeley's hand.

"Thanks, John," Day said. "I hope it'll be all right for you."

"Don't worry about us," the farmer said. "Ireland owes everything to you men."

"Thank you." Day nodded toward the door, and the others walked out. MJ joined Monohan. As they left the house, the rain, driven by a fresh gust of wind, beat against their shoulders.

They walked several minutes, until they came to the River Blackwater, which paralleled the road for a mile. The river was about twenty feet below them, and in the darkness they could not see it. Day was anxious to move along as quickly as possible. But Monohan had difficulty keeping up, and he leaned against MJ, gasping.

"Sorry," he said. "Cooped up in that cellar all this time, old sot like myself. I'm too weak for it."

MJ took him by the arm, and they rounded a turn in the road, past a long stone wall.

"We're going to be picked up ahead, if the arrangements have been made," Day said. "Damn them, they'd better have been made." He, too, was out of breath. So darkened in the storm, he and the others appeared lumpish and heavy. The backs of their coats were like rough slabs. After another turn, the road straightened and descended toward a bridge across the Blackwater. Day stopped as soon as he saw it. There was a roadblock.

Four British soldiers stood at the bridge. A lantern cast harsh light, continuously streaked with rain, about their feet. Day whispered for quiet, but it was obvious that the soldiers had heard their approach. The man holding the lantern lifted it high, for more light. Each soldier carried a rifle.

"Shall we give 'em a fight?" Costello whispered.

"No," Day quickly responded. "They don't know who we are. We'll just be on our way back down the road." He turned away.

The soldiers started walking toward them.

"Help me!" Monohan suddenly shouted.

Day pulled a pistol from the pocket of his overcoat.

"They're going to kill me!"

Day aimed at the soldiers and fired. In seconds, there was gunfire everywhere.

"It's all up!" Day shouted. "Run!"

Monohan cried out and ran toward the side of the road. MJ, his heart beating violently, followed close behind. Gunshots lit the darkness. MJ took Monohan in his arms and pushed him to the bank above the river. They struggled, Monohan shouting at him to let go.

"You'll be killed!" MJ shouted. They rolled down the bank, MJ's hands caught in the folds of Monohan's coat.

Monohan put his hands up over his head. The heavy gunfire lasted only a moment. Then the noise dispersed as the others escaped across the fields. For several minutes, MJ and Monohan remained in the ditch. Both men cowered as a pair of shots up the road was followed by garbled, anguished shouts. MJ could not make them out, or who it was now screaming in pain. His throat filled with bile, and he struggled to swallow it. His gut felt like it would break.

Heavy rain ricocheted from the mud into MJ's face. The river below fell noisily over the rocks. MJ's hands still clutched the sleeves of Monohan's coat, and Monohan himself was breathing with difficulty. His face was half-buried in the folds of the coat.

MJ let go of him and crawled to the top of the embankment. The road appeared deserted in both directions.

"Mr. Monohan," he called after a moment. "Come up."

The old man came out of the darkness, brushing mud from his coat. Despite the gloom, MJ could make out his face. As Monohan approached, MJ saw that his clothes had been soiled. His hands were muddied as well by his fall into the ditch. Running his hands over his own coat, MJ found that it was badly splotched, and ripped above the left pocket.

For a moment, neither man spoke. Monohan seemed to shelter himself next to MJ, as though awaiting the younger man's protective lead. MJ stepped to the side of the road and stared down toward the river. When he looked about, he saw that Monohan's face was drawn with exhaustion. Beneath his crumpled hat, he seemed lost, a discomforting mask.

"Go on, then," MJ said. He turned away. Hearing no reply, he glanced back over his shoulder.

Monohan's face, looking up into MJ's, was so wrinkled that his spectacles appeared over-precise and severe.

"Down there. To the river." MJ pointed from the road. "You can follow the embankment. I'll tell them you escaped in the fight."

Monohan's cheeks trembled. The distance between the two men—Monohan's boniness and sparse hair, an elderly man who was feeble by comparison to the youth in the wool coat next to him—sickened MJ. He hated the despair of the old man's loss. He hated Monohan himself for his suffering, when all Monohan had done, in his utilitarian way, like millions of others, was to serve the bloody queen and then her son. As well, the memory of Captain Monohan's bicycle, one wheel twirling like an ornament on a Christmas tree, remained on MJ's mind, an emblem of the Rising.

Monohan wiped the rain from his spectacles with his fingertips. He looked down the bank. Both men heard the river, but in the darkness they could not see it. There was simply a void at their feet. The run of the water over the stones far below seemed to intimidate the old man. Rain fell across the weeds.

Afraid, MJ pushed Monohan by the arm.

"Damn it, get on with it," he said.

"But there's nothing down there," Monohan protested.

MJ looked about. The others—either the soldiers or Day and his men—would be coming back soon to look for them.

"There's nothing to see," MJ said. "Just go!"

Monohan took in a breath. Suddenly he reached for MJ's hand and shook it.

"Thank you," he whispered. "Michael, isn't it?"

"Go on!"

Monohan descended the bank. He fell once, backwards, and stood up, wiping his hands. A few more steps, and he disappeared into the blackness. His footfalls through the brush grew faint. A branch snapped. Slowly the sound of the river enveloped his escape, and he was gone.

MJ turned away, anxious to escape himself. But he did not know in what direction he *could* escape. The gunfire had been so terrifying that he had clung to Monohan on the embankment, certain that he was going to die. He did not know where everyone had gone. He walked up the road ten yards, in the direction of Charleville. There was a light in the distance—a house, probably—and he stopped, afraid he would be seen. The rain had almost soaked his overcoat, and his efforts to pull it more tightly to his chest did nothing to alleviate the cold. He felt suspended in the darkness.

"Michael!"

MJ clutched his coat. It was Monohan's voice, coming up from the river.

"Michael!"

The second utterance was lost in the riffling noise of the water, so that, for a moment, MJ was not sure he had even heard it.

He looked up and down the road, seeing nothing. Abruptly he hurried down the bank, slipping and tumbling on his side, almost to the water itself. The pistol scraped against his belly, and he took it from his pocket, tossing it toward the sound of the river. He pulled himself to his knees, sightlessly recoiling from the darkness around him. But he could go nowhere. The black was complete. MJ heard only the shallow river, grovelling past him. He crawled several feet downstream, whispering Monohan's name. The weeds were glasslike and cold, and he fell forward as his hands slipped over a clump of rocks. He rolled into some thorn bushes and moaned with the bright pain they caused in his face. He pulled himself to his hands and knees again. Blood trailed down his cheek, and he tried to brush it away.

"Mr. Monohan," MJ said. There was no response. His face brushed the thorns once more. "Mr. Monohan!"

He descended into the stream itself. The frigid water ran over his legs and hands.

"Mr. Monohan. Please!"

He crawled over the rocks. Anguished, he felt his hands being bloodied as they slipped from stone to stone. He fell forward and, to his horror, his cheek fell against a swatch of cloth, a soaked sleeve, an arm askew and motionless in the dark. MJ pulled away from the body, terrified that it might rise up to attack him. But it remained inert, face down in the water.

Screaming, MJ stood and lurched to the riverbank.

He ascended to the road on his hands and feet. His breath came in quick, aspirated gulps that ached in his chest. He turned up the road and stumbled, swearing at the mud. He turned back.

He worried that he could not possibly get away. Each side now had reason to apprehend him. He had helped murder a policeman. But when Emmett Day returned, he could easily think that MJ had let Monohan go, that Monohan had escaped. That MJ was a collaborator, surely. MJ stayed close to the edge of the road, ready to jump a wall and disappear into the fields.

But it was not just the police or Day's men that frightened MJ. He ran from the phantom of Monohan's voice, calling to him from the river. Feeling the rain across his back, he was confronted by the memory of the poor old man and his drowning in the cold night. You fool, MJ thought. You sent him to his death. As he lowered his head against a gust of rain, he remembered how Monohan, with such perverse humor, had cursed him. You'll never be forgiven, he had said.

Lying in bed, one hand pressing against his chest, MJ gritted his teeth with pain. He might as well have said that you'll never forgive yourself, he thought.

Everything in the store appeared gray in the new morning light, without features, old or aging. But there were no rats, and the bok choy lay quietly in the bin. Pearse, looking out from the storeroom, saw that it was safe to move. He heard footsteps in the apartment upstairs. Recalling Forrest's anxiety, he folded the blanket and replaced it behind the table. He stacked the cardboard on the floor, where Forrest had found it, and entered the store.

Walking past the fruit bins, Pearse yawned, stretched, and picked up two bananas, which he ate hurriedly. Not knowing what to do with the skins, he remembered the wastebasket that Mr. Yick kept beneath the cash register. He threw them into the basket, then peered over the top of the register into the store. Everything was in order.

He turned toward the front door, where Sergeant Rye stood looking in.

Rye's face was red, a familiarity to Pearse, who had often seen him after a few whiskies at his father's meetings. When he saw Pearse standing before the cash register, he waved at the boy, gesturing to him to open the door.

"Pearse, you've got to come with me, right now," Sergeant Rye said. He took the boy's hand and pulled him through the doorway. "Don't argue with me." The hair that showed beneath his dark blue cap was graying and overlong. Rye's huge back seemed to house some kind of engine, from which great clouds of breath swirled about the policeman's head. Pearse stumbled along behind.

They crossed Mason Street and walked up the hill to Pearse's home. Standing on the front stoop, Sergeant Rye rang the doorbell several times. As they waited for someone to open the door, Rye leaned over and straightened the collar of Pearse's jacket.

"Are you OK?" he asked. The intimacy of his gruff voice surprised Pearse. Sergeant Rye did not seem angry with him at all, now.

Pearse nodded.

"You didn't get hurt?"

"No. But it was kind of scary," Pearse muttered.

The door opened.

"Hello, Mimi," Sergeant Rye said. "I've got him."

"Oh, Pearse!" Mimi knelt before the boy and embraced him. Pearse kept his hands at his sides a moment. Then, sensing Mimi's anguish, he raised his hands to her waist and held on to her. Sergeant Rye placed a hand on Pearse's head. They remained on the porch a moment.

"Pearse, I was so worried," Mimi said.

"I'm OK, Mom."

They ascended the stairs and turned into the living room. Pearse's father sat on a chair in the bay window. His face sagged when he saw Pearse, and he closed his eyes. Tim stood before the fireplace. He wore his bathrobe and slippers, and he appeared hardly to have slept at all. The air of dismay that hung in the room made it colorless, as though any light that there had been had now gone out of it. The organdy curtains hung before the windows like wet sheets.

"Where'd you go?" Joe asked.

Pearse swallowed. "I was across the street, in Mr. Yick's market."

"Did he know you were there?"

"No. I kind of snuck in."

There was a silence.

"Are you mad at me?" Pearse asked.

Again, no one spoke.

"I didn't mean it!" Pearse shouted.

Joe nodded and held out a hand. Pearse stepped toward him, not certain what his father would do. Joe took the boy in his arms and embraced him.

"Pearse," Joe said. "There's terrible news. MJ has . . ."

Pearse felt a watery hum in his father's breathing.

"He had a heart attack. Last night."

Pearse's cheek was pressed so tightly against his father's chest that he could barely breathe.

"Your grandfather's dead," Joe continued. "I'm so sorry, Pearse. He's gone."

« 5 »

SLIVERS OF PAIN

Already the wake had taken on a broken manner, so that the mourning seemed abrasive to Pearse. There was too much laughter and too much whisky. Even his father had been laughing with several of his friends in the living room of MJ's house, as though this were no funeral at all, rather just a party where everyone got to have a wonderful time. Dozens of guests stood at the dining room table, sampling from platters of food they had brought to the wake. There were crumpled napkins stained with mustard, piles of ham on rye, empty Guinness bottles, plates of fat-mottled beef . . . It made Pearse sick. It was too festive. It wasn't fair.

Sister Marie George, accompanied by Sister Miriam, asked for Pearse the moment she entered the house. He was hanging Mr. Doherty's coat on the rack at the foot of the stairs. Turning toward her, he saw her glistening eyes. He went to her and took her hand, and she embraced him. Her wimple crinkled against Pearse's cheek.

"Pearse, we loved your grandfather."

Anger had enveloped Pearse all day. He had wandered through the preparations for the wake, trying to keep himself intact by helping his mother and her friends. She had excused him from many of the activities, sensing how gravely sad he was. She even had to intercede once, when Joe, who was distressed and mournful himself, criticized Pearse and Tim for the slowness with which they dressed for the funeral. Pearse, in the middle of tying a shoe, fumbled hurriedly to complete the task, and failed as his father stood in the doorway.

For the two days since MJ's death, Joe's accusatory voice had sounded wounded, with a downturn in every utterance that had convinced Pearse of his father's disapproval of him. That Pearse had run away from home had been spoken of neglectfully, if at all. The talk during the few days' preparations for the funeral was of other things . . . flowers and priests, coffins and music. Really, no one seemed to care that Pearse had run away. The only person who did so was Pearse himself.

The morning of his return home, he had gone to bed exhausted, yet unable to sleep. "MJ searched for you for hours," Mimi had explained. "And he looked so tired when he went home that I knew something was wrong." She caressed her forehead with the fingers of one hand, then rubbed her eyes. "If only I'd asked him to stay here, maybe he'd have been all right."

But Pearse knew that it was not his mother's inaction that had caused MJ's death. MJ had died stricken by Pearse's disappearance. It was Pearse's fault.

On the way home from the Rosary, Mimi had assured the boy that MJ and Doll were together once more, and that news at least had softened Pearse's guilt. The image she presented of his grandparents—gray and elegant in their Sunday clothes, Doll in a feathered pillbox hat with a little lace veil over her spectacled eyes, MJ in his fine brown suit and dark fedora from Marshall Field and Company in Chicago, walking around in the clouds with the angels, buttery-fat and pink—that image had provided Pearse with some solace, even some humor. His hand in his mother's, he imagined MJ looking down upon him from the cupola at Saints Peter and Paul, a Garcia y Vega between the fingers of one hand, as snowlike feathers flowed from his K of C hat *and* from his archangelic shoulders.

But an image of MJ's actual death also cluttered Pearse's thoughts, like the images he had seen in old vampire movies on TV, of Bela Lugosi in fetid rags getting a stake through his heart. Those movies had always terrified Pearse. When he imagined his grandfather stiffening on his bed, his heart exploding, he cried out in his own bed and pulled the blanket over his head. He felt the stake between his hands, pulsing with MJ's efforts to push it from his heart. What must that feel like, Pearse wondered, the slivers of pain?

They buried MJ in a Catholic cemetery in South San Francisco. Monsignor said the Requiem, and he asked that Pearse serve the Mass with him. But Pearse refused. Standing at the graveside, his hand held tightly in Mimi's, he wept with doubt. He stood on a patch of wet grass, the mud radiating cold through the sides of his shoes. Monsignor's mechanical Latin sent him into a rage. As Monsignor read from the prayer book, a cold breeze caused the sleeve of his vestment to obscure the pages. The priest's own sorrow was evident as his voice rose and fell in an almost silent monotone. But Pearse grumbled to himself that these were not prayers. They were just sounds. He took the handkerchief his mother handed him and pressed it against his eyes. He felt that if he pressed hard enough, the tears would stop. But they came out of him freely. He feared they would always come from him like that, guiltful liquid, forever.

Lowered into the ground, the polished wood coffin seemed to contain nothing at all. It was antiseptic. It gleamed . . . like a speedboat, Pearse thought. The sports clippings MJ had saved for Pearse, the angry defense he had provided Pearse upon his expulsion from the altar boys, the lemon crunch, the paper rings from his Garcia y Vegas . . . the coffin contained none of those. It was just a box disappearing in the ground, and Pearse was convinced that it was empty of kindness because he had so foolishly abandoned his grandfather.

"Will you sit with me a moment?" Sister Marie George asked. She turned, with Pearse, toward the living room. The other guests standing in the crowded hallway made room for Pearse and the nun. They offered respectful greetings, and Pearse hoped that the grace that accompanied Sister Marie George everywhere was protecting him for the moment as well.

"I said an extra prayer for your grandfather at the funeral Mass this morning," Sister Marie George said.

Pearse could not reply.

"And all the sisters lit candles for him." Sister Marie George's fingers lay on Pearse's, and her small face puffed from beneath her veil. Finally Pearse started to speak. But he winced as he heard an outburst of talk from across the room. His father was conversing with several men from his office. They all were laughing, and when Joe added something, his hand on the shoulder of one of the others, there was more gleeful noise.

"I know your father will miss him, too," Sister Marie George said.

"But why does he have to laugh?"

"Oh, he does it to calm his suffering, poor man," the nun replied.

It was an answer that astonished Pearse. He could not imagine that his father was suffering at all. It seemed so improper, his drinking so much and greeting people at the door with hefty claps to the shoulder, handshakes, patter, and cigar smoke.

"It's true, Pearse," Sister Marie George said. "When you

lose your father, as he has, it's a terrible thing. And so soon after his mother. Just terrible.''

Though wounded by Joe's criticism, Pearse had admired how burly and handsome his father looked at the cemetery. There, Joe had seemed sad in the way Pearse was, in pain as they lowered the coffin. Joe's crumpled black suit had made him appear larger than normal, and his solitude had dignified him remarkably. But now all that had disappeared. His face was red as he lifted his whisky to his lips. The memory of MJ seemed to have disappeared. MJ had been forgotten.

The doorbell rang, and after a moment Mimi entered the living room, her fingers wrapped in a small kitchen towel. She searched out Joe, and when she spotted him she hurried through the crowd of guests toward him. The entry from the hall to the living room was a high moorish arch, lined with two lengths of curved molding. The hallway itself had a polished oak floor and a long oriental runner. Several other guests in the hallway were looking in the direction of the front door. There was a threatened stillness in the way their conversation paused, as though an explanation were required of the phantom that stood before them. Several other guests turned to look, and Pearse himself stood up to see.

Tim appeared in the entry to the living room, with Debbie Mariano. He looked for Joe, and when he saw Mimi whispering to him, he lowered his head and moved with Debbie toward the dining room.

A voice called out. "Is Pearse . . . is Pearse here?"

Joe turned toward the hallway, and Ed Finney appeared beneath the arch.

"What does he want?" Joe asked. He pushed through the guests toward Ed. His voice was immediate with anger.

Pearse leapt from the couch. "Ed!" He too hurried across the room.

"Look, Mr. Pearse," Ed said, as Joe approached. "I know this is a sad time for your family." He twisted his beret between his fingers. "But I wonder if you could let me say something to Pearse. Just for a moment. I knew your father."

"I know that."

"Ed!" Pearse approached the two men. Ed pushed his beret into his coat pocket. He saw Pearse from the corner of his eye, and smiled as the boy approached.

"I don't think you have the right to come here," Joe said. "To interfere in something like this."

"But I was a friend of your father," Ed persisted.

Joe, a hand in one pocket, sipped from his whisky. His impatience had a sloppy, edgy persistence, and at that moment Ed seemed intimidated by him.

"You weren't invited," Joe said.

"I know," Ed replied, "but Tim came and told me about it."

"Tim!" Joe shouted. He looked over his shoulder toward the kitchen. Tim, standing in the doorway, retreated.

"Yeah, he and his girlfriend. They came to the Caffè Trieste, Pearse, to tell me about MJ," Ed said, looking down at the boy. He reached toward Pearse's shoulder.

Joe brushed the hand away. "Don't touch him," he said.

"Dad! Stop it!" Pearse reached out to push Joe away, but knocked the drink from his hand. The glass broke, splattering whisky and ice across the floor. Ignoring it, Joe took Ed's coat in his hands and pushed him back. But Pearse forced his way between the two men, until, lurching about, he and Joe fell to the floor. A shout rose up from the crowd.

Covered by his father's body, Pearse struggled to free himself. He could not breathe.

Pearse rolled away, then turned over and raised himself to his hands and knees. His tie hung to the floor. The knuckles of his right hand, where they had scraped against the rug, were abraded. His fury remained as he stood up.

But he had never seen his father appear so helpless. Joe's mouth was closed, his lips white. Pearse's heart beat with such splintered discomfort that he wished he could make it stop. Embarrassed, Joe stood and walked toward the front door.

"I'll be home, Mimi," he said.

There was the sound of defeat in his voice, the same defeat Pearse heard from himself when he was being criticized by his parents. Joe was indeed running away. He was embarrassed and drunk. He took his keys from his jacket pocket and descended the stairs. Hurrying down the brick path toward the sidewalk, he did not look back. He was quite angry, though there was obvious bereavement in his retreat. Pearse stood with his mother on the porch and watched.

He was glad to see his father gone.

The Fairlane pulled away from the curb and turned the corner toward California Street.

When Pearse and Mimi returned to the house, Sergeant Rye stood at the door.

"I think somebody should go after him," he said. "I'll be glad to do it, Mimi."

"One of us should go too," Mimi replied.

Pearse turned toward the living room, wishing to find Ed.

"Joe's so unhappy that MJ's gone," Mimi muttered.

"Of course," Sergeant Rye said. "Any son would be."

Pearse paused at the entry to the living room. Ed stood alone in a corner, ignored by the other guests.

"Oh, but there's more than just that, Marvin," Mimi continued.

Pearse glanced back at his mother, and she lowered her head. He did not know what she intended. He hoped she would say more, but the dismay that now overtook her made it impossible for her to speak. As he waited, he felt someone's hand on his own shoulder. He looked back. Ed stood behind him, his beret in his hand.

"I'm sorry, Pearse," he said. He exhaled, and placed the beret on his head.

"Pearse can go with you, maybe," Mimi said, and Sergeant Rye nodded agreement.

"Me?!" Pearse turned about.

"Yes, Pearse. Won't you, to make sure your father's all right?"

"No!" The muscles of his face tightened. "I don't want to go!"

"Oh, Pearse," Mimi replied. "Don't be so . . ."

Pearse covered his wounded fingers, sheltering the knuckles with his other hand.

"Don't be so angry with your father all the time," Mimi said. "You're just being cruel, that's all."

"But I don't want to!"

"Pearse!"

Pearse hurried toward the door and ran out into Lake Street. He scurried through the darkness and fog, and the humiliation he felt at being so accused by Mimi grew as he ran. He turned toward California Street, where he knew there was a bus stop, and the faster he ran, the worse his heart felt. The headlamps of the passing cars were diffused by the fog, and the cars themselves could not be seen, so that they passed Pearse by in a glare, like disks of flurrying ice. He threw himself onto the bus stop bench, pulling his feet up so that he could rest his chin on his knees. He lowered his head, frightened by the lights.

"Pearse, is that you?"

He looked up. Ed, gasping for breath, his shirt hanging out in front, leaned on the back of the bench.

"Jesus, who do you think you are? Y. A. Tittle or someone?"

Swearing, Pearse lowered his head once more. A bus arrived, heading downtown. To his surprise, Ed pulled Pearse from the bench and forced him up the steps.

"Go on back and sit down," Ed said, as he took change from his pocket. He placed the money in the coin box, then pushed Pearse toward the rear. The bus was empty of other passengers, though Pearse did not notice that as he tried to remove Ed's hand from his shoulder.

"Sit down," Ed said, and Pearse gathered himself into the corner of the rear seat, looking out the window. They rode in silence until Ed, unwilling to put up with Pearse's wordlessness, finally spoke.

"So, what are you going to do about your father?" he asked.

"I don't want to help him," Pearse yelled. He leaned his head against the window. "He doesn't care whether I help him or not."

Ed folded his arms. Pearse noticed that he carried a program from the funeral service.

"He's just an old . . . fascist, that's all," Pearse said.

Ed's head snapped about, and he stared at Pearse. A moment's humor appeared in his face, but he suppressed it. Pearse, who had expected immediate agreement, was unprepared for Ed's silence, and felt compelled to keep talking.

"Tells me what to do all the time," Pearse muttered.

"I know what it's like."

Pearse looked out the window. They passed the corner of Polk Street, and Blum's. Pearse craned his neck to look in the window, but the sweetshop was closed. Sighing, he faced forward again.

"I'd rather go to the Trieste, anyway," he said, "with you."

"I guess we could do that," Ed replied.

"We could?"

"Sure. Have an espresso, maybe a piece of pie or something." Ed's throat rumbled as he exhaled. He reached into his coat pocket and brought out a packet of Gauloises.

"I guess so," Pearse said. His voice weakened, and he swallowed. An unusual fear had risen up in him during the conversation, bringing with it a kind of distaste that he did not understand. The freedom Ed was offering him actually felt friendless to Pearse. An image of the piece of pie appeared in his mind, a lump of sweet on a dark plate. It had none of the joy that a piece of pie at the Trieste should possess.

Confused, Pearse joined his hands on his lap. They rode all the way downtown, then transferred to the Kearny Street bus, which they rode to North Beach. Pearse's enthusiasm for the Trieste fell away through the journey, like eroding sand.

The bus stopped at the corner of Columbus and Broadway.

"Let's go," Ed said, moving toward the front door. Pearse remained seated. Ed stopped and turned back. He stood in the aisle, his hand holding the leather overhead strap. His coat hung open, revealing his black turtleneck T-shirt.

"You coming?"

Pearse looked down at his hands. "I don't think the Trieste is open," he mumbled.

"Sure it is. It's always open this time of night."

"But . . ."

"You guys goin', or what?" the driver shouted. He looked to the back of the bus in his rearview mirror. Ed shook his head.

The bus moved from the stop. Losing his balance a moment, Ed took hold of the seatback before Pearse. He reached up to pull the cord for the next stop.

"You get to fight with your family, Pearse," he said. "It's allowed."

"Yes, but . . ."

"You don't have to agree with them."

Pearse could not bear being criticized by Ed, but he felt that that was what Ed was doing. His advice was agreeable enough. It gave Pearse permission to remain furious with his father if he wished. But it felt, nonetheless, like scolding.

"I don't want to go to the Trieste," Pearse said.

The bus came to a halt at the next stop. In the wordlessness that ensued, Pearse hoped for some sort of release from Ed. He wished to abandon Ed and go home.

"Hey!" the driver shouted, looking again into the mirror. "You guys want to stay or go?"

Ed turned toward the front and waved once to the driver, as though asking him to wait a moment longer. Turning back to Pearse, he tapped the boy's knee.

"Pearse, I lied to you, didn't I?"

"Yes."

"But here's something that's the truth. The truth, you know what I mean?"

"Yeah, the truth!"

Ed took off his beret and examined it.

"It's just that . . . look, I don't think the Caffè Trieste is worth abandoning *anything* for," he said.

Pearse stood and ran toward the front door. Descending to the curb, he waited as the bus began moving away. Ed sat back in the seat and adjusted his beret. Looking out the window, he spotted Pearse, who abruptly waved. Ed's clenched fist appeared in the window, and after a moment he raised it in the air. The bus rumbled into the traffic. To Pearse, Ed's receding gesture looked like a salute.

He ran up Columbus to Mason Street. A single light shone in the bay window of his parents' flat. Pearse hurried up the front steps. As he closed the door behind him he paused a moment, looking into the darkness. He gathered a breath, frightened by the gloom, then moved slowly up the stairs. He turned into the living room, where his father sat in an armchair. Joe had not removed his coat. The fingers of his hands were intertwined with one another. His tie was twisted unevenly and hung down above his hands.

"Hi, Dad," Pearse said. He stood in the entry to the room and removed his jacket. Joe's acknowledging gesture fell to sadness, and he moved his hands about, studying them, trying to get control of himself.

Pearse realized that his father was unable to speak. He went into the kitchen and placed a pot of water on the stove. The cupboards were beyond his reach, and he decided to go to his mother's china cabinet, in the dining room. Opening the glass door, he took out a white porcelain cup and saucer and brought it to the kitchen. The cup was his mother's favorite, one of a set given to her by MJ after Doll's death. It was delicately shaped porcelain, so thin that light could actually be seen through it. Two strips of gold filigree circled the cup, inside and out.

Waiting for the water to boil, Pearse rehearsed what he wanted to say to his father. But always it ended in complaint, and he did not want another fight. Finally, Pearse poured the water into the pot, dropped a teabag into it, and placed the pot and the cup and saucer on a small wooden tray. He reached for the breadbox, near the sink, and the lid fell open. Swearing at the clatter, Pearse took two pieces of Langendorf bread from the waxed-paper bag and dropped them into the toaster, then got some butter from the refrigerator.

Once the toast was ready, Pearse carried the tray up the hall to the living room.

Joe sat in the chair, slumped to one side. He had taken off his coat, and his white shirt, so carefully pressed by Mimi that morning, now appeared awash with wrinkles. Here and there it was soiled. His downcast eyes were red-lined, lost in the drink. Pearse passed him the cup of tea. Sloppily, Joe raised it to his lips.

"The odd thing, Pearse," Joe said, after a moment, "is that when Doll died, I thought it didn't matter much to my father."

He placed the cup and saucer on the table and began rubbing his hands together. Shaking his head, he brought a hand to his forehead. His fingers formed crooked bars across his brow. When he spoke again, Joe's voice had weakened.

"Sometimes, you know . . ." He looked to the side. "Jesus. Sometimes I hated him."

Delivered with such finality, the last sentence so shocked Pearse that his own bitterness against Joe resurfaced. He bit his lower lip. How could anyone hate my grandfather?

"He didn't pay a lot of attention to me when I was growing up, you know," Joe said. He seemed to have forgotten that Pearse was even in the room. "Didn't have a lot of feeling for me. He always wanted to avoid me, especially when I tried to learn things that I thought would please him."

Pearse's breath shook in his throat. He wanted to shout at his father that he was not being fair.

"And yet today I felt like I was the only one who knew who he really was. And that he was gone," Joe continued.

He lifted a hand, gesturing across the empty room, then rejoined his hands and stared at them. He was slurring his words, so that Pearse had to listen carefully.

"All those people, our friends, eating and drinking. What did it matter to them that my father was gone? What did they know about him?" Joe continued, blinking his eyes.

"What about me?" Pearse asked.

Appearing offended, Joe moved to speak. But Pearse, just as quickly, turned away and pushed his fists into the pockets of his pants.

"You? Of course, you knew," Joe said.

"What?" The cold air in the room pressed against Pearse's shoulders.

"You knew how important he was, Pearse. You remembered that he was your grandfather, and how much he meant to you. And I envied you for that."

"But . . ."

"You always knew."

Joe's eyes settled on Pearse's.

"It's one of the things that made me feel so guilty about the way I thought of him," he said.

There was, for a moment, a look of such sensibility on Joe's face that Pearse's anger retreated in confusion. He recalled following Joe up the stairs to Doll's room the night of her funeral. Sitting in MJ's rocker, staring at Doll's bed, his father had crumpled forward in the chair, his elbows on his knees. His back had seemed to the boy reduced in size, as though Joe had suddenly grown old himself. Now, watching as Joe lowered his eyes with such dismay, Pearse realized that his father *was* saddened by MJ's passing. Maybe even as saddened as he had been when Doll had died.

Joe's shoulders began shaking. There was no heat on in the house, and Joe brought his hands together gingerly, rubbing them to get some heat from them.

"Are you OK?" Pearse asked.

"Just cold," Joe said. Overcome with chills, he took in a breath and held it, trying to quell the movement through his body. He sat back on the couch and folded his arms before him, to cadge some heat from them. He lowered his chin to his chest.

Pearse stood and went into the hall to his bedroom. He got the K of C blanket from the foot of his bed and returned to the living room.

"Here, Dad," he said, unfolding the blanket and wrapping it about his father's shoulders. Joe allowed Pearse's careful adjustment of the blanket as the boy pulled it down behind him and around his waist. He took the cup of tea from Pearse once more, and the boy sat down on the couch. Sipping from the tea, Joe's mouth turned up in a smile. Its appearance, from such sorrow, was unexpected and strangely joyful.

"Thanks," Joe said. His fingers gripped the cup. He appeared, simply, lonely. "Will you sit with me, please?"

He lifted one arm, making room within the blanket for Pearse. For the moment, Joe seemed to have set aside his son's failure to tie his shoe before the funeral. Pearse sensed that Joe had forgiven his running away, as well, and Halloween at the beach. He had let go of the memory of Pearse as a renegade and a beatnik and a bum . . . lost to the faith, fallen away. Pearse suspected that now none of those things even mattered to his father.

But still Pearse did not move.

"It *is* cold, isn't it?" Joe asked. There was fresh disappointment in his voice. He dropped his arm and leaned forward to replace the cup of tea on the table.

Faltering, Pearse looked down. The tea was very clear, and gave a precise view of the gold-leaf design that circled the interior of the porcelain cup, just below the rim. There was nothing else to be seen. Just the intertwined meanders of gold.

Agitated by the remains of his anger, Pearse stood and moved to his father's side.

Joe brought the blanket about them both, and Pearse leaned his head against his father's chest. Joe took the cup of tea in his free hand. A swirl of steam rose into the air, making a flawed loop above Joe's fingers.

ACKNOWLEDGMENTS

Grateful acknowledgment is made for permission to reprint from the following works:

page 80, 157 — "Charlie Brown" by Jerry Leiber and Mike Stoller. © 1959 Jerry Leiber Music & Mike Stoller Music & Chappell & Co. (renewed). All rights on behalf of Jerry Leiber Music & Mike Stoller Music for the U.S.A. and Canada administered by Chappell & Co. All rights reserved. Used by permission.

page 90 — "Lucille" by Richard Penniman and Albert Collins © 1957, 1960, renewed 1985, 1988 Venice Music, Inc. All rights controlled and administered by EMI Blackwood, Inc. Under license from ATV Music (Venice). All rights reserved. International copyright secured. Used by permission.

page 91 — "Great Balls of Fire" by Otis Blackwell and Jack Hammer. © 1957 Unichappell Music, Inc. & Chappell & Co. (renewed). All rights reserved. Used by permission.

page 91, 125 — "Splish, Splash" by Darin and Murray, published by Portrait Music. © 1958, renewed 1986 Unart Music Corp. Rights assigned to EMI Catalogue Partnership. All rights controlled and administered by EMI Unart Catalog Inc. All rights reserved. International copyright secured. Used by permission.

page 124 — "Poison Ivy" by Jerry Leiber and Mike Stroller. © 1959 Mike Stoller Music & Jerry Leiber Music (renewed). All rights on behalf of Mike Stoller Music & Jerry Leiber Music for the U.S.A., Canada, and Japan only administered by WB Music Corp. All rights reserved. Used by permission.

page 184–5 — "Ode to Coit Tower," *Gasoline & The Vestal Lady on Brattle* by Gregory Corso. Copyright © 1955, 1958 by Gregory Corso. Reprinted by permission of City Lights Books.

About the Author

Terence Clarke is the author of *The Day Nothing Happened*. His fiction has appeared in numerous literary magazines across the country, including the *Yale Review*, the *Denver Quarterly*, and the *Antioch Review*. Clarke lives in San Francisco.